UNCHARTED SEAS

DENNIS WHEATLEY

DENNIS WHEATLEY

UNCHARTED SEAS

Frontispiece Portrait by
MARK GERSON

Original Illustrations by
JOHN ROBERTS

*Published by arrangement with
Hutchinson and Co. (Publishers) Ltd.*

© Brook-Richleau Ltd.
© 1972, Illustrations, Edito-Service S.A., Geneva

To my charming and gifted stepson
W. A. YOUNGER
of
Christ Church, Oxford

Whose first book of poems

'INCONSTANT CONQUEROR'

has just appeared. I have the honour to introduce his work to my readers in the three poems, written by him, which grace the pages of this book.

CONTENTS

CHAPTER I

THE HURRICANE

ANOTHER great wave hit the ship a resounding thud. She gave a sickening lurch, lifted with alarming rapidity, hovered a moment, shuddering through all her length as the screws raced wildly, and plunged again—down, down, down—so that the passengers scattered about her lounge felt once more the horrible sensation of dropping in a brakeless lift.

The *Gafelborg* was no luxury liner but a Swedish cargo vessel of 3,600 tons carrying twenty cabin-class passengers. She was seven days out from Cape Town, bound for Rio de Janeiro, the ports along the north-east coast of South America, and the West Indies. Twenty-four hours earlier she had hit the hurricane. Since then life had been hell for all on board.

That morning, such passengers as could still stand had staggered up the companionway to the small lounge and remained there ever since. The hatches were battened down, the decks awash and impassable, except for officers and crew who ran the risk of being swept overboard every time their duties made it necessary for them to fight their way through the foaming waters. No hot meals could be served even if the hardier travellers could have faced them and even the bravest preferred the upper-deck lounge, which seemed less of a death-trap, to the narrow dining-saloon or their cabins on the decks below. Those who felt hungry had picnicked on cold meat sandwiches.

Basil Sutherland stood up and lurched towards the bar. No one could have accused him of being drunk on account of his unsteady gait; the roll and pitch of the ship easily accounted for that, but his voice was thick as he said to the barman: ' 'nother whisky, Hansie—make it a double.'

The pale-faced, blue-eyed Swede steadied himself and poured the drink with his free hand.

Basil grabbed the tumbler but did not lift it. With an effort he brought his brown eyes into focus and stared at the pale golden liquid. As the ship rolled, the whisky in the glass tilted smoothly, first to one side then to the other. 'Twenty-five degrees roll,' he announced; 'at thirty we turn over and go under—don' we?'

'I wouldn't reckon we've touched twenty-five yet, Mister Sutherland,' the bartender smiled deprecatingly.

'Good for you, Hansie, you ol' liar, but what the hell! Who cares anyway? Drowning's a pleasant death they tell me.' The young Englishman did not really believe there was any serious risk of the ship sinking. They had weathered the storm for a night and a day so in another twelve hours they would probably run out of it. Yet a morbid streak in him, brought to the surface perhaps by heavy drinking, made him toy with the possibility that death was closing in on them and that before morning they might all be drowned.

He picked up his drink, tossed off half of it and swinging round spread his legs wide, dug his heels into the deck, propped his back against the bar, and surveyed the occupants of the saloon.

Rotten lot of blighters, was his mental comment. Not a decent feller among them, except the Frenchman. What was his name— De Brissac, that was it—Captain Jean De Brissac. But he was doing a shift on the pumps at the moment. A plate in the ship's bows having sprung a leak owing to the heavy seas, all the male passengers had been pressed into service since midday.

The two old nuns were putting up a pretty good show, Basil ruminated. Sitting bolt upright on that hard settee, clicking over the black beads of their rosaries as though it weren't a fifty-fifty chance that their mouths would be full of more salt water than they could swallow before morning. Wonderful thing religion. Insurance for Heaven and a certain place in the far, far better world to come—if you could believe in it.

Swisssh—thump! Basil reeled, steadied himself by grabbing at a screwed-down table and tensed his muscles; the ship was climbing again as though she never meant to stop. The groaning of the girders increased to a scream, an awful sideways wriggle ensued while the screws beat the air, then she sank like a stone for minutes on end so that it seemed utterly impossible that she was not just diving straight to the bottom of the Atlantic.

'Coffee?' said a voice beside him.

With an effort he swung round and stared into the pale face of Unity Carden. She held a big jug in one hand and a clutch of thick cups in the other. 'I've just made it in the galley—do you good,' she added.

2

'No—no thanks,' he muttered, and, taking advantage of a momentary righting of the ship, she slid across to two bronze-faced Portuguese traders.

His eyes followed her, admiration struggling with contempt in their expression. She reminded him of a season years ago when, just down from Oxford, he had danced with dozens of her kind, stupid, empty-headed little ninnys, whose conversation was confined, through lack of experience, to finishing abroad and hearty chatter about horses. Well, Barbara had got him out of that. She'd cost him a packet, but he didn't grudge a penny of it. What a summer they'd had in that little place he'd taken for her down on the river. There wasn't a millionaire, even, who could boast of having kept Barbara La Sarle for a solid twelve-month. She'd ditched him in the end as he'd always known she would, but if he were drowned tonight the memory of her radiant face and low-pitched voice in the days when she simply couldn't keep her hands off him was something worth having lived for.

He watched Unity Carden's erratic progress from group to group and if he'd had a Union Jack with him he would have waved it, half-derisively, half in genuine pride. Good old England! That's the stuff to give 'em! Cold as an icicle, stupid as an oaf, loathing all these foreigners without the faintest reason, yet bringing them sustenance when every other woman in the ship, except the nuns, had gone under with sickness or given way to hysterical despair.

He saw her complete her round and reach her father. Colonel Carden, with his gammy leg stretched out in front of him, was as calm as though he was sitting in his club. An insufferable old bore, thought Basil, narrow as they make 'em, and stupid to a degree. No one but a criminal lunatic could ever have allowed him to hold the lives of a thousand men in the hollow of his hand, yet he possessed a code as straightforward as that of a boy who had been taught the rules in his first term at a public school. Basil recalled his own ideals at the age of thirteen, and grinned wryly. He slammed down his tumbler on the bar. 'Gi-me-another, Hansie.'

Countering a heavy lurch of the ship, he snatched back the refilled glass and his glance fell upon Synolda Ortello. She appeared to be asleep, or comatose, stretched out at full length on a divan. In the last few days he'd wondered a lot about her. She was a South African of British extraction; twenty-eight or thirty perhaps and, rumour had it, the widow of a Spaniard. She was pretty good to look at, or had been a few years before; vaguely reminiscent of Marlene Dietrich, but Marlene in a part where she was a bit shop-soiled and prematurely old. Much too much make-up and a shade careless about her clothes; troubled, too, apparently about some secret worry of her own, so very reticent and difficult to get to know. She'd lived in Rio with that Spanish husband for several years, so she said, and the passenger list showed her to be returning there, presumably to her home. All the other women on board had hated her on sight. That wasn't her fault as she'd done nothing to encourage any man's attentions, rather the reverse, but half the men in the ship, from the youngest officer to the senile-looking old Greek, could hardly keep their eyes off her whenever she appeared.

Between bouts of drunkenness Basil had watched the comedy of their advances with much amusement. Watching other people, getting blind most nights, and occasionally turning a pretty piece of satirical verse, which he destroyed immediately afterwards, was about all the fun he had in life.

If only his uncle's money had come to him when he was a little older things might have been different. As it was, with the reckless-ness of youth and a few people like Barbara La Sarle to help him, he had blown the lot.

After two marvellous years he had woken up one morning to find himself bankrupt without really understanding how such a thing could have come about. The friends of yesterday had melted away like snow under a summer sun; nothing remained of his handsome legacy except outrageously extravagant tastes.

He had turned to and got a job on the strength of his having been supposed to know everyone in Mayfair; but it was with the wrong kind of people. A criminal prosecution had followed as a result of which a parchment-faced judge had sent most of Basil's share-pushing associates to push needles through thick canvas, an operation necessary to the making of mail-bags in His Majesty's prisons, but the shrewd old man had sensed that Basil was an innocent party to the frauds and directed the jury so that he was let off with a caution.

The family had then loomed up again; aged aunts and uncles, neglected during those hectic years. Their offer had been con-siderably better than going on the dole; £400 a year paid to any bank he chose, provided he kept out of Europe and prison; they wanted no further scandals connected with the family name. Hating the thought of going into exile, his fight to retain his independence had caused them to increase their offer to £500.

Four weeks later, absolute necessity forced him to accept their terms and he had gone abroad.

During the last three years he had made his way via South Africa, India, and the Straits Settlements to China and back. For a month or two here and there he had managed to get a job, but he loathed routine and the practical side of business. In every case he had either been sacked or anticipated his dismissal by walking out. If there had been no allowance coming from home he would have had to stick it, but with £10 a week he could afford to slack when he got bored or move on by cheap routes to fresh places in the vague hope that he might find them more congenial.

The wind howled and blustered through the rigging overhead, the spray hissed against the portholes like driven rain, every piece of woodwork creaked infernally under the frightful tension. The ship was rolling with a horrible twisting motion caused by her pitching as the Swedish skipper fought to keep her head-on to the storm.

Half a dozen dripping figures, oilskin-clad, lurched up the companionway at the far end of the lounge. Their leader, Juhani Luvia, a herculean young Finn, was the ship's Second Engineer. He had served four years in a United States shipping company and so spoke passably good English with an American accent.

'Next spell,' he bellowed above the thunder of the rushing waters, and repeated his demand in German and bad French.

Basil knew his turn at the pumps had come and slithered half the length of the narrow room to take over a suit of oilskins from the French Army Captain, Jean De Brissac, who was wriggling out of them. 'Well, how are things?' he muttered.

'Not good,' the Frenchman shook his head. 'The water in the forehold gains a little always in spite of our great efforts.'

'D—d'you think she's going down?'

Jean De Brissac shrugged his well-set shoulders. 'Who shall say, *mon ami*. I would prefer to be in the deserts of North Africa, facing half a dozen hostile Toureg—but then I am no sailor.'

The Finnish Engineer overheard his words and smiled. 'The water wouldn't be gaining any if we had a dozen men like you among the passengers, *Monsieur le Capitaine*. We've no cause to get rattled though and your chances are plenty better than they would be in North Africa.'

He turned and favoured Basil with a disapproving stare. 'Come, Mr. Sutherland, we must get to it.'

Another of the pumping squad who had just come off duty

gripped the Finn by the arm. 'Chances?' he repeated in a guttural voice, 'surely you do not mean there is *any* chance that the ship should sink?'

'Certainly not, Señor Vedras.' Juhani Luvia looked down from his great height on the squat middle-aged Venezuelan who had spoken. 'I've been in ships that have weathered much worse storms.'

'Yes, but they were bigger and better ships—not little old tubs like this,' Basil Sutherland snapped. 'Still, go ahead. Lead me back to your filthy pump.'

A door banged loudly somewhere and there was the sound of smashing crockery. Luvia cocked a blue eye in the direction of the galley, then took the new shift below.

Jean De Brissac and Vicente Vedras commenced a zigzag course towards the bar. The Venezuelan was a man of forty-five who had lived well; showing it by his heavy jowl and increasing waistline. He was very dark with a swarthy complexion, and heavy black eyebrows that almost met in the middle of his forehead.

The Frenchman was ten years younger; dark, too, but of a finer mould. His skin was tanned a healthy nut-brown from the years he had spent as a member of the Military Mission in Madagascar; his brown eyes held a laughing impudence that had made many a lovely lady eager to know him.

As French officers habitually wear uniform, their wardrobe of civilian clothes is small, so, although he was sailing under the Swedish flag, *en route* for Guadaloupe, he had obtained the Captain's permission to wear his military kit. A little vain by nature, he was conscious, even in these anxious hours while the ship was battling against the hurricane, that he cut a dashing figure in his breeches and tunic of horizon blue.

'You will drink?' he asked the Venezuelan courteously.

'*Mille gracia, une Cognac.*'

'*Deux fines,*' De Brissac told the white-coated Hansie.

Vicente Vedras's eyes flickered in the direction of Synolda Ortello, the South African girl. He leaned over to the barman. 'For me separately, a bottle of champagne also. Two glasses. I take it to the Señorita there who is not well.'

The Swede pushed a bottle of Hennessy towards De Brissac. Judging the roll of the ship with commendable accuracy, he poured two portions.

Vedras took his glass and bowed politely. 'This storm—it is 'orrible, but that we are in no danger is good news. For some little

6

moments I was afraid.' With a quick movement he tossed off his drink.

'So was I,' confessed De Brissac. 'But these heavy seas will probably go down by morning. Here's to better weather!'

He drank more slowly and glanced round the saloon. It was not a pretty spectacle. The dozen odd passengers were lolling about in various degrees of discomfort and abandon, their canvas-covered cork life belts near at hand. The elderly Greek was being abominably sick. A plate of stale sandwiches, with their pointed ends curling upward, reposed on a near-by table. The air was heavy with tobacco smoke. As the ship's only common room and bar it was the natural refuge of the men who had been working at the pumps, and for hours on end they had been cooped up there smoking at an abnormal rate owing to the tension of their nerves.

With a muttered: 'You will excuse, *mon Capitaine*,' the Vene-zuelan signed his chit, clutched the bottle of champagne to his breast, and stuffed two glasses in his pockets. Making a sudden dash across the room he landed up beside Synolda.

Jean De Brissac advanced with a more cautious step towards the two nuns. He brought himself up a little unsteadily before them.

'*Mes sœurs*,' he said, and continued in French, 'if I can be of any service to you I pray you to command me.'

Neither of the women looked up from their rosaries, but they knew him by his polished riding-boots and beautifully cut breeches.

'Thank you, *Monsieur le Capitaine*,' the eldest murmured, and he could only just catch her words above the pandemonium of the storm. 'But we have placed ourselves in the hands of the Holy Virgin. You can only add your prayers to ours.'

He managed a bow, rocked unsteadily for a moment, and in two quick strides was back clutching the bar. '*Encore une fine*,' he grinned at Hansie, showing his magnificent white teeth.

Turning, he stared again at the groups of miserable passengers. Unity Carden was sitting bolt upright beside her father. Game little devil—De Brissac thought—queer people the English, and particularly their colourless, flat-chested women. Looked as though they would faint at the sight of a spider, but actually tough as the horses they rode so well. She was pretty in her way, he con-ceded, but she lacked nearly all the feminine attributes which appealed to his Latin temperament. He wondered if she'd ever see those friends with whom she and her father were intending to

7

spend a pleasant month in Jamaica before returning home to the English spring.

Personally, he would not have staked a fortune on her chances, or his own of reporting for duty to the Military Commandant's office in the French colony of Guadaloupe. It was all very well for that hulking Finn to keep a stiff upper lip and talk optimistically. He was one of the ship's officers, so it was his job to do so, but M. le Capitaine De Brissac had travelled a bit in his time and he didn't at all like the way things were shaping. The *Gafelborg* was an old ship and it was no reflection on her officers that she could not face up to these devilish seas which were throwing her about as if she were a cork in a mill-race.

He stroked his small D'Artagnan moustache and began to make a mental list of the really vital things to collect from his cabin if it did come to the point where they had to abandon ship. There seemed no immediate urgency about the matter. The old tub was probably good for a few hours yet, but if the storm didn't ease, the constant pounding on the sprung plate would loosen it further, and once the forehold had filled with water the position might become critical.

A sudden thought caused his handsome face to cloud with acute annoyance. Among his heavy luggage in the hold there was a packing-case containing the parts of a new type of machine-gun; his own invention upon which he had been working for over two years. It was impossible to get the crate up now; if the ship did go down the precious gun would be lost. He decided swiftly that he had much better put any nightmare pictures of the ship actually sinking out of his mind, and at that moment his eyes fell on Synolda.

She was sitting up now talking to the Venezuelan. De Brissac wondered vaguely what she could possibly see in such a bounder. He thought her most attractive and would have liked to have known her better but she had been almost offensively curt on the few occasions he had spoken to her, whereas she had accepted Vicente Vedras's attentions right from the first day of the voyage.

'Please, Synolda,' Vicente was saying, his words inaudible to the others in the roar of the storm. 'A little champagne and a dry biscuit. Something to fortify you and keep your insides going. Champagne of the best and the little biscuit; believe me that is the thing, 'owever bad the sickness.'

She looked at him through half-closed eyes. 'I feel so ill I wish

I were dead. We're all going to die—aren't we? The ship'll be shaken to bits if this goes on much longer.'

'No, no, no!' he protested. 'Things are not so bad. The Second Engineer 'as said there is no danger. 'E can judge—that one—the big, blond man.'

Vicente was so passionately anxious to believe the best that he had accepted Luvia's statement without question. The future was rich for him, rich beyond his wildest dreams with the gold just discovered on his brother's farm in South Africa; rich, too, in hopes of getting his way with Synolda whose beauty had inflamed his desires to fever pitch. He leant toward her:

'Be of good cheer, little one. The storm by morning will be finish. Soon your Vicente will make for you a paradise in Venezuela.'

She screwed up her wide mouth and shrugged slightly. 'I've told you twenty times I'm leaving the ship at Rio.'

'Oh, no,' he said with sudden firmness. 'You come on with me to Caracas, otherwise it may be that you will meet bad trouble.'

Her eyes hardened. 'You've hinted at that sort of thing before, but laughed it off each time I've questioned you. Just what do you mean?'

'You know, my beautiful Synolda. I am not one to threaten. I 'oped you would appreciate my delicacy—my patience—in the week of days since we left Cape Town. A week is a long time for us Venezuelans who are 'ot-blooded people; particularly when the sun shines as it did until—until, yes, the day that preceded yesterday. You are the loveliest woman I 'ave ever seen. You will be kind to Vicente or there will be questions. The people at Rio will want to know things about your 'usband.'

'He's dead,' she declared sullenly.

Vicente nodded. 'But it might be that some curious people would make the inquiry to know why you left South Africa without any luggage and all that—eh?'

Synolda's eyelids quivered. For the thousandth time in a hundred and fifty hours she wondered anxiously how much the dark-faced man opposite her really knew. Certainly that he knew something had kept her civil to him—but what? Her home was actually in Caracas; not Rio as she had given out, although she meant to leave the ship there. He might perhaps have known her by sight when she was living in the Venezuelan capital, but she could not swear she had not set eyes on him during her recent visit to South Africa so how could he know anything of her recent

9

past? She had made a bad slip though in giving it out that she was a widow.

He nodded again. 'You be a good girl and nice to Vicente when the storm is gone—yes—it is better so.'

Suddenly, above the muffled howling of the wind something hit the ship with a boom like thunder; the reverberation of the shock echoed for at least a minute. The timbers groaned, the bolts grated in the girders as though about to be torn out of their sockets; the deck reared up aft to so sharp an angle that the passengers would have been thrown from the settees unless they had clung to the screwed-down tables.

De Brissac knew the ship had taken another giant wave on her for'ard well-deck; that sunken space between the fo'c'sle and the bridge would now be four feet deep in water and she must lift again before it could pour off through the storm ports.

The *Gafelborg* rose once more, yet the deck of the lounge continued to slant steeply up towards the companionway at its after end. De Brissac waited, imagining that the volume of water was too great for the scuppers to carry it off so soon, but the lounge remained tilted permanently. He knew then that she had been seriously damaged.

That knowledge was reflected in the faces of the other passengers; all but a few showed varying degrees of fear from a furtive, hunted look to one of stark terror.

'Dear God! Dear God we're going to drown,' wailed a middle-aged woman, in Spanish; flinging herself on her knees beside the two nuns.

The elderly Greek wrung his hands in an agony of misery. He was not frightened for himself, but he knew that if he was drowned his rascally half-brother would contrive some means to cheat his wife and son out of their share of the family business.

The screws were vibrating like electric drills; at shorter intervals now as the stern was tossed for longer periods from the water. The old cargo carrier began to wallow horribly and it seemed that at any moment she might turn turtle.

Basil Sutherland came scampering up the companionway on all fours; pitched into the lounge, and slithered down the slope towards the bar. De Brissac caught him by an elbow and steadied him. 'Back already, eh! What happened just now?'

'A hundred tons of briny smashed in the fore-hatch. No more use to go on pumping than it would be to try and ladle out the contents of a swimming bath with a soup spoon.'

'The forehold is full up with water then?'

'Yes.' Basil was sober enough now. 'Fortunately her forward bulkhead is holding, but she's badly down at the head. She's so sluggish in the troughs that her nose'll hardly lift before another comber crashes over her fo'c'sle head.'

'It looks, then, that we are for it.'

A report penetrated the hubbub and Basil nodded. ' 'Fraid so. Hear that? They're beginning to send up their rockets. They've been keeping the distress signals for an emergency.'

'*Mon Dieu!* What is the good of rockets when there is so little shipping here in the South Atlantic?'

Basil grinned mirthlessly. 'And we're over a thousand miles from the nearest land.'

'I shall see you!' The Frenchman ran up the deck, slipped, caught at the banister-rail of the companionway, and plunged down it.

Bang! Smash! The ship reeled again under another sledge-hammer blow. For a moment the dark green sea covered the starboard ports of the lounge, although it was up on the boat-deck. The shock and following dip to port were so acute that a number of bottles were jolted from the racks of the bar. Hansie's face took on a greenish tinge as they smashed behind him.

Even he was scared now. In a mental flash he saw a young girl nursing a baby. The child was his and he was doing the right thing by the girl, although he could not marry her because he had a wife already. What would happen to both of them if the sea got him and he could never send poor little Hildagrad any more money?

Another of the women suddenly jumped to her feet and screamed. Instantly she was flung full length to the deck and rolled across it until brought up by the legs of a port-side table. Vicente and some others, swaying like a Rugby scrum, managed to get her up between them.

Colonel Carden braced his good leg against a table to prevent himself from slipping off the settee. Beside him, Unity, still outwardly calm, felt as though her heart was rising into her throat to choke her. She feared that at any moment she would give way at last to an unsuppressible fit of terror. Grabbing her father's hand, she pressed it and he turned to look at her.

'Cheer up, Daddy,' she said, striving to reassure herself. 'We'll be all right.'

'Of course we will,' he replied gruffly. 'I'd be happier if we were

11

in a British ship, but these Swedes are first-class sailors. The Viking blood, you know; we've got a dash of it ourselves.'

The heaving deck had assumed a new angle. It sloped now towards the port bow. The forehold being full of water weighed them down by the head and something else had given them a permanent list to port.

De Brissac, frantically grabbing the most important items of his kit down below in his cabin, rightly suspected a shifting of the cargo.

Crack! Something snapped on the deck outside. The despairing wail of a human being penetrated to the lounge. Vump—smack —sisss! They were hit again.

Jean De Brissac's head suddenly shot up from the companion-way. It hovered for a moment. As the ship rode on the crest of the next wave he seemed to bounce up the last few steps. He was wearing his military cloak and had a rubber rainproof over the crook of his arm.

The *Gafelborg* heeled over. The Frenchman lost his grip on the banisters and came crashing into the settee where Unity was crouching. His white teeth, set tight, flashed below his little dark moustache. She managed a feeble smile as he shouted an apology.

The racing screws seemed as if they must be tearing the bowels out of the ship. She staggered, plunged, rolled in the troughs and was cast upward only to bump again on the next wave. The spray scurried past the ports incessantly. The passengers who could still think at all realized that the ship was now out of control; they were at the mercy of a crazy thing.

Juhani Luvia, the blue-eyed Finn, suddenly appeared among them; his face was tense; with him were the Swedish First and Third Officers; the water was pouring from their oilskins. The ship's siren began to wail piercingly overhead.

'Get your lifebelts!' bellowed the First Officer above the din. 'You know your boat stations—go to them!'

CHAPTER II

TO THE BOATS

'To the boats—to the boats!' the cry was taken up in half a dozen languages. The passengers snatched their cork life-jackets and hastily set about adjusting them.

In two groups they scrambled towards the entrances of the lounge which gave direct on to the boat deck. The English-speaking passengers had all been allotted to the port boat aft, which was the Third Officer's and also Juhani Luvia's. The Finnish Engineer grabbed Unity Carden's arm with one hand and Synolda Ortello's with the other. As the port entrance was the more sheltered of the two the little crowd had no difficulty in pressing through it.

De Brissac's place was in the starboard boat aft with the First Officer. They had to wait for a moment until a lull in the storm gave them a chance to fling open the door without fear of a sea driving them backwards. The Frenchman had hold of the elder of the two nuns, and, supporting her as best he could, he began to stagger up the slanting deck.

Above him, to the right, the insistent buzz of the wireless in the operator's cabin momentarily caught his ear; S O S—S O S—S O S; as the ether waves stabbed the dark night with their urgent call for help.

The piercing note of the ship's siren cut through the thunder of the storm; it was sounding an unceasing succession of short blasts. Another rocket was fired with a loud report; it burst in the blackness above and for a second De Brissac glimpsed its coloured stars before they went out.

The *Gafelborg* plunged again; a sea of terrifying height loomed up out of the darkness to starboard. It swept forward, hovered like a towering cliff, then broke and came rushing down to engulf them.

He flung his right arm round a staunchion and clung to it with all his might. With his left, he clutched the frail body of the nun. For a moment they were both entirely submerged by the torrent of water. The ship lifted again and they gasped for breath while the flood seeped back over the side, sucking and gurgling and almost pulling them over with it.

They caught a glimpse of a figure being whirled away behind them. It was the other nun. She crashed against the rail, doubled up, and fell limply. Someone sprang after her and dragged her to her feet, but she could not stand and was carried along in their rear.

The boat was already swung out on its davits. The First Officer and a number of the crew, all wearing lifebelts, stood by it. Some of them were crouching in the boat ready to help the passengers aboard.

A lesser wave scudded round their ankles and poured away in foaming cascades, the phosphorus in the spume temporarily lighting up the deck. Owing to their list to port and downward tilt for'ard, the starboard boat aft was higher than the others. Swaying drunkenly, half fainting and wholly terrified, the women were passed into it like so many bundles. The screaming of the wind drowned all efforts at speech except the stentorian bellowings of the Officer through his megaphone.

Another big wave surged over them and they all clung blindly to the nearest gear that offered. The boat's complement was nearly completed when the Officer made an imperative gesture to Jean De Brissac, but the Frenchman backed away.

Some instinct warned him not to commit himself to this timbered cockleshell, packed with drenched, bemused humanity, which hung at what seemed to him so perilous an angle over the slanting side of the ship.

In a flash of memory he recalled the advice of a man who had survived three shipwrecks. 'Never try for a place in a boat. They so often prove death-traps when lowered in a storm, and even if a boat's launched safely there's danger of its becoming overloaded through picking up people who're struggling in the water, or capsizing in a heavy sea. Far better avoid the crowd and play a lone hand. Lash yourself to a collapsible raft and wait until you're floated off as the ship goes down. A raft rides the waves like a great lump of cork, so you can't possibly drown. It's only a question of endurance; just sticking the cold and discomfort till daylight comes and you're spotted from one of the other ships the S O S has brought to the scene of the wreck.'

Three sailors who were standing by to lower the boat flung themselves upon De Brissac and began to drag him towards it.

The arrival of another wave forced them to loose their hold on him and grab at the davits for their own preservation. He was nearly swept overboard, but managed to clutch the rail and clung to it with straining fingers.

The spume-spattered water was still streaming fi om the deck when the First Officer passed within a foot of him, shrugged angrily, and clambered into the boat. It was not his duty to rescue grown men who were crazy and refused to take such steps for their own salvation; he had the women and the boat's crew to think of.

The sheaves in the blocks of the boat tackle screamed as the Swede raised his arm. The boat sank from sight, smacked into the water, a tiny toy affair, it seemed now, in the horrid blackness of the gulf below.

Suddenly a huge sea lifted it and cast it up against the steel side of the ship before it could get away. It was smashed like an egg-shell—splintered into bits. The men and women in it were flung into the seething waters and its shattered timbers were whipped away up the slopes of those mountains of blackness that rose on every side.

For a second, as the sea receded, De Brissac glimpsed a white face on its surface, and the two arms lifted in mute appeal, then he was blinded by the flying, dust-like froth. When he could look again no trace of the boat or its occupants was there below him in the space to show that he had not dreamed that swift fatality. He staggered back, clutching frantically at the deck-house rail behind him.

Numb, cold, soaked to the skin, he hung there waiting for the sea's next subsidence; when it came he staggered through a narrow alleyway between two deck houses to the port side of the ship.

Vaguely his mind was still revolving about the project of getting himself a raft. He would have done so without hesitation had he been north of the equator where the most important trade routes in the world are constantly traversed by quantities of shipping, but here, in the great wastes of the South Atlantic, it seemed certain that even if he could survive these tremendous seas he would die of thirst and starvation, alone upon a raft, long before there could be any reasonable hope of his being picked up.

The loss of his machine-gun down in the hold flashed into his mind again. It was complete and fit for action when assembled. He had refrained from dispatching it to the Ministry of War in Paris before leaving Madagascar only because he had not had time to carry out the final tests for heat by prolonged firing. Its

15

acceptance by his Government would mean promotion, a handsome grant, and, far more important in his eyes, a deadlier weapon for the defence of his beloved France than any of its kind possessed by other nations. He had plans of it, of course, actually on him in an oilskin wallet, so he could get another made—if he survived—if he survived. He began to upbraid himself furiously for his lack of forethought in not having deposited a duplicate set of plans with the authorities before sailing.

Next moment he stumbled into the Third Officer who was superintending the swinging out of the port boat aft and the party scheduled to go off in it.

Most of the boat's complement was already aboard. In the coloured light which flickered momentarily from the falling stars of another rocket, turning white faces to a ghastly hue, De Brissac glimpsed Unity Carden sitting bolt upright in the stern, next to her father.

Synolda Ortello was between old Colonel Carden and Basil Sutherland. Her fair hair, caught in the violent wind, was whipping about in wild disorder; her blue eyes were wide and terrified. Some of her eyelash black had run where she had tried to wipe the flying spray from her chalk-white face. Vicente Vedras had attempted to force his way into the boat with her, but as he was listed for the port boat for'ard, which was taking off the Portuguese-speaking passengers, the Third Officer had refused to allow him to board.

As De Brissac came staggering into them the Venezuelan was still pleading with the Swede to be allowed to join the young widow for whom he had developed such a desperate passion.

'Wait!' shouted the officer. 'I must check my crew—if there's room I'll take you.'

Juhani Luvia was standing in the bow of the boat. He and the young Third Officer yelled at each other, cupping their hands about their mouths like megaphones to make themselves heard above the screaming of the straining timbers and constant hiss of rushing water.

It was found that three sailors were missing from their posts. One was a Quartermaster who had been carried overboard earlier in the day; another lay dead in the fo'c'sle, killed an hour before by the snapping of a wire rope under tremendous strain which had flown back with such force that it had nearly severed his head from his body; the third was a young apprentice who had just disappeared—no one knew where.

The officer swung round on the Venezuelan. 'All right—up you go!'

The siren blared incessantly; shouts and curses sounded faintly above the howling storm.

A lurch of the ship sent De Brissac reeling a dozen paces forward, so that he came just opposite the bow of the boat; it was above him, but only a few feet beyond the ship's rail where he brought up. Peering down on to the deck, Luvia recognized him, and, leaning out, yelled at the top of his voice: 'Why the hell aren't you in your boat, man?'

'Boat's gone!' De Brissac roared back. 'I'd thought of waiting till she goes under and floating off on one of the rafts.'

'You're nuts!'

'I'm not—the other boat was smashed to bits against the ship—everyone drowned. I doubt if you'll be any luckier.'

'We're better off here—the list to port'll help us drop clear—no alternative worth trying.'

'You're full up, aren't you?' De Brissac hesitated.

The tall Finn smiled, leaned further over, grabbed him and drew him up. 'Even if we are, we'd take you—we can do with real men. *Vite, mon Capitaine!* We haven't a chance in a hundred, but we'll take it together.' De Brissac scrambled on to the rail and was hauled over the gunwale by willing hands.

The Third Officer clambered into the stern at the same moment. 'Lower away,' he thundered in Swedish; and the sailors remaining on the ship's deck paid out the falls.

A merciful, but all-too-short, silence ensued as they sank under the lee of the vessel, protected momentarily from the driving spray and cutting wind by its black bulk towering beside them. Entirely out of control, the *Gafelborg* had swung round a little and was wallowing beam-on to the tempest.

The sailors got out their long, heavy oars and those to starboard used them to fend off the boat from the ship's side, which, with its portholes still brightly lit, now sloped above, seeming as if about to fall upon them. The others were holding their oars aloft awaiting the Officer's order to lower them to the tholes.

Suddenly a swell carried the boat up until it was almost level with the ship's deck. It rocked violently, and, as without warning the sea sank again, almost turned over.

Several of the standing men stumbled; a negro stoker tripped over the after thwart, lost his grip on an oar he had been holding, and fell against the Officer. The Swede staggered uncertainly,

17

clutched wildly at the empty air, and, with a piercing cry, pitched backwards overboard.

At the same second the oar came crashing down among the forward passengers of the boat. Its blade caught De Brissac on the head before he could twist aside. A thousand stars circled and vibrated before his eyes, a suffocating blackness smothered him, and he slid down like a pole-axed ox between the struggling seamen.

Juhani Luvia flung himself half out of the boat in an attempt to grasp the Officer, but the Swede was swept past out of his reach and whirled away to death in the raging, foam-flecked torrent.

While Luvia was making his futile attempt at rescue, the sailors had begun to ply their oars; three to starboard, two to port. Colonel Carden grasped the tiller and turned the boat's nose away from the ship's side.

De Brissac was hauled to his feet, but he hung as a sack between those who held him, and blood trickled down his face—he was dead or unconscious. Luvia ordered the lifeless body to be passed along to the stern sheets and laid out there on the bottom boards. He followed it aft, plunging recklessly over the bent backs of the oarsmen. Now that the Third Officer was dead it fell to him, although an engineer, to take command of the boat. With a nod he relieved the Colonel of the tiller and sat down between him and Basil Sutherland.

Basil knew that he ought to be very, very drunk indeed. Convinced that there was not a shadow of a hope that any of them could live, once they were ordered to take to the boats in what seemed to be the very centre of the cyclone, he had snatched up a bottle of brandy and emptied its remaining contents down his throat before leaving the lounge. He was still gasping from the effects of the fiery liquor which burned in his chest and threatened him with the agonizing pains of the most acute indigestion, but he was not drunk. Far from it, the stress of the crisis seemed instantly to have dissipated the fumes of the alcohol, or made his brain impervious to them. His senses had quickened so that he seemed to be reeling, seeing, and hearing every phase of the drama that was being played out around him, with abnormal clarity.

He found himself contemplating his own fate with astonishing detachment. Long since, he had ceased to have any illusions about his personal importance in the scheme of things. He was a failure, that's all there was to it; although perhaps deep down he had always had a vague idea that somehow, somewhere, sometime, an

John Roberts.

opportunity would be given to play a better role than that of an unwanted waster. He'd often regretted not having gone on the Everest trip when he'd had the chance. Expert mountaineers had considered his climbing showed exceptional promise as a young man, but more facile excitement had kept him at home. It was too late now to recall lost opportunities, and they would come no more. He was still only twenty-six, but life was ending—ending—the sands were running out while he sat there silent and acquiescent in the crowded boat.

The sky was black as ink; not a cloud's edge silvered by moonlight nor the pinprick of a star broke the universal canopy of darkness above them. The only lights came from the *Gafelborg*; a line of yellow moons amidships, a few more about the bridge and the abandoned lounge, the navigation lights in the rigging and a brilliant flare that someone was holding on the after-deck.

Forward, on the side of the ship nearest to them, the other port boat was now being manned. Dark figures silhouetted for seconds only in the glare of torches moved swiftly about it. Suddenly it seemed to fall stern first towards the water.

Carried on the terrific wind which roared over them at a hundred miles an hour, they clearly heard the shrieks and imprecations of the wretched people who had been pitched out into the boiling sea.

With swift presence of mind some sailor, who had retained a precarious hold on the other boat, hacked through the bow falls with his knife. It flopped into the water sending up a great sheet of spray.

Luvia's men were endeavouring to keep their boat steady and give it way. They were already fifty yards from the *Gafelborg*, although they could only dip their oars on alternate sides at one time owing to the constantly changing slope of the dark swell.

Rockets were still sailing upward and detonating with loud reports above the ship. Game to the last, the Swedish Captain was firing his whole stock before going over the side to take command of his own cutter.

'*Dios! Dios!*' cried Vicente Vedras, burying his head in his hand. He had seen the other boat, in which he should have been, now under-manned through its mishap in launching, picked up on a wave-crest and capsized. In the constantly shifting reflections from the ports they could see it floating upside down with one little figure clinging to it before it was swept away into the darkness.

The blaring of the siren ceased; a last rocket flung out its coloured stars in a graceful curve high overhead; the blue flashes from the signal lamp in the rigging suddenly stopped. The Captain and those remaining on the *Gafelborg* were now taking their lives in their hands as they attempted to get away in the forward boat to starboard. The little company in Luvia's boat, who were watching, could not see if the attempt was successful because they were on the far side of the ship.

'I'll never see daylight again,' thought Unity Carden, 'never live to ride another horse. It's no good fooling myself any more. We'll be swamped inside ten minutes; the boat will sink and we'll all be struggling in the sea. God! how I wish I'd let George make love to me when he wanted to so badly. Now I'll die without ever having known what love is like.'

Basil's mouth was set in a cynical grin. He was just thinking that there was not a single soul in the world who would be really hit by the news of his death, except perhaps Barbara, now a big noise in Hollywood. She might even sling back a few extra cocktails because she wouldn't care to think of the young man she'd loved for a brief season floating bloated and swollen a few feet below the surface of the ocean with the fishes nibbling at his eyes.

As they drifted and paddled farther from the abandoned ship they left the shelter she had temporarily given them. Fierce drifts of spray, stinging as April sleet in the Highlands of Scotland, beat in their faces. The boat slid up a watery mountain until its occupants felt that it would take off like a seaplane and zoom up into the dark heaven. For a second it hovered, poised in the tempestuous breaking waters on the summit, then slithered down a natural watershoot to unseen depths.

Carried skyward once again to a mighty crest, they could see a score of other white-topped peaks separated by awful gulfs and the *Gafelborg* a hundred feet below, heaving slowly in a watery valley. They were high above her mastheads and still rising. The lights from her line of ports amidships showed by their slant that she was heavily down by the bow. A great sea broke over her, the wash gleaming dully with phosphorescent light. There was no sign of the Captain's boat; nothing but the derelict ship was visible except for patches of angry foam on the surface of the storm-tossed waters.

Suddenly Luvia's boat began to rush down the precipitous farther side of the mountainous wave that had caught them up.

20

As though catapulted forward by the unleashed force of a ten thousand horse-power engine, they were carried headlong into the black void. When they rose again on the ridge of another terrific sea the *Gafelborg* had disappeared behind them and they were utterly alone on the raging waters of the mighty ocean.

CHAPTER III

ADRIFT

How they survived the remaining hours of the night none of them could afterwards have said. Many times they were within an ace of capsizing; often the boat reared up on end so that it seemed to be almost standing on its bow or stern. The weaker members of the party had to be tied down to prevent their being flung out; the stronger worked at the bailers, waging an unceasing battle with the incoming spray which washed ankle deep about the bottom boards, until they were blind and stupid with fatigue. Yet, by its buoyancy the lifeboat continued to ride the waves and miraculously weathered the storm. Dawn found them chilled to the marrow, drenched to the skin, and huddled in grotesque attitudes where they had fallen when too exhausted to carry on the struggle further, but still alive.

Alone among them, Juhani Luvia saw the coming of the dawn. He had not closed an eye all night. In the long hours of duty, while the hurricane raged, it had hardly occurred to him that things would go so badly they might have to abandon ship. Later, when the crisis came, his every thought was concerned with saving the passengers and crew allotted to his boat from the fresh perils which beset them every moment. It was only when the last of his men had given in that he began to think of the death he had fought off and another, more terrible, form of death which would soon be creeping on him.

He was not afraid to die, but he would have preferred drowning to the grim end he now foresaw he might have to face, adrift in an open boat, in the near future. He was glad now that he had never married; at least he had no wife and children to worry over.

Athletics had taken most of his spare time while he was studying to become an engineer, and, since he had been at sea, his affairs with women, apart from one long, drawn-out sentimental attachment to a German girl in Hamburg, who had married the

22

year before, had been limited to a few short-lived romances in various ports.

Juhani's mother would be the only sufferer from his death. His father had owned a prosperous timber business until the collapse of the Swedish match combine had ruined him and subsequent worry had led to his early death. Since then the young engineer had contributed to his mother's support. She lived now in a pleasant apartment overlooking the river and with a fine view of the old castle at Viipuri, a port near the head of the Gulf of Finland, where Juhani had been born. He was her only son and very devoted to her. It was a bitter thought to him that in addition to mourning his loss the poor lady would have to move to less comfortable quarters if death robbed her of him.

The pale greyness of the eastern sky was soon touched with gold: the colour deepened and spread until it looked as though a great bonfire was burning there miles away under the horizon. Sunrise was no unusual sight for a sea-going engineer, but it never failed to remind Luvia of his summer holidays in boyhood spent among Finland's ten thousand lakes and their hundred thousand wooded islands where short nights give place to daybreaks of stupendous beauty.

A fresh wind was blowing, but the hurricane was past. Great seas were still running and continued to carry them up and down on the bosom of a long, rolling swell. Luvia could not see any great distance, but as far as he could see no sign of life showed on the grey-green waters. He leant over and undid the knot of the line that was holding Basil Sutherland in place on the seat beside him.

As the line came loose from round his waist Basil slipped forward and fell with a bump on the bottom boards. His eyelids flickered and he came out of black unconsciousness.

He felt ghastly. His mouth was dry and evil tasting, his head heavy and throbbing dully, his eyes were aching in a way that told from experience, without the aid of any mirror, that they must be terribly bloodshot; he was suffering every symptom of a first-class hangover.

That was no new sensation as during the last year or two he had gone to bed in varying degrees of tightness more often than not. However, he was still young and blessed with a good consti-tution, so his drinking had not yet seriously undermined his health and he knew just what he wanted to make himself his own man again—a good hot bath with its accompanying rituals, and two large cups of China tea. Thus fortified he would normally have appeared spruce, amiable, and ready to talk with reasonable intelligence to anyone congenial.

His eyes had not been open ten seconds when he realized that his chances of obtaining either a hot bath or China tea were about as remote as his coming into another comfortable fortune like that the rash expenditure of which was the prime cause of his being where he was at the moment.

When he had tilted that half-bottle of brandy down his throat before abandoning ship he had been convinced they were all about to die. He remembered feeling strangely sober when they piled into the boat; but shortly afterwards the huge quantity of neat spirit, taken at a draught on top of all he had drunk before, had done its work; he had lapsed into a drunken stupor. Now, it seemed, by some act of God or fantastic freak of chance, the boat had not gone down after all. He was ill, wretchedly ill, but still very much alive—that was quite certain.

De Brissac's body lay stretched out at full length beside him. During the night someone had tied a handkerchief round the Frenchman's head and in the dawn light patches of dried blood stood out darkly on it. His handsome face was a chalk-blue and he lay so still it seemed certain he was dead. Basil stretched out a hand and touched him gently on the shoulder.

'Leave him alone, you young fool,' growled Colonel Carden. 'Can't you see he's sleeping?' The old man was wide awake, having only dropped into an uneasy doze just before the dawn. His daughter, in spite of the apparent discomfort of her position, bent over at an angle, was sleeping soundly, with her head in his lap.

Basil murmured an apology, rolled his tongue round his evil-tasting mouth, and lifted himself back on to the seat from which he had slipped. He was already beginning to feel that Fate would have been kinder to allow him to drown while dead drunk on good Hennessy rather than to preserve him for the sort of end he could expect in an open boat at sea. There was, he supposed, an outside chance that they might be picked up, but the unnatural existence he had led for the past two years had veiled his naturally cheerful nature with a pessimistic outlook.

At the sound of Colonel Carden's growling reprimand, Vicente Vedras sat up with a start. He had been dreaming of all the gold that lay under his brother's farm in South Africa. In the dream he had already sold his coffee business in Venezuela and returned with the money to Johannesburg. The two of them had bought all the necessary mining machinery and installed it; they were actually drilling the new reef which would make them both multi-millionaires. He had been telling his brother how wise he had been to send for him, Vicente, instead of getting the capital, which he needed to exploit his discovery, from strangers. Now they would keep it all in the family. All that rich, red gold that would buy women and cattle and plantations, and women and horses, and yet more women.

Vicente stared across the boat at Synolda, sleeping still. Her golden hair, escaped from under a sou'wester, tumbled about her white face and neck. That one first, he thought, she is lovely—lovely as the Madonna in the painting that hangs in the side chapel of the church at El Perso. Then he shivered in his sodden clothes and wakened to grim reality. His dark eyes became shadowed and he began to wring his hands.

Luvia had stood up to get a wider view and was searching the horizon on every side with his binoculars. At last he lowered them and looked down at the boat's company.

'Not a sail in sight,' Basil remarked before the Finn had a chance to speak. 'That's the correct expression—isn't it?'

'You've said it,' Luvia snapped, 'but I don't see it's anything to go making wisecracks about.'

Colonel Carden did not like Basil. In fact he and his daughter were at one in regarding the young man as a disgrace to his class, but the old man would not stand by and see one of his own countrymen snubbed without reason.

'You don't understand our English character, sir,' he shot at Luvia. 'It's our habit to make jokes when we find ourselves up against it—and a very good habit too.'

'Right-oh, Colonel, joke away if you want to—and welcome.' The tall young Finn shrugged his broad shoulders and began to check up the boat's company. Some had oilskins, others not, but all of them looked blue with cold, miserable and dejected.

He was the only officer in it, but he had Jansen, the ship's carpenter, and four other Swedes—Bremer, an elderly reliable man; red-headed Steffens; young Largertöf, and Hansie, the lounge steward; also a half-caste seaman named Gietto Nudäa. The passengers were Colonel Carden and his daughter, Basil Sutherland, Vicente Vedras, Captain Jean De Brissac, and Synolda Ortello. They also carried four stokers from the engine-room, all negroes. That made a total of fifteen men and two

25

women, but two of the men were as good as useless—old Colonel Carden with his gammy leg and the wounded De Brissac.

As he glanced down on the comatose French Army Captain, Luvia frowned. He felt it a particularly evil stroke of luck that the falling oar should have knocked out the man who was so obviously best fitted to be his right hand during the hours or days of terrible uncertainty and appalling strain which lay ahead.

The breeze was dropping rapidly and the boat rocked idly on the long, gentle swell, drifting mainly with the current. Best try and warm them up a bit, Luvia thought, and raising his voice he shouted to the crew in Swedish.

As the men roused and got out the oars he tapped Colonel Carden on the shoulder. 'Did you understand what I said, Colonel?'

'No—er—I—er don't speak any foreign languages.'

'That's just too bad, because we Finns like to pull one now and again when we're in a spot, as well as you English. I've just told the boys they'd best put their backs into it or we won't make the coast of South America by lunch time.'

Basil managed a sickly grin. 'You mean by Christmas. With eleven months to go we might manage that.'

The Colonel grunted but turned to his daughter who had been woken by Luvia's shouted orders. 'Well, Unity, how're you feeling?' he asked with forced cheerfulness.

She gazed round, her grey eyes dull with great purple shadows beneath them. 'Not too bad,' she replied a trifle hoarsely, and she began to tidy herself as best she could.

Synolda had woken at the same moment. She was staring at her face in a little mirror she had taken from her bag.

'Oh, God!' she exclaimed miserably, and rubbing the brine from her face with a rag of handkerchief she set to work to repair the ravages of the storm by heavy application of powder, rouge and lipstick.

Basil's teeth began to chatter. He remembered now having given the suit of oilskins that he had been wearing when they left the pumps to Synolda just before he passed out. His clothes were soaked through from the spray that had driven gustily over them all night. He was chilled to the marrow of his bones and had a thirst on him which he felt could hardly have been quenched by the contents of the Great Tun of Heidelberg.

'Go get on to one of the oars,' said Luvia. 'That'll put some warmth into you.'

'All right,' Basil lurched to his feet. 'For God's sake give me a drink first though. Got any brandy in the locker you're sitting on? If not, rum'll do.'

The Finn's fair-skinned, freckled face set grimly. 'I'm afraid you'll have to cut out the drinking for a while. I've had no chance to examine our stores as yet, but if there's any spirits they'll be held for medicinal purposes. Maybe you'll get a half-cup of water when I issue the morning rations.'

'Thank you, my brave Viking. There's no need to be so darned pleased and pious about our lack of civilized liquor though. I'm a medical case at the moment if ever there was one. Come on, give me a swig of something to pull me together.'

'You heard me!'

'I heard you talking like a pussyfoot schoolboy who doesn't understand the needs of a grown man.'

'Sir! You forget yourself,' Colonel Carden interposed sharply. 'Mr. Luvia is the officer in charge of this boat. To his skill in handling her, his example, and the manner in which he kept his men at bailing her out all night, while you were in a disgusting, drunken sleep, we owe our lives.'

'Oh, Lord, defend me from these thy heroes,' muttered Basil: upon which the Colonel's face turned a bright brick red.

'Now, Daddy, now!' Unity exclaimed, clutching at the old man's arm as he began to struggle to his feet. 'Don't take any notice of him—he's not worth it.'

'Your servant, Madam,' Basil bowed unsteadily, 'and my congratulations on your perspicacity.'

As he turned away he felt a touch on his elbow. Synolda was holding out a small flask which she had taken from her bag. 'It's Van der Hum,' she said. 'I can guess what you must be feeling like. Go ahead.'

He took the flask, swallowed two medium-sized gulps, and, screwing the top on again, handed it back to her. The rich tangerine-orange flavoured South African liqueur brought new life to him. It warmed his inner man and sent the blood coursing more rapidly through his veins. He smiled down at the girl who looked like a rather shop-soiled Marlene Dietrich.

'That was darned decent of you. I'm very, very grateful.'

She pursed the full lips of her now reddened mouth, and shook her head. 'It was decent of you to wrap me up in your oilskins last night. I should have died of cold if you hadn't, and one good turn deserves another.'

'It very seldom gets it though. Anyhow, you're a darling!' Cheered by that brief, friendly encounter in this little crowd of people made unnaturally hostile by misery and dejection, he stumbled forward across two thwarts and sat down on the third, next to Hansie, the fat barman.

There was ample room on the thwarts for two men to pull at each of the big oars, and all six were already in motion. Basil had chosen to double bank Hansie because, as the barman's best customer on the seven days' run from Cape Town, he had come to know him well.

'Glad to see you with us, Hansie,' he remarked, grabbing the oar as it swung back in the tholes, and lending his weight on the next stroke.

'Glad ter be here, Mister Sutherland. 'Fraid I can't offer to fix you an eye-opener this morning, though.' Like most Swedes, the little man was multilingual. He had served in many ships and his English had an indefinable accent, something between that of a Bowery American and a London Cockney. 'How d'you figure we'll make out?'

'Lord knows! There's not much shipping in this area.'

'And no islands neither.'

'Where does the Second Engineer think he's taking us, I wonder?'

'Sun's in yer eye, so we're moving due west, seein' it's only just risen. If we keep pulling long enough we'll hit the coast of South America.'

'If?' Basil repeated sceptically. 'We're a thousand—perhaps fifteen hundred—miles from land. Allowing for winds and currents we couldn't row that distance in a month. We'll be sunk by another storm or dead of thirst long before that.'

'Sure, Mister Sutherland, sure. We're in pretty bad unless we get picked up.'

'What sort of stores do these lifeboats carry?'

'Keg of water, jar of rum, tinned beef and biscuits. That's about the usual in most freighters where I've done stooard; though I've never had to quit ship before.'

'The more I think about this party, the less I like it.'

'I like it so mighty little I'm jus' not thinking about it at all. I'm lying doggo and saving my strength for when the real trouble starts.'

'You mean when the water runs short?'

'Ai—an' worse as a result of that.'

'Just what are you hinting at, Hansie?'

The barman lowered his voice. 'Keep the soft pedal on the organ, Mister Sutherland. All these fellars understand a bit of English, knocking around in all sorts of ships as they do, an' the nigger stokers come from the Southern States. It's them I'm scared of. We got a sight too big a coloured quota in this outfit. You see, we lost the Third Officer last night; besides a Quartermaster, a white seaman and an apprentice, who should be with us, bein' dead 'fore we quit the ship. That puts the niggers' odds up considerable, seein' one of the seamen's a mulatto too.'

'Oh, come,' Basil protested. 'There are only five of them including the half-caste, whereas we've three white A.B.s, the carpenter, Mr. Luvia, Mr. Vedras, you and me. That's eight without counting the old Colonel and poor De Brissac, who seems to have passed out. They'd be crazy to start anything when we outnumber them by practically two to one.'

'Sure, Mister Sutherland, sure. They wouldn't risk a beating-up as long as we're awake, but we've got to sleep sometimes. What's to prevent them rushing us when most of our bunch is having a shut-eye in the middle of the night?'

'Have you got any grounds for the mutiny bogey you're trying to scare me with, Hansie? Any of them say anything during the night to make you suspicious? Or were the officers having trouble with the engine-room staff before we left the ship?'

'You've guessed it. Don't go looking over yer shoulder now; but later on take a squint at the big buck nigger who's pulling bow. That's Harlem Joe. Used ter be in the boxing racket they tell me, but got slung out because he did some bigger fellar dirt. Next heard of doing a stretch for homicide in a jail down Missouri way. Broke prison during the 1937 floods and got signed on in the stokehold of a Dutchman outward bound from St. Louis. He——'

'Half a minute,' Basil muttered. 'How d'you know all this?'

'Picked it up from the other fellars in the fo'c'sle. Harlem's the boastful kind an' he knows no one'd do a split.'

'D'you mean to tell me that, knowing you had an escaped convict on board, none of you had the guts to report it to your officers?'

'Sure, Mister Sutherland,' Hansie's voice was as low and even as ever. It only just reached Basil's ear, and was drowned for the others by the constant tapping of the oars as they moved in the tholes. 'Life's not easy for poor sailormen. Plenty of fellars before the mast have records that wouldn't show too good if they was looked into, but they may have been unlucky and be decent scouts all the same.' '

'Yes, I understand that; and naturally you hang together. But in a case like this . . . well, homicide's murder, isn't it?'

'That's so. All the same, the unwritten law holds and anyone who goes back on it 'ud be asking for a knife in 'is ribs from one of the others the next dark night he went ashore.'

'D'you think he's got the others under his thumb?'

'I certainly do. He's one of these wise guys—considers himself educated because he's lived in Noo York. When he hands out the dope about all men being brothers and gives them the Communist angle on equality they just lap it up. Them three black buddies of his, Lem Williamson, Isiah Meek, and the one they call Corncob, eat right out of his hand.'

'That may be, Hansie; but what are you afraid they'll try anyway?'

'Why, Mister Sutherland, I can't rightly say. But some of us may get a knife in our ribs should Harlem get it into his nob that he'll stand a better chance himself if he can seize control of the boat.'

'But surely you're not suggesting that these five blacks would cut all our throats and chuck us overboard if they could take us by surprise? I can't believe they're as bad as that.'

'Can't you? Well, Harlem gave the Third Officer his last night. Oh, I can't prove it, and I'm not going to try; but when the Third slipped Harlem was just behind him. As sure as you like your gin fizz sweet, Mister Sutherland, that nigger fell against him on purpose, so as to send him over the side.'

'The devil he did! But why? Surely he must have known that by bumping off the officer in charge at a time like that he was adding enormously to the chance of the whole boat's company being drowned, including himself? It just doesn't make sense.'

Hansie spat nonchalantly over the side of the boat. 'Niggers don't have no sense—not like civilized people leastways. They're primitives—just big children with out-sized appetites; kind and jolly as God made 'em, or evil and dangerous scum of Satan's brew.'

'Does Mr. Luvia know any of these bedtime stories with which you've been trying to cheer me up?' Basil asked quietly.

'No, he wouldn't know anything, 'cept that Harlem's been

making trouble in the engine-room, and there's nothing much unusual in that.'

'Well, I'll tip him off to be on the look-out. Don't worry, Hansie; with the odds so much in our favour we'll be able to take care of ourselves all right.'

The sun had now risen well over the horizon. Its rays were not yet strong but carried a welcome warmth. Several members of the party took off their sea-soaked jackets and spread them out to dry. The sharp work at the oars was getting the men's circulation going, and they were already more cheerful than they had been a quarter of an hour before.

In the stern, Juhani Luvia had been making an inspection of the emergency stores, which proved considerably better than Hansie had led Basil to suppose. They consisted of a six-gallon cask of water, a half-gallon jar of rum, a canister of tea, three pounds of sugar, three tins of condensed milk, eight of corned beef, and a large supply of ship's biscuits. In addition there was a primus stove, methylated spirit, paraffin, a kettle, and a small medicine chest.

Basil was horribly out of condition, and a quarter of an hour's pulling proved as much as he could manage without suffering acute discomfort. He left Hansie and scrambled back into the stern. Vicente had taken his old place next to Synolda and, puffing like a grampus, he subsided on her other side.

Unity was busy with the primus and her father was helping to measure out the water for the kettle. Synolda was cutting thin slices of corned beef from a square block out of one of the tins.

'Feeling better now?' she asked Basil as he sat down.

'Yes,' he held his breath; 'warmer, anyway. You're looking fine—just as though you enjoyed this sort of thing.'

Actually, she was looking awful. Having made up her face for the day without any of her usual facilities, the cosmetics with which she had daubed it, lacking ground-work, stood out harsh and crude in the strong light of the morning sunshine; but he had lied deliberately, knowing that a compliment on her appearance was the best possible way to cheer her.

Her chin went up a trifle and she smiled. 'It's nice to know I look all right, because I'm feeling just like hell.'

Luvia gave the order to cease rowing and ship the oars. He was perfectly well aware that any progress they could make that way was so infinitesimal as to be virtually useless, and had only set them to pulling in the first place to put a little life into his men.

31

Now he called old Jansen, the carpenter, aft to take the tiller while he went forward himself to superintend the stepping of the short mast through a hole in the central thwart, and the setting of the single sail.

By the time the job was completed, and the boat rippling through the water at a steady pace, Unity had made the tea and all hands were called aft to receive rations.

Synolda had cut the block of bully beef into seventeen slices with scrupulous fairness, and each of them received one of these with a large ship's biscuit. De Brissac's was put aside, as he was still sleeping, in the hope that he might be able to manage it later.

Most of the sailors had brought mess tins in their hastily packed bundles, and there were half a dozen tin pannikins in the locker which served for the passengers. Luvia had them all set out in a row, and Unity, measuring the hot tea with one, distributed it equally among the rest.

The last to come up for his tin was Harlem Joe. Basil studied him with special interest now he could see him at close quarters. The negro was a huge man, weighing at least sixteen stone. He was wearing only a pair of canvas trousers and a dirty cotton singlet. The muscles of his biceps stood out under the black, shiny skin of his bare arms in great knotted cords. His forehead had none of the breadth seen in the musical type of jazz-band player, and sloped back to an ugly, high, pointed crown. His lips were thinner than is usual in his race and his nose straighter, but the eyes had a shifty look and the general expression was one of cunning blended with a certain brutal power.

For a moment he paused opposite Luvia, then he pointed with a thick beringed forefinger; first to his own pannikin, then to Luvia's, the only two remaining. 'Fair do's, Bass.'

Luvia looked down. There was very little in it, but just enough for anyone to have agreed that there was a spoonful or two more tea in his pannikin than in the negro's. Without a word he changed them over, giving the stoker the larger portion.

Having dealt equitably with a quite unintentional injustice, Luvia turned away; but Basil, who had watched the whole episode closely, kept his glance fixed on the negro's face. What he saw there brought home to him very strongly that Hansie had real grounds for his anxious forebodings.

Harlem Joe said nothing, but the half sly, half arrogant, smile which he gave his coloured companions as they moved forward held a world of meaning. 'You see,' it said as plainly as if he had

32

spoken, 'dat white swine would cheat us if he could, but I'se not the one to let him. I browbeat him into giving me his own ration —didn't I! He's got no guts.'

It was Monday, January the 10th, and they had been thirteen hours in the boat when, at midday, Luvia shot the sun with the dead Third Officer's sextant and, after a short calculation, announced that their latitude was in the neighbourhood of 35° South.

'Clever boy,' remarked Basil acidly. 'I didn't know you were a navigator as well as an engineer.'

'I'm not,' replied the Finn with a good-natured smile, 'but even an apprentice knows how to fix a sextant.'

'Christoforo Colo discover America before the instrument was invent at all,' Vicente said hopefully.

Unity nodded. 'And the Carthaginians circumnavigated Africa in one of their galleys nearly two thousand years before that.'

'Phoenicians,' Basil corrected. 'You're confusing Hanno's voyage with the sailors sent by Pharaoh Necho who sailed out of the Mediterranean from Egypt and returned nearly three years later up the Red Sea. They landed each year to sow and harvest a crop of wheat before going on; but where's all this erudition getting us? What does 35° South mean in terms that the lay mind can understand?'

Luvia spread out a chart he had taken from the locker and placed a square-ended forefinger in the middle of the South Atlantic. 'We're somewhere here, 'bout level with Cape Town in the east and Buenos Aires in the west. Just on the line that shows the limit to which drift ice comes north from the Antarctic.'

Fortunately for them it was early January, high summer in the southern hemisphere, at which season the nearest icebergs were many hundreds of miles to the south, so they had no cause to fear the intense cold they would have suffered had they chanced to drift into an archipelago of bergs at night.

On the contrary, the January temperature in that latitude was much the same as it would have been at sea in July off the coast of Morocco, and they were finding the strong sunshine a mixed blessing. In the mid-morning hours it had dried their clothes and cheered their spirits, but now it was grilling down on their backs and shoulders with uncomfortable persistence.

To protect the two girls from it, and give them a little privacy, a low, tent-like tarpaulin-covered shelter, with a flap that could be lowered, had been rigged up from spare gear at the extreme stern of the boat.

It was little more than a cubby-hole, dark, uncomfortable and awkward to move in, as the tiller, now artificially lengthened by a boathook lashed to it, ran through the centre of the space and out at the forward end; but it afforded a refuge from the eyes of the men, and in order to tend the unconscious De Brissac better Unity had him carried into it.

The Frenchman had roused just after breakfast. He had lost a great deal of blood and was delirious. After bathing and re-bandaging his head, they had forced some condensed milk diluted with water down his throat, and two tablets of medinol from the medicine chest, soon after which he had fallen into another heavy sleep.

At twelve-thirty Luvia issued rations again: half a cup of water all round and two biscuits apiece. He told them they would not feel so thirsty if they had no meat in the middle of the day and promised them a slice of corned beef a head with their evening meal.

Afterwards, the girls retired to try and snatch a nap in their shelter during the heat of the afternoon, and the crew set to work on making another low tent in the bows of the boat. Luvia decided the time had come to hold a conference, so he gathered Jansen, Vicente, Basil, and the Colonel round him in the stern.

'I think I ought to tell you people just where we stand,' he opened up at once, in a voice carefully lowered so that the women on the far side of the tarpaulin should not hear him. 'We're over a thousand miles from the nearest land, and I'd be a liar if I told you I thought there was the least chance of our making it.'

'Why not?' asked the Colonel gruffly. 'Lieutenant Bligh of the *Bounty* covered a greater distance than that in an open boat.'

'Did he? Well, maybe he did. I don't remember hearing about it; unless he's the guy who crossed the Atlantic in a canoe a year or two back. Anyhow, that's neither here nor there. The point is that whatever he did he was properly provisioned for the job—whereas we're not.'

' 'Ow many days' sail you need to arrive South America?' Vicente inquired.

'Even with a favourable wind I doubt if we could do it under fourteen days. As it is, the wind's next to useless. That's why we're tacking about so. We're constantly losing way to the south as it is.'

'And for 'ow many days 'ave we provision?'

'If we go easy we might make the food hang out a week. Water's the trouble. That cask holds six gallons, but it's lost about a gallon by evaporation. Four quarts to a gallon—that's twenty quarts. Two pints to the quart—forty pints. Say we allow ourselves three rations each per day of one-third of a pint: there are seventeen of us, so that's seventeen pints a day. We'll have used the lot by midday the day after tomorrow.'

'We could distil fresh water by boiling sea-water in the kettle,' suggested the Colonel.

'Only as long as our fuel lasts, and our supply of paraffin is pretty meagre.' Basil shrugged gloomily.

Vicente groaned. His dark eyes held the expression of a spaniel that has been unjustly punished. Life was so very good and would be infinitely better once they had mined the gold that lay under his brother's farm. It was unfair; unreasonable that death should come to claim him out here in the desolate wastes of the ocean when fortune promised him so many favours.

'How about cutting the ration down a bit?' asked Basil.

Luvia shook his head. 'I might a little, but not much. If we were in a cooler climate we could do on less, but we'll be burnt up on under a pint a day beneath a sun like this. Don't you agree, Jansen?'

'*Ja, ja*, Mister Luvia. I was in a boat myself one time off the Canaries. My, it was no joke that, and a pint a day we have to have, else we go mad of the heat. Fortunately, we do not run out and are picked up the third day.'

'You definitely state that it's impossible to reach the coast, Mr. Luvia?' the Colonel asked abruptly.

'Yes, unless we were blown there by another gale, and in that case it's a thousand to one only the boat would be swept up. She'd have capsized and we'd be drowned.'

'Then we must pin our hopes upon being sighted by a passing ship?'

'That's about it, but here again I don't want you to go counting any chickens. We're three thousand miles south of the great traffic lanes connecting the principal ports of the world across the North Atlantic, and the hurricane swep' us five hundred miles south of the lesser routes linking up Africa with Rio and the Indies.'

Basil made a grimace. 'So the hurricane carried us off the track as far as that?'

35

'Yep, and we're still drifting southward, caught up in the main current that runs parallel with the coast of South America and then swings across to pass south of the African peninsula.'

'We're right out in the blue then?'

'You've said it! If we go on this way we'll be south of south-ward, if you get what I mean; beyond the waters in which any ships ever sail except for whalers and Antarctic expeditions.'

'Well!'—the Colonel tapped his sound foot sharply on the bottom boards—'What d'you propose to do?'

Luvia's kind blue eyes regarded the old man a little pitifully. 'I had a hunch I was making things pretty plain, Colonel. There's nothing I can do—nothing that anyone could do, except hope we'll sight a ship in the next two days. I thought it right to let you know how we stand though—that's all.'

There ensued a few moments' gloomy silence, then Basil broke up the meeting. The afternoon sun was beating down so fiercely on his head and back that he feared he would get heat-stroke if he didn't move. As it was, he had covered up every portion of himself that he could to prevent sunburn and blistering. Now, wiping the perspiration from his face, he crossed a couple of thwarts and lowered himself on to the bottom boards to get in the shadow of the sail.

He was feeling rotten again. The tonic effect of finding himself still alive when he woke in the morning had worn off. He needed a drink. He would have needed one anyway, having been deprived of his normal before-lunch cocktails; but facing the grim pros-pects his imagination conjured up as a result of Luvia's statement made him need one extra badly.

The temptation to go aft and plead with Luvia for a tot of rum was a strong one, but he knew the Finn would refuse him and it seemed senseless to submit to such humiliation to no purpose. He thought of Synolda and her flask of Van der Hum, but could not bring himself to ask her for a pull at it. It wasn't fair to rob the girl when she might need the stuff herself later on.

He tried to sleep, but could not. His mind seemed obsessed with the craving. As he dozed, visions of iced horses' necks, gin-slings, whisky-sours and planters' punch came up before him —all those long, cool, spirituous concoctions which men drink in the tropics directly the sun goes down. Again and again he roused up just as he was dropping off to pass his tongue round his dry mouth and face reality.

A movement near by caused him to turn over. Hansie, having

36

helped to complete the men's shelter in the bow, was settling down in the shade beside him.

'Well, Mister Sutherland, hot enough for you?'

'Too hot by half,' Basil muttered. 'I wonder you weren't burnt to a cinder up in the bow there.'

Hansie regarded the backs of his hands ruefully, and began to feel his cheeks, ears and neck. They were a bright brick red, glowing hot to the touch, and the skin seemed to be stretched abnormally taut across the red patches. 'I've caught it,' he declared bitterly. 'It'll start in about two hours' time—burn like I was being held in front of a red-hot fire. Ain't life hell!'

'Hell's the word,' agreed Basil, 'and it's triple hell not being able to get a drink.'

The barman looked at him thoughtfully. 'Of course, you've been used to your bottle a day, Mister Sutherland, haven't you? It's not easy to go on the wagon all at once. Here, don't let the others see you, but take a pull at this.'

With a cautious movement Hansie extracted a large flat flask of Bourbon from under his jacket and passed it beneath Basil's upraised leg.

Basil reached down a hand and gripped it, turning slowly over on one side. Hansie leant above him, shielding his head from view as he unscrewed the cap and sucked down a couple of gulps of the fiery liquid.

'Bless you, Hansie,' he said, when the flask was safely back in the barman's pocket. 'God! that was good. I'll manage to keep sane until sundown now.'

To while away the time he amused himself composing some lines of poetry; a cynical summing up of his companions in misfortune which he scribbled in a notebook he had on him. They ran:

> *To these ends did I carve you said our Maker,*
> *you dozen painted dolls within a boat.*
> *(I was an Artist; your lives brand me Faker.)*
>
> *Carden, a man borne brave, grown old a goat;*
> *Hans with his soul behind a steward's coat*
> *mixing oblivion in a cocktail-shaker;*
> *Vicente with a purse around his heart;*
> *Synolda, shop-soiled by exchange and mart;*
> *Four negroes, children who would not grow old*

till civilization gave them guns and gold;
Basil, a scarecrow, dressed in the ragged tatters
of love and genius—and of all that matters.

Such lives are jangled mockeries of my craft,
poems so out of tune they will not scan.
My last gift to you then—your epitaph;
'the improper image of mankind is man.'

Luvia came towards him some time afterward. 'You were saying this morning that you'd done some yacht sailing, Mr. Sutherland—isn't that so?'

Basil nodded.

'Good. Then you'll take the tiller for the next hour. The men passengers must break even with the crew. The Colonel's coming forward to do a spell at look-out and Mr. Vedras will take over from him later.'

'The old man will be fried like a fritter up there in the bow,' Basil grinned.

'Not he,' Luvia smiled back. 'He'll have gotten the hide of an elephant after all those years in Burma.'

Basil stood up and went off to take over the tiller from Jansen. Having surrendered it, the carpenter accompanied the Colonel forward to his post.

Just as the change-overs were being effected Synolda popped her head out of the low tent where she and Unity were sheltering. Vicente seized the opportunity to produce a pack of cards from his pocket.

'You're very bored, eh?' he smiled. 'Let me tell your fortunes. Vicente is very good fortune-teller with 'is cards.'

Synolda spoke to Unity, and then turned back to him. 'All right. You'd better come in here out of the sun. If we squeeze up we can just make room for you.'

'*Gracia, gracia,*' he accepted the invitation instantly, and eagerly scrambled in beside them.

He told Synolda's fortune first and muttered a lot over it rather unhappily. The King of Spades, which obviously represented himself, was constantly in her vicinity, but the King of Diamonds persistently came between them. It appears that she had just escaped from a grave danger and others threatened her. However, she had all the 'luck' cards, and so he was able to promise her health, wealth, and a happy marriage.

Unity's cards troubled him much more; not from his own point of view, as he had no personal interest in her, but from hers. He told her of an unhappy love affair in the recent past and spoke of a Club man in her future; but he stuttered, became tongue-tied and so obviously agitated, that both the girls insisted on his telling them what else he could see. At last, unwillingly, he confessed it. 'Death comes up next to you again and again.'

Meanwhile, only a couple of feet further forward, Basil was at the artificially lengthened tiller, with Luvia beside him. Ever since his talk with Hansie in the early morning he had been watching for a chance to get the Finn for a few moments on his own; at last luck had favoured him.

In a low voice he gave a detailed account of Hansie's disquieting information about Harlem Joe.

Luvia heard him out and sat silent for a little. 'So the man's a killer, eh!' he said slowly. 'Doesn't exactly add to the gaiety of nations having a guy like that along—does it?'

Basil had little time for large, blond, hearty men in the ordinary way, but he looked at the strong-featured Finn now with considerable sympathy. He had been so immersed in his own personal misery that he had not given a thought before to what Luvia must be feeling. The situation was bad enough for any of them individually, but the young Engineer had in addition the responsibility of keeping discipline, navigating the boat, and looking after them all; a responsibility which seemed almost certain to bring hideously increased anxieties the further one looked into the desperately uncertain future. 'I'll keep an eye on Harlem as far as I can,' he volunteered.

'Thanks. I'll tip off the Colonel and Mr. Vedras too. Between us we'll watch him plenty.' Luvia yawned and lowered himself to the bottom of the boat. It was many hours since he had closed an eye and almost instantly he was asleep.

Through the long hours of the afternoon the whole party tried to make the most of every inch of shadow, and where it was insufficient they hid themselves under blankets or odd pieces of clothing from their bundles. They sweltered there in acute discomfort, but that was better than suffering the agony of being blistered by the relentless sun.

Unceasing watch was kept for smoke trails or any other sign of shipping, but when sundown came, and the shadows crept in upon them from the surrounding emptiness, there had not even been a false alarm from the look-outs during the whole day.

By the light of a hurricane lantern Luvia superintended the distribution of the evening ration; a slice of meat, a biscuit and half a mug of tea laced with a dash of rum. The men could hardly restrain themselves from snatching at the pannikins. It was over seven hours since they had sipped down their third of a pint of water, and in the baking heat of the afternoon the thoughts of all of them had become centred in wishing away the crawling minutes which separated them from their next drink.

When the other members of the crew had gone forward Harlem Joe remained behind and sat himself down on the rear thwart. Having drunk his tea and rum in sips, rolling each noisily round his mouth, he looked at Luvia and said, 'Der boys had a li'l meetin' dis afternoon, Bass. Dey 'pointed me dair spooksman to ask yoo one or two questions.'

'Ask away,' Luvia replied quietly.

'Jus' where d'you reckon we is right now?'

'About a thousand miles from the coast of South America.'

'Is dat so! An' how do we go fer der eats?'

'Our stores will last us about two more days.'

'We'll need to be a whole lot faster dan we are to git der in dat time.'

'We may be picked up.'

'Shoo—but say we ain't?'

'Well—what then?'

Harlem cocked his head on one side. 'If der was less folks dey could make der eats last longer. Den dey'd stan' a better chance o' commin' to der land.'

'Perhaps, but fate's already fixed our number for us.'

'Fate! dat's jus' another word fer God. Well, Harlem don't believe in God. No sur! He's seen der mighty cities o' der world an' lived rich like der white people do. All dat Hosanna an' der Lawd business is jus' fer der poor coloured folk what don't know no better.'

'The fellow's crazy,' boomed the Colonel. 'Never heard such blasphemous nonsense in my life. Send him about his business, Luvia.'

'I'll have you leave this to me, Colonel,' Luvia replied evenly. 'Go on, Harlem, but make it snappy.'

'Shoo, Bass. I'd jus' hate to make you late if yoo's goin' some place—yoo's got a date with a dame, maybe? I'se a great one for der dames myself.'

A little titter of laughter greeted the negro's sally. The rest of the men had come quietly up behind him and settled themselves just beyond the circle of light on the midships thwarts, where they were listening to the conversation.

Luvia's eyes narrowed. At that moment he would have given a lot for the apt retort that would turn Harlem into a figure of ridicule in front of the others, but unfortunately he lacked the gift of repartee. He itched to exercise his authority in a curt reprimand, but he was no longer on the *Gafelborg* and knew by what a slender thread that authority remained attached to him in these very different circumstances. If it was to be put to the test, it must be on some major issue where he could depend on the support of all the best elements of the boat's company—not because this nigger had raised a laugh at his expense.

'Never mind dates and dames, Harlem,' he said mildly. 'I was only trying to keep you to the point. You don't believe in God you say—so what?'

'Dat's so, Bass, but I believe in Man—man an' Nature. It's Man who is Nature's greatest creation an' he shoo is her master. Maybe yoo's heard o' dat old proverb, "Man proposes an' God disposes". Well, dat li'l old proverb ought to be rewrit, "Nature arranges an' Man rearranges".'

'What's all this leading to?'

'You says, Bass, dat 'cause Fate or God or whatever yoo call it has fix der number o' folks in dis boat dat can't be altered. I'm sayin' dat Man bein' Man wi' all der freewill in der world—it can.'

'How?'

'Der shoo is a variety o' ways.'

'Let's hear 'em.'

'Only der strong guys is goin' to make der grade dis trip, Bass. I's sorry fer der dames an' der feller who got smacked down by dat oar, and der ole puss here with der dicky leg, but dey ain't got no chance nohow. Der grub dey's eatin' would keep us tough fellers goin' another day or maybe two. Six folks less in dis boat 'ud give us an extra thirty per cent chance o' gettin' some place or bein' picked up alive; so der six weakest folks is jus' unfortunate. Dey got to liquidate or be liquidated, like dem Russian Communist guys say—see?'

'Harlem's right, mister,' the half-caste Gietto Nudäa backed him up.

'You infernal scoundrels,' Colonel Carden lurched forward and raised his fist to shake it in the negro's face. Basil grabbed his shoulder and forcibly pulled him back again.

41

'Take your hands off me, sir!' the Colonel bellowed, turning furiously upon the young man. 'If you had a spark of manliness in your drink-sodden carcase you'd help me throw this murderous devil out of the boat.'

'Oh, dear no!' Basil laughed lightly. 'I'm a bit of a gourmet you know and I've never eaten Colonel. If we let him have his way I'll be able to try a slice of Colonel's saddle naturally pickled for forty years in port. I really couldn't resist that.'

It was Tuesday, 11th January, and they had been thirty-two hours in the boat when they roused next morning, but there was no bright dawn to wake them; the sky was overcast, and the daylight filtered through grey banks of cloud.

Watches had been kept throughout the night in case the lights of a passing ship showed on the horizon, so that they could be roused immediately to pull towards it while the look-out signalled with the lantern, but no friendly glimmer had appeared to bring them hope.

Basil's sally the night before had mortally offended the Colonel, but that was of little moment as the old man had never regarded him with anything except cordial dislike. What did matter was that, temporarily at all events, it had dissipated a very tense and dangerous atmosphere. Not a man in the boat, apart from Harlem, was yet so mentally warped by thirst and privation as even to dream of laying a hand on one of the passengers, and Basil's purposely ludicrous suggestion that they should eat the old boy had been followed by a sudden roar of laughter. Angry and discomforted, Harlem had abandoned the discussion and shuffled off forward with his tittering cronies to settle down for the night.

When daylight brought the boat's company back to consciousness they roused up listlessly from a comfortless, unrefreshing sleep taken in snatches on the hard bottom boards with bundles for pillows and a ship's blanket or odd piece of tarpaulin for bedding.

It was calmer than the day before. The breeze had dropped to light airs that barely rippled the surface of the water; the long rolling swell had disappeared.

The sail was set again, but except for an occasional puff of wind which billowed it out to carry them a few fathoms it flapped noisily against the mast or hung slack and useless.

The morning ration was issued and eaten in despondent silence. The sun broke through the clouds and gradually the sky cleared until it was once more a hard, bright blue. Luvia knew that during the night the current must have carried them many miles still further south, but the sun's rays seemed no less powerful. By ten o'clock they were taking advantage of every scrap of cover, and by midday they were panting where they sat, like so many dogs after a long, exciting chase.

The only cheerful person in the company was Jean De Brissac. Having been unconscious or asleep practically the entire time since they had left the sinking *Gafelborg*, he had escaped thirty-six hours of acute anxiety which had already undermined the resistance of the others.

When he awoke after his long sleep he felt very weak and his head pained him, but the gentle lapping of the waters against the boat's timbers and a patch of bright blue sky that he could see through a gap in the tarpaulin tent where he lay informed him that the storm was over. Having escaped the tempest there seemed no reason to him why, given good weather the boat should not carry them safely to land. He had no idea what had laid him out, but previous experience of wounds had taught him that complete inactivity, mental and physical, was the quickest road to recovery. As he was a casualty he could not assist his companions in handling the boat, but he could help them by worrying neither himself nor them and by being as little bother as possible.

Unity had constituted herself his nurse; a position which Synolda, decorative but incompetent, was incapable of filling. As De Brissac eased his position a little Unity saw that his quick brown eyes were open, and bent over him.

'What happened?' he murmured, economizing words and effort.

'You were hit on the head by an oar the night before last. Your scalp's badly cut, but as you bled like a pig you may have escaped concussion. Now you're awake I'd better do your head again.'

With deft fingers she undid the bandage and began to bathe the wound. Fresh water could not be spared for the purpose, but Unity thought sea water even better on account of the healing properties of its salt. The treatment caused De Brissac to wince and make a feeble protest, but she smiled reassuringly.

'Stinging you up a bit, eh? I'm afraid it's bound to as long as the wound remains open. Still, it's a clean, healthy sort of gash and it's looking much better than it did yesterday. If you're a good patient we'll have you up and about again within a week.'

She was determined to conceal the fact from him as long as possible that their water supply would be exhausted in another twenty-four hours. The horrors which might ensue did not bear contemplation, and were certainly not the thoughts to put into the head of a sick man.

In consequence, after she had washed his face and made him as comfortable as she could he thanked her with a little compliment on her gentleness and drifted into a semi-doze happily ignorant of their true situation.

The appearance of the party was going rapidly from bad to worse. None of the men had shaved now for two days and the heat had increased the growth of dirty-looking stubble on their cheeks and chins. Several also had angry red patches on their noses, foreheads, and necks, where the sun had caught them during their turns at look-out the day before.

Having lost most of her hairpins Synolda had abandoned her attempts to keep her long hair up and, in an endeavour to make the best of a bad job, appeared that morning with it flowing down over her shoulders. She looked very attractive like that and well she knew it.

To her surprise and indignation Luvia ordered her curtly to tie it up in a bun or conceal it under a handkerchief head-dress. He knew that all the men, and particularly the negroes, would become abnormal once thirst and despair began to affect them seriously. The last thing he meant to have was anything like a display of Synolda's golden tresses which might excite their lust when they became unbalanced.

Grudgingly, with a sullen glance from her blue eyes, she returned to the tent and when she reappeared some moments later he saw that she had met his order by a compromise, having braided her hair into two long plaits. As her face was still heavily made up the result was not a happy one; she looked like a middle-aged actress playing the part of a schoolgirl in some third-rate revue.

For a company of fourteen, not counting the women or De Brissac, the duties were light. Luvia, Jansen and Basil took turns at the tiller; from the remainder shifts of three—one to do the look-out and two to handle the sail each time the boat went about—were all that was necessary.

With monotonous regularity they tacked from one side to the other, making the best of the light breeze and creeping gradually a few miles further westward. Luvia knew that even if they had

had provisions for a month they could never have reached the coast of South America at this pace, but it was better for everybody's morale that they should appear to be making some attempt to get somewhere rather than confess complete impotence and just let the boat drift.

When he took an observation of the sun at midday he found that the current had carried them still further southward; the wind was too light for him to counteract the movement.

As he remarked on it Unity said: 'There is land at the Antarctic—isn't there?'

He nodded. 'There certainly is. Several pretty useful islands still lie south of us. South Georgia and the South Orkney group; then there's Graham Land, a long, coastal region of the Antarctic continent itself.'

'I suppose there's nothing but snow and ice there, though?'

'You're wrong to suppose that at this season. Graham Land's only about sixty-five south, same as my own homeland, Finland, in the northern hemisphere. It's grand there in summer; the lakes and woods are just wonderful. Such carpets of wild flowers, too, as you never see in other places except, perhaps, Siberia. We get a twenty-hour day to enjoy them in, what's more. You see, Nature makes up to us a bit for the long, dark night she hands us out in winter and, although I don't know a thing about Graham Land, I figure it must be much the same.'

'Really!' Unity brightened instantly. 'Are there settlers there then—little towns and villages?'

'A few maybe; but the Antarctic's so cut off from the rest of the world it's only been explored in quite recent times. I don't think there's any native population, and Europeans have hardly woken up yet to its possibilities. Still, there'd certainly be settlements of sorts round the whaling stations.'

'Then we'd be all right if we got there; even if we had to rough it for a bit before we could find a ship to take us home?'

'That's so, we'd be as well off there as we would be in Patagonia or the Falklands—if only we could make it.'

'How far south of us is Graham Land, and these islands?'

'Oh, quite a way,' Luvia answered casually. He had not the heart to tell her that the Antarctic coast was even further off than that of South America.

During the hottest hours those who were not on duty endeavoured to doze again but, unlike the previous day, when they had needed sleep after their ordeal, they found it difficult to escape their misery in slumber. Even so there was less talk among the men and, although little was said, it was obvious from their strained faces that every one of them was the prey of the same desperate anxiety.

Basil alone roamed the boat from stem to stern, exchanging small talk with all and sundry. His craving for what he termed a civilized drink made him restless and irritable. He stubbornly refused to allow himself to cadge a further peg from Synolda or Hansie, but he could see no earthly reason why Luvia should not allow him a tot of the boat's rum. In his view it was absurd to hold the stuff for medical purposes when the only invalid among them was the Frenchman, who was not allowed it anyway because Unity forbade him alcohol, fearing he might have delayed concussion. The rest of them were as fit as could be expected; the nights were warm so there was no question of reserving it to revive sufferers chilled by exposure, and as they had only sufficient water to last them another twenty-four hours it was quite unreasonable to assume that a number of cases would call for special treatment in that time. Once the water had given out the rum would be of little use anyway as it would not quench thirst taken neat, but if used now, Basil argued to himself, it would strengthen and fortify them.

Luvia's reason for refusing it was the perfectly sound one that if he let Basil have a tot he could not refuse to let the others do the same, and he feared the effect that strong spirits might have on Harlem and his companions when taken on almost empty stomachs.

Basil was too preoccupied with his longing to think of that. He could not get the rum jar out of his mind and, as the afternoon wore on, he gradually formed a resolution to circumvent Luvia's ban, however irate the Finn might prove afterwards.

His plan was a simple one. The rum was in the after locker, now forming the rear portion of the girls' quarters. He would wait until Luvia went to the small shelter at the forward end of the boat, as they all did from time to time, push the girls out of the way and snatch the coveted jar before anyone could stop him.

Once he had made up his mind to this flagrant breach of discipline he began to watch Luvia cautiously, but over an hour and a half crawled by, every moment of which held added torture now that he could almost feel by anticipation the glow of the reviving spirit in his chest.

At last the Finn handed over the tiller to Jansen and began to clamber over the thwarts towards the bow. The half-caste sailor, Gietto Nudäa, and Harlem Joe were on duty amidships at the sail, but intent on his raid Basil never gave them a thought. He waited until Luvia was out of sight forward of the mast then thrust his head into the girl's shelter.

'How's old De Brissac getting on?' he asked briskly.

'Hush!' Unity exclaimed. 'You'll wake him. He's——'

'Sorry!' His apology, cutting her short, could be taken to refer either to her protest or the fact that in leaning over the recumbent Frenchman his shoulder struck her in the chest. Next moment he had the locker open and his hand on the rum jar.

'What are you up to?' Unity's voice held a sharp, suspicious note, but he ignored the question, murmured a bland, 'Excuse me,' and with one heave lifted the heavy jar over De Brissac's body.

Synolda laughed; a low delicious chuckle was not the least of her attractions, but as Basil pulled his prize past the flap of the shelter Colonel Carden gave a gasp of surprise and anger.

'Hi! Stop that! Put that jar back at once, sir,' he ordered tersely.

Giving him a swift, malicious grin, Basil wrenched out the bung and lifted the jar with both hands, bringing its mouth up to his lips.

'Mr. Luvia!' bawled the Colonel, scrambling to his feet. 'Here! quick! Sutherland's getting at the rum!' Still shouting for Luvia he grabbed Basil by the elbow and tried to pull the jar away.

Basil had taken one great gulp. His eyes were starting from their sockets as the neat spirit ran down his throat but, with a dexterous twist, he shook off the Colonel's grip and tilted the jar again. Some of the rum spilled down his chest, but he sucked in another mouthful.

It was barely a minute since Basil had thrust his head into the tent but the Colonel's bellowing had already roused the whole boat's company. All those abaft the sail took in the situation instantly; others came tumbling aft to find out the cause of the disturbance.

Next moment the ill-considered action to which Basil's craving had driven him precipitated open mutiny.

CHAPTER IV

MUTINY ON THE HIGH SEAS

HARLEM JOE had seen the passengers quarrelling among them-selves. For him it was a God-sent opportunity. He would kill if need be, but he had already determined to seize the stores and particularly the precious keg of water for his cronies and himself next time Luvia snatched a nap.

Gietto Nudäa had also grasped the possibilities of the situation; the eyes of the two men met in a glance of swift understanding.

'Dat cask, pal—now.' Harlem roared, and with eyes aflame for battle the two men came crashing over the intervening thwarts towards the stern-sheets.

Basil lowered the jar with quick apprehension. He had had all the rum he ever meant to take and was prepared for trouble with Luvia, but the trouble rushing towards him now was very different.

Luvia's voice reached them in a shout from beyond the sail. 'Hang on, Colonel—I'm coming.'

Halting in his tracks, Harlem turned and yelled: 'Lem—Isiah —Corncob—grab de Bass an' give him de works.' In a flash he swung back and hit out at Basil.

The negro's great fist would have sent Basil spinning into the stern tent if it had landed square, but he ducked in time and it only grazed his ear. The rum jar slid from his grasp and fell with a thud on the bottom boards; it's precious contents gushed out over the Colonel's feet.

A commotion had started in the bow of the boat. Harlem's cronies had obeyed his instructions and set on Luvia before he could make his way aft.

Jansen, already on his feet to help the Colonel prevent Basil's raid on the rum, now abandoned the tiller and flung himself at Gietto. The two went down together with a terrific crash, the tough old carpenter on top.

Vicente Vedras, until Harlem's attack a neutral spectator of the scene, now dived at the negro from behind, catching at his legs in an attempt to pitch him overboard, but the great black had his feet planted well apart and stood steady as a rock. The only result of Vicente's assault was to divert Harlem's attention momentarily from Basil.

The negro swivelled round, stooped suddenly, and grasping the Venezuelan, forced him away. An instant later Vicente was struggling wildly in the air, gripped by one ankle and his neck. Harlem rose again to his full magnificent height, heaved his attacker up over his head and with a cackle of evil laughter, chucked him green-faced and screaming, right over the stern tent into the sea.

'Dat's where yo'll all go soon,' he bellowed as Vicente, a whirling mass of arms and legs, spun through the air; but Vicente's misfortune had given the others a chance to act.

As Harlem's head came down just after his mighty throw the Colonel's stick caught him a terrific wallop right across the eyes. At the same second a tin of bully beef thrown by Unity thudded into his left shoulder and Basil landed a welt like the kick of a mule in the pit of his stomach.

The black colossus possessed enormous strength and had lost little of his ring-craft; but he had allowed himself to go soft. He could have stood up to the whack from the Colonel's stick and the impact of the heavy tin, alone, but Basil's blow found his weakest spot. Under the triple assault he staggered, doubled up, and suddenly went down.

For the moment it looked as if the forces of order were victorious. Steffens, the red-headed sailor, had come to Jansen's assistance and between them they were holding Gietto Nudäa down. Harlem lay squirming, mouth agape, white eyeballs popping, his limbs twisted in knots as he gasped and fought to get his wind back.

'Jansen! Sutherland! Steffens! lend a hand here!' Luvia's voice came urgently from the far side of the sail. Jansen was astride Nudäa's chest and the half-caste had ceased to struggle so he sent Steffens forward at once.

Basil grabbed a hatchet with intent to finish Harlem, while he had the chance. In his view only further trouble could come of letting the black live and this was no time for scruples. But Colonel Carden stepped between them and the flash of his rheumy old eyes showed clearly that he did not mean to see murder done.

His ill-judged interference proved their undoing. Supple as a snake, swift as a mongoose, Harlem rolled over, grabbed the ankle of the Colonel's gammy leg and twisted it with all his force.

The old man let out a roar of pain, clutched wildly at the air and fell, cannoning full into Basil and bringing him down as well.

Instantly Harlem was on his knees. With a murderous backwards stroke he cut Jansen, who was just behind him, across the nape of the neck with the outer edge of his hand. The carpenter fell forward as though he had been pole-axed; slumping without a sound limply on to Nudäa's body.

In falling the Colonel had struck his head on the tiller. He was not knocked unconscious but momentarily dazed and lay where he had fallen. Thrusting the Colonel aside, Basil struggled to his feet. Harlem rose to his full height at the same moment.

For a fraction of time they stood glaring at each other. Basil, half crouching, wary, flaying his wits for some trick, no matter how dirty, by which he might kill or maim his far more powerful antagonist; the negro grinning evilly, gloating in anticipation over the victim he was about to crush. For that blow in the stomach he meant to break every bone in Basil's body before he flung him, a bleeding mass of pulp, to the sharks.

Basil had dropped the hatchet when he fell. His hands clenched spasmodically. He would have given another fortune, had he had it, to have felt the comforting grip of its smooth handle now.

The negro ceased smiling. His greenish eyes, veined and flecked a bilious yellow in their whites, gleamed balefully; brutality, sadism, murder, stared out of their muddied depths, all the bestiality and evil of a being cast in human form but nearer in mentality to the gorilla, the jackal, and the snake.

His mouth dry, beads of sweat gathering thick upon his forehead, Basil stared back; and suddenly he knew that he was afraid, desperately afraid.

As Harlem moved, Basil stepped back. He was brought up sharply by the calves of his legs knocking against the edge of the stern seat. He was trapped. Nothing could save him. A strangled call to Luvia for help died in his parched throat; shouts and curses coming from beyond the sail showed that the Finn was still fighting his own battle in the bow.

Aid came from an unexpected quarter. The primus stove, hurled by Unity, hurtled past Basil's shoulder and caught the black full in the chest.

Its weight, and the force with which it was thrown would have

50

knocked any ordinary man off his feet; Harlem only grunted and gaped in fierce surprise, but his attention was diverted just long enough for Basil to decide on diving at the hatchet.

He stooped, but too late: the black recovered and came at him before his fingers had a firm hold of the handle. Terror-stricken, he half-rose again, cowered back, felt the edge of the seat catch him sharply behind the knees, lost his balance and went overboard.

The semi-tropical waters held a pleasant warmth, but the fierce excitement of the mutiny and the scorching sun under which it was being fought had both contributed to drench him in a bath of sweat. As he plunged downwards he felt as if he had suddenly been submerged in the icy waters of a polar sea. His heart seemed to contract with the shock and he came up gasping like a man who, without warning, has had a bucket of cold water thrown at his naked back.

Only two yards away the boat was rocking violently as the fight raged on. A dark blob showed under its stern—Vicente's head as he trod water there, clinging to one of the life-lines fixed to the boat's gunwale.

A new fear gripped Basil—sharks. He twisted swiftly in the water and struck out for the boat. Grabbing a life-line amidships he looked hurriedly round, peering as far as he could see into the green depths below. He expected great, dark shadows to be moving there, or a flash of white as one of the brutes turned over on its back and opened its huge jaws to snap off his feet, but to his infinite relief he could see no sign of life other than a million molecules that danced and shimmered as they caught the light.

Hand over hand he pulled himself rapidly along the side of the boat away from the fiendish negro in the stern. He thought of the two girls but he knew he was powerless to help them, and that any attempt to board the boat again there would be simply asking to have his head bashed in. The only course seemed to be to reach Luvia in the bow, get hauled aboard, and when they had armed themselves with makeshift cudgels, to attack Harlem from the rear.

So much had happened since Basil's raid on the rum he wondered that Luvia, with the aid of the loyal seamen, had been so long in getting the situation forward of the mast in hand, but, in reality the whole desperate encounter had occupied less than five minutes. As Basil pulled himself up and peered over the gunwale he saw why Luvia had been detained even that length of time. One of the black stokers was down, but the other two were still fighting and each was whirling an open razor over the back of his clenched right hand.

Luvia had Hansie with him and the three other Swedes, Steffens, Largertöf and Bremer. The unfortunate Steffens had received a frightful cut right across his cheek and mouth. Faint, sick and bleeding like a pig, he was lying collapsed half out of the boat. Largertöf held Corncob down right up in the bow, and was battering his woolly head. Hansie was vainly trying to staunch the bleeding from a badly slashed arm, while Luvia and Bremer were striving to get in under the guard of the two other blacks.

Lem and Isiah were both big men and they wielded their horrible weapons with practised skill. Luvia and Bremer were hard put to it to hold their own.

Basil, clinging to the far side of the boat, was well out of reach of the negroes and as he was unable to hoist himself over the gunwale he could not give active help, but the result of the scrap meant life or death to him and his wits were still working.

'Don't try to rush them, you fool,' he shouted to Luvia. 'Get an oar and ram them in their stomachs.'

Hansie stopped dabbing at his arm and lifted the nearest oar. Luvia and Bremer jumped back and got hands on it. There was not much room to use such an unwieldy weapon but the three of them jabbed its blade hard into Isiah's midriff. He gulped, goggled horribly and fell. Lem sprang forward at the same second, slashing at Bremer with his razor. Hansie gave the negro a terrific kick behind the knee which threw him off his balance. The oar was brought into play again and caught him on the side of the neck, sending him spinning.

Largertöf's blows with a knotted rope-end on Corncob's thick skull had at last rendered the black unconscious. The young Swede jumped to help his comrades who were disarming Lem and Isiah. Luvia turned to pull Basil in over the side. The sound of screams now reached them from the stern.

'Haven't you got a gun?' gasped Basil.

'Yes, but it's in the locker aft,' Luvia replied swiftly as he straddled a thwart.

'Get aft then! For God's sake get aft and stop that devil murdering those women.'

Luvia gave one glance round. Hansie had fainted from loss of blood. Steffens had slipped down into the bottom of the boat and was whimpering pitifully. Largertöf and Bremer were needed there to tend them and secure the temporarily disabled mutineers. He slipped under the sail and scrambled towards the stern alone.

Basil's eyes were just level with the gunwale of the boat and it took all the strength of his arms to raise himself so far out of the water. He made a desperate effort to lift himself further and scramble over but he could not manage it. The side of the boat sloped away from under him and he could get no purchase for his feet. He realized too late that if Luvia had delayed a moment to help him in it would have been time well spent as there would have been two of them then to go aft and tackle Harlem.

In an effort to catch the Finn he pulled himself back along the boat's side again, yelling 'Luvia—Luvia!' but the curses of the negroes and the shrieks of the two girls drowned his shouts.

When he came opposite the mast amidships and could see round the sail Luvia was already charging into the stern.

Another brutal scene was being enacted there. The Colonel still lay on his back; Gietto Nudäa was standing astride of him and he had the two girls each by a wrist. They were both kicking and struggling to get away from him while he gave the wrist of first one and then the other a violent twist, striving to force them overboard. He could have managed it with either of them separately but could not exert quite enough pressure on one to snap her arm or throw her while he had to hold off the other fighting like a wildcat. Harlem, meanwhile, had half wrecked their tarpaulin shelter and was just carrying off the precious keg of water.

'Drop that!' roared Luvia. 'D'you hear me. Drop that or I'll knock your block off.'

Harlem put down the little cask, but gently, and squared up to the Engineer. 'It's yo's head'll be fo' de knocking, Bass,' he spat out as he made a sudden pass with his big fist.

The muscles in Basil's arms were strained to breaking point; the pain was so acute that he was compelled to relax and let himself slip back into the water where the high side of the boat cut off his view. When he had strength enough to pull himself up again the most terrific fist fight he had ever seen was in progress.

In height and weight the two men were matched pretty evenly. The negro had the big advantage of his training as a professional boxer, but it was obvious that the herculean Finn was no mean amateur and he was in better condition.

There was little room to manœuvre and no clinching so it was

53

literally a stand-up fight where sledge-hammer blows were given and taken without cessation.

Harlem got a left in early, nearly closing Luvia's right eye, but the Finn covered it up skilfully after that and got his own back twenty seconds later by landing a punch which had every ounce of his great weight behind it over the black man's heart.

The strain on Basil's arms forced him to drop down for the next half-minute and when he was able to look again Luvia had given back a pace. He was still getting in telling blows on the negro's body, but Harlem seemed capable of taking plenty of punishment and was striking again and again at his opponent's head. Basil knew that if one of those hammer-blows got through Luvia's guard it would be the end; and the defeat of Luvia would be the end of them all.

The Colonel had grasped that too apparently as, in spite of a savage kick in the ribs from Nudäa, who was still struggling with the two girls, he had succeeded in wriggling out from under the half-caste and now grasped the hatchet dropped by Basil in the earlier scuffle.

With a groan Basil dropped to the water level once more. He counted ten before gritting his teeth and hoisting himself up again. The Colonel was on his feet behind Harlem with the hatchet raised to cleave his skull in two. But Nudäa suddenly flung the girls from him and, lugging something from his belt, spun round. There was a crack, a spurt of flame, and the hatchet dropped from the Colonel's nerveless fingers. Shot through the chest, he pitched forward at the half-caste's feet.

Nudäa had fired at point-blank range and within two feet of Harlem's back. The sudden shattering report threw the negro off his guard for a second and involuntarily he half turned about. Instantly, Luvia sent a mighty right to the point of his jaw and followed it with a left to the solar plexus. The black dropped to his knees and slumped forward senseless. Without a pause Luvia rushed the half-caste, but Nudäa had no guts without his leader. He threw down the gun he had just stolen from the after locker and put up his hands.

The mutiny was over: Basil and Vicente were hauled aboard, but they had lost the primus, Synolda's vanity case, the kettle and one tin of bully, all of which had gone overboard in the scrimmage, in addition to wasting the rum; Steffens was seriously wounded and Colonel Carden died that night. He was buried at sea; the first of several in the boat's company who were soon to go on that longest of all journeys, from which there is no return.

It was Wednesday, 12th January, and they had been sixty-six hours in the boat, as they crouched parched and sweltering on their third afternoon since abandoning the *Gafelborg*.

The unleashing of so much violent emotion during the mutiny twenty-four hours earlier seemed to have exhausted all their energies. A terrible lassitude had fallen upon them; moreover, they were conserving all their strength now, not for any set purpose but instinctively and because of the secret knowledge each of them had that they were already weaker. Under-nourishment, lack of water, and exposure were steadily sapping their vitality. With the last flicker of it they would die.

Even Juhani Luvia had succumbed under the hideous creeping of despair to the extent of not bothering to take the elevation of the sun at midday before sharing out the last drops of water from the cask. He knew that the sail could not make much difference to their continued southerly drift with the current, and it seemed of little moment if they died a few miles nearer to the South American coast or not when so many hundreds separated them from it.

Two and a half days soon pass in normal surroundings, and often all too quickly; but in that period a heart beats over a quarter of a million times. Each beat is time enough for a separate thought to pass through the brain, and when physical movement is restricted, mental occupations nil, discomfort such that even proper sleep becomes an impossibility, the brain is at liberty to consider the miserable situation of its owner with almost un-broken continuity.

For more than two hundred and fifty thousand heart-beats very similar chains of thoughts had been repeating themselves with horrible persistence in each of their minds, almost entirely to the exclusion of all else.

Shall we be picked up?

I do wish I could have a drink.

How devilish hard this seat is.

Surely we'll sight a steamer soon.

If only I could get to sleep.

This sitting still is driving me mad.

Will the sun never go down?

It'll be hours yet before I get another go of water.

Oh God, I'm tired!

We can't possibly be going to die here like this.

What wouldn't I give for a decent meal.

Hell! how my bones ache.

Will the night never end?

Tomorrow—tomorrow we'll sight a ship.

If only I could walk about.

I mustn't panic—but I'm afraid!

Damn it, I'm getting cramp again.

What will the end be like?

A drink—I *must* have a drink.

Do people really go mad of thirst?

Shall we all go mad?

God, this is awful!

I'll go mad if I don't get a drink!

We're going to die.

I'm afraid! I'm afraid! *I'm afraid!*

Over and over went those thoughts almost ceaselessly and
varied slightly only according to the time of day. Even the

stoutest-hearted among them quailed at the thought of the torture they must suffer before dying of thirst, and the conviction that there was no escape had been growing upon them all.

The ex-mutineers were the greatest sufferers. Fearing another outbreak during the night, Luvia had had them all bound hand and foot and laid out in the bottom of the boat. Even when daylight came again they were not allowed the full use of their limbs, but occupied the five starboard seats on five of the thwarts, and the feet of each were lashed to an oar which passed beneath them, making it impossible for them to move from their places except when specially released to do so. At intervals they were freed one at a time and allowed to stretch their legs in the bow, but for hours they were forced to sit with their ankles roped in the same position. Sullen, resentful, glowering, they sat there cursing in their hearts and casting occasional glances full of hate at the whites.

De Brissac was better. Protected from exposure, lying in such comfort as the collected resources of the boat could afford, and cared for by the two girls, the invalid had an easier time of it than the others; besides which he had been either unconscious or in a drug-induced sleep for the greater part of the time since they had put off from the *Gafelborg*. Nevertheless, he spoke little and was now fully aware of the terrible end that faced them.

Basil sat with his back against the lower part of the mast amidships. Since the previous evening he had spoken to no one except to decline a pull at Hansie's flask. Luvia had seen the futility of taking him to task for his raid on the rum, and when he had begun a tentative apology had turned contemptuously away from him.

The Finn had known that Harlem would make trouble sooner or later and regarded Basil's part in precipitating it as incidental, but he did not attempt to hide his scorn of a man whose craving for drink had led him to forget common decency. Basil, on the other hand, considered himself directly responsible for the outbreak and consequently the Colonel's death. The fact that he had disliked and despised the pompous old man did not ease his conscience at all; on the contrary, and, illogical though it might be, it made him feel almost as guilty as if he had deliberately engineered the fracas to get an enemy out of the way by treachery.

Under normal conditions he would have been far too well-balanced to allow sentimental remorse for his part in the unpremeditated death of a comparative stranger to influence his future actions, but here, where stark tragedy had gripped them under a cloudless sky in the vast empty wastes of the ocean, and perhaps because he was already a little light-headed from privation, he had formed the quixotic resolve that to punish himself he would not touch another drop of spirit, even if it was offered to him.

Having once made the resolution he experienced almost immediately an unexpected relief from his craving. To his amazement he found that he could regard Synolda now without thinking of her little flask of Van der Hum, and when Hansie offered him a tot of Bourbon he felt a curious joy in refusing it.

He could not bring himself to talk to the others yet as in some ways he was extremely sensitive. The poor view that Luvia took of him was plain to see and he guessed that the rest of them shared the Finn's condemnation of his conduct. He preferred to deprive himself of their fellowship rather than risk giving them an opportunity to show their feelings openly.

To keep his thoughts off the Colonel's death and his own misery he wrote some more verses, but they were in a very different strain from those he had written on the previous afternoon.

A constant grim reminder of the previous evening's events was the presence, some thirty yards astern of the boat, of three triangular fins which cut the water with a steady ripple. No sharks had been in their vicinity before, but blood had been spilled over the side from Steffen's terribly cut face, and, by some strange mystery of nature, that had brought them racing to the scene.

All the men knew, and hoped the girls did not, that Colonel Carden's body must have provided a midnight meal for them after Luvia had consigned it to the deep by the light of the hurricane lantern, having spoken a short prayer over it in which the other whites joined.

The long afternoon seemed never-ending. The blacks drooped in their seats under the rays of the strong sunshine; the rest, seeking what shade they could, lolled listlessly, rolling over occasionally to ease their aching limbs.

It was a little after five o'clock when Basil looked up to see Unity coming towards him from the stern. As she crossed the intervening thwarts he was filled with dismay, fearing that she was about to upbraid him for the part he had played in the death of her father.

'I see you've sent yourself to Coventry,' she opened up quite calmly as she sat down on the bottom boards beside him.

'Well, more or less,' he admitted. 'I didn't think my society would be particularly welcome in the stern after——'

'You needn't have,' she cut in, 'at least as far as I'm concerned. I can quite understand the temptation to have a go at that rum proving too much for you.'

'Thanks,' his voice was bitter. 'In that case it would be kinder if you refrained from heaping coals of fire on my unworthy head.'

'But I mean it,' she protested, 'and seeing you look so miserable I wanted you to know that I *do* understand how a person can want a thing most terribly and decide to take it even when they shouldn't.'

'Do you?' Basil raised his eyebrows. 'Really? Well, it was an appalling weakness on my part, anyhow.'

'Of course, but we all give way to things at times.'

'I suppose we do, but it isn't everybody who'll admit it.'

'Perhaps, but it happens that I remember just what the after-effects are like.'

To his amazement he caught a sudden twinkle in her grey eyes as he murmured, 'I'm afraid I don't quite understand.'

'How should you? But we can speak frankly now. I mean, there doesn't seem to be much chance of our being picked up alive, does there?'

'To be honest, no.'

'And one's done so many stupid, harmful things; and left undone so many decent things. Though it sounds pretty sloppy put that way.'

'It's true all the same,' Basil agreed, shooting a quick glance at the face of the girl beside him. He hesitated a second then, on a sudden impulse, pulled out the notebook in which he had been writing. 'Queer you should say that. It's just what I've been thinking all the afternoon. Care to look at a whine that might be entitled "Lost Opportunities"?'

She took the open book and read the pencilled scrawl:

> *Our days have been the bones of nothingness*
> *dressed in a scarecrow dress of patchworked tatters;*
> *we tore up all our nights in restlessness,*
> *filled them with the dropping spindles of our chatter;*
> *our lives are the aimless turning of broken looms,*
> *the rustling of beetles' wings in empty rooms.*

Faces have mocked us down our broken ways,
the backless masks of our bent chivalries
as empty as the rent cloak of our days;
flame-like, the clearness of their lips' dead laughter
came after us, speaking of bittered memories
which had belonged to us, life's mercenaries.

And yet we could have torn the world apart
if we had loved; we could have rolled the days
back on the nights, lived in another's heart,
and shod our lips with laughter caught amazed
on the sudden quivering of another's smile;
. . . or, as at Troy, have thrown a wave of spears
crescendo-ed in silver against the walls of years.

We could have taught this other, had we won
our way to her, the woven, darling rhyme
which bound our ways together—then undone
our days and slipped them from the leash of time.

. . . But these are fantasies
Maimed by the masks of our lost opportunities.

'Thank you,' she said slowly. 'That is very beautiful and it was kind of you to show it to me. I had no idea you—well, were the sort of person who had those sort of thoughts, or such a wonderful gift for expressing them.'

'I don't, often—have those sort of thoughts, I mean. You'd hate most of the things I jot down at odd moments. Still, there's some good in the worst of us and a streak of bad in the best of us, I suppose, as the old cliché has it.'

'Of course there is.' Unity's grey eyes held his steadily. 'I never meant to speak of it again until I saw you looking so miserable; but I thought it might make you feel less bad to hear about my frightful lapse from virtue. I was in Selfridges one morning and I saw a lovely fur. It wasn't particularly big or valuable, but I couldn't possibly afford to buy it and quite suddenly I wanted that fur more than anything I've ever wanted in my life. My upbringing was very strict and I'd never stolen so much as a peppermint bull's-eye from anyone before, but I just had to have that fur even if hell's flames had suddenly leapt up to get me from a crack in the floor. I bagged it and got pinched for shop-lifting.'

60

'Good Lord! How frightful for you!' he exclaimed.

'Yes it was grim—absolutely grim. But I escaped the worst, as Daddy was in Burma at the time and he never got to know. Anyhow, you'll see now that I really do understand what you felt about the rum.'

He smiled. 'It's most awfully decent of you to tell me about your brainstorm so that I shan't feel quite such a spineless fool. I don't normally give way to my worst impulses and I'm sure you don't either.'

'Of course not.' She passed her tongue over her dry lips. 'We're in a bad enough way without holding things up against each other. Let's forget it.'

'I wish I could, but it's what followed that makes me feel so awful.'

'You weren't to know that your grabbing the rum would prove like putting a match to a powder-barrel.'

'I ought to have thought of it. You see, I *did* know that the stokers were ripe for mutiny.'

'Even so, father's death was an accident. Nudäa swears by all his gods he was only holding the pistol as a threat and never meant to pull the trigger.'

Basil shrugged. 'I wouldn't give a bean for anything that slimy rascal says—or his gods. The fact is I was directly responsible for your father getting killed, and, believe me, I'm most desperately sorry.'

'Why? You never liked him—did you?'

He turned and stared at her in surprise. 'No, quite frankly, I did not. I've known lots of soldiers I do like—and admire, but your father got something in me on the raw. I may be entirely wrong, of course, but he seemed to me the absolute personification of the old style, pompous, narrow, self-opinionated martinet; the type that caused my older friends to hate and despise so many of the professional soldiers they met in the war. It's not much fun, you know, for an intelligent young man to suddenly find himself under an ill-informed old bigot; particularly when he has to watch good lives being chucked away through his senior's hidebound stupidity. . . .'

Basil broke off suddenly and mentally kicked himself for having expressed his views so freely. Unity was silent for a moment, and during it he was so horribly conscious of the ill return he had made to her generous gesture of coming over to rehabilitate him in his self-esteem.

At last she said very quietly: 'You're quite right, and since we're being so frank I'll tell you something. You'll probably think it horrible of me to admit it, but he was all you say. Worse, he was not only stupid but mean and beastly. If you want the truth, I hated him more than any man I've ever met.'·

Suppressing an exclamation, Basil sat quite still. It occurred to him that the heat had got her or that brooding on their desperate situation had already turned her brain, but he was soon convinced of her normality by the sober bitterness which throbbed in her low voice as she went on:

' "Daddy knows best, my dear!" That was his parrot cry. "Daddy knows best." I could have screamed sometimes when he brought out that unctuous anachronism as the invariable last word in any argument. He hadn't imbibed a new idea since he left Sandhurst. Even the war taught him nothing. For him the world was still peopled with only two sorts of men—gentlemen and cads. That's why your baiting in the saloon of the ship used to drive him into such a frenzy. You're so obviously the kind of young man his snob mind would place in the category of "gent"; yet you mocked at the old school tie business and all the ballyhoo he held sacred, just as though you were the most utter "cad". There were times when I'd have given anything to back you up.'

'I wish I'd known that,' Basil said quickly. 'I'm afraid I was far from polite to you once or twice, but that was only because I thought you were tarred with the same brush. You might have given me a hint.'

She shrugged her slim shoulders. 'I was quite as rude to you as you were to me and I had two perfectly good reasons for not making myself pleasant.'

'Really! Do tell me what they were.'

'Well, for one, I didn't like your habits.'

'Of course. It seems so long ago that I'd almost forgotten, but I was drinking like a fish—wasn't I?'

'You were. I'm not a teetotaller or anything when I'm away from the family; though one of father's nasty little meannesses was that he didn't approve of women having anything to drink. "Daddy knew best" what was good for me in that as in everything else. But, all the same, I've never had any time for drunks.'

'Quite understandable. What was the other reason?'

'My life wouldn't have been worth living if I'd shown the least sign of encouraging your cynical digs at him after the first night out.'

62

'Why? What happened then?'

'Don't you remember? You said at dinner the reason they couldn't get all the recruits they wanted for the Army was because young men didn't mind fighting for their country, but they kicked at the idea of being pushed into impassable mud-swamps by incompetents like some of the Generals in the last Great War.'

'Generals who have failed in a supreme trust and thrown the lives of their men away to no purpose should not be allowed to pass into history with glory.'

'You seem so bitter about it though, and, after all, you could only have been a boy at the time.'

'I was nine in the summer of the great slaughter. My father, an uncle, and my elder brother were in the same battalion; they all choked out their lives within a few days of each other—just three little units out of the mighty host that were mown down by machine-guns from the almost impregnable pill-boxes they'd been sent to attack across a sea of mud at Passchendaele. Indirectly, too, I probably wouldn't have made such a mucker of my own life if one of them had been spared to keep an eye on me.'

'I'm sorry,' she said softly. 'No wonder you feel so strongly. Anyhow, it doesn't matter much what you said now, but I thought father would have apoplexy at the time and I wasn't taking any chances of adding fuel to the fire. I was in his black books badly enough already.'

'Were you—why?'

She laughed a little ruefully and then swallowed hard because her mouth was so dry. 'I fell in love with a "cad" last summer. Ghastly, wasn't it? A board-school boy who's earning his living as an artist. He was spending his holiday sketching near my home in Norfolk because he's mad on landscapes, although ordinarily he does poster work. He's not making a fortune, but enough for us to have married on, and I've got a little money of my own. I was quite mad about him; I still am, a bit, and he was crazy about me.'

'What happened? I suppose your father kicked?'

'Yes. My happiness didn't count, of course, and "Daddy knew best" as usual. I don't come into my money till I'm twenty-five and he's my sole trustee; so he sold out some of my shares and made me come on this trip with him.'

'Could he do that? It hardly sounds legal.'

'He had power to use part of the money for my education, and travel's education, isn't it? Anyhow, I couldn't stop him without taking action and I hadn't the courage to burn my boats by running away.'

'You poor dear. I can imagine him being pretty terrifying to anyone he'd had under his thumb for years.'

'That's just it. I knew well enough that he was only a stupid, narrow old man, but there was something about those stony eyes of his that used to freeze the marrow of my bones. He'd already arranged a round of visits in South Africa and Jamaica for this winter so it suited him splendidly to break up my affair and at the same time have me around to do his packing and all the odd jobs he hated doing himself. You must think it pretty beastly of me to say this sort of thing about him now he's dead, though.'

'Not at all! "We choose our friends, but our parents are thrust upon us", as somebody once said very truthfully. It's quite illogical that we should be expected to love people if they do nothing to earn our affection. Hadn't you a mother, though, to help you out?'

'No, mother died when I was sixteen. His selfish slave-driving wore the poor darling out and. . . . Hallo! What's that?'

A shout had come from forward of the sail. It was followed immediately by a loud splash and then excited cries in Swedish.

Basil jumped to his feet and pressed forward to see what had happened. At the same moment Unity saw an arm suddenly protrude from the water about ten feet from the side of the boat: it was swept past and disappeared again within a few seconds.

Luvia yelled an order from the stern and the boat was put about; but the triangular fins which had followed in their wake so sinisterly all day had disappeared. A little cloud of bubbles and a sudden reddening of the water in the place where Unity had seen the arm told the rest of the grim story. Further efforts at rescue were quite useless.

'It was that poor devil Steffens,' Basil said as he rejoined Unity. 'The fellow who was cut about the face so badly in the scrap last night.'

'Oh, dear! He's been feverish all day and he was feeling the lack of water more than any of us. I was going along in a few minutes' time to re-do his bandages. What happened?'

'He couldn't stand the strain any longer, I suppose. His friend Largertöf says they've twice had to prevent him by force from drinking sea-water, but the first time he swallowed quite a lot before they could stop him.'

'Drinking sea-water sends people mad doesn't it?'

'So they say. He suddenly jumped up and chucked himself overboard.'

'Oh, how horrible!' Unity covered her face with her hands and burst into tears.

'Steady—steady on.' Basil put his arm round her. 'You've been so splendid all this time. Don't give way now.'

After a moment she checked her sobbing and he helped her back to the stern. The others there had noticed them during their long talk together, so Basil's presence was accepted without comment.

For a short spell the new tragedy had roused the whole boat's company to frantic activity, but now they subsided in their places again, a hapless prey to the gnawing misery of their thoughts.

Largertöf wept for his friend Steffens and would not be comforted. He was a young fellow, little more than a muscular, well-grown boy, and the older man, a seaman of twenty years' standing, had become his hero through having protected him in the rough life of the fo'c'sle. The others sat glum and silent; some of them wondering with good reason if Steffens had not taken the wiser course in making a sudden end of himself.

The sun, now a red-gold disc, touched the horizon. The long, low layers of cloud gathered about it were lit for a few moments into a glory of crimson, orange, and rose. With lack-lustre eyes they watched it sink into that underworld which the ancients believed to contain only death and eternal night. Another day was gone, and the passing of the supreme symbol of all life and virility left them doubly conscious of their ever-increasing-weakness.

When the hurricane lantern was lit, Luvia issued rations. The cask was now empty as a hollow drum, and owing to the loss of the kettle and stove in the mutiny no sea-water could now be boiled to distil fresh with the limited amount of paraffin still at their disposal, but the fat of the corned beef contained a small amount of moisture and the condensed milk, of which he allowed them two spoonfuls apiece, was a semi-liquid.

After the long day of sunshine their throats were so dry and parched that it was a struggle to get down the sticky mess, but they masticated the ration doggedly; conscious that it would give them a little strength—a few hours more of the life for which they were so greedy now that its sands were running out with such terrifying speed.

Before they settled down to the long hours of darkness Juhani Luvia joined them all in prayer as he had done each morning and evening since they had been in the open boat. None of the company had a prayer-book with them, but Juhani's mother had brought him up in the faith she held very dear, and on his leave he still accompanied her to an old church in Viipuri, so he experienced little difficulty in leading a simple appeal for help, guidance and fortitude to the Maker of them all.

The night proved calm, and had they been in comfortable berths after an ample meal they would normally have enjoyed a dreamless slumber, but their seats on the hard boards and lack of nourishment kept them wakeful. The gentle rocking of the boat and the monotonous lapping of the water against the sides became a torture to their frayed nerves. Towards midnight one of the negroes began to pray aloud, a semi-incoherent rambling argument with God, it seemed, in which the man alternately reasoned and pleaded that he had done nothing to deserve such chastisement. Luvia was in two minds whether to stop it with an abrupt order, but, knowing that none of the others were really sleeping, could not bring himself to do so.

The coloured man was not the only one to become light-headed. Suddenly, without warning, Synolda began to scream and bang her head against the woodwork in the stern. It took twenty minutes' patient handling on the part of Unity, Luvia, Vicente and Basil to restore her to sanity, and when the hard tears came at last to her dry eyes they thought her rasping sobs would never cease.

Starlight of a brightness unbelievable to those who have always lived in cities lit the scene. The Southern Cross gleamed high in the heavens to the south, yet moved in its orbit as the night crawled on with what seemed to them incredible slowness. Like points of light in a high canopy of dark purple, the countless stars winked and twinkled above them, so that each shape in the boat could be recognized as an individual by their gentle radiance. When the negro had fallen into an uneasy slumber and Synolda had been quieted, a great silence was all about them. In the mysterious twilight of the stars they crouched, suffering there until the sky paled and out of its greyness came another dawn.

The night had not been cold, but their lowered resistance had made them more susceptible to the chill of a light breeze that had sprung up in the early hours. Their muscles ached almost unendurably from the strain of trying to keep in one position for

66

any length of time: their heads were heavy from fatigue and sleeplessness, yet curiously clear in the matter of awareness concerning their surroundings.

Water, condensed milk and rum were now all exhausted, so the only issue for the morning meal was the last tin of corned beef. Slowly they chewed it, but Unity found hers impossible to swallow and had to dispose of it over the side of the boat. Hardly a word was spoken; it was an effort for them to croak out more than a sentence from their leather-dry throats.

Anyone who had seen them go on board at Cape Town would hardly have recognized them on this, the fourth morning of their ordeal. Their eyes were sunken in their sockets; their cheeks leaden, where they were not covered with a coarse stubble.

Synolda's vanity case had been sent spinning overboard during the upset of the mutiny. At the time her fury at its loss had caused her to become almost blasphemous, but now she no longer cared. Curiously enough, without her make-up she seemed years younger, but she had the pale-faced, hectic-eyed look of a consumptive rather than the robust freshness of a healthy girl.

After the ration of bully had been dispensed it was found that one portion remained over. At first Luvia feared that their depleted company of fifteen had been further reduced by yet another fatality unwitnessed by them during the night, but Hansie was discovered curled up sound asleep in the bow.

All efforts to arouse him proved fruitless and his big flask lay beside him quite empty. It was obvious that he had sought temporary oblivion in his supply of Bourbon and, on a practically empty stomach, the strong spirit had overcome him to an extreme degree. He was dead drunk, and, having rolled up his eyelids, Basil came to the conclusion that the ex-bartender would not regain consciousness before midday.

Four hours of the morning drifted by and for all of them each hour seemed like a month in hell. At a little before eleven o'clock the woolly-pated Lem, who had rambled so wildly in the night, went insane. Cursing, screaming, blaspheming, he suddenly dived at his feet and attempted to tear away the ropes that held them. The sailors tried to restrain him, but, wild-eyed and foaming at the mouth, he fought them off with superhuman strength. Luvia went forward and, thinking it the most humane thing to do, hit him a smashing blow under the jaw that knocked him out.

Just as Lem sagged and slid down in a heap, Vicente, who was doing look-out, gave a croaking yell.

'A ship! I see her! Blessed Madonna! A ship to left there! A ship, Luvia—a ship!'

Instantly every neck was craned in the direction he had pointed. A groan of disappointment went up—the horizon was blank and empty.

'Oh, how could you!' Synolda's cry of protest came huskily from between her cracked lips.

'He wasn't trying to be funny,' said Basil bitterly. 'The poor chap's gone off his rocker.'

Vicente's expression suddenly changed from delirious joy to utter despair. He ceased waving his arms and stood staring, mouth agape, at the unbroken seascape with its monotonous expanse of bobbing wavelets. 'She is gone!' he wailed. 'She is gone. Yet I swear I see her this moment back.'

'What was it you thought you saw?' Luvia asked soberly.

'Two masts—their top staffs—also, between, for a second, a black patch I think is a funnel tip.'

'He's higher than we are and can see further,' Unity muttered just as Luvia pushed past her, and, jumping up on to the thwart beside Vicente, cried, 'Hi you, give me those glasses.'

With a dazed look on his face the Venezuelan handed over the binoculars which Luvia lent to each look-out for his turn of duty.

For two breathless moments the whole company remained absolutely motionless, their hearts gripped by the most appalling suspense. Not a murmur escaped them while they awaited the verdict which meant for them life or death.

Luvia held the glasses firmly to his eyes, yet he could not keep his hands from trembling. Slowly he lowered them and turned to look at the group who stood in the well of the boat, their anxious faces all strained up towards him.

His mouth twitched spasmodically before he spoke. 'We win. Vedras is right. There's a steamer to sou'-west of us. I can see her topmasts and the tip of her funnel when we rise on the swell.'

It was Thursday, 13th January, and they had been eighty-four hours in the boat. The tension snapped. Some portion of their inexpressible relief was manifest in a sudden outpouring of emotion. Synolda flung her arms round Vicente's neck and kissed him. Basil led a husky cheer. Unity fainted. Jansen slipped to his knees and began to render thanks to God aloud. Luvia sat down on the thwart, put his head between his hands and burst into tears.

Within five minutes Unity had come round and Luvia was back

in the stern rapping out orders. The rest, having regained control of themselves, were springing to obey him; their languor gone; galvanized into a fierce activity by the miraculous promise of succour which had come to them when hope seemed past even praying for.

The mutineers were released; the sail was set. Jansen was sent forward with the glasses to keep watch upon the ship. Basil shinned up the mast and tied a long streamer of white material which Synolda had ripped from her underskirt to the spar.

'How far off is she?' he asked Luvia when he had finished fixing the pennant which he hoped might attract the attention of the look-out on the ship to them.

'Difficult to say,' the Finn replied. 'Her funnel tip, which I could just make out, must be fifty feet above the water; a man sitting on it could see our sail each time she rises if he had glasses. At that height his horizon would be close on ten miles away. Maybe the funnel's higher though. If so, we're farther off.'

'How long d'you reckon it'll take us to come up with her?'

'God knows! It's a bad break her being almost dead to wind-ward. Can't sail within seven points of the wind, you see, so we'll have to tack first one way then another to get nearer.'

'With any luck she'll spot us and turn out of her course to pick us up.'

Luvia shook his head. 'I doubt that; anyway till we're much closer. They'd never sight a small boat like this such a distance away. There's so little shipping in these waters, too, the look-out knows it's a cinch there'll be nothing to report so the odds are he's some lazy bum who's sitting up in the crow's-nest half asleep.'

A hoarse voice behind them asked anxiously: 'In which direction is she going?' It was De Brissac; his head still swathed in bandages, but well enough to lie propped up now.

'I don't know,' Luvia grunted. 'I couldn't see the slant of her masts sufficiently to judge; but she's practically broadside-on to us.'

Synolda grabbed his arm. 'But if she's ten miles away and not coming towards us she may disappear again before we get near enough to signal her.'

'Yes,' Luvia agreed soberly. 'I'm afraid that is so. We're not out of the wood yet.' He had already visualized such a possibility, but forborne to mention it.

At the awful thought that they might not be rescued after all a quick reaction set in. They fell silent, strained their eyes in the

69

direction of the ship they could not see, and watched the maddeningly slow progress of the boat through the water with the acutest anxiety.

The life-boat was a heavy, broad-waisted vessel, built to survive in rough seas and not for speed. With a good wind she could not have done much more than six knots an hour and the light breeze which played about it at the moment was carrying it along at less than three. The necessity for tacking further reduced their actual progress towards the ship and when midday came Jansen reported that while the steamer did not appear to be any farther away he did not think they were much nearer to her.

As they were tacking all the time at an angle to their true course, it was difficult to observe in which direction the vessel was moving. A second and longer study of her through the glasses had convinced Luvia that she was not broadside, but three-quarters-on, with her stern towards them. He could see no smoke rising from the funnel tip and concluded that she was cruising very slowly away to the southward. Jansen and the oldest sailor, Bremer, agreed with him.

Speculation was rife among them as to what the ship could be doing in such a lonely area of the ocean. From the little they could judge, without seeing her hull and at such a distance, she seemed too big for a whaler, while a tramp or passenger ship would hardly have been likely to be cruising at a few knots an hour in the empty spaces of the South Atlantic.

They were in no state to talk much, however, as, after the first excitement of sighting their possible rescuer had subsided, they suffered a relapse to their previous state of weakness. Even a few words meant an effort, and now the sun was over the meridian the real torture of thirst had them all firmly in its grip.

Since there were no liquid rations left to issue, old Jansen had the idea of breaking up the cask. Its wood retained a little moisture and when he had knocked off the iron hoops they eagerly shared out the curved staves. By hacking off small pieces of the wood with their knives they were able to chew it for the pitifully small amount of water it still held before spitting out the evil-tasting residue. Though it did not even serve to wet their throats it occupied them for a while and gave them the illusion that they had had a meagre ration.

By one o'clock they still seemed to have made little progress and the light wind was dying fast. Luvia judged that they could not have made more than a mile in the direction of the ship in

70

the past hour, and, whatever might be her mysterious mission, cruising so slowly in these wastes, he feared every moment that she would put on steam and sail away. In a cracked voice he ordered the sail to be lowered and the men to get out their oars.

They obeyed willingly enough, only too glad, in spite of their physical distress, to be able to lend a hand towards their own salvation, rather than remain idle in such frightful suspense.

Luvia took the stroke oar himself; Basil, Bremer, Largertöf, Harlem, and Corncob made up the rest of the crew. Jansen, at the tiller, turned the boat's bow dead towards their goal and Unity relieved him of his job of look-out with the glasses.

An hour's rowing brought them perceptibly nearer to the steamer. Occasional glimpses of her mast and funnel tops could now be caught when standing up in the boat, and from Unity's perch on the bow thwarts she could keep them under constant observation, even when the ship sank a little in the gentle swell. But that hour had taken the go out of the best men in the boat.

It was over twenty-four hours since any of them had tasted water and for nearly four days they had subsisted on the barest minimum of food.

As in a nightmare, Synolda watched them from the stern; their faces grimed and furrowed, or red and puffy where the sun had caught them; their breath coming in painful gasps at each tug on the heavy oars; their eyes protruding unnaturally from black-ringed sockets. Nearest her, Luvia was sticking it manfully; the muscles in his cheeks tightening under his four-days' growth of golden stubble every time he threw his weight into a long, steady stroke. His fine head and splendid physique had attracted her from the beginning, and in these days of stress she had come to admire his courage and fortitude as well. Now, her heart bled for him as she realized that the rest of the oarsmen were quite incapable of adequately supporting his splendid effort.

Bitterly he realized that too. Their strokes were becoming ragged and uneven; their oars dipped into the water but there was little power behind the blades. Now and again one of them caught a crab, impeded the others, and checked the way of the boat. It was not that they were slacking, but too weary and feeble to row better even though their lives depended on it.

At half past two he replaced Bremer, Largertöf, Corncob and Basil with Isiah, Nudäa, Vicente and Jansen.

Another hour of dogged rowing and Unity reported that she could see most of the funnel and the upper bridge-works of the ship. It had turned a little and was now heading dead away from them, but must be proceeding very slowly as they were certainly decreasing their distance from it.

At four o'clock Basil went up into the bow and found Hansie, about whom they'd all forgotten, lying there wide awake staring up at the sky. The ex-barman had come out of his drunken stupor some time earlier, but was suffering from such an appalling hangover as well as ravaging thirst that he had no idea a ship had been sighted and the fact that the others were rowing had not even impinged on his consciousness.

Basil dipped a canvas bucket over the side, and, filling it with sea-water, flung its contents over Hansie to rouse him fully. It then occurred to him to take a look at Lem. After Luvia had knocked the negro out in the morning they had tied him up and gagged him to prevent his screaming tearing all that remained of their nerves to pieces when he came to again. Basil found him still and stiff, with his eyeballs staring; he was quite dead. His body meant so many stone of weight in the boat; so much extra to pull when every ounce mattered to the aching muscles of the rowers. Without the least compunction Basil heaved up the dead negro's body and, with an effort, pushed it overboard

With Hansie's revival Luvia decided on another change of crew. The ex-barman, Basil, Bremer and Largertöf, relieved Isiah, Nudäa, Vicente and Jansen. Harlem refused to be relieved although he had been rowing from the first like Luvia, and Luvia himself would not hear of taking a spell. The leader of the mutiny had stamina and a perverse pride of his own; he wished to show that he was just as good a man as the Finnish Engineer.

By five o'clock Jansen said that through the glasses he could now make out the deck-houses of the steamer when standing on a thwart and insisted that Luvia should have his place taken at the stroke oar if only long enough to have a good look at the ship.

Luvia's back was nearly breaking under the strain and the palms of his hands were half raw where they had chafed in his hours of strenuous pulling. He was not beaten yet but honestly glad of the excuse to give up for a while at least. Ordering Isiah to take Harlem's place and Nudäa his own, he joined Jansen in the bow.

'Yes,' he agreed thickly after he had trained the binoculars on the steamer. 'We're nearer, much nearer. Not more than five miles from her. Difficult to tell what she is though with her stern turned towards us like that. She's pretty high out of the water—a cargo boat with ballast probably. Too far off still for us to see any of the people on her decks and unfortunately it's unlikely they'll spot us yet either. If only she were broadside-on or coming across our bows there'd be so much more chance, but who the hell ever looks out over the stern of a vessel?'

'The thing is, can we get so near to hail before we lose her in the darkness, sir?' the old carpenter asked despondently.

Luvia turned to look at the exhausted rowers. 'We've got to, Jansen,' he rasped. 'We've damn' well got to.'

During the next hour some of the oarsmen had to be changed three times. Their swollen tongues were like thick lumps of leather in their mouths, they could no longer draw breath properly through the closing passages of their throats, their faces were blackened and discoloured, their palms a mass of blisters from constant tugging at the oars so that the shafts now felt red hot to their touch.

Largertöf had fallen forward, sobbing on his oar, crying out in Swedish, 'Kill me! Kill me! I cannot bear it any more.' Hansie, Isiah and Vicente Vedras had all collapsed and lay gasping in the bottom of the boat. Gietto Nudäa was suffering from a violent bout of vomiting, as a result of having gulped down half a pint of paraffin from the supply for the lost primus stove in a crazy attempt to quench his thirst. Synolda was comatose; a white huddle tumbled in disarray at the stern of the boat.

Luvia carried on with the rest somehow. Old Jansen was at the tiller and Unity had the glasses again. She could observe the ship quite clearly now nearly down to her water line, but only her stern was visible and in that portion of her she could see no movement.

Low on the horizon a cloud passed in front of the sun; a light mist was rising and gradually the shadows closed around them. Basil fainted and there was no one left to take his place. While they were shifting him out of the way Isiah doubled up and fell beside him. The rowers were reduced to four.

'We're—not—far off,' Unity managed to choke out as the survivors settled to their oars again, 'but—it's getting difficult to see her.'

'She'll show her lights—any minute . . .' Luvia croaked back. 'Stick to it boys—cheat the devil yet.'

For another twenty minutes Unity continued to stare through the glasses. It was quite dark now but through the mist she could not make out any lights yet in the ship ahead. She was only a black patch, a little darker than the surrounding gloom. Suddenly Unity lost sight of her altogether.

Frantically she began to sweep the darkness ahead, trying to pick it up again, and not daring to tell the others of this overwhelming calamity which threatened to cheat them at the last when they were so near to victory.

In vain she peered and peered, the ship's lights would certainly be on by this time, but the mist must have thickened considerably and was hiding them from her; only a dense, uniform blackness showed ahead.

At last Luvia ceased rowing and turned round. 'How much farther?' he gasped. 'Where is she?'

'I've lost her,' Unity choked.

'Oh, God!' groaned Luvia.

'There she is—there!' Bremer suddenly sprang up and pointed, not ahead but over their starboard side, and through the mist they all made out the faint dark outline of the steamer. They were less than a hundred yards away but had nearly passed her in the darkness.

They tried to hail her, but none of them had sufficient voice left to raise a shout, so they wearily took to the oars again and pulled until they came up to within a few feet of her side.

The ship was not moving and showed not a single light. A strange uncanny silence, intensified by the mist, wrapped her round.

'Something queer about her,' Luvia muttered, 'and she's got a nasty list to port.' Suddenly his voice rose to a hoarse shout. 'By God! it's the old *Gafelborg*. She didn't go down after all!'

CHAPTER V

THE SEA GIVES UP ITS DEAD

AT THIS amazing discovery the feelings of the little party who still remained conscious in the boat were distinctly mixed.

For the last hour Corncob had sustained himself entirely on a pleasing vision. Its principal ingredients were a mighty meal, followed by unlimited supplies of hot grog while an eager crowd in the fo'c'sle of the stranger ship listened with rapt attention to his recital of their adventures. Like the big, black child he was, he burst into dry, hoarse sobs at his bitter disappointment.

Unity's first thought was the happy one that she would be able to get all the things she had been compelled to leave in her cabin when they abandoned ship; her own hair tonic, brushes, bath salts; sleep the clock round in her favourite nightdress, and revel in clean undies when she got up.

Harlem felt a grim satisfaction. He had rowed so desperately only because his very life depended on it; but knew that when they reached the ship he would be put in irons and have to face his trial for mutiny on the high seas immediately they touched a port. In the old *Gafelborg* there was food and drink, but nothing to fear. He'd broken prison in the States and wriggled out of plenty of tough spots since. Many things might happen before Luvia got a chance to hand him over to the authorities, and he'd have skipped long before then.

Knowing the *Gafelborg* to have been seriously disabled, Jansen was frankly dismayed. He considered it little short of a miracle that she had survived the cyclone or not gone down since; and he realized that her being still afloat was due to the exceptionally calm weather of the last four days. He gloomily foresaw a short sojourn in her revictualling, then her sinking with the first puff of wind, and their having to face the horrors of the open boat again. Bremer's thoughts were very much the same.

Luvia, on the other hand, was seized with a wild elation. As she had remained afloat for four days he felt there was a good chance of her lasting a few more. If only the weather held he might be able to patch her up and run her into port. That would mean a small fortune in salvage money for him, praise from his owners, and certain promotion to a better berth in a new ship.

He was cautious enough to realize, however, that the *Gafelborg* might suddenly slide under at any moment, and checked the impetuosity of the others who were frantic to get on board. They were already man-handling the boat along the side of the ship to some rope falls which hung slack from the davits where one of the boats had been lowered.

'You'll stay put,' he told them as he grabbed the metal block which dangled at the end of the tackle. 'The least thing may send her plunging—even the extra weight of a bunch of us all boarding her at one point at the same time. I'll be back with water just as soon as I can.' He swarmed up the falls, clambered down the davit, and disappeared over the ship's side.

As he was well acquainted with the *Gafelborg's* geography, he was able to make straight for the pantry, draw off a large copper can of drinking-water and return with it without the least delay. Taking one big, glorious gulp himself he bent a line through the handle of the can and lowered it to the tortured sufferers in the boat.

'Don't drink too much at once,' he called, 'else you'll get belly-ache. No one's to come aboard before I give the word. I want to have a look round first.'

Returning to the pantry, he poured himself a pint of water, and savoured to the full the luxury of sipping it slowly down while he thought over the situation.

The *Gafelborg* still had a heavy list to port and was dangerously down at the head. If she was repairable it would take days, weeks perhaps, to make her really seaworthy. In the meantime there was always the chance that a sudden squall might send her to the bottom or that a slight infiltration, which was probably in progress through the forward bulkhead shutting off the water-logged compartments, might accumulate enough weight in her main holds to tip the scale so that she would go down without the slightest warning.

His normal caution made him feel that he ought not to allow any of the others on board at all. Once in the ship they might be trapped like rats and drowned, whereas while they remained in the boat they could draw supplies from the *Gafelborg* and would be safe from anything short of another cyclone.

On the other hand, he had to face the fact that most of the party were half-dead already. If they were to repair the ship sufficiently for her to remain afloat, and it seemed now that their chances of life mainly depended on their being able to do so, he would need every man he had in fit condition for the labour. Plenty of good food and a long sleep in comfortable bunks was undoubtedly the quickest road to their full recovery. The lowering of hot victuals to the boat seemed a pretty problem and its hard bottom boards, as he knew well enough, were no place for refreshing slumber. Finishing up his glass of water he made his decision. He must chance the ship going down with them in it and have them all on board.

Collecting a canvas sling from one of the deck lockers, he returned to the ship's side. 'Hallo there!' he called. 'Harlem, you come up here to me. Jansen, Bremer, stay in the boat and fix the casualties to be hoisted in this sling I'm sending down to you.'

As soon as Harlem had shinned up the falls Luvia hauled in the block, attached the sling to it, and lowered away. By means of the block and tackle hanging from the davit the two of them raised all the boat's company to the deck. Jansen arrived last, having made the lifeboat fast so that it would not drift away during the night but be ready for any fresh emergency which might overtake them.

Basil, Synolda and Isiah had already been revived with some of the water in the can that Luvia had lowered; but Vicente, Larger-töf, Hansie and Nudäa were still incapable of using their own legs. De Brissac, too, although conscious and less exhausted than some of the others, was standing upright for the first time since the oar fell on his head, so found it impossible to stagger more than a few steps. As they came aboard Luvia sent them to the lounge and those who could walk carried in the grimly sagging figures of the remainder.

Unity took one of the hurricane lamps and went straight to the after galley. Finding some large tins of soup in a cupboard, she opened four of them, tipped their contents into a big saucepan, and mechanically set it on the stove. She was so dazed with fatigue it never even occurred to her as queer that the fire should still be going although the ship had been abandoned four days before, and twenty minutes later Basil discovered her curled up in a corner of the galley sound asleep. He roused her with some difficulty and together they carried the soup and plates to the lounge.

Meanwhile Luvia and Synolda had been busy on the casualties. With the aid of brandy from the bar they had succeeded in restoring all of them except Nudäa, who was still desperately ill and could keep nothing down.

The soup was handed round, and, although several of them were sick afterwards owing to the frightful state of their distended stomachs, even those who were felt the better for its comforting warmth as it trickled down their gullets.

All of them were much too worn out to attempt cooking anything further that night, so the hardier ones supplemented the soup with some bananas and a tin of cheese biscuits which Hansie produced from a locker in the saloon. Afterwards, Luvia thought for a moment of getting bedding up from the cabins, so that they could sleep nearer the deck and have more chance of saving themselves if the ship began to sink, but even that small effort was now obviously quite beyond them. It was as much as they could do to support the invalids down the companionway and stagger with them to the nearest bunks.

Almost blind with fatigue, Unity found her own cabin. The electric light was not working. All thoughts of a hot bath and the pretty nightdress had left her. She ripped off her clothes in the dark, crawled between the cool sheets naked, and, next moment was sound asleep.

When she awoke the strong, midday sunshine was streaming through the porthole. Her own belongings were set out about her in the small, familiar cabin, and, for a second, she thought the events of the last five days had occurred only in a frightful dream. Yet her heavy head, rough tongue, nakedness, and the sloping angle of the cabin, immediately convinced her of their reality.

'Missie wantum bleak'fas—lunch?' a sibilant voice asked from the doorway.

She jerked her head round and to her amazement saw a smooth-faced Chinaman standing there.

'Yoh clom topsides. Li Foo mek heap plenty bacon-eggs an' veh good tea.'

Without a sound the yellow-faced vision drew to the door and disappeared.

Unity stared after him, realizing it was his coming which must have wakened her, but uncertain yet if he were man or ghost. He certainly had not been with them during their nightmare existence in the boat and she was sure she had not seen him on the ship during the run from Cape Town. However, he seemed a very friendly apparition and promised unbelievably good things.

Deciding to accept his invitation without delay, she slipped out of the bunk. The water in the cabin basin was cold, so she contented herself with sluicing her face and washing the grime off her hands; determining to have a hot bath later, even if she had to boil every kettle of water for it and carry them to the bathroom. All the men having seen her so recently in such a hopelessly bedraggled state, she wasted little time in dressing, but, with the heavenly thought of fresh, hot tea spurring her on, combed her hair, pulled on some clothes, and hurried to the saloon.

Basil was there, but so changed she hardly recognized him. The grubby-looking ruffian of the day before had been transformed into a lean, brown-faced young man; freshly shaved and immaculately dressed in a light grey lounge suit. His old slouch of the pre-storm days was gone too; his complexion was healthier and his eyes clear. Four days' privation and acute mental stress had made a different man of him.

'Top of the morning to you,' he greeted her.

'Same to you, but I should have thought it was getting on for afternoon,' she smiled, sitting down opposite him.

'It is. You've had a good sixteen hours' sleep; although I'll bet it didn't feel like more than a ten minute nap to you, any more than it did to me.'

'It didn't. I just fell asleep and seemed to wake up again immediately. I shan't find any difficulty in getting off tonight either. Where are the others?'

'A few of them are too ill still to leave their cabins. You'll have to do the Florence Nightingale act again when you've fed. Luvia and the rest have been about for the last three hours or more, doing things to the ship.'

'Why are you slacking then?'

'I'm not,' he protested as the Chinaman appeared and set a plate of sizzling bacon and eggs before her. 'I'm "Sparks", the wireless man from now on, and I've been doing my damnedest to repair the outfit. The deckhouse was stove in and half the gear wrecked in the storm. But even wireless men must eat, and all workers are entitled to a second breakfast.'

Unity glanced over her shoulder as the Chinaman left them. 'Where in the world's he sprung from?'

'Oh, that's Li Foo; the ship's second cook. Extraordinary luck

79

the fellow's had—or fate—whichever you like to call it. Apparently some fortune-telling bird in his own country drew the bamboos for him once and told him he'd die in a boat; so when everybody else abandoned ship he wasn't having any and hid himself in case they took him off by force.'

'What! he's been here all the time? But, of course, he must have. That's why the fire was going in the galley when we came on board last night. My brain was almost giving out but I'd just remembered and was beginning to puzzle about it.'

'Yes, and living like a fighting-cock while we were chewing our fingernails in that damn' boat. He says the storm ceased within an hour of our leaving the ship and it's been like a millpond ever since.'

Synolda appeared at that moment; her fair hair tumbling over her shoulders and a silk wrap partially concealing her pale blue pyjamas.

'Thank God you're here!' she exclaimed. 'I've had such a fright. I was woken by a Chinaman. He just popped his head into my cabin and out again and—and—well, none of our coloured men were Chinese, were they?'

Basil laughed and explained about Li Foo.

'I see,' she hesitated, 'then I suppose I'd better go back and get some clothes on—although I'm absolutely dying for breakfast.'

'Why bother?' he replied lightly. 'None of the negroes will come in here and I've seen you with lots less on than you've got now when we used to sunbathe before the storm.'

'If Unity doesn't mind.' Synolda was still a little frightened of the disapproval of the younger girl, although necessity had forced them to bury their prejudices against each other during the last few days.

'Of course not!' Unity smiled. 'Let me pour you out some tea. I expect Li Foo will bring you some bacon and eggs in a moment.'

'Thanks.' Synolda sat down. 'As a matter of fact my clothes are in rags anyhow. You see, I sailed in rather a hurry and lost my luggage at the last moment, so I only had the dress I stood up in and a case containing my night-things.'

'I should think my things would fit you fairly well and I've plenty of clothes. Would you like me to lend you some?'

'Would you?' Synolda's blue eyes widened with surprise. 'I'd be terribly grateful if you would.'

'Certainly I will. Because we didn't—er—talk to each other much on those few days out from Cape Town, that's no reason we shouldn't pool our resources now. It may be quite a time yet before we get back to a port.'

Synolda eagerly accepted the proffered olive branch. She knew only too well the effect which the extraordinary magnetism her presence exercised over men had on other women, although she never sought to trespass on their preserves. It caused her to aggravate the position by being abnormally suspicious and on the defensive even when she would have liked to make friends, but here, she felt, was a really welcome chance to make herself pleasant. Now that the immediate dangers of the last few days were past both girls were able to relax and, over breakfast, Synolda came right out of her shell.

Just as they were finishing Luvia joined them and Basil said at once: 'I take it you've finished your inspection. Let's hear the best and the worst.'

The tall Finn sat down and poured himself a cup of tea. 'Things are O.K. for the moment. The for'ard bulkheads are holding and there's very little water coming through into the main hold. Our first job is to shift the cargo. Luck's with us that it's general merchandise, most of which can be manhandled. I've got the boys on it right now.'

'How long'll that take?'

'Couple of days, I reckon, before we can shift enough to counteract this dangerous list and right her. Then we'll have to shift the fo'c'sle gear and anything else that's movable as far aft as possible, so as to raise her bow out of the water. If we can do that maybe I can get down to patch the strained plate for'ard that's been the cause of all the trouble.'

'How about the water that's in there though?'

'I've got the auxiliary boiler going, so we should be able to pump it clear, if we can once stop the leak, now there's no big seas pouring down the forward hatch. How'd you make out with the radio?'

Basil madé a grimace. 'I'm not at all happy about it. One side of the deck-house was completely carried away. I've only managed to clear part of the wreckage, so I don't know if any of the essential parts have been damaged yet, but the apparatus looks in a pretty nasty mess.'

'That's not so hot. I was kinda counting on that radio to S O S some shipping. You see, we'll be safe enough here as long as it's like this. I'm easy about that now. But it won't be so funny if bad weather blows up.'

Synolda grabbed his arm. 'We won't—we won't have to take to that awful boat again?'

'If we can't call another ship to pick us up and this one looks like sinking on us, we will.'

'I'll be able to let you know for certain about the wireless by tea time,' Basil cut in. 'What an extraordinary thing it is, though, that we should have run into the old *Gafelborg* again.'

Luvia shrugged. 'It's not so queer as it looks on first sight. She's probably never been much over twenty miles from us—just under our horizon, perhaps, which wasn't all that wide from the boat. The hurricane drove her the same way as us that first night and, after, winds and tides would have carried the boat and ship in the same direction.'

'How're the invalids?' Unity asked suddenly. 'I've had no chance yet to have a look at them today.'

He shrugged again. 'Neither have I. Plenty more urgent things to see to. De Brissac's in his cabin, of course, and Vedras and Hansie are too sick to show a leg—so the Chink tells me. That little dirt—Gietto Nudäa, is all washed up as well. It's on you dames to snap into getting them fit again just as quick as you can. I must ask you to do our cooking, too, since I'll want the Chink. I need every hand I can get for shifting cargo in the hold.'

'I'll do the nursing,' Unity agreed, 'but my cooking's not too good. How about yours, Synolda?'

'Mine's not up to much either. I've hardly boiled an egg since I finished the cooking course at my school in Johannesburg. But, of course, I'll do what I can.'

The Finn stood up. 'Well, whatever you can manage will be good enough for us. Li Foo'll show you things and give you the keys of the store. I'm for a shave now, then I must get back to keep the boys at it and lend a hand myself.'

'Oh, no—please don't. Shave, I mean,' Synolda protested. 'You're growing the most lovely golden beard. It'd be an absolute sin to cut it off now the worst's over. In another few days you'll look just like a Viking.'

Doubtfully, Luvia stroked the yellow stubble on his chin. In the five days his beard had grown a lot and it was by no means unsightly now he had washed. Suddenly he smiled. 'I'll make a bargain with you.'

'Well?' she asked.

'You haven't made your face up today, although I expect you've got lots more muck in your cabin, same as you lost the time we had that scrap in the boat. You keep your face free of the fixings and I'll retain the beard.'

She looked down and her mouth twitched humorously. 'It's very flattering that you should take so much interest in my face.'

'I don't. I'm thinking of the men. I can't be around all the time and conditions here are far from normal. To have you mixing in with them all painted up is just asking for trouble.'

Her mouth went sulky. 'Thanks; I can look after myself, and you can do what you like with your damn' beard.'

'Don't get all het up. I'm not being fresh, but sensible. I like your face the way it is better too. Honest I do.'

'Really.' She was slightly mollified. 'I must powder though.'

'I'd rather you didn't.'

'Oh, come,' Unity interrupted, 'you can't reasonably expect a girl not to powder her nose. She hasn't asked you not to trim your beard when it grows longer.'

'O.K. Powder on the nose but not elsewhere. Will you play ball on that?'

Synolda nodded. 'All right. It's a deal.'

'Fine! I must be getting back to the men and I'm trusting you passengers to give me all the help you can. We're not out of the wood yet by a long way, so if you don't want another trip in the open boat you'll work till you drop.'

As he left the dining-saloon Basil grinned at Synolda. 'I believe you've made a conquest.'

She was not given to blushing very readily, but she did on this occasion, although she protested quickly: 'What nonsense! Plenty of men do seem to take an interest in me—far too many, as a matter of fact. But he's not that sort.'

Throughout the afternoon and evening Luvia kept all the able-bodied men hard at it in the hold. It was tiring work unstacking the heavy bales and boxes from the great, jumbled heap into which they had slid on the port side and lugging them over to starboard, but none of the men complained. Harlem had spoken privately to his coloured cronies and told them that if they valued their lives they had better obey Luvia's orders for the moment, so the negroes put their backs into it as heartily as the rest.

Vedras, Nudäa and Hansie were still too sick for such arduous labour, but Unity insisted that they were fit enough to come on deck, and Luvia set them to chipping away paintwork with

83

chisels and hammers from the screws and bolts which held all the gear on the fo'c'sle head. It was only about two feet above the waterline and his main hope of raising it lay in stripping it of everything movable; even the heavy winches which he could lift further aft when he got the derricks going.

De Brissac was still weak, but could now walk alone. The climb to the crow's-nest was impossible for him, but Luvia posted him on the bridge in an easy chair with a telescope through which he could keep a look-out for other shipping. Basil struggled with the wreckage in the wireless room, but by six o'clock he was compelled to report that the apparatus was smashed beyond repair and, since certain of the spare parts he needed to make it good were not in the storeroom, he had to abandon it altogether.

The girls took over the stores and galley from Li Foo. They found that with the reduced ship's company there was enough food to last them, even if they lived extravagantly, for a month and, with reasonable care, for two. The Chinaman was a perpetually smiling person and his serenity was only ruffled by the thought of the honourable Missies demeaning themselves to soil their hands by working in his galley. Almost instantly he developed a doglike devotion to Synolda and, when Luvia carried him off to work in the hold, displayed a remarkable degree of cunning in slipping back each hour or so for a few moments to stoke the fire, open tins, and implore her not to fatigue herself.

The fo'c'sle being uninhabitable, it was arranged that the dining-saloon on the main deck should be given over to the crew and that the passengers should mess in the bar lounge on the upper deck immediately above it. With the loss of three-quarters of the ship's original complement in the hurricane there were cabins enough and to spare for all.

That night they fed late, at ten o'clock, but Luvia and his squad of nine having worked like Trojans for the best part of twelve hours in the hold, the slant of the decks showed a decided improvement. They were all so dead beat that they ate almost in silence and, immediately after, tumbled into their bunks to fall into a dreamless sleep.

On the following morning, to their immense relief, the weather was fine again and showed no sign of breaking. They were drifting southward with the current still, but the sun was hot on the decks and, normally, they would have revelled in the beauty of the southern summer day. Most of them spent it again in the semi-darkness of the hold, however, choking in thick clouds of dust as they sweated there, straining to lift and trundle the weighty packages of merchandise.

By eight o'clock that evening the work was done. The *Gafelborg* still dipped heavily at the bow, but she was once more upon an even keel and they all felt heartened in consequence.

After the evening meal De Brissac asked Luvia if he had any idea where they were.

'Not a notion,' the Finn replied shortly. 'Far too many urgent jobs need my attention to splash time on taking observations. South Georgia's our nearest land now, I'd say. With luck we may drift down to it or hit one of the Sandwich group farther east. On the other hand, we may pass miles away from either.'

'What do you intend to do if you can succeed in getting the ship under way?'

'Head her dead west until we strike the coast of Patagonia.'

'In that direction the Falklands must be much nearer,' hazarded Basil.

'Maybe. I doubt if we're that far south yet though. South Georgia's farther south still, and I only spoke of it as being nearer than the coast of South America.'

'If only the weather keeps good,' Unity murmured.

'Yes—if only it does,' Luvia agreed, and with that prayer in all their hearts they went to their bunks.

CHAPTER VI

INTO THE MIST

THEIR third morning in the ship the arduous task was undertaken of clearing the fo'c'sle of its gear. By means of the auxiliary boiler Luvia had steam up to one of the winches. The high derricks in front of the foremast swung back and forth, lifting the anchors, great bundles of weighty chain, bollards, deck plates, and every possible thing which could be dismantled, to positions as far aft as possible. Hansie, Vedras and Nudäa were fit again and in the past two days they had succeeded in undoing all the fitments. Throughout the whole of the long morning the winch clattered and rattled while load after load of metal was made fast to the big dangling hook and afterwards thumped upon the deck as it was lowered.

By the early afternoon all the heavy stuff had been cleared, but the bow of the ship had only risen three feet out of the water, and under the stern, which rode high in the air, the propellers were still showing.

As the for'ard well was now only just awash Luvia sent the men into the fo'c'sle with orders to clear it entirely. Slopping about, they rescued their saturated belongings and then set to breaking up the furnishings with axes. Ladders, bunks, planking, lockers were all smashed to matchwood and the débris carried aft. By sundown the forepart of the ship had been completely gutted, yet they had only succeeded in raising the bow a further fifteen inches.

At supper that night Luvia expressed his anxiety. He did not see what else he could shift, yet it was useless to attempt to get the engines going as long as two-thirds of the propellers remained in the air. Moreover, it was vital to repair the leaky plate and pump out the forehold.

'These negro stokers,' De Brissac inquired, 'from where do they come?'

'The Southern States,' Luvia informed him.

'That is a pity but, even so, if one of them is from a coast town he may be a diver.'

'I don't quite get you.'

'If they came from the West Indies or the African seaboard they would swim like fishes.'

'Of course,' Basil nodded. 'You're thinking of the fellows who dive for coral, oysters, pennies.'

'*Certainement*, and everyone who swims that well could take down the hook on the rope of the derrick, hitch it to a bale underwater: then, hey presto! up she comes. So we could lighten the forehold of its cargo.'

'Gee!' Luvia hit the table. 'That's the whale of an idea. If only all those black swabs weren't raised in cities or inland among the cotton I'll get 'em on to it first thing tomorrow.'

Unable to contain his impatience he hurried off to the men's quarters and returned, ten minutes later, with the news that Corncob had once been employed on the Florida coast in a sponge fishery. The others were quite useless and could not even swim, but one good diver would enable them to try out De Brissac's scheme.

That night they slept uneasily. It seemed that the weather had broken at last. Clouds hid the young moon and stars; rain began to fall before they went to their cabins and continued to patter ominously upon the decks above, a constant reminder that, in its present state, the ship only afforded them temporary security.

Next morning the skies were grey; the rain still falling. Small, choppy waves slopped against the ship's sides and she was rolling slightly.

More anxious now than at any time since they had boarded her, Luvia at once set about De Brissac's plan for raising the submerged cargo.

For this operation the usual rope sling which is twisted round a bale for lifting was useless; instead four short chains attached to a ring, which was slipped over the big hook from the derrick, were used. Each chain had a small hook at its end and Corncob's business was to wedge the small hooks wherever he could under the corners of the cases, or into the wires and bands that bound them.

The work was arduous, but the big negro seemed to enjoy it. His naked body black and glistening, he plunged again and again into the greenish water which slopped in the open square of the fore-hatch, disappeared with his greyish feet wavering froglike

87

into the darkness of the hold, and emerged a few moments later blowing like a grampus as he waved a cheerful signal to hoist away.

Package after package came dripping from the hold, sometimes on four chains, sometimes, perilously, hooked by only one; twice the cords to which Corncob had attached the hooks burst under the strain and heavy crates plopped back into the water, but steady progress was made, which delighted Luvia who was keeping an anxious eye on the weather.

The rest of the crew were not idle. As each case was landed they flung it on a low-wheeled trolley they had got up from the store-room and ran it along to the after well, where they were stacking the salvaged cargo. By these means the ship was not only lightened at her head as each load came up, but weight added in her stern which further helped to restore her length to horizontal.

A sea mist had risen with the rain and following on the heat of previous days it clung warm and damp about them. Luvia's shouted orders were muffled and the figures of the toilers shrouded in its greyness appeared strangely ghostlike.

During the afternoon Corncob's vigour began to fail him. He was forced to dive deeper to get at lower cargo and sometimes it took three or more dives to get the hooks fast in a bale where in the morning it had required only one. The periods of rest he had to take between each dive grew longer and each time he came up he clung to the combings of the hatch grey-faced and gasping.

Luvia saw that the man was nearing the end of his tether and, at four o'clock, ordered him out of the water; giving him a few words of hearty praise for sticking it so long, and a promise that a triple ration of rum should be brought with a hot meal to his bunk where he was to tuck himself up immediately.

As no more cargo could be raised that day, Luvia turned his attention to getting out some of the water. The pumps were set going and in addition two chains of men with buckets organized. It was slow work as each bucket of water had to be drawn up on the end of a rope before it could be passed along and slung over the side, but by evening the water was five feet below the rim of the hatch and as a result of the day's labour the bow of the ship was now a good twelve feet clear of the sea level.

That night Luvia arranged for all his men, except De Brissac, to take short watches in couples, so that the boiler furnace might be fed and the pumps kept going. In the morning it was found that a further eight feet of water had been sucked up from the hold and, with comparative ease. Corncob was able to reach cargo which had been extremely difficult for him to get at the day before.

Just before midday Jansen spotted the leak. It was about fifteen feet down on the port side and as the water in the hold seeped away with each slight movement of the ship the pressure of the sea on the far side of the plate forced a jet through the gap.

That leak had gradually waterlogged the forehold in the first place; the water already pumped out had entered from above only after the great wave had smashed in the fore-hatch.

Luvia and the carpenter went down to inspect it. They could not repair the sprung plate with the limited equipment at their disposal, but both agreed that the leak could be stopped up. A weighted canvas awning was lowered over the ship's side to lessen the pressure from without, so that the jet became a dribble; the under edge of the plate was caulked with oakum well hammered home until the dribble ceased, a tarred mattress boarded over it and the boards braced by staves to the staunchions and deck beams.

It was a rough-and-ready job, although it took them all the afternoon, but when it was finished they were confident that, short of another storm which might spring the plate still further, any water that trickled through their tar-and-canvas plaster would not be more than the pumps could cope with.

After it was done Luvia called the whole company together and thanked them for their herculean labour which had enabled him to salvage the ship. He declared that for the first time since they had abandoned the *Gafelborg*, ten nights before, they could now consider themselves reasonably safe. The pumps must be kept going in order to clear the forehold entirely of water; so short watches of two men each would continue until the morning, but the rest could knock off for a lazy evening. Extra rations were issued for a celebration and, in the best of good spirits, the men gave him a rousing cheer.

Li Foo insisted on cooking dinner that night, and Hansie voluntarily returned to his old post of passengers' steward. He opened the bar again officially for the first time and Luvia ordered champagne with the meal to be at the ship's charge.

'Tomorrow,' he announced as they sat down, 'I mean to get the boilers going. We're short handed, but I think we'll make it. Here's to another few days seeing us safe in port.'

They drank the toast with enthusiasm and De Brissac made a short speech expressing the feelings of them all that they owed their lives to Luvia's tireless energy and unflinching devotion to duty.

The big man smiled uncomfortably and came as near to blushing as he ever had, under his short golden beard. 'Oh shucks!' he shrugged. 'Maybe I haven't done too badly for an Engineer, but every one of you's given all the help you could so let's cut out the bouquets; forget it, and enjoy ourselves.'

Willingly enough they agreed and, relaxing after the long days of strain, made it a gala night. The sparkling wine warmed them to carefree conviviality; each member of the party now knew all the others intimately, so they bandied jests without restraint and laughed uproariously.

In the saloon below the men were singing. Knowing the value of good feeling, Luvia agreed to Basil's suggestion of taking a couple of bottles of whisky down to them with the best wishes of the passengers. He drank a glass to their health himself and brought old Jansen up to drink another in the lounge, so that the carpenter could convey the compliments of the men to the ladies and the passengers.

The party did not break up until eleven, when De Brissac, now almost well again but still needing to take care of himself, said he thought he would get to bed; Basil and Unity went below with him. Luvia left at the same time to go forward and see how the pumping was going before turning in, so Vicente Vedras and Synolda were left on their own.

Both had imbibed pretty freely of the champagne. Synolda liked her drink and plenty of it. She was a little flushed, but showed no other signs of having partaken liberally, except that her easy-going good nature was even more apparent than usual. Vicente was outwardly quite calm, but his hands trembled slightly and his dark eyes caressed her with a hungry look. His passion for her had been gaining force again these last few days, since his recovery, and this evening the wine had inflamed it to fever pitch.

They were seated side by side and now that they were alone together his heart was pounding like a hammer; he could hear it beating and his chest seemed about to burst with its steady throbbing.

Suddenly he threw his arm around her shoulders, leaned over, and kissed her hard on the cheek.

She did not struggle, but pushed him away gently as she murmured, 'Don't be an idiot.'

He seized her again and got his lips firmly on her mouth. For a moment, her head thrown back, she let them remain there, surrendering to his kiss and enjoying it herself, but with a quick jerk she broke away and thrust him back into his chair, 'Vicente!' she said a little breathlessly, 'you mustn't do that. I don't want you.'

'Why?' he burst out. 'You 'ave been kissed before—plenty. Is it not so?'

'Oh, yes. I've been kissed before. More times than I care to remember—and sometimes by men I didn't like.'

'Then, Synolda *mia*, why not me?'

'Because I don't want you.'

'But I 'ave love you ever since I see you first.'

'I'm sorry, but I don't want you,' she repeated stubbornly.

'Listen please.' He spread out his thick hands. 'You 'ave for me no love—yes—that I understand. But the love it comes presently.'

'No, Vicente, no. I'm sorry, but it won't in this case. I know myself.'

'Yet yourself you say you 'ave been kiss by men you love not at the first time.'

'I didn't come to love them afterwards either. The thought of them makes me hate men so much sometimes that I feel I never want to have anything to do with a man again.'

'Ah, my poor beautiful, that will pass. You 'ave 'ad bad experience, eh? Tell me then of it and ease yourself.'

She shook her head. 'I'd rather not. I want to forget it.'

'The way to forget it is in the love of one who is tender for you. I love with gentleness—yes. I would not harm one 'airs of your 'ead.'

'I'm sure you could be very kind, but I don't want you, Vicente.'

'You are 'ard—'ard as the iron nail.'

'I'm not. I'd like to be friends with you, but I just don't want you the other way; that's all.'

'Friends!' he stamped his foot angrily. 'Friends! What is that? Between man and woman it is never to be. A pretence only: a fooling of themselves when very young. A cover up necessary for peoples of position sometimes. What interest 'as each in each but one—that which the good God 'as made natural to them?'

91

Synolda could appreciate his Latin point of view. She knew that in her own Anglo-Saxon race genuine friendships were quite common, but such an experience had never come her way. Almost since she could remember anything, boys had done crazy things for the chance to kiss and maul her; later on, a hundred different men had pleaded, threatened, schemed with the object of inducing her to submit to their caresses, but if their efforts failed they soon showed that they had no other use for her. 'I'm sorry, Vicente,' she repeated once more, 'but I don't *want* you.'

His face became sullen as he leant towards her. 'You are 'ard —all right then; I will be 'ard too.'

She shrugged and lit a cigarette. 'Surely you're not going to start all that old business over again?'

'In love as in war all is fair play. We are derelict no more. Tomorrow we sail again. For what port who can say? but in three, five, six days we get there. You are not so foolish you make me so desperate and tell the police what I 'ave to say.'

'You've never told me what you could say yet.'

'Once I start—much. One little word and the police press to know all.'

'All what?'

'First place—why do you come on board last moment with no luggage?'

'I had a perfectly good reason.'

He nodded his dark head. 'Yes—I know it.'

Synolda paled and with unnatural calmness picked up her glass to drink some champagne. 'If you do, I wonder that you're so keen to have an affair with me.'

'That you sail without your 'usband makes you not less desirable.'

'I've told you again and again that I only decided to make the trip on the spur of the moment and the fool porter at the hotel must have taken my luggage to the wrong quay. I've told you, too, countless times, that I have no husband. I'm a widow.'

'When since? The very day before we sail I see you with your 'usband at the St. James 'otel, Muizenberg.'

'What nonsense! You may have seen me with a man, perhaps, but that doesn't say he was my husband.'

'Ha!' he jerked forward. 'You make admission you was in Muizenberg then. That you deny before.'

'I neither deny nor admit it, since it's no concern of yours.'

'But you have done so and now I tell you something. On the

92

terrace of the St. James I see you with 'im. You, I admire—I
become loving instantly. 'Im I recognize: 'is face, yes, I know it
well, but 'is name elude. Who is 'e? I ask, that I may make re-
acquaintance and so meet you; for I am certain that I've spoken
with 'im before. But 'is name—no, it refuses to come. I would
make inquiry at the 'otel, but business friends arrive and at once
I 'ave to drive back with them to Cape Town. The opportunity is
gone from me. I think of you all night and puzzle for 'is name,
but it is useless. Next morning I come on board. Before the ship
sail I buy a paper. There I see the name plain to my eyes, 'Enriques
Ortello. That night, when the ship is well at sea, the beautiful
Señora Ortello, she appear suddenly at the dinner-table. She is
wife to my acquaintance of old days in Venezuela—'Enriques.
She travels in this name because it is on 'er passport and she can
use no other. When I learn that she comes 'urriedly to sea without
luggage I know for certain the thing that 'as 'appened.'

For a moment Synolda was silent. She drew heavily on her
cigarette before crushing it out. 'I see,' she said softly. 'I didn't
know about the paper. What was in it?'

'You can make the guess.'

'Yes, I can guess. They must have got on to it very quickly.'

'Truly. And you, I think, must 'ave laid a false trail with
much skill. I fear each day they broadcast for you by radio.'

'They have by now, I expect, but they left it too late. Those
first few days they were probably chasing somebody they thought
was me over half South Africa.'

There was a long pause until she asked, 'And you're quite
determined to hand me over to the police when we reach port?'

'That I would 'ate to do. But it is my nature to want what I
want most badly.'

'So, if you don't get it?'

'My 'eart would break, I think, but you are 'ard so I must be
'ard also.'

'It's only your word against mine and I've always found that
a man will give the benefit of the doubt to a pretty woman. The
police wouldn't believe you.'

Vicente pursed his lips and shook his head. 'You go wrong
there. I keep the newspaper an 'ave it still in my cabin. Once I
show that, your sweetest smile, it will get you nowhere.'

'What d'you want me to do?' she asked a little hoarsely.

His hand trembled on her shoulder. 'Tonight we are cele-
brating—yes? Let us keep up the celebrations. Over there is one

fine bottle of champagne unopened. We will take 'im down to your cabin and when it is drunk up you shall forget all your troubles there in my arms.'

'You're taking a pretty mean advantage—aren't you?'

'No, for I will run much risk to 'elp you afterwards. I force your 'ands only because I love you.'

'If you do you'll destroy that paper?'

'Yes, and be a slave to you in all things if you will let me love you.'

Once again Synolda fell silent.

Vicente had played his last card, but knew it to be a good one. From the age of fifteen a long succession of women had occupied an almost regular and very considerable percentage of his time. The majority of them had been Latins with the warm temperament which quite naturally made them regard physical love as the most important thing in life. Circumstances, rather than morals, governed their chastity.

The better class were hedged about with the restrictions common in Spanish-speaking countries to protect them from the carnal temptations normally resulting from enforced idleness. Few of them would have risked serious trouble with their husbands to satisfy a peccadillo, but nearly all the husbands kept mistresses as an accepted custom. Many were complacent after the first few years of marriage, and others had to be away from their homes at times for considerable periods. In consequence, these idle, amorous ladies almost invariably welcomed an intrigue if it could be conducted with discretion, and from generations of tradition would have considered themselves grossly insulted if any potential gallant had addressed them in terms of platonic love.

The women of the lower classes, with whom Vicente had had even more frequent dealings, were much easier of access, no less hot-blooded, and prone to satisfy their passions on impulse with the promiscuity common in tropical countries. Many of these were half-breeds without even a pretence of morality, and nearly all could be bought, bullied, or beguiled into a surrender which, once made, rarely failed to excite a passionate response.

With such a wealth of fortunate adventure behind him Vicente could only wonder why Synolda had not given in to him before. He failed entirely to take into account the fact that his experience was almost confined to a single country where climate and the conditions of an earlier age combined to make women easy game.

It did not even occur to him that the emancipation of women in most civilized nations had turned their thoughts into a hundred other channels away from sex, or that Synolda, being an Anglo-Saxon, might be less eager to indulge her appetite than the olive-skinned beauties he had known.

As a young man, though short, he had been handsome. In recent years he had put on weight, he knew, but he still regarded himself as an attractive fellow, and was extremely proud of his virility, which he had come to believe was the one thing that women really cared about in a man.

Had Synolda been a young, unmarried girl, a pious devotee who had foresworn the lusts of the flesh for the sake of the Kingdom to come, or even been vowed to temporary chastity by a romantic attachment to another man, he would have acted in accordance with his code; respected her and left her alone. But she was none of these things. On the contrary, she was a woman of the world, had no husband or relatives who might have embarrassed her freedom travelling with her, and nobody to whom she was morally bound to account for her actions at her journey's end.

Vicente felt bitterly resentful that she should have compelled him to force her hand. It would have been so much pleasanter if she had taken him as her lover willingly, but luck having given him the means to make her, he considered himself perfectly justified in using them. Having no real grounds, other than an unflattering lack of interest, for refusing him in the first place, he was certain she would come to heel rather than face all that exposure entailed, and was confident in his own ability to please her as a lover once she had surrendered.

He did not hurry her, but sat there silent; giving her plenty of time to visualize the consequences of a refusal while he dwelt in anticipation upon all the joys her beauty would afford him.

Synolda's thoughts during those tense moments were very different. She, too, had an ample experience behind her. There had been times when she had almost fainted with pleasure in a man's embrace, but others when her whole body had cried out in loathing.

She had done what she had done in order that she might never be forced to suffer that hate, indignity, and shame again. Yet here she was, free for such a little while before necessity compelled her to submit to another man against her will.

In an effort to view the situation calmly she examined her

feelings for Vicente. She certainly did not hate him; she did not even blame him for taking advantage of the information which enabled him to bring pressure to bear on her. Most of the men she had met would have done the same, she knew. In her experience men were like that when they wanted a woman really badly. Honest enough in their calling but quite unscrupulous about blackmailing a wife into sleeping with them if they had the power to check or assist her husband's advancement.

No, it was not that Vicente was actively repellent to her. He was getting on in years, of course, but still muscular and healthy; at times he was even passably good-looking and must have been quite attractive when he was a younger man. He was quite amusing, too, when his sense of humour was not submerged by his passion for her, and he was kind. She recalled his eager solicitude for her comfort during their first days on the ship and the many ways in which he had sought to make her ordeal in the boat more endurable.

If only she had had one spark of desire it would have been different, she felt. She was a free agent, responsible to no one, and she would have gone through with it without any qualms. But she hadn't; that was the trouble.

She began to visualize what it would be like down there in her cabin. The plump Vicente undressing near her. He probably wore woollen combinations. She'd be spared the sight of him taking off his clothes though, as she could see to it they did that in the dark. Instead, his thick hands would fumble for her in the bunk; she could almost hear his heavy breathing, and then. . . . Speculation ran riot in her mind as to what he might require of her. Her husband Henriques Ortello had been a Venezuelan and she was well versed in their idiosyncrasies.

No, she decided, she wouldn't do it. Why the hell should she? And yet he had the whip hand over her. If she didn't, in a few more days she might find herself in a prison cell. Prisons in South America were not nice places. Few people in Europe or the States had any conception of the horrors practised in the secret cells under the protection of a heavy censorship by some of the officials of the smaller Republics. She had once visited a prison in Caracas before the death of the tyrant Gomez. The barbarities which took place during the times of his Presidency were unmentionable.

If she landed in a place like that, and was unable to claim the protection of a Consul, she knew exactly what the warders would do to her. Most of the women prisoners were willing enough to sell themselves after a few days in the lice-infested cells for a transfer to better quarters and good rations which would save them from the almost universal dysentery. Good-lookers who were stubborn could be brought to heel in other ways. She might scream and kick until she burst her lungs, but that wouldn't help; they'd only think it funny or use a whip to tame her. One of them would probably give her a child or something worse before her trial came on, and with all the graft that was practised there was never any way of getting back on those devilish gaolers if they were like the ones she'd heard of at first hand in Caracas. They knew it and boasted openly of the sport they had with the helpless women behind the closely guarded walls.

Much better take on Vicente. It might not be so bad perhaps if she could stop him talking and try and think of him as someone else when they were in the dark together. Better put a cheerful face on it too. That paid. It would make him more considerate and she'd be able to get rid of him sooner.

At last she stood up and went over to the upright piano which occupied a corner of the small lounge. Idly she began to strum upon it.

'What is that you play?' asked Vicente.

'Oh, just a little ditty that tells the oldest story in the world.' In a husky contralto Synolda began to sing:

> *She was poor but she was honest*
> *Victim of a village crime*
> *For the Squire's cruel passion*
> *Robbed her of her honest name.*

> *Then she came right up to London*
> *There to hide her grief and shame*
> *But she met another Squire*
> *And she lost her name again.*

Synolda stopped playing and gently shut down the lid of the piano. 'That second verse is rather appropriate, don't you think? Fix me a double brandy and bring down the champagne.'

CHAPTER VII

THE WEED

THAT night the ship drifted on through the mist, and when morning came she was still shrouded in its grey, ghost-like wisps.

It muffled the footsteps of those walking on the decks, made wood and metal fitments damp to the touch, covering them with fine beads of moisture like sweat, and gave the passengers an eerie feeling.

Luvia took scant notice of it. He knew that in these desolate seas there was little likelihood of another ship being within a hundred miles of them, so the risk of a collision was entirely negligible.

Taking the bulk of the crew with him he went down to the engine-room; he was overjoyed to have the chance of working again in his own special domain. To rake out the fires and get them going up to the point where sufficient pressure of steam had been generated for the propellers to turn over at a normal speed would require many hours of heavy labour, but the men set to with a will.

Vicente was among them; stripped to the waist and ready to take his turn at the shovels with the others. Basil, who was also there, looked at him curiously. The Venezuelan was broad and squat, but in spite of his little paunch he looked vigorous and muscular; for some inexplicable reason, too, he appeared to be half a dozen years younger this morning.

Between-decks in the galley Unity was peeling potatoes while Synolda was making pastry for a pie. She showed no trace of the night's events except that she was a little more silent than usual.

'Penny for your thoughts,' Unity asked with no object but to make conversation.

'I was thinking,' said Synolda slowly, 'how strange it is thàt things you dread are never quite so bad, when you really come to them, as you imagine beforehand.'

Unity laughed. 'There's a pavement artist at Hyde Park Corner

98

who does a scrawl which says, "Today is the tomorrow you were worrying about yesterday", and it's quite true. Even when the future appears incredibly grim we get through it somehow. In fact, people often derive a certain amount of enjoyment from periods in which they had visualized themselves committing suicide through bitterness and disillusion. But what makes you think about that?'

'Oh, nothing particular,' Synolda hedged. 'Just being here a thousand miles from anywhere cooking for sailors in a derelict ship, yet not feeling particularly unhappy all the same—if you know what I mean. Just think how worried we'd have been if we'd been told the sort of voyage we'd have to face before we left Cape Town.'

'Yes, we'd have been horrified and refused to sail, of course, although now we're more or less out of danger I wouldn't have missed the experience for anything.'

There was a pause in the conversation before Unity went on: 'D'you know what I'd have said you were thinking about, if you'd given me the usual three guesses?'

'No, what?'

'Oh, Juhani.'

Synolda turned to stare and opened wide her heavily lidded blue eyes in genuine surprise. 'Juhani Luvia—but, good God, why?'

'Well, you've made a pretty sweeping conquest there, haven't you?'

'What, I? Gracious, what nonsense!'

Unity stiffened slightly. 'I'm sorry. I haven't the least desire to pry into your personal affairs. Of course, I should never have mentioned it.'

'Oh, please!' Synolda dusted the flour quickly from her plump white arms and abandoned her pastry-making. 'I'm not offended. Not a bit. You've been so sweet to me, how could I be? But, honestly, I haven't even looked at Juhani. I thought you were just pulling my leg.'

Unity smiled. 'I wasn't, and if you haven't looked at him he certainly spends most of his time, when he's taking a spell from work, looking at you.'

'Really! How queer. I've never noticed it.'

'Then it's quite time you did—that is unless you dislike him.'

'Oh, I don't dislike him in the least. In fact, I admire him a lot and think him rather a hero. He's behaved splendidly all through, but he's so off-hand. I had no idea he was interested in anything except his job of salvaging the ship and getting us safely back to land again.'

'Well, you can take it from me, he's just crazy about you. Like the great big baby he is, he tries to conceal it, but I know from the way he follows you about with his eyes whenever you move out of his vicinity; and he's jealous as hell of Vicente.'

'Is he?—but he has no cause to be,' Synolda replied innocently.

'No, none,' Unity agreed, 'since for some obscure reason he conceals his interest in you. All the same I should probably be jealous, too, if I were in his shoes. Ever since we sailed from Cape Town you've shown pretty plainly that you prefer Vicente's company to anybody else's.'

'Oh, well, he lays himself out to be pleasant,' Synolda hurriedly turned back to her pastry-making. 'You see, he knew my late husband years ago in Caracas.'

'Caracas!' echoed Unity a trifle puzzled. 'I'm afraid I'm frightfully ignorant, but where exactly is that?'

'It's the capital of Venezuela. I lived there for nearly seven years.'

'How interesting. You've only been on a visit to South Africa, then?'

'That's all. I was born and brought up there, but my first husband—I've been married twice, you know—was an engineer named Piet Brendon. He had a job in Venezuela so he took me out there, but he died after we'd been married only a year and left me more or less high and dry. I could have gone back to my people in Johannesburg, of course, but I didn't want to—then.'

'So you married again.'

'Yes. I was still under twenty. My second husband, Henriques Ortello, was pretty well off and very persistent. I knew the language enough to talk it fairly fluently by then, and as I'm the lazy kind I preferred an easy life to going home where I should have had to do some sort of job.'

'What is Caracas like to live in?'

'Not bad, provided you steer clear of politics. Of course, no girl can go about the streets alone there, even after she's married. Upper-class women are treated in the old Spanish fashion and almost as carefully guarded as if they were in a harem. They have their affairs just the same, though, because the men come in over their garden walls at night.'

'It sounds most romantic.'

'I thought that too at first, but Venezuela has its drawbacks. All the men are absolutely crazy about politics, and it's not much fun never knowing when your boy friend's going to be bumped off as a Liberal or something. Everyone lived in terror of that until the old Catfish died.'

'The Catfish?' Unity murmured. 'Who was he?'

'That was their nickname for the Dictator Gomez. He was an incredible old man who ran the country as though it was his own private boozing-den and brothel from 1890 right up to 1935. No woman was safe from him however highly placed, and he had over a hundred illegitimate children; but his power was so great that nobody could break it. He made the cattle-market his own personal monopoly and millions out of the oilfields, so he was able to keep an army strong enough to terrorize the whole country. They just imprisoned anyone they suspected was anti-Gomez, without trial; men and women alike; and nine-tenths of the prisoners died in their cells from disease or torture.'

Unity stared at her in amazement. 'D'you mean to tell me that sort of thing was still going on in 1935—the year of King George's Jubilee?'

'Yes. It may sound a bit far-fetched, but it's perfectly true. All news that reached the outside world was frightfully strictly censored, and although most of the European Governments must have known what was happening they were much too busy with their own affairs to interfere.'

'But torture—in these days?'

'They used to put leg-irons weighing seventy pounds on all the prisoners and hang them up to the ceiling with ropes by their tenderest parts. If the women were attractive they were raped first by the officers and then by the half-breed soldiery.'

'It sounds simply too frightful.'

'Things weren't so bad if you could keep out of prison and out of the way of the old man's innumerable hangers-on. They were naturally all tarred with the same brush as their lord and master. If one of them took a fancy to a girl she had to make up her mind to a party, or risk herself and her whole family suffering God-knows-what awful fate through being slung into prison on a false accusation of conspiracy.'

'My dear, you *have* seen life with a vengeance.'

'I didn't have. . . .'

Synolda stopped short. De Brissac had suddenly flung open the door and thrust his head into the galley.

'Land—land!' he shouted. 'Get out on deck—we may run ashore any moment.'

He dashed away and began to bellow down through the fiddley of the engine-room hatch amidships.

Both girls abandoned their preparations for the midday meal and ran after him. Young Largertöf, who was greasing some gear half-way down the shaft, heard his shouts and attracted Luvia's attention. The whole party came clattering up the iron ladders on to the deck.

'Land!' panted Luvia. 'Where—where?'

De Brissac led them to the side of the ship and pointed downwards. The mist still shut them in, but it was not too thick for them to see a great patch of seaweed floating alongside.

'You see it,' exclaimed De Brissac. '*Algue*—seaweed—washed from the rocks by a storm. Where there is weed there must be a coast not far distant.'

Luvia shook his head dubiously. 'That doesn't follow. I'm afraid. I'll have to have a look—see what sort of weed it is before we know for certain. Anyway this stuff might have been washed scores of miles from the rocks on which it grew.'

He ordered the men below again, with the exception of Basil, and together they hauled the boat up alongside by the rope which kept it trailing in the ship's wake whichever way she drifted. The two of them went over the side into it and rowed the few strokes necessary to bring them within reach of the patch of weed.

Leaning over the bow, Luvia thrust his hand into the weed and pulled up a great bunch of it. Basil saw that it was a bright grass-green and grew in long, spiky trails inextricably interwoven. The Finn threw it back into the water and made a grimace.

'De Brissac's barked up the wrong tree,' he grunted. 'This stuff's called algæ, I think. Anyhow, it's the sort of weed that's often seen right out in the middle of the ocean.'

'Well?' Unity called down impatiently as they clambered up the rope ladder again.

'No luck,' Luvia told her. 'It's just ocean weed and we're probably drifting through a big belt of it.'

'But from where does it come?' inquired De Brissac.

'That sure is a mystery; nobody seems to know. There's masses of it in the North Atlantic, about five hundred miles off the coast of Florida, and it's met with right down to the south-west of Australia, too. They even mark these areas on the map. Come up to the chart-room and I'll show you.'

They followed him up the bridge ladder, and, in the deck-house he produced a big map of the world, showing the principal prevailing winds, ocean currents, and seasonal limits of drift ice. Weed seas were clearly marked upon it by hundreds of tiny horizontal black strokes forming irregular patches on the blue grounds of the oceans, with the word 'weed' printed across them. North of the equator lay one between the Azores and the West Indies, another to the south-east of Greenland, and a third in the Pacific, north of Hawaii. In the southern hemisphere the weed seemed to be even more prolific. A big patch of it lay to the east of New Zealand, and about a thousand miles south-west of Australia a vast weed continent as large as Germany, France and Italy put together occupied a huge area of those rarely travelled seas. From it, a belt several hundred miles in depth spread out westward, across the great waste of waters girdling the earth for over seven thousand miles, in a wavy streak roughly following the forty-fifth parallel of latitude and passing south of Africa to end off the eastern coast of South America.

Luvia placed a large finger on the spot. 'See the weed here; a thousand miles from Patagonia. That's our position—roughly. I can only guess our longitude as somewhere between thirty degrees and fifty degrees west, but our latitude must be about forty-five degrees south as we're just entering the weed belt.'

'Does it get thicker as we go further in?' Unity asked.

'Not a lot if it's anything like the patch up here,' he pointed to the seaward area, as big as Spain, which lay north-east of the West Indies. 'I've sailed those waters plenty and for a couple of days or more you see great banks of it drifting with the wind if you're running down from Europe to Havana.'

De Brissac peered over his shoulder. 'That is the Sargasso Sea. I have heard of it, but did not realize that there were others like it elsewhere. Columbus was delayed by it on his voyage to discover America—was he not?'

'I couldn't say,' Luvia shrugged. 'Though I've heard tell lots of those old navigators had trouble with the weed. You meet up with it in banks a mile long at times, and that's not so funny if you're in a sailing ship with only light winds to help you. Steamers can avoid the big patches and cut through the little ones, so it presents no problem at the present day.'

'De Brissac's right,' Basil cut in. 'Columbus did get stuck there for some time on one of his voyages, so did lots of the other early adventurers. There grew up to be quite a legend about it.

103

For centuries people believed that there was a great, central mass of weed and that many ships which were reported lost had got caught in it for good and all.'

'I've heard that too,' Unity agreed. 'It was thought that the hulks remained there derelict for years and years after their crews had died from lack of food and water, until the timbers rotted and they sank. There were supposed to be Spanish galleons with cargoes of golden doubloons and pieces of eight trapped in the Sargasso Sea.'

Luvia laughed. 'That's all boloney. A Danish research ship charted the whole area in the '80s and they would sure have found any place such as you speak of if it existed. The weed in the Sargasso just drifts around in chunks as the wind blows it, and there's no central mass anywhere. By all the rules it'll be just the same here. Come on, Sutherland, let's get back to the engine-room.'

'Right-oh,' replied Basil cheerfully, and, leaving the girls with De Brissac, they went below.

By midday Luvia had the boiler-fires raked out and re-lighted. It was now only a question of steady stoking until a sufficient head of steam could be maintained to get the ship under way.

After the meal he assembled the passengers and crew, told them that hitherto they'd all had to work as many hours as they were able and get what sleep they could between times; but that now he proposed to divide them into watches; upon which he set about the business.

The watches consisted of six men apiece. Vicente Vedras, Largertöf, Hansie, Harlem Joe and Isiah Meek forming the starboard watch under Jansen; and Basil, Bremer, Li Foo, Gietto Nudäa and Corncob being drafted to port under Jean De Brissac.

Luvia gave a watch to the Frenchman in preference to any of the others because his army experience had accustomed him to the command of men, and the rest, knowing that, were unlikely to resent it; but he placed with him Bremer, who was the most experienced of the two seamen. The arrangement also separated the two most likely elements of trouble, Harlem and Nudäa. All the ex-mutineers had become models of good behaviour since they had reboarded the ship, but Luvia was perfectly well aware that appearances were deceptive in such a case and it was all the more likely that they would try and stage something before he could hand them over to the authorities on land.

He did not propose to take a watch himself as he would have all his work cut out to both navigate the ship and superintend the shifts in the engine-room, so he would have to snatch an hour's sleep when he could. Synolda and Unity were also excluded from the watches; it being understood that they would continue to work in the galley during the daytime and get a clear rest at nights.

Jansen's party went on duty while De Brissac slept, until, at eight bells, he took over for the first dog-watch. When he arrived on deck he saw that the mist had lightened during the afternoon. From the bridge a considerable area of the surrounding sea was now visible. Upon it on every side, like islands in an archipelago, floated large patches of the weed. Many of them were several hundred yards in length and all tailed out like long streamers parallel with the direction of the wind. The ship was drifting nearly broadside-on between two big banks, but a little faster owing to the greater area her hull and tophamper offered to the pressure of the light breeze. There were no wavelets as the weed checked any free movement of the waters and it heaved upon them in a slow, oily swell.

A great silence brooded over the strange seascape. It seemed incredibly desolate in the evening light and there was something sinister about it. Although all was well on board and there was the cheering prospect that the ship would soon be under way again, heading for a port, De Brissac felt unaccountably depressed and was troubled by the queer imaginative notion that he was no longer living in the twentieth century, but had passed out of time into a dateless period when there was neither land nor sea, only weed and water, so that he gazed on no normal phenomenon, but Earth as it was at the beginning, or might be at the end of the world.

CHAPTER VIII

SOMEWHERE SOUTH OF SOUTHWARD

WHEN De Brissac's short watch came to an end at six o'clock he was glad to be relieved by Jansen, and went at once to the lounge in search of Basil who had been working below decks.

They fed at seven, the passengers' mess being as usual except for the absence of Vicente, who was a member of the duty watch. Luvia told them that he hoped to have steam up before midnight, but would not set a course before the following morning as the weed here was thicker than he had ever seen it in the Sargasso Sea, and he did not want to pile great heaps of it up against the bow. By waiting till morning he would be able to steer her through the wide channels of clear water which lay between the banks and avoid running into the densest of them.

When dinner was over Synolda asked him if he hadn't earned a rest from his labours in the engine-room.

'I certainly have,' he replied promptly, 'and I mean to take it. This is the last good night's sleep I'll be getting for some time.'

'Come out and get some fresh air before you turn in then,' she suggested. 'You've had little enough all day.' The devil inside her prompted the invitation. Unity's remarks that morning had stirred her curiosity about the big Finn and she could not resist the itch to see how he would behave if she gave him the chance to be alone with her.

He stood up at once. 'Sure, that'd be grand. Let's go to it right away.'

Side by side they walked along to the deserted fo'c'sle. The ladder leading up to it had been ripped away when the whole forepart of the ship was dismantled, but he put his foot on a projecting bolt, grabbed the edge of the deck above, and in one spring had landed sitting on it.

'Give me your hands,' he laughed, leaning down, 'now, one foot on the bolt and up you come.'

It hardly looked possible, but she obediently lifted her arms towards him. He could only just touch her fingertips, but gripped her wrists as she jumped and drew her up towards him. Next second he had released one wrist to catch her round the waist and she found herself pressed against him, her face on a level with his, her legs dangling between his as he sat perched on the fo'c'sle break. She was quite helpless even if she had wanted to resist and instinctively flung her free arm round his neck to save herself from falling. Suddenly she felt a terrific thrill as his golden beard came in contact with her skin, and, finding her lips, he kissed her.

'Oh!' she gasped when at last he drew back. 'Oh, you shouldn't do that.'

He laughed again. 'Why not? You didn't ask me out here to talk engineering, did you?'

'I didn't ask you out here. But pull me up—pull me up—I'm falling.'

'You did,' he declared, taking not the least notice of her plea. 'If you want to be pulled up you'd best confess it.'

'I won't. I didn't. All right, I did if you insist—but only to talk to.'

'Why?'

'Because I like you.'

'Good girl,' he grinned. 'That's better,' and he drew her up sideways across his knee so that she could sit beside him.

They continued to sit there with their arms round each other's waists and their legs dangling for a long time. She told him a lot about her girlhood in South Africa, a little of her two husbands, and practically nothing of her life in Caracas. Somehow she did not want to talk to him about that black chapter in her history. It was not a pleasant story and she wanted him to think well of her, although she knew that she was living in a fool's paradise. If nothing worse came out he would be sure to learn sooner or later about Vicente Vedras.

He scarcely noticed the omissions in her disconnected story for he was busy talking about himself. She encouraged him, and finding her such a sympathetic listener he spoke of things he rarely mentioned. Finland in the springtime after the great thaw had come; green and beautiful with a million lakes and wooded islands bursting into leaf and blossoms almost overnight; the old town of Viipuri and his mother who still lived there. He did not attempt to kiss her again, but talked on as though that single contact had sealed their friendship and made them intimates;

107

telling her of his ambitions as an engineer, and his hopes of reward and promotion if he could bring the salvaged *Gafelborg* safely into port.

The moon was rising watery and haloed through the faint haze that still obscured the stars, and they might have sat there until the small hours of the morning if they had not been interrupted. Footsteps sounded below them in the forewell of the ship and a bulky figure emerged from the shadows. It was Vicente.

He had come off duty at eight o'clock, had a bath to cleanse himself after his labour in the stokehold, changed into clean clothes, and scented his person lavishly in preparation for another *tête-à-tête* with Synolda. Not finding her in the lounge he had dined there on his own and spent the last twenty minutes searching the ship for her.

' 'Ullo!' he said.

'Hello!' replied Luvia cheerfully. 'What d'you want?'

'It becomes late—yes.'

'Well, what about it?'

'It comes to me that the Señora would like to know that it is nearly ten o'clock.'

'Thanks, Grandpa. If there's going to be any curfew on this ship it's Juhani Luvia who'll order it.'

'But the Señora likes 'er sleep now that she 'as much work to which she is not accustomed.'

Luvia frowned. 'I guess you'd better get some sleep yourself since you go on again at midnight.'

'That I know; but I require little sleep and I was looking forward to a few minutes' talk with the Señora before she turn in.'

'Well, I'm afraid you won't get it. You can see for yourself she's busy. G'night.'

'As the Señora wishes. Good night, then.' The Venezuelan bowed courteously to each of them in turn, swung on his heel, and, with fury in his heart, walked slowly away.

'What a neck!' exclaimed Luvia as Vicente disappeared from sight. 'Damn the fellow, he's always monopolizing your time. Acts just as though he had some claim on you. Well, he won't get you to himself much after tonight; I mean to see to that.'

Synolda laughed, but she didn't feel like laughing. The big man at her side had quite unconsciously come too near the truth. Vicente *had* got a claim on her, and there was going to be the most awful trouble if Luvia started in to try and keep her to himself. She knew she had been acting like a fool to even let herself get interested in the good-looking Finn, and a double fool to encourage him by sitting up there on the fo'c'sle with him all this time, but it would make things too obvious now if she left him suddenly.

They talked for another half-hour, but the charm of their earlier conversation had vanished with its interruption. By half past ten they had fallen silent and shortly afterwards decided to break up the party. He took her below by a ladder under the bridge-deck so they did not pass the entrance to the lounge where Vicente was sitting, waiting for her. The passageway to her cabin was empty, so Luvia kissed her before saying good night, and this time she responded warmly to his embrace.

Once in her cabin reaction gripped her. She felt certain that Vicente was furiously angry; policy demanded that she should soothe him down as soon as possible; yet she could not bring herself to face a row that night.

Having succeeded in avoiding him on her way below she thought it a safe bet that he would continue to assume that she was still occupied on the fo'c'sle until he had to go on duty at twelve o'clock; from then until four he would be hard at it in the stokehold. After that, as he had been up since soon after dawn, he would need to get some sleep.

As a precaution against his invading her cabin in the early hours she locked the door behind her. She knew she had got herself into an unholy mess and must pay for her fun in the morning, but in spite of her anxiety she fell asleep feeling happier than she had for a long time.

The following morning broke fairly clear but a distant mist still shut out the horizon. Luvia was on the bridge by six studying the surrounding scene with De Brissac. They could now rake the seas for some miles on every side with their glasses. Both of them had long since given up all hope of sighting a ship in this limitless expanse of watery desert to which the hurricane and southward currents had carried the *Gafelborg*, but they searched the great emptiness with no less anxiety.

During the night the weed had thickened. It no longer presented the appearance of islands in an archipelago, but rather a low, coastal region intersected, here and there, with winding creeks. Down one of these, almost stern first now, the *Gafelborg* was drifting. The two men strained their eyes to catch a glimpse of the open sea, but it seemed they had been borne away from it during the hours of darkness, and, as the ship had turned, they were no longer quite certain in which direction it lay.

De Brissac pointed. 'The weed seems to be most broken over there.'

'But that's the south-west,' Luvia protested. 'We're wise to that from the sun. The open ocean must be somewhere to the north.'

'I know it. Yet to go due north you must cut directly across these great fields of weed. The channels seem to run roughly east and west twisting gradually to southward as far ahead as we can see. Is it not possible that we are nearly through this big weed area and shall strike open water again if we head south-west?'

'More than likely, I'd say. I've never seen the damn' stuff so massed as this any place before. It can't be anything but local, though, and a decent wind would disperse it.'

De Brissac sighed. 'A wind, yes. How I would welcome a good fresh breeze. There is something unnatural about this stillness. I don't know why, but it makes me unquiet in my mind.'

'So you've felt that too, eh?' Luvia gave a quick glance at the Frenchman; a virile, wiry figure having still an air of dash and gallantry in spite of the stains that now marred his once spotless uniform of horizon blue. 'Queer, isn't it? This devilish quiet kind of gives you the jitters.'

'It is not the quiet only, but a feeling that one must get away; a sense of panic almost. I do not understand myself because it is not usual for me to be afraid.'

'I get you. Sort of wanting to cut and run with no pausing to look over the shoulder for fear what you might see. The moment I came on deck I had an impulse to put on full steam ahead and snap right out of this unhealthy spot just as quick as I could.'

'Why do you not do that then? You said yesterday that steam-ships could easily cut through such weed.'

'Sure. So they can. I'm not batting my head about that, but the quickest way to make it. If we head north, as I'd like to, we'll make mighty slow progress nosing our way through chunks of solid weed. I'd a hope we could get back to good blue water quicker some other way. I'll shin up to the crow's nest and have a look-see from there.'

While he was gone De Brissac slowly paced the bridge, a prey to nameless forebodings. The solitude and utter dreariness of the scene weighed upon his volatile spirit. He examined the channels on either side through his glasses again, and wondered if he only

110

imagined it or if they were in fact growing gradually narrower as the ship drifted on.

When Luvia returned there was a serious set expression on his bearded face. He had made his decision.

'I'm going south-west,' he said. 'There's not a sign of a break to north or east, and it looks as if this channel's closing in a couple of miles behind us. When we're through this first wide bank on the starboard beam we'll strike that broader waterway and run down it a few miles. From what I can see it'll lead us into that less congested area you spotted.'

He gave careful instructions to Bremer, who was at the wheel, put his hand on the engine-room telegraph, and turned it to 'Slow Ahead'. It rang for the first time in eleven days.

The *Gafelborg's* propellers began to thresh the water. Slowly she moved forward until her nose had made a deep indentation in the opposite bank of weed. The telegraph rang again and she backed away. The process was repeated until Luvia had brought her round. She was now headed due south-west with a clear two hundred yards of open water in front of her. He switched the telegraph to full speed ahead and she throbbed to the beat of her engines.

Soundlessly and without the slightest impact she hit the weed at an angle. For a hundred yards she ploughed through it without a perceptible decrease in her speed, then she began gradually to slow down. When she had covered less than a quarter of a mile her way was checked entirely although her engines were still turning over at full speed.

Luvia swore profoundly, rang the telegraph to 'Stop' and went forward to the fo'c'sle to see what was baulking her.

De Brissac accompanied him and, looking over the bow, they saw that a great heap of the weed had been forced up out of the water so that its countless tendrils were holding the ship back like the tangled skein of a vast, many-stringed bow.

Returning to the bridge Luvia threw the engines into reverse. The wake of the ship was almost free of weed as she had cleared a narrow waterway by her passage. The propellers churned and she slowly backed out into the main channel.

The failure of the *Gafelborg* to cut through the weed surprised and annoyed Luvia. It was denser, and its main growths very much thicker, than he had imagined. Some stalks that he had caught a glimpse of in the tangle beyond the bow had been fully as large as a woman's wrist. He did not relish the idea of being hung up there for several days pushing and nosing his way from one small lagoon to another before he could set a course for South America.

After another visit to the crow's nest he said to De Brissac abruptly: 'We'd best follow the creek westward. Farther on it bends a bit towards the south. Maybe we'll reach the open that way.'

For over an hour they steamed in the direction they had been drifting earlier in the morning. Eight bells sounded and Jansen joined them on the bridge, but De Brissac did not go below to get his breakfast. A vague alarm was steadily growing in him and he was already too troubled to think of food. Gradually all the other members of the off-duty watch straggled up on deck and stood in the fore part of the ship, studying the uniform surface of the weed on either hand and speculating in low voices about it.

Just before ten they came to a place where the creek was split by a peninsula of weed and a choice of two waterways lay before them. A fresh survey from the look-out of the scene ahead convinced Luvia that the left-hand fork offered the best prospect. It was the southernmost and although slightly narrower it appeared to lead almost directly to the broken water that De Brissac had sighted in the far distance that morning. This watery area in the continent of weed was now only about four miles away on their port bow and it seemed to stretch as far as they could see.

Still at half-speed, they crept towards it, but when they had covered about two-thirds of the distance the channel they were following suddenly began to narrow. Half a mile farther on it petered out altogether.

The sight of the free water, dotted only with islands of the weed, now no more than three-quarters of a mile distant, decided Luvia on another attempt to force a passage. Where the channel should have continued the weed seemed less dense than at all other points, so he headed the *Gafelborg* for it.

She progressed easily for five hundred yards and then slowed down again; a further two hundred and she was stuck. Backing her a little, he turned her slightly so as to clear her bows of the weed she had piled up, and made another attempt. But now that they were in the thick of the weed she was checked almost at once. Again and again he drove her forward, first at one angle then at another, but each time the great mass of weed she pushed before her brought the ship to a halt until a great ridge of it, wet, green and glistening, had been forced up in a rough semicircle, barring the way to the more open water as effectively as if it had been a twenty-foot-thick stone wall. Much time had been taken by their efforts and it was long after midday when he was at last forced to give up.

They suddenly discovered that they were desperately hungry, and, as there was no point in leaving anyone to watch, all snatched a hasty meal together. In depressed silence they ate until they had satisfied their appetites, and, the moment they were done, hurried back on deck.

During the morning their attention had been so fully concentrated on endeavouring to force a way forward that they had neglected to keep a watch astern. Now, when Luvia went aft to signal directions for backing out into the channel he saw that, unnoticed by them, the weed had closed in across their wake. He stared at it glumly for a moment and was then seized with a sudden feeling of panic. It could not be his imagination; the main masses of weed had shifted and the channel itself lay much farther away than it was before.

Hurrying up to the bridge he put the ship's engines into reverse and edged her backwards till her rudder just touched the weed, then he brought her forward again at dead slow. In three-quarters of an hour he had succeeded in turning her right round and had her headed back to the now distant channel, but the weed in her old wake had thickened and it was no longer possible to force a passage even with her bow.

The broken area they had striven so desperately hard to reach lay tantalizingly no more than a quarter of a mile away towards their stern; but the banks they had piled up in the morning had now seeped back so that the clear water around them was reduced to a mere two ship's lengths.

All through the afternoon and early evening Luvia manœuvred and charged the weed which always gave under the pressure, but never broke. Twilight fell; the open water with its archipelago of islands appeared to be farther off than when they had first tried to break through it. The drear, eerie silence of the weed continent seemed to become intensified with the failing day. When the sun sank down under the horizon there was no longer room to manœuvre, and with sinking hearts they knew that they were trapped.

CHAPTER IX

THE FLOATING PRISON

THAT night was not one for love-making. Owing to the nervous tension which had beset them all day Synolda had so far escaped the interview with Vicente she so much dreaded. Both their minds had been occupied so fully in following Luvia's efforts to get the ship into free water that little time had been left for thinking of anything else.

Since there was no necessity for a watch Luvia and all the passengers dined together. Immediately after the meal Synolda declared that the strain of the day had completely worn her out and that she meant to take three Aspros to ensure herself a few hours free from worry. Vicente could hardly protest and Luvia was so troubled by his own disquieting thoughts that he scarcely noticed her leave the table.

The Venezuelan's first anger at her treatment of him had already cooled off. When he went below ten minutes later he paused for a moment outside her cabin door, but he was desperately tired and horribly depressed, so, with a little shrug of his broad shoulders, he refrained from knocking and passed on.

Luvia bid a curt good night to the others and went off to his cabin; not to sleep but to badger his wits for a way of getting the ship out of the weed when daylight came again.

When he had gone, the remaining three, Basil, De Brissac and Unity, stared at each other in silence for a space.

Unity had been very quiet all day and had said little during the meal. She looked now from side to side studying the grave faces of the two men who were with her, and hoping for a word of comfort; but neither of them had any to give her.

'Oh God!' she burst out suddenly. 'What're we going to do? What *are* we going to do?'

'Steady on,' Basil caught one of her wrists and held it. 'None of us can do any good by panicking.'

'But don't you understand?' Her voice rose to an hysterical note. 'We're trapped—caught in this devilish weed. If we don't do something we'll die here.'

De Brissac moved over to the bar. He returned with a small glass of liqueur brandy. 'Please, Mademoiselle, you have been so brave. You will not add to our distress by breaking down. Drink this; it will warm your heart and calm your nerves.'

Unity shut her eyes and fought to control herself. When she opened them again two large tears glistened on her lashes. 'Thanks,' she said hoarsely, 'I'll be all right in a minute. I'm sorry.'

'That's better.' Basil managed a smile. 'We're not dead yet and nothing like as near it as we were a few days ago.'

'In that ghastly boat—yes, I suppose so. Yet somehow this seems more horrible. Then, we couldn't have lasted much longer. Just before we reached the ship we were all desperately weak, and it was the sort of end we had at least read about in newspapers and books. Now we're all fit as fiddles again. We've space to walk about and comfortable beds to sleep in. But we've less chance of escape than we should have in any bastille. Think of living like this for weeks, months, perhaps; eking out our provisions and knowing that once they're gone there's not the faintest hope of obtaining any more. Dying of slow starvation in this frightful solitude and watching death creep nearer day after day—day after day.'

'No, no. Our case is not as bad as all that.' De Brissac shook his head. 'We may have to possess our souls in patience for some days—a week or more perhaps. But we have enough food to last us a long time yet and plenty of water. If we need more, why, we can distil some now we are in the ship. Sooner or later a storm will come. The weed will be tossed about—broken up again. When that happens we sail away into the open sea.'

'You think so—really?' she asked doubtfully.

'*Certainement*. Did not Luvia tell us that these great weed belts have no fixed centre? It is our bad luck only that we struck this unusually thick patch. In a heavy sea even this is bound to tear and scatter. Be of good cheer, Mademoiselle, I beg. Our imprisonment is only temporary.'

'That's right,' Basil agreed. 'Look at the way the end of the creek moved away from us without our having noticed it while we were trying to break through in the opposite direction. The stuff is shifting all the time. Even without a storm we may wake up tomorrow or the next day to find ourselves in a clear space again.'

Unity swallowed the last of the brandy in her glass. 'Well, perhaps you're right,' she said a little more cheerfully. 'I only hope so. Anyway, I'm going to follow Synolda's example—and go to bed. It's the atmosphere of this place, I think, that gets me down.'

The two men stood up with her and, almost directly, followed her below. Both had done their best to appear optimistic for her sake, but somehow neither of them believed in their hearts one word that they had said. The utter stillness of their strange surroundings that were neither sea nor land made a storm in such a place seem quite unthinkable. They had a horrid feeling that she was right, and that the *Gafelborg* would never come free of the weed to plough once more the open seas.

Next morning visibility was bad; a haze rather than a mist obscured distant objects, although the immediate surroundings of the ship were comparatively clear.

Luvia had been up on deck twice during the night and said at breakfast that, although they appeared to be fast in the weed, they were actually still moving; the whole mass was drifting roughly southward as he had observed from careful watching of their masts against the stars.

'There you are,' Basil looked across at Unity, 'what did I tell you last night. We're not really stuck at all. It only needs a bit of a breeze and the weed will automatically break up into patches.'

'I'm not waiting for any breeze,' declared Luvia. 'I mean to cut my way out.'

'How will you?' asked Vicente quickly.

'By using her stern instead of her bow. God knows why I didn't think of it yesterday, but the hunch came to me last night just when I was chucking in my hand as beat. If we go dead slow astern the propellers'll cut a path for us through the weed instead of piling it up into a barrier. Get the idea?' He smiled round at them with pardonable pride.

'Oh, but how marvellous!' Synolda exclaimed, clapping her hands together. Luvia basked for a moment in the glow of her admiration, but she caught Vicente's black eyes fixed upon her stonily, and her enthusiasm ebbed as quickly as it had risen.

'Sounds a good scheme,' agreed Basil, 'as long as there's no risk of your breaking your propellers.'

'What! break my propellers on this pulpy muck?' Luvia

laughed. 'Not likely! Why the blades will chop it to ribbons—
you'll see. Come on, let's go get on the job.'

They swallowed their coffee and followed him up to the bridge.
The channel by which they had penetrated so deeply into the
weed had disappeared altogether. No others could be seen in that
direction, and the weed presented a uniform, bright-green surface
for as far as they could see before the haze baffled their vision.
The other sectors showed the same dreary uniformity with the
one exception of that over the port beam. Here, just where the
haze limited their outlook, broken water varied the scene. During
the night the ship had turned a little, but that was undoubtedly
the open, island-dotted area they had attempted to reach the
day before.

Luvia gave his orders and placed Basil at the starboard side of
the stern rail, taking up a similar position to port himself. He
waved his arm, and De Brissac, at the extreme port end of the
bridge, acknowledged his signal; the ship slowly began to move.

By hanging right over the rail the two men in the stern could
each keep an eye on one of the propellers. They were churning
the water into foam and severing the weed like two huge chaff
cutters; great hunks of it, wet and glistening, were continually
cast up and thrown outward by the force of the strokes, to splash
a dozen yards away.

For ten minutes all went well; the ship made slow but encouraging progress. Suddenly Basil saw the starboard screw stop
turning. Instantly he flung up his arm, and Jansen, watching from
his side of the bridge, cut off the engine.

'Propeller fouled eh?' Luvia said, coming across. 'The main
stems of this dratted weed are thicker than I thought, but we don't
have to worry. Vedras and a couple of men can pull themselves
round in the boat and cut it free. Even if we're held up this way
a couple of dozen times we'll make the open water before
evening.'

The boat was already alongside as it had never been hoisted
from the water since they had reboarded the *Gafelborg*, but
towed astern of them on a long painter.

Vicente, Largertöf and Isiah went down the rope ladder to it;
they poled and paddled with the oars the short distance until they
were right under the stern. With hatchets and sheath-knives they
succeeded in cutting away the thick stem which had become
entangled in the screw.

'A piece great and fleshy of a thickness as of my arm above the

elbow,' Vicente described it when he was back on board. Luvia
signalled 'Slow Astern' again and the vessel proceeded.

Another useful distance was covered before the ship was
brought up short for the second time; the starboard propeller
was fouled again, and Vicente again went over the side with his
crew of two.

Basil and Luvia leaned together over the stern rail watching the
men at work.

Vicente looked up and called to them: 'This is a worse one; he
is much greater round,' and they saw that the mighty weed trunk
the screw had raked up was nearly as thick as a man's thigh.

As the axes cut into it the great stem squelched and bubbled,
but it was tough, like rubber, and appeared to have a hard,
sinewy core.

Suddenly a long, brown, slimy tentacle reached up out of the
weed and inward over the gunwale of the boat. Luvia saw it
flickering there for an instant blindly searching, rippling like a
snake, and yelled a warning. Next second it touched Isiah and
circled round his waist.

At Luvia's shout the men in the boat had looked upward
instead of down, and their backs were towards the octopus that
had come upon them. Isiah was caught before he even realized
the danger and when the others swung round he was already in
the grip of the tentacle.

Having felt its prey the great sea beast suddenly became
violently active. There was a mighty flurry in the weed which
scattered it in all directions. Another glistening arm shot up,
another and another, so that in less than a minute a whole
multitude of them appeared to be waving and diving here, there
and everywhere. Only the tip of one tentacle had appeared at
first, but, as the brute rose out of the water, its great size became
apparent. Each arm was as big as a full-grown python, and on its
inner side it had a graduated row of saucer-like suckers.

'It's a squid,' shouted Luvia, 'a great squid. I must get the guns
—nothing else any good,' and he darted away aft to get them
from the arms locker of which he held the key.

Isiah was screaming with uncontrollable terror as he clung for
his life to one of the thwarts. Young Largertöf lifted his axe, but
panicking, misjudged his stroke so that in bringing it down on
the greater feeler it also cut into Isiah's ribs.

Vicente pulled from his pocket an automatic that he had left in
his cabin when abandoning the ship. The noise of its explosions

drowned the shouting as he emptied the whole of its contents into a great limb that was reaching out for him.

The boat rocked violently, the octopus had one feeler round its bow and another curled about a thwart. It was so powerful that it could have upset the heavy life-boat if that had been its purpose.

Basil stood helpless on the deck above, paralyzed with terror for the men below, but only for a second, the next he had seized a rope and flung it over the stern. It hit Largertöf on the head; he swayed back and caught it.

'Hitch it to a thwart,' yelled Basil. 'Hitch it to the stern thwart.' He knew that there was no time to pull each man up separately.

At that moment the boat almost turned over as the face of the brute appeared over the gunwale and it attempted to heave itself right out of the water. Two enormous, soulless eyes as big as plates stared up at the ship fixed and unwinking; between them was an evil, dull white, parrot-like beak.

Isiah was still clinging to the thwart; blood was dripping from his side and he moaned unceasingly. The wounded tentacle which gripped his waist seemed to have little strength left in it, but stark terror had robbed him of the power to free himself from it and rise.

Another of the octopus's waving, leathery arms suddenly whipped round his neck; his hold on the thwart was broken and he was drawn upright. The negro's eyes seemed to start out of his grey face as he was lifted right out of the boat. His legs waved grotesquely, and Vicente flung himself forward to grab the nearest of them, but it was too late. For a second Isiah dangled from the end of the tentacle, like a hanged man, almost on a level with the stern of the ship, then the lower part of the great arm relaxed and the wretched man disappeared with a loud plop into the weed.

Basil succeeded in taking a couple of turns with the rope round the nearest winch. Darting to the ship's side he saw that Largertöf had managed to hitch his end to the after thwart. The negro had vanished.

'Hang on,' shouted Basil, 'hang on. I'm going to tilt up the boat.' He rushed back to the winch and thrust over the lever.

Luvia and De Brissac came pounding up, each holding a Winchester. They saw Largertöf cowering back in the stern as a wriggling tentacle reached after him and Vicente, stretched straight out clinging to one thwart with his arms and another with his crossed legs, while one of the brute's feelers twisted sinuously about his body.

'A devil-fish,' panted De Brissac. 'Fire at his eyes—the only spot he is vulnerable.'

Luvia's Winchester cracked as the Frenchman spoke. The bullet smacked on to the octopus's cuttle beak, ricocheted, and whined away into the distance.

The winch clattered, the rope strained until it seemed certain that it would part, but with a great sucking sound the stern of the boat suddenly left the water. Its bow dipped and, as the winch wound in the rope the life-boat tilted at a steeper and steeper angle, but the great cuttlefish maintained its hold, and was coming up with it. One of the feelers, thirty feet in length, reached out, flicked through the deck-rail and made a grab at Luvia.

He leapt aside just as De Brissac fired. The Frenchman had taken careful aim and got a bull. A jet of filthy blackish-red liquid spurted up from the creature's left eye, which shuddered like a mass of jelly. The tentacle that had sought for Luvia found a hold on De Brissac's leg, but he did not lose his nerve. Remaining steady at the rail he fired again and again straight down into the eyes of the monster. Gradually its hold relaxed, its tentacles began to thrash wildly, and, with a terrific splash, it fell back into the sea.

CHAPTER X

THE THING THAT CAME
IN THE NIGHT

ATTRACTED by shouts and firing the rest of the party had now arrived upon the scene. The boat was up as far as it could go, hanging bow downwards. Immediately he saw its stern appear Basil had shut off the winch. Largertöf and Vicente were hanging on to prevent themselves falling out into the weed below. More dead than alive from shock, strained muscles and bruises, they were helped aboard and carried down to their cabins.

The boat was lowered again at once before the rope parted under the strain, but its oars had been flung out and lay in a criss-crossed pile, like spillikins, floating on the weed just under the ship's stern.

By means of a running bowline Luvia managed to lasso them one by one, and, with the others' help, drew them up on deck. The job took a good half-hour, and during it they spoke in hushed tones of Isiah's death and this new menace to their operations.

Vicente's party had not succeeded in freeing the propeller, and it was obviously too great a risk to send another party over the side. After their promising start of the morning they were stuck again, and, it seemed, stuck for good this time.

Lunch was a gloomy meal, and as no one could think of any other expedient for freeing the ship they began to resign themselves to remaining inactive until rough weather broke the vast tangles of weed into sections for them. She was still drifting and altering her direction slightly from time to time as she moved, so Luvia felt there was a small chance, at least, of her working herself free if she came into a less congested area.

The amusements provided for the passengers when the ship left Cape Town still being available, Basil carried Unity off for a game of ping-pong. The table, with some basket chairs, occupied a small deck-house.

He beat her three—love, and as they finished the third game she exclaimed: 'You have come on! I used to be able to beat you easily. D'you remember? That first afternoon at sea when we

121

played together—before father found out what a rotter you were?'

Basil laughed. 'Poor old chap, he couldn't bear to have his pet ideas ridiculed, could he? Yet I'm just as patriotic a Briton as he was, in my own way.'

'You're a more agile one than you were, anyhow.'

'Think so?'

'Certain of it. Look at the beating you've just given me. We're all a good bit thinner, of course, after our four days' enforced slimming in the boat. But you look altogether different. Ever so much healthier.'

'Thank you.' He smiled. 'I've been hoping for these words of praise on the outward and visible signs of my regeneration.'

'Have you?'

'Well, haven't you noticed anything else about me?'

'Yes. Since we got back to the ship you've given up drinking—at least—except for a glass of wine now and then.'

'That's right—d'you know why?'

'Because you've had to do your share of the work and you knew you'd be fitter without it.'

'Good Lord, no. I'd have seen old Juhani to the devil before I stopped drinking on that account.'

'Why then?' Unity looked quickly away as she asked the question, because she already guessed the answer.

'Because I thought it'd please you, of course.'

'Really?'

'Yes. Does it?'

'Of course it does. I like you ever so much better. Before, you know, joking apart, you were a bit of a blackguard.'

'My dear, I know it. But this thing's changed us all. It's changed you a lot.'

'Changed me!' She looked up in surprise.

'Rather. You were a most awful little prig, whereas now you're quite human—you've even taken to drink—at least you appear to enjoy a glass of wine now and then.'

It was Unity's turn to smile. 'I always did, but father was so damned mean about letting me have it.'

'That's not the only thing. You were a pinch-faced prude before, even when your father wasn't present. Now, you're so much gayer, in spite of everything, and perfectly natural.'

'I was full of inhibitions, I suppose. If you'd lived in constant fear of a man like that you wouldn't have been so cheerful either.'

She made a mocking little curtsy. 'Thank you, sir, for your compliments on my improvement.'

He laughed. 'You're a darling. D'you know I don't mind really if we are stuck here for a time now we can take things a bit easier.'

'Don't you!' Her eyes opened wider. 'But there's such a beastly feeling about the place. The silence, and these miles of weed with God-knows-what horrible creatures in it. Think of that poor wretch who died this morning.'

'Yes. It was a pretty beastly death, wasn't it. Still he escaped a long stretch in prison for mutiny and that's something. Luvia'll hand all these coloured men over to be tried directly we make a port, you know.'

She nodded. 'I suppose he will, but if they continue to do their job as they have done this last week I expect there'll be a recommendation to mercy. Anyhow, I'm not one of them, and I'd give a lot to be safe in a civilized town.'

'Um,' he murmured doubtfully. 'I can't say I like this place exactly myself, but I haven't quite the same inducement as you for wanting to get anywhere particular. Naturally you're anxious to get home as quick as you can to your family and friends.'

'I haven't got much family now father's dead. My mother died years ago, as I told you. I haven't very many friends either. Ours wasn't quite the jolly, carefree household that a girl feels happy about inviting her friends to, so I never had the chance of making many.'

'There's the painter chap.'

'Yes, but that was finished as far as he was concerned when father made me cut him out.'

'You could always dig him up again.'

'I've thought of that, but I'm not betting on it in case he's got interested in somebody else.'

'Anyhow, you'll have your independence.'

'Yes, that's what I'm really looking forward to. Life'll be fun now I'm my own mistress, and I'll have enough money of my own to keep me comfortably.'

'God, how lucky you are!' he burst out suddenly. 'I'd give anything now to be able to go home to England and settle down to a steady job. It's not much fun being a remittance man. I'm paying for the follies of my youth with a vengeance.'

She pulled up a chair. 'I don't know why we're standing up. Come and sit down and tell me about it. This is the first chance

I've had to ask you about yourself. You're quite young and clever and attractive. What on earth started you off drinking like a fish? Was it a girl?'

He flung himself down in the chair beside hers and stretched his legs. 'No, it wasn't a girl. Nothing so romantic. Just my own damned stupidity. You won't think any the better of me when you've heard about it; but I'd like you to know the worst because you're much too decent to judge me entirely on the past.'

Time slipped by unnoticed while he told her of his inheritance and how he had frittered it away; then of his narrow escape from imprisonment and the useless sort of life he had led since, kicking his heels up and down the world. They were so immersed in their conversation and each other that they would probably have sat on there until dinner-time if a clear hail from the bridge had not brought them back to their present situation.

Full watches were not being kept, but Luvia had detailed the men to take turns at look-out and Hansie was on duty. His shout brought Luvia running up from below.

'By Jove! It's nearly sunset,' Basil exclaimed as he hurried after Unity out of the deck-house. 'We forgot all about our tea.'

Unity laughed. 'Poor Synolda. She'll have had to do all the dirty work for once. Anyhow, I don't mind. I'll do it for her another time. What's Hansie shouting about?'

They walked quickly towards the bridge together and ran up the ladder. Luvia was there with Hansie and De Brissac beside him. Several of the men had come up on deck.

Hansie was pointing excited, while the other two men on the bridge were both peering through their glasses.

'I can't make it out,' Luvia muttered.

'What is it? What're you looking at?' Unity asked eagerly.

'There's something moving on the weed.'

'Where? Oh, yes, I see it. That little black dot.' Basil nodded.

'I'd say it's some kind of bird,' Luvia remarked a moment later.

'No, no. It is not a bird.' De Brissac disagreed; and with his powerful military binoculars still glued to his eyes he went on. 'It has a large black body—quite round. From that stretch down to the weed four slender legs like spindles. At the extremity of each is a black blob. Not feet or claws, but balls rather. Look—it is hopping across the weed like some gigantic flea—yet it moves quite slowly. It is coming nearer.'

Soon, even those without glasses could make out the strange creature fairly clearly, although the sun was setting behind a low cloud and the mist which had hung about all day still obscured the horizon.

Luvia and De Brissac could now see the strange animal in more detail through their glasses. The body was elongated with a vast round head as big as a small motor car; the two front legs appeared crooked at their tops, but the back ones tapered straight down into bone-like spines before meeting the ball-like feet. It appeared to prod the weed with all four feet simultaneously; the two back legs then shot forward between the two front legs in the manner of a giraffe, which animal was a good comparison with it for height. After each stab at the weed it sailed right up into the air for about fifteen feet, as far as they could judge, drifted slowly down, and repeated the prodding process with its ball-like feet which sent it sailing up again. It was like nothing they had ever seen before and they could not make up their minds if it was a bird, animal, or some gigantic unknown species of insect.

It was still the best part of a mile away when De Brissac gave a shout: 'Look! a devil-fish attacks it!'

At the same instant the others had also seen the huge tentacle of an octopus shoot up out of the weed and wrap itself round one of the creature's spindly legs. The nameless beast stabbed violently at the devil-fish with its other three feet for a few seconds, but suddenly seemed to collapse. Next moment it had been drawn under, and in the semi-darkness of the falling night the weed once more appeared to be an empty, lifeless expanse.

The strange tragedy they had witnessed out in the grim weed-land and the nature of the curious creature which had fallen a victim to the great octopus, provided them with food for much talk and speculation during dinner.

Vicente was too sore and bruised from his mauling by the octopus to put in an appearance, so Synolda was able to evade his unwelcome attentions again. With Luvia beside her she sat for a long time that night up on the break of the fo'c'sle, and when they parted at her cabin door their last embrace had a warmth about it that left the big, blond Finnish engineer dazed but happy.

Singly the men kept watch for an hour apiece during the night. It was a little before the dawn that Harlem Joe roused Luvia.

'Well—what is it?' asked the Finn.

'Bremer, Baas,' said the negro. He was shaking slightly. 'I's his relief, but he don' come give me der call bes part of dis hour back as he should. I wakes by myself, and t'inks maybe he's laid down on de job. Get me, baas? Sleepin' or somethin'; but when I makes der bridge he jus' ain't dere.'

Luvia tumbled out of his bunk and soon verified the stoker's statement. Shouts and hails failed to bring any response from the Swedish seaman. Everyone was roused out and a systematic search of the ship began. It was quite fruitless; the fellow seemed to have vanished into thin air.

Synolda said she remembered vaguely hearing someone call out in her sleep, but thought it was only a dream. No one else had heard anything.

After the unavailing search had been completed and the others had gone below, De Brissac took Luvia by the arm and led him along to a spot on the port side of the ship just below the bridge. He said nothing but switched on his torch and pointed with it.

Luvia stared at the thing upon the deck. He stood very still, his hands felt cold and clammy. It was a single, long tendril of wet, bright-green weed to which De Brissac pointed.

Bremer was gone, and both men knew that in the darkness of the night some stealthy, hideous thing had come up out of the sea to get him.

CHAPTER XI

THE COMING OF THE REFUGEE

DAWN was breaking. De Brissac and Luvia faced each other in the grey early light. The strip of bright-green seaweed which told such a terrible story lay on the deck between them.

'Golly!' Juhani gulped, 'I thought my nerve was pretty good, but this scares me more than somewhat.'

The Frenchman nodded. 'It is uncanny this; horrible to think of that poor fellow pacing the deck here only an hour or so ago and now . . .' He left the sentence unfinished, twisting his handsome face into an expressive grimace.

Luvia picked up the trail of seaweed and flung it over the side. 'Poor Bremer. A darn good seaman too. We'd best not let on to the others about this or they'll get the jitters.'

'I agree. In future, too, it would be best that no one is allowed on deck alone—even in the daytime.' De Brissac turned and together the two men went along to the deck lounge where Unity and Synolda, having been roused early with the rest, were serving morning coffee.

The warm brew raised their spirits a little and De Brissac put an end to speculation about Bremer's disappearance by announcing: 'I do not think there can be much doubt about what happened. The nerves of all of us are frayed to breaking point. This horrible quiet is enough to drive anyone insane. Poor Bremer must have had a brainstorm and decided to end it all by throwing himself overboard.'

The explanation was accepted by the others as plausible. Those among them who had done night-duty as watchmen since the ship had been caught in the weed knew, well enough, the strain of standing about, peering out into the darkness trying to focus the hidden landscapes of this desolate sea which seemed to be the very end of the world; startled by the least plop as some fish or animal stirred in it, and unutterably depressed by the thought that their fate might be to die there, prisoners of the slimy weed.

After breakfast they all went out on deck. It was very early still but the day had broken fine and the mist had lifted. Synolda was leading, and the second she stepped through the doorway of the lounge she grabbed at Luvia with a shrill exclamation.

'Look, look, land!'

The others saw it almost at the same second, and in a cluster they rushed to the ship's rail, staring out with eager eyes across the calm stretch of watery vegetation.

Now that the mist had dispersed land was clearly discernible. There were two pieces, one to the south-west, an irregular cape of greyish colour, low on the horizon, which Luvia judged to be seven miles distant; and another larger stretch almost due south of them about five miles away. Between the two the weed showed unbroken, covering a channel some three miles in width.

De Brissac hurried back into the lounge to get his binoculars; Luvia ran up to the bridge. Two minutes later they were together there while the rest crowded round them pressing to hear what they could make out with their glasses of these islands in the middle of the weed continent.

'No trees,' murmured De Brissac, 'and a shelving rocky-looking coast. Anything but hospitable, I'm afraid. The near island looks a good size and, I don't know if it's cloud, but I can see something which looks as though it might be higher ground some miles inland.'

'Sure,' agreed Luvia. 'If it's not cloud it might be a small, flat-topped mountain. No sign of habitation on either of them, though. Just a muddy foreshore and then rocks—not even a thorn-bush, as far as I can see.'

'Sounds a bit disappointing,' Basil murmured, 'but don't let's get too depressed. Most coastlines are barren except just round the ports and fishing villages, yet often enough they conceal habitable areas inland. The climate here isn't so bad and if we could only get ashore I should think there's a chance we might find wild fruit trees, birds and game even if the place is uninhabited.'

Unity laughed uncertainly. 'Perhaps, but we've got to get ashore, haven't we?'

'We're still drifting,' Luvia remarked, 'and drifting in the direction of these islands. If only we don't pass down the middle of the channel between them we might fix some way of getting ashore. I'm going aloft to the crow's-nest. I'll get a better look-see from there.'

He was away about twenty minutes, and when he rejoined them he said: 'There's a third island 'way over towards the farther one—ə bit more to the west. It's only a few hundred yards in length and quite barren—low in the water too—I wouldn't think its highest point is more than twenty feet above the weed. I could see trees on the biggest island, about half a mile inland, unless I'm much mistaken, so maybe there's fruit and nuts to be had if we could get ashore.'

'Focus on the other one,' said De Brissac swiftly. 'There's movement of sorts just by the coastline on the eastern side of the point.'

They all strained their eyes in the direction he indicated. After a moment Luvia exclaimed: 'Yep. I get you. On the point there nearest to the other island—tiny black specks that seem to be dancing up and down on the weed just off the shore.'

'Perhaps they are more things like we saw yesterday,' Synolda suggested, 'you know, the queer beast with the big black body and head all in one and four spines for legs.'

Luvia lowered his glasses. 'You've got it. That's what they are. A whole swarm of them, and it looks as if they're crossing the channel towards the island nearest us.'

For the best part of half an hour they remained clustered on the bridge passing the binoculars from hand to hand and studying the strange creatures in the far distance. As they approached the island it became easier to see them, and De Brissac estimated their number at well over a hundred. In front, leading the swarm, three of the animals appeared to be bunched together springing up from the weed simultaneously in a series of bounds as they crossed it. The rest were dotted about in an irregular formation behind.

A quarter of an hour later the swarm had almost reached the nearer island and individual creatures could be picked out clearly with the human eye. So far they had been coming towards the ship on a diagonal line, but now they turned a little to the eastward to cover the last hundred yards or so to the coast to which they had been moving.

Suddenly the watchers in the ship saw a short scrimmage take place among the three animals in front. Their stilt-like legs seemed to get mixed up; the one on the left toppled over and fell into the weed. The central creature detached itself, and swerving sharply, bounded away northwards towards the ship, while the third hopped about its fallen comrade endeavouring to raise it from the weed.

129

The swarm was still a long way off, but a sea breeze coming from the island carried a faint crying sound as the whole lot turned parallel to the coastline of the island and followed its leader in the direction of the *Gafelborg*.

'They're heading dead for us,' Luvia grunted. 'Wonder if they mean mischief.'

'We'd better get out the arms and be on the safe side,' De Brissac replied promptly.

The little crowd on the bridge scattered and ran down the ladders to the deck. Since the affray with the octopus on the previous day Luvia had kept handy the two Winchesters which he and De Brissac had used, but now he hurried along to the armament store with Largertöf and Basil, and got out the four others that the ship carried, with a good supply of ammunition.

De Brissac, Vicente and Luvia had pistols, so, with six rifles, there were nine firearms between the eleven men. In any other circumstance Luvia would have thought twice before arming Harlem Joe but, with over a hundred of these strange and probably hostile creatures advancing on the ship, he felt that he must take a chance, so only Corncob and Nudäa were left without weapons.

De Brissac, as a military man, took command of the situation and Luvia willingly allowed him to do so. The two girls were ordered to their cabins and told to lock themselves in; but neither of them would hear of going below and, when Unity pointed out that if they were shown how to handle the Winchesters they could act as loaders, it was agreed that they should remain with the men.

Luvia suggested they should divide themselves into three groups—one to hold the fo'c'sle, one the poop, and the third the bridge—but De Brissac overruled him, pointing out that a small party might be overwhelmed whereas if they concentrated the whole of their forces on the bridge, they would be in a much stronger position. It was unthinkable that the creatures had any means of attacking them other than with their claws and beaks, if they had them, so in one compact group the ship's company would be better able to resist an assault.

The nine armed men took up their positions round the bridge rail on the side of the ship nearest to the oncoming swarm, while Nudäa, Corncob, Unity and Synolda stood just in the rear ready to reload their weapons.

By the time the arrangements were completed the strange

beasts had covered about half the distance between the island and
the ship with the leading creature bounding along about a hundred
yards ahead of the rest. The swarm presented a most curious
spectacle as each of the creatures kept prodding the weed with
its four ball-like feet and floating up into the air like a gigantic
flea in slow motion. Their elongated bodies were now clearly
perceptible, and the great black heads that rose above them each
seemed as large as an Austin Seven. The leader of the swarm
appeared to have a whitish blotch in the middle of its head, but
the others showed no marking and in colour were a uniform
blackish grey. They were within a mile of the ship when De
Brissac suddenly sent up a shout:

'*Mon Dieu!* I believe they are men.'

'What the hell . . .' exclaimed Basil.

'Yes, yes,' the Frenchman went on excitedly, 'I am sure of it.
Regardez-moi-ça! What we think are heads are not heads at all
but big balloons, strapped on to the backs of their shoulders—
and round ball-like feet—those are balloons also. The back legs
of each one are real legs fastened to stilts and the front legs,
which you see form angles near the body, are arms and things
like ski-sticks.'

'Holy Mike! You're right.' Luvia passed his glasses over to
Basil. 'They're humans, sure enough, by all that's wonderful!
The balloons must be filled with gas, I reckon, to support their
weight as they hop over this devilish weed.'

'That's it, that's it,' Basil muttered. 'How positively extraordinary—no limit to the invention of man, is there? These are
the inhabitants of the islands, evidently; as they can't get from
one to another by swimming or boats, because of the octopuses, they tap some natural gas to fill balloons and flit over the
weed from place to place.'

'Of course that's it,' Synolda added. 'Have you ever done
ballon-jumping? I have. It's grand fun. You have a gas-filled
envelope strapped to your back which just about carries your
weight. One kick of your foot's enough to send you ten feet in the
air and right over a hedge. It's best of all when you're on top of a
hill. You can kick off and sail gently down a couple of hundred
yards of slope before landing again.'

While they were talking the irregular mob of island balloon-
hoppers had covered another half-mile and their limbs could be
made out quite clearly.

'*Sacré Nom!*' muttered De Brissac, 'the one in front is a white

131

man. Look at his pale face and arms. The others are all blacks.'

'White *woman*,' corrected Unity, who had Luvia's glasses. 'She's got long hair and a sort of short skirt that reaches only to her knees. The others, as you say, are all negroes.'

'D'you know what I believe?' Basil said suddenly. 'They're not coming to attack us but are chasing the girl. She's trying to escape from them. Remember how she broke away from two of the others just as they reached the island.'

'Yes, yes,' De Brissac took him up. 'I can see terror on her face now and she looks constantly over her shoulder. Her lead, too, has much decreased. It is no more than twenty yards that she has in advance of the others.'

'Oh, come on! Come on!' Synolda began to shout in swift excitement. She swung round on Luvia: 'Do something, do something quick! Why don't you fire at those negroes who're after her?'

Luvia shook his head. 'Hang on a minute. She's leading still. We don't want to scare her into thinking we're hostile, and it's a hundred to one against her speaking our language.'

Unity's eyes were bright with anxiety. She clasped the bridge rail and stamped her foot impatiently. 'Oh, the poor darling! She's quite a little thing—almost a child—and pretty too.'

The girl from the island was now no more than a hundred yards away. The nearest negro was springing along ten yards behind her. Not a sound came from the hunters or hunted. Their every effort was concentrated in straining on the stilts and ski-sticks which propelled them. The pursuing negroes were almost naked and their powerful ebony bodies glistened with sweat as the grim chase proceeded in deadly silence.

De Brissac raised his Winchester. 'Ready now? I'm going to give the leading black a warning shot through his balloon. If that doesn't halt them you'll each pick your man and come into action with my second shot. Aim for their balloons with the first round; we do not wish to take life unnecessarily.'

His rifle cracked. There was a soft answering plop as the bullet struck the balloon just above the negro's head. At fifty paces from the ship the whole line suddenly halted. Only the girl still came on. With one last bound she sailed into the air, tripped with her sticks on the ship's rail, and came drifting head first down on to the deck.

Unity ran towards the bridge ladder to go down and help her but De Brissac barked, 'Stay where you are,' and she halted, irresolute, at his order.

The blacks could not remain still as their gas balloons did not carry sufficient weight-lifting power to support them entirely. They came no nearer to the ship for the moment but hopped up and down in the weed presenting the queer spectacle of a great crowd of dancing Jennies.

Suddenly they began to yell in some strange unknown tongue, a series of barbarous, blood-curdling shrieks and, prodding the weed to get themselves into a rough line facing the ship, they bounded forward.

'Fire!' yelled De Brissac and a burst of flame flashed from the line of weapons on the bridge.

One negro staggered and fell. The other bullets went wide or hit the balloons, but the volley did not stop the charge.

'Independent fire. Aim for the men,' shouted De Brissac, and an uneven crackle of rifle and revolver fire came in response to his order.

Half a dozen of the negroes lurched, spun about and went headlong into the weed, but at least fifty had reached the ship and, clinging to its rails, were untying the cords that attached their feet to the awkward stilts. All of them were naked except for a loin cloth, and belts in which each carried an array of primitive but ugly weapons; knobkerries, long knives, assegais, and here and there an old-fashioned sword. Ugly, brutal, screaming their war cries, the savages swarmed on to the decks. De Brissac's voice rose above the din:

'Keep firing! Shoot to kill or those devils will murder us all. I'll be back in a second.'

He thrust his Winchester into Largertöf's hands, and snatched his own revolver which he had lent to the seaman. Bounding down the bridge ladder he leapt towards the girl from the island.

She was moaning loudly but sitting up and frantically endeavouring to get her feet free of her stilts.

As De Brissac raced up to her two negroes sprang at him from the rail. He pistolled the nearest, shooting him through the throat, and turned to face the other. His automatic clicked uselessly. The ammunition in the clip had been exhausted.

The ferocious-looking black giant came at him with a broad-bladed cutlass but he had dropped his ski-sticks on the deck and stooping swiftly, De Brissac grabbed one of them. He was just in time to jab the negro with its pointed end in the left side of the belly.

The black let out a howl of rage, bent double, straightened up, and came on again; but De Brissac had more time to aim his second thrust and landed the point of the ski-stick in the man's right eye. With a wail of pain the savage dropped his cutlass and staggered away towards the side of the ship.

Other negroes came roaring at De Brissac, brandishing their knives and clubs; two pitched forward shot down from the bridge, another checked hit through the shoulder. Next second the Frenchman had his arm round the girl and was lugging her, stilts and all, up the ladder to the bridge. Basil fired over De Brissac's shoulder and dropped another black, who was grabbing at the girl's legs.

Fortunately the savages had no firearms, so the *Gafelborg's* company suffered no casualties at all whereas, in the couple of minutes since the island horde had reached the ship, the execution among them had been appalling. The rearmost ranks of the attackers, seeing the fate that was overtaking their comrades, refrained from boarding the ship and, jumping up and down in the weed some twenty feet away, shouted abuse in their strange tongue, hideous and threatening, but fearful of following their fellows on deck.

Those who had boarded the *Gafelborg* in their frenzied pursuit of the young girl had either been shot down or were hurriedly lashing on their stilts again, in such cover as they could find, and slipping over the side into the weed to escape the devastating fire from the rifles and revolvers of the whites.

A further horror now overtook the attackers and demoralized them entirely. Several of those whose balloons had been shot through could no longer support themselves; with others who had been killed, they lost their balance and fell headlong in the weed. The disturbance of its surface attracted a giant squid. Its grey-white, leathery tentacles shot up, waving and flickering in the air, searching for victims among the fallen.

Having no wish to massacre the wretched savages now that they had been driven off, De Brissac gave the order to cease fire, and the little company on the bridge stood staring at a horrifying spectacle. Half a dozen of the unfortunate black men were in the grip of the octopus's giant tentacles, some seized by a leg, others by the neck, others again round the waist; while a score more were attacking the creature with great courage.

The negroes were at a big disadvantage as they could not stand still but they seemed to have had considerable practice in managing their stilts and ski-sticks since they leapt from place to place with great agility, each man grasping both ski-sticks in his left hand and in his right brandishing a spear, knife or cutlass, with which he made sudden swoops at the snake-like tentacles.

The octopus began to thresh the weed, tossing it in all directions; one of its tentacles was severed completely about three feet from the tip and several others were cut and slashed with jagged wounds in a dozen places. The great brute suddenly leapt half out of the weed, then dived; disappearing under the surface and dragging four of its victims with it.

The negroes rescued their fallen comrades, and others that had been hit but succeeded in getting away from the ship. Two or three unwounded men supported each of the casualties and with a few last howls of hate and defiance at the people on board they made off towards their island.

Eight or ten of their number were left killed or badly wounded on the *Gafelborg*; great splodges of red blood stained the white decks where they lay, but the interest of her passengers and crew was now centred in the young girl they had rescued.

After De Brissac had dragged her up on the bridge she had fainted, so, without any rudeness, they were able to stare their fill at her. She was a slim little creature, less than five feet in height, but with well-developed breasts which made them guess her to be a girl of nineteen or twenty. She was nearly naked, being dressed only in a short, kilted skirt of some homespun material and a vest of lighter stuff which had been neatly darned. Her hair was dark, parted in the centre and floated down to her shoulders in long curls. Her face had something of a Spanish look with its small aquiline nose and pointed chin. She was undoubtedly a white woman, although her skin had been tanned to a rich golden brown, and a small crucifix dangling from her neck on a thin gold chain showed her to be a Christian.

What strange story of shipwreck or life in the weed-surrounded island would she tell them when she came out of her swoon? That was the thought that filled their minds as they carried her down to the lounge.

CHAPTER XII

THE SECRET OF THE ISLANDS

THEY made a careful examination of the girl directly they got her along to the lounge and found that she was only slightly bruised from her fall. With Synolda's help Unity set about reviving her, while the men went off to clear the decks of the casualties in the recent battle.

Altogether nine negroes were found in various parts of the ship; five were dead, two more had been shot through the stomach and were obviously in a dying condition, while of the remaining two one had been stunned by a bullet passing under the skin of his scalp and the other was moaning from the pain of a smashed thigh-bone. The rest of the victims of the whites' guns had either escaped or disappeared under the weed.

The dead were thrown overboard, the four wounded carried to a deck-house on the poop which had previously served as part of the officers' quarters. Their wounds were bandaged, drugs administered to them from the medical store, and Hansie was told off to watch by them.

Luvia had the decks swabbed down to clean up, as far as possible, the horrible patches of gore which stained them, and when the arms had been collected and returned to a locker of which he had the key, with De Brissac, Vicente and Basil he went back to the lounge to hear the rescued girl's story.

She had been badly shaken by her fall and was only just recovering from her terrible experience, but as soon as she had opened her eyes, which were brown lit with golden lights, she began to speak in English to the joy of the other girls who were able to comfort and reassure her.

As the men filed into the lounge, she gave them an enchanting smile and said at once: 'Gentlemen, you and your ladies must be wondering who I am that I should seek refuge in your ship. Permit me to present myself and, if you have leisure to hear it, recount something of my history.'

The gallant De Brissac caressed his little dark moustache with one brown hand and bowed courteously. 'We are dying to hear all about you, Mademoiselle, if it will not fatigue you.'

She shrugged and spread out her hands with a little foreign gesture. 'To you I owe special thanks, Monsieur, for saving me on the deck there. I am a little bruised and shall be stiff tomorrow, but am quite enough recovered to tell you my strange story.'

The Frenchman bowed again and sat down beside her while the others settled themselves in a semicircle near by.

'My name is Yonita Van der Veldt.' She began and continued with considerable vivacity but often using old-fashioned phrases. 'I am half of Dutch and half of Spanish extraction, although I have English blood in my veins also and speak English as my natural language. Most of my forebears have lived on the smaller of these two islands during the last two hundred and fifty years. As you may surmise, we are a colony made up of the survivors of several shipwrecks, and we number now one hundred and twenty-seven men, women and children. All of us are the prisoners of the weed sea which holds many horrors.'

'Doesn't it ever break up when there's a storm?' Juhani interrupted.

Yonita shook her head. 'For some strange reason we are never plagued with violent storms here. Now and again in winter inclement weather churns the weed up into a long, rolling swell for a few days, but there is such a vast extent of it that the great waves of the ocean are smothered in its weight long before they can reach our shores. The weed is not even agitated by a swell for more than perhaps ten days in any year and for the rest of the time it is just atrocious, still and silent, as you see it now.'

Basil grimaced. 'That doesn't sound as though we have much chance of getting out of it again.'

'I fear me, sir, you have no chance at all,' she told him solemnly. 'Through the centuries many ships have been caught in this pernicious web of weed but none that have been driven past the fringe have ever come free to set their sails again. There is a current under the weed which passes through the channel separating the two islands, and the ships that are caught are carried by it until they beach upon the one or the other. 'Tis impossible to see them from here, but round the corner of Satan's Island there are a half-dozen ships which have gone aground in the shallow water, and the remains of several more which beached themselves there in long-past generations.'

'Satan's Island, Mademoiselle?' De Brissac asked interrogatively.

'Thus we have named the one nearest to you which is inhabited by these devilish negroes. Farther along the coast of our own island there is yet another shallow beach where you will find more ships aground in a wide bay. 'Twould be an even wager to which of those strange graveyards of shipping your vessel will go.'

'I knew we were drifting south,' Luvia remarked. 'It was misty yesterday so we couldn't have seen the islands anyway, but I'm dead sure we've drifted farther in during the night. How long d'you reckon it'll take us to make one of these beaches?'

'My opinion is scarce worth the having, but the denseness of the weed slows up the progress of vessels as they get nearer to the land. It looks no great distance, but methinks not less than ten days or at most a month. How long is it since your ship was snared in the weed?'

'It's four days since we first struck it.'

Yonita nodded. 'You have been very speedy then to get so far in so short a time. Most ships drift for weeks in the weed before they come so close in as this. That is why very few of the crews ever survive to land. Often they die of starvation, if their supplies are short when they first enter the weed, or go mad through the terrors of living week after week imprisoned in it. The few who do survive tell always that they have lost many men snatched from their decks by the giant devil-fish that live under the weed.'

'Bremer!' exclaimed Basil.

De Brissac shrugged, '*Oui*, Luvia and I guessed that, although we did not like to tell you. Please proceed, Mademoiselle, and tell us more of your strange life in these uncharted seas.'

'The weed sea is a thing of dread,' she went on slowly, 'yet our island is by no means unpleasant. In winter it is very cold but we have abundance of wood for fires to warm us and for the building of comfortable houses. In summer it is most agreeable here, and with the stores salvaged from ships we have been able to raise crops of Indian corn, wheat, potatoes, tomatoes and other vegetables. Also we have planted orchards of apples, pears, plums and cherries. Our livestock is confined to pigs and chickens, those being the only animals we have been able to salvage in sufficient numbers to breed from. I claim to be of Spanish and Dutch descent but actually our population is a very mixed one; although the predominant strain of our blood is English.

'The first people to be cast away on our island were Sir Deveril Barthorne, the Royalist buccaneer, and his crew, in 1680. They had with them at the time two Spanish ladies whom they had recently captured, together with their negress waiting-women, from the Spanish Main. The first Sir Deveril married the lovelier of these Spaniards, and they established what might be termed a Royal Line. There has been a Sir Deveril in the island ever since, and I am betrothed to the present holder of the title.'

'How many other ships have arrived with living people on board since the first lot?' Unity asked.

'Eight altogether, madam. A Dutch officer named Van der Veldt, who was my ancestor, and two Dutch sailors were cast up as the sole survivors on a wrecked Dutch-warship in 1703. It is from this officer and the daughter of the other Spanish lady that I am descended.

'In 1726 a French merchant ship arrived. There was one officer on it, who died, the Doctor, the Captain's wife, and the daughter of the Governor of one of the French islands in the West Indies; also two loyal seamen. There had been a mutiny on board and the mutineers had gone ashore in the boats. 'Twas for that reason the ship became unmanageable and drifted down into the weed sea. The Governor's daughter married the grandson of the original Sir Deveril. Then in 1744 there was almost an invasion.' Yonita paused.

'A famous pirate of that time called the "Red Barracuda" reached the island in a dismasted ship after a terrific sea-fight with an English man-of-war. Thirty-three men of the crew survived, also the Barracuda's Portuguese mistress and a dozen other women who like the pirates, were of a mixed nationality, some of them being mulatto and two of them South American Indians. After that two Spanish sailors reached us in a small sloop which had been badly battered in a hurricane; all the rest of the crew had been swept overboard or taken by the octopuses. That was in 1810. In 1828 another small barque arrived with three Portuguese, a mulatto and a Chinaman. 1862 brought us a Norwegian officer and five Scandinavian sailors, and 1879 the crew of an American whaler, consisting of seventeen men. Our last arrivals came in the first steamship that we had ever seen. It was a small German gunboat which was snared for three months in the weed and could not get free owing to some trouble with its machinery. Only two of the Germans were alive when it reached us, so you see, with all the intermarriage which has been going on, we are a very mixed community.'

'It certainly sounds so,' Luvia agreed, 'but what about all these niggers who were chasing you this morning?'

Yonita gave a little shudder. 'They come from the other island, and are the descendants of a cargo of slaves in a ship that was on its way from Africa to the American plantations in the eighteenth century. As we have never been able to cross the weed we did not even know of their existence until 1854 when, one night without the least warning they appeared among us, set fire to several of our houses, and carried off some of our women. Our men could not go in pursuit because, alas, we do not have any of the natural gas in our island with which the negroes fill the balloons that enable them to cross the weed.

'Since 1854 there have been repetitions of that raid from time to time. Sometimes they happen twice in one year, but often three or four years go by without any raid at all. They are governed, methinks, by the negroes' desire to secure fresh women getting to a pitch when it overrules their fear of casualties, because, of course, we have firearms. Although they are much more numerous than we are, we generally succeed in killing a number of them before they can get away to the beach—where they leave their balloons under guard—with prisoners.'

'Why do you not live inside a stockade and post sentries each night so that they cannot surprise you?' De Brissac asked.

'If the raids were more frequent we should do so, but to cultivate our land we must live in different parts of the island, so the farthest houses are several miles apart. We lack horses or any other means of transport, so if we lived in one fortress village we should have a long way to walk to and from our work each morning and evening. Besides, we have special hiding-holes for the women in our farms and a system of alarms by which we can come to one another's assistance. The negroes have only succeeded in capturing three women in the last ten years.'

'It seems, Mademoiselle, that you were exceptionally unlucky then,' De Brissac murmured.

She smiled. 'Indeed, sir, I was caught only through a quite unusual circumstance. My uncle, with whom I live, was from home last night, a thing which does not happen more than once in six or eight months, and the three farm-hands who live with us celebrated an anniversary. They got tipsy and were sleeping off their drink, methinks, so did not hear the natives until too late. Had I had the least warning I could have slipped into the hiding-hole which all the females of the island have in their rooms for just such an emergency. As it was they had broken down the door almost before I roused, and I had only time to don these garments before they were upon me. They dragged me down to the beach and strapped one of the spare balloons they had brought upon my back. With two of them gripping my arms, I was forced to hop along across the weed, utterly undone, and nearly frantic with fright.'

'I wonder, though, that you were able to manage your ski-sticks and stilts well enough to get away if you've never had any practice,' remarked Basil.

'I was wondrous struck how simple it is with one of those balloons which buoy one up so splendidly. Thus when I saw the ship, being frantic with despair I formed the resolution to break away, even at the risk of a most gruesome death by falling into the weed and becoming the victim of an octopus. Once I had tripped one of the negroes and pulled away from the other it was amazing easy. I am so much lighter than any of the creatures that I could take longer hops without the ball feet on the sticks and stilts sinking so far into the weed. Yet they would have caught me if it had been a greater distance for I was near dead of exhaustion when I reached the ship.'

'Any idea how many of these niggers there are?' Luvia asked.

'There were some hundred and fifty of them in the raid; but there are many more on the island. None of the females they have taken prisoner has ever escaped so we know little of them except what Father Jerome has told us.

'He was a Catholic missionary on a ship that reached Satan's Island in 1874,' Yonita continued in explanation. 'His account of the negroes' customs is too terrible to dwell upon. They live in a great village, sheltered by a mountain cliff at the far end of their island, some seven miles from the coastline you can see. Near by the village there is a prison compound with a stockade all round it which is called the "Marriage House".

'Whenever a ship drifts up to their coast they crucify all white men that are in it and any women are carried off to this vile den of vice where they are shut up as the negroes' concubines for the remainder of their lives. Any male children born to these poor creatures are killed at birth, since the blacks do not wish to bring

141

white blood into their strain, but the girl-children are kept and reared there until they are old enough to be subjected to the same horrible fate as their poor mamas.

'Father Jerome was voyaging to South Africa and landed there with seven other survivors. His fellows were tortured to death before his eyes, and he himself was only saved by a miracle. He tried reason, pleading and threats in vain; then he called on God to punish these loathsome savages. A thunderstorm broke and one of the headmen of the black tribe was killed by lightning only a few paces from him. The others were so terrified they lacked the courage to kill him, and holding a council decided that he was much too dangerous a witch-doctor to keep, even as a captive. A score of them trussed him up and carried him by night over the weed; leaving him on the beach of our island where some of our people discovered him the following day.'

The company of the *Gafelborg* plied Yonita with innumerable other questions about the life of the strange community, product of many shipwrecks, which inhabited her island and, over lunch, they continued with unabated curiosity until at last she said:

'My betrothed and my family will be monstrous put about. By now they will be mourning in the belief that they will never see me again and that I shall endure untold horrors in that iniquitous "Marriage House" to which all the blacks have equal right of access; and that I'll remain a prisoner there for the rest of my life. I must get back to my own island as soon as possible now so as to alleviate their distress and enable them to rejoice at my escape.'

'I quite see that,' Luvia agreed. 'I suppose you mean to make it by using one of the blacks' balloons. What about the octopuses, though? We saw one of the blacks pulled down into the weed yesterday, although it was so far off we didn't realize he was a man.'

'I am not afraid,' she smiled. 'He must have landed directly on an octopus to be caught. Ordinarily they hardly touch the weed with the ball feet, and not a single one of the great crowd that captured me this morning was attacked until some of them fell into the weed after you shot at them from the ship.'

'It is not right that you should take such a risk alone, Mademoiselle,' De Brissac said quickly. 'I will willingly come with you.'

Luvia nodded. 'That's sound. In fact I think three or four of us ought to go. They can be hitched to each other then with good long lengths of line, like a chain of mountaineers, and if one slips, the others will be able to pull him up again. I can't go because I'm in command of the ship. I'll not be able to spare too many whites, either, in case I have more trouble from our ex-mutineers. They're pretty certain to be boiled up again now on account of seeing all those niggers this afternoon. I noticed Harlem didn't shoot, although I loaned him my gun before we knew just what sort of trouble there was going to be. If the negroes' attack had proved a piece more successful I wouldn't have put it past him to turn his gun on us; except that I had him in front of me all along and he must have savvied I'd have plugged him like a dog if he'd tried a fast one. There's Corncob, though. He played up all right and doesn't seem a bad sort of nigger. You could take him if you like. That gets one black out of the ship and you'd better have another white. What about you, Sutherland?'

'By all means,' Basil agreed. 'I'm quite willing to go.'

Unity lowered her eyes to the table. She had no grounds for protesting his going, but the idea of his running the risk of crossing the horrible weed-sea distressed her terribly. For the first time she realized that she regarded him now as something much more than a friend.

Synolda looked at Yonita: 'You've been through an awful experience, my dear, and it must have tired you, too, answering all our questions this morning. Your people fear you are lost for good, so surely an extra few hours here won't make very much difference. I do think you ought to lie down and get a rest this afternoon before you set out on your journey.'

'I should return as soon as possible,' Yonita said, but her voice was a little uncertain. She had been dragged from her bed at about four o'clock, and she was now beginning to feel the reaction from the terror and fatigue of the early hours of the morning.

'Synolda's perfectly right,' Unity cut in. 'There's the best part of seven miles of weed to cover before you can get to your own island, and you can't halt on the way, even for a moment. That means a big strain, although, I suppose, you'll be able to make the journey in about an hour. I do think it'd be ever so much better if you rested until—say five o'clock. There'll be plenty of time for you to make the crossing between then and sundown.'

'You're very kind to be so thoughtful for me,' Yonita smiled, 'and really, I suppose, it would be best to do what you say.'

Synolda went down to her own cabin with the island girl and tucked her up. The others remained in the lounge talking of the extraordinary history Yonita had related to them and wondering how they could ensure the *Gafelborg*'s beaching on the white man's island instead of the blacks'. Soon, however, Unity and Basil retired again to the deck-house which contained the ping-pong table.

They played two games, but at the end of the second Unity threw her bat down declaring that she did not want to play any more.

'What's up?' Basil asked. 'You've become awfully solemn. Aren't you feeling well?'

She shrugged. 'Oh, I'm well enough, but worried.'

'Why?'

'Because of you, of course. I simply hate the thought of your risking your life by crossing this beastly weed.'

'Do you? It's not much of a risk really. I'll be all right. But Unity——'

'Yes?'

'I hate to have you worry for me, but it's nice all the same.' He stepped forward and took both her hands in his. 'You know the worst about me now. Does it mean, in spite of that, you——'

'Of course I do.' She suddenly pulled away her hands and flung her arms round his neck.

'Say it,' he murmured, drawing his head back from a long, violent kiss. 'Go on say it—do.'

She tried to laugh but the laugh caught in her throat. 'All right,' she said distinctly, smiling into his eyes, 'I confess it. I love you—there!'

They clung together breathlessly for a few moments while he caressed her. All the false prudery she had imbibed through her stern upbringing was gone to the winds and, like a normal healthy girl who is stirred to genuine passion for the first time, she returned his caresses with an equal fervour.

'I've got something for you,' he said at last, drawing back a little and fumbling in his pocket. 'I didn't mean to show it to you —not yet anyway—but I will now.'

'Is it—a poem?' She looked up with flushed face and shining eyes. 'Do let me see.'

'Yes, here it is. I've been burning the midnight oil on it between spells of duty these last two nights.'

THE SECRET OF THE ISLAND

With his arm about her shoulders she unfolded the sheet of paper and slowly read the lines, savouring every facet of their beauty.

I know two handfuls of the evening smoke
stole while you slept into your waiting eyes
and filled them with a dreamers' drifting cloak
of deeper grey, as quiet and old and wise
as all the world's forgotten dynasties.

But in that smoke which drowned your eyes with grey
were all the things my life had tried to say
and failed: so I went to discover
the dreaming eyes of you, my unseen lover.

Then we undid the world and threw aside
the stars that we might meet; we never met,
though you were standing, watching at the side
and saw the deep hill-passes torn to flame
by banked spear-blades whose silver rode in pride
to meet the end of some forlorn crusade
and I marched in the ranks of that brigade.

We knew the lovers of a thousand years
and learnt with them; we had felt all their laughter
tangled with threads of pain, fretted with tears,
the falling-fading of their dreams; and after
the broken mirrors of their memories.

We saw them die and learnt the storming power
of love made from such loved inconstancies;
yet neither of us loved until this hour.

We sought each other over doomed defeats,
in the ashes of a song that once was flame,
behind the masks of constant counterfeits,
the burnt-out mockeries of men's love and shame,
in the fairy tales that whispered round our feet.

Yet through it all your grey eyes were the same,
the shuttle worked always beneath your lips,
weaving your smile; your dark hair waved that way

when the first bent wind danced it to proud display;
startling your mouth with unplacated white
your skin rebels against your dark hair's flight . . .

and I would always have you this same way . . .

the way you looked when I rode to discover
the unseen eyes of you, my dreaming lover.

As she finished she turned up her face and kissed him gently.

'Like it?' he asked smiling.

'How could I help liking it?' she murmured. 'It makes me a little nervous, though. I'm such an ordinary person really and it's a sort of miracle that anyone could think such wonderful thoughts about me.'

'It's you who's the miracle, darling,' he cried, seizing her to kiss her lips again.

It was very silent there in the deck-house. As there was no work to do in the ship most of the others were sleeping in their bunks or talking idly in the lounge. The great weed continent, full of mystery and foreboding, wrapped them round, but the two lovers ignored it in their happiness and the long hours of the afternoon drifted by unnoticed.

They were still entwined in one of the big basket armchairs, her head resting on his shoulder, when Luvia came to find them. He paused in the doorway, a little embarrassed, as they started up.

'Sorry,' he murmured, 'I didn't mean to disturb you; but it's five o'clock and you'd best have a bite to eat, Sutherland, before hitting the trail.'

Unity smiled at him, radiant with health and happiness.

'Don't be so horror-struck, please. Basil and I have just got engaged. We've been planning what we'll do if ever we get back to England.'

Basil nodded. 'Yes, I don't suppose you knew it; I'm a poor devil of a remittance man. But I think my family'll take me back and give me another chance if Unity vouches for my new-found respectability.'

She laughed. 'If they don't, they can go to the devil, darling, because I've got money of my own to set you up in anything you'd like to do, and I'll have more than ever now father's dead.'

'I wouldn't count too much on getting back to England,' Luvia grinned. 'I've pretty well given up any hope of that myself. But you can settle down together on Yonita's island—if we can only reach it. Anyhow, all the best of luck. Perhaps you'd rather not make this trip now, Sutherland—seeing how things are?'

Basil glanced at Unity and, catching her faint nod, he said what he felt expressed her wish: 'I think I'd better since I agreed to do it. It's hardly fair to back out now. There's not much risk and I'm the obvious person to go with De Brissac. Vicente's hardly got over his mauling by the octopus yet and you'll want Hansie and Largertöf for jobs about the ship.'

'O.K. then. Let's get going. There's a bit of a mist coming up; not much to worry about but I'd like to see you well on your way before it has a chance to thicken.'

As they followed Luvia out of the deck-house they saw that the farther island, to which Basil was going, was now no more than a smudge on the horizon and hurried along to the lounge where a high tea had been prepared for him.

Luvia had examined the balloons left by the negroes after the fight that morning. Two of them had been shot through and had deflated but, including Yonita's, there had been ten altogether and the remaining eight appeared to be in perfectly good condition. De Brissac and Corncob, already equipped with the strange gear, were making a preliminary trial fifty yards away from the ship.

Twenty minutes later, just as Basil was finishing his tea, Luvia came into the lounge. 'Come on, Sutherland, make it as snappy as you can, there's a good guy.'

'Why—what's the hurry?'

'De Brissac's anxious to get off before the mist thickens.'

'Right-oh! just two minutes and I'll be there.' Basil kissed Unity very tenderly, and went out on deck. A balloon was strapped on his back and he made the circuit of the *Gafelborg*, finding the ski-sticks and stilts much easier to manipulate than he had expected.

It was nearly a quarter to six by the time Yonita went over the side to join the men, and another ten minutes were occupied in getting the party roped together at thirty-foot intervals on a long line. Sunset was not due for over an hour and a half yet but with the coming of the mist the westering sun had disappeared behind a bank of clouds and twilight was creeping down upon them. The mist had thickened slightly, almost obscuring Yonita's island, but it did not look as if they would have any difficulty in reaching the shore before the light had gone.

Watched by the whole ship's company and sent on their way with hearty shouts of farewell the four who were to make the journey set out in a string, with De Brissac leading, across the dree, eerie weed sea into the shadows of the coming night.

CHAPTER XIII

THE ISLAND OF FEAR

DE BRISSAC found the balloon-jumping a delightful experience. They did not make as rapid progress as he had expected from having watched the negroes' advance that morning; their pace was only about twice as fast as a man could walk; but there was something extraordinarily exhilarating in propelling oneself up into the air and floating gently forward through it. The feeling was something like that of a dream he had had once or twice in which he had felt himself to be gliding effortlessly along a few feet off the ground, right down the little street of the village which lay near his home in Gascony.

They had not gone very far before his thoughts were occupied with much more serious matters. All about them the dead-flat sea of weed seemed as though it was smoking, little curling wisps of mist were rising from it and ahead of them Yonita's island had now become entirely obscured. Mentally he cursed the delay which had prevented their starting earlier. They should have set off promptly at five o'clock, but Basil had disappeared and Luvia had spent quite a time hunting the ship for him. Basil had had to have a meal and there had been the further business of getting into their strange equipment and trying it out before they had set off, so, after all, they had not started on their journey much before six. De Brissac reckoned the seven miles to Yonita's island as only an hour's journey, but now the twilight of the summer evening added to the difficulty of seeing through the rapidly increasing mist.

Basil, bringing up the rear, was hardly conscious of the changing of the conditions in the light and atmosphere. His heart was too full of happiness from having so recently discovered that Unity loved him. His only thought was to get this job of seeing Yonita home over as quickly as possible so as to be free to return to the ship.

Before they had gone two miles De Brissac was really worried. Glancing over his shoulder he saw that the ship was now entirely hidden behind them and that they were utterly alone on the open weed hedged in by the damp, grey shroud which had risen all about them. He was a brave man, but, like all good commanders, cautious, and he never ran any unnecessary risks. If the ship had still been visible he would certainly have turned round and gone back to it, telling Yonita that, sorry as he was, her friends must grieve for her until the following morning; but he realized that if he turned round he might miss the ship, upon which they would be faced with the awful fate of staggering round and round above the weed all night until they were too exhausted to propel themselves farther and fell into it.

He saw that they must go on but he felt a constant, gnawing anxiety that in the fog they might miss the island by going either too far east of it or too far west. It was vain for him to reproach himself with not having brought his prismatic compass which was stowed away with his other military gear in his cabin. With that he could have taken a bearing of the island before they started and gone forward with complete confidence, but with every jump he took he feared now that, in spite of his concentrated effort to move only in a straight line, they might be making a curve which would carry them away from their destination. When serving in Algeria with the French African forces he had been lost on one occasion with a small party in the Sahara; he remembered then how they had gone up and down interminable sandhills thinking that they were moving east but all the time going round in a circle until at last they stumbled upon their own tracks. During his service in Madagascar, too, he knew that people who got lost in the bush almost invariably went round in a curve, however hard they endeavoured to keep moving in a straight line.

They had been going for something over half an hour when he spotted a rise in the weed just in front of him and shouted a warning to the others. Next minute he was floating down, not on to weed but on to a smooth rocky shore that rose out of it. Dropping his ski-sticks he put out his hands to save himself and landed with an awkward tumble. A moment later Yonita descended on top of him, and, before they could get up, Corncob and Basil had joined the tangled heap.

Owing to the gentleness with which their balloons let them down none of them was hurt, and, sorting themselves out, they sat up in a row with the long stilts attached to their feet stretched out in front of them.

De Brissàc heaved a sigh. 'What luck! We should all thank *le bon Dieu* for this piece of fortune.'

'Piece of fortune!' Basil echoed in protest. 'I don't see much to be thankful about. One of us might have hurt himself darn badly on these rocks. It's not going to be so easy getting off again either with stilts on our feet and these footballs at the end of them.'

'We're not going to get off again, *mon vieux*,' De Brissac said quietly. 'Not till tomorrow morning, and, believe me, I am heartily glad that we should have stumbled on this piece of *terra firma*.'

'Is we goin' to stay in dis place orl night, Bass?' Corncob inquired anxiously. 'Dis ain't no place for a guy to sleep at all.'

'Maybe not,' De Brissac told him, 'but we're going to stay here just the same.'

'No! no!' little Yonita protested quickly. 'These rocks are evil like all the land that is near the weed. I vow I should die of fright if we must stay here through the night.'

De Brissac put out a hand and patted her shoulder. 'Please don't worry, Mademoiselle. It will be uncomfortable, I know, but we will take good care of you.'

'But damn it all,' Basil expostulated, 'why should we stay? This must be the third island, the little one about four hundred yards long, that we spotted from the ship this morning. We're half-way to Yonita's island now—another half-hour and we'll be there. The mist's a bit nasty, I know, but it'll probably clear soon after sundown, and I was betting on being able to get back to the ship by moonlight tonight.'

'I am sorry,' De Brissac said firmly, 'but you do not realize the danger we were in ten minutes ago. Like a fool I never thought to bring a compass, and there isn't a man living who can keep his direction over a distance of several miles without landmarks or heavenly bodies to guide himself by. If you remember, this small island is quite a bit to the westward of the other, and had we not had the good fortune to come right on it we should have curved away, missing Yonita's island by at least a mile, and gone floundering on all night, utterly lost, until we dropped in this foul weed from sheer exhaustion. I am in command of this expedition. We are not moving from this place until daylight; and not even then unless we can see the coastline of Yonita's island with much clarity.'

'But we must go on, indeed we must!' Yonita insisted. 'We are too near the weed here to be safe for the night. We know the position of my island from this one and can start out from it in a new direction which will bring us safely to the shore.'

De Brissac shrugged: 'We know the position of this island from the ship and from yours in daylight when we can see all three places, but are you so certain that we can judge its position accurately now that we can see neither of the others? Just show me where you think the ship is.'

' 'Tis out there,' she said decisively, pointing to their front.

'No, no, missie,' Corncob disagreed. 'De ship's way over to de left dere. I'se sure of dat 'cos we was comin' right from her an' I fell sideways on dis rock.'

'There you are,' De Brissac smiled to himself. 'Two of you do not even agree exactly on the direction from which we were coming when we all fell down here in a heap. The curve of the shore here puts you out a bit, I expect. Anyhow, if you are not certain about that, I certainly would not trust myself to guess just where that narrow headland of your island is we wish to reach. I'm sorry, but I'm afraid there's nothing else for it. We must stay here the night. Let's see if we can find any kind of shelter.'

They unlaced the stilts from their legs and De Brissac got out his torch to lead the way inland. He switched it on but muttered an inaudible profanity as it failed to light. Shaking it beside his ear he heard a faint tinkle and knew that the electric bulb had broken in his recent fall. None of the others had a torch upon them so they had to hop and drift gently forward in the foggy semi-darkness, dragging their stilts and ski-sticks behind them.

First they made the circuit of the island's low, rocky shore to ascertain its extent and found it to be, as they had supposed, about four hundred yards long by two hundred yards wide. They then moved diagonally across it. There was not a single tree or shrub of any kind on the whole of its barren surface. It was just bare, inhospitable rock, but here and there the higher ground towards its centre was split and broken into fissures. The thickness of the mist limited their range of vision and as the sun, hidden from their view by the gloomy pall, sank to the horizon, darkness closed in; but before the failing light finally disappeared they succeeded in finding a shallow cave among the bigger rocks in the island's centre.

Stowing away their cumbersome balloons, ski-sticks and stilts and carefully weighing them down with loose rocks so that they should not be blown away, they settled in to try to make themselves as comfortable as they could in the deepest portion of the cave.

The business was a far from happy one as there was not even a little sand on the floor of the cave to soften the hard stone upon which they had to sit; their only comfort was that they had the gas balloons to lean against. Basil had a box of matches but the island contained no wood or dried sticks with which to make a fire, and, as they had counted upon dining with Yonita's people, they had brought no provisions with them. De Brissac, being an old soldier, had a flask of brandy and a packet of chocolate on him. They passed round the flask and divided the chocolate, nibbling it slowly to while away the time since it was still early and none of them felt like sleep.

The mist was all about them, thick, dank, and oppressive. In the shallow cave they could only just make out each other's form for a little time and soon dead night had descended on them, wrapping them in Stygian blackness.

For a while they talked, encouraging Yonita to give them further descriptions of life on her island and her friends among the people there; not only out of genuine interest but to try to keep her thoughts from the discomfort and uncertainties of their position which showed little likelihood of improving for the best part of ten hours to come.

After a time their conversation flagged and each of them might have been utterly alone. De Brissac would not allow smoking for fear a leak in one of the gas balloons might lead to an explosion, so they had not even the glow of each other's cigarette-tips to comfort them in the darkness.

As night deepened the dead silence of the horrid weed world gave way to occasional queer little noises—a soft plop as some creature moved under the green jungle that obscured the face of the sea—a little hissing noise, faint but insistent and quite inexplicable—the fall of a pebble upon the rocky foreshore, making them suppress a start and turn their heads in the direction of the sound, fearful that some vile thing was creeping upon them out of the deep.

Corncob, a healthy child of nature, untroubled by the subtle imagination of the more sensitive whites, had buried his head in a balloon, and, curled up into a ball, had gone off to sleep in spite of his strange surroundings. He began to snore with a long, low, nasal trumpeting, the monotonous repetition of which irritated the others, yet they had not the heart to wake him, knowing that he might not be able to get off to sleep again.

De Brissac declared his intention of staying awake all night to watch. There was no land animal of any size on the island, as, had there been, they would almost certainly have seen it during their tour of the small barren space, in spite of the mist. They could think of nothing which could possibly come up out of the sea to attack them, yet this terrible, eerie waste was so utterly unlike any ordinary shore that they were filled with a sinister foreboding. Much as Yonita and Basil would have liked to have slept, both protested that they would find it impossible.

From time to time De Brissac glanced at the luminous dial of his wrist-watch. The hands crept on with deadly slowness; it was past midnight when he spoke in a low voice to Basil, and, receiving no reply, guessed that his friend had, after all, dropped into a doze, but Yonita answered him in a soft whisper.

'You were so quiet I thought you too had fallen asleep, and that I was watching for you instead.'

'No,' he smiled in the darkness, 'I'm used to long spells of duty, so I don't find it very irksome to watch all night; but you, I had hoped you were asleep. Try counting sheep jumping over a hedge. If you could sleep a little it would shorten this time of waiting so much for you.'

'I cannot,' she muttered, 'in our present pass I do not think I could sleep if we were here for a week. I'm frightened, and I'm cold. Oh, so cold.'

He stretched out his hand, and, putting it round her shoulders drew her towards him. '*Ma pauvre petite*, cuddle up to me; that will make you a little warmer. If he could know how we're having to pass the night I don't think your *fiancé* would mind, do you?'

She crept gratefully into his embrace and snuggled her head down just below his chin so that he could feel her dark, silky hair against the lower side of his right cheek. 'My *fiancé*?' she asked, in a surprised tone, 'why should he mind?'

De Brissac was silent for a moment. He knew quite well that if he were engaged to a young woman he would mind her snuggling up to another man as quickly and warmly as Yonita had

done to him, very much indeed, unless it were in equally exceptional circumstances; but her innocence seemed so transparent
that he was loath to put his thoughts into words. After all, she
was little more than a child, although an exceptionally well-
developed one. '*Je ne sais pas*,' he replied vaguely, 'but *fiancés*
are sometimes apt to be jealous without reason.'

She gave a funny little laugh and said: 'We are aware, in some
degree of the customs of the outside world through the American
whaling men and the two German sailors, who are the most
recently come amongst us. I had forgotten that your ways are
somewhat different from ours where love-making is concerned.'

'*Vraiment!*' De Brissac slowly moved his chin, lightly caressing
her dark head that lay beneath it. 'Do tell me in what way your
customs differ from ours. Like many Frenchmen, I think that
love is one of the most important things in life, and I am tremendously interested in all the forms it takes. Apart from—shall
we say—just a little practice on my own account, I've studied the
native customs in all the countries where I've been stationed
as a soldier.'

Yonita chuckled again. 'Just a little practice! Methinks you
are being too modest, *Monsieur le Capitaine*. 'Twould not be the
first time, I vow, that a woman has told you how very good-
looking you are, with your nice, bronzed face and merry eyes.
You are brave, too. I have had proof of that—in fact you are
altogether a very nice person indeed. I do not believe this story
that women have been so cruel to you that you have only had just
a *little* practice in making love.'

De Brissac grinned to himself in the darkness and pressed
Yonita more closely to him. 'If you will, then, I confess, Mademoiselle, that I have had my fair share of the joy of life; in fact, I
have never lost an opportunity of making love to any girl who
pleased me, providing my honour was not concerned. I would
be making love to you at this very moment, uncomfortable as
we are, if it were not that you had spoken of your engagement.'

'I have a particular regard for Deveril,' said Yonita solemnly.
'I am more devoted to him than I am or could be to anyone
else in the world, but, all the same, as I was about to tell you, our
ideas about these things in my island are quite different from
yours.'

'You excite my curiosity, Mademoiselle. Also, I will freely
confess, my hopes, since I thought you utterly adorable from the
very first moment I set eyes upon you.'

155

'I do not wish to forfeit your good opinion of me, *Monsieur le Capitaine*, but in our island. . . . Hush! What is that?'

For a moment they sat silent, listening intently. From somewhere out upon the rocky foreshore there came a stealthy tap—tap—tap.

Yonita let out a muffled cry and drew herself sharply free of De Brissac's embrace. He kept a firm hold on her with one hand, but leaned forward peering into the darkness.

'What is it?' murmured Basil starting up from his uneasy doze.

'Silence,' snapped De Brissac. 'Listen!'

This time all three of them heard it—a sudden slither of stones and then again the horrid tap—tap—tap.

In an instant they were on their feet, and De Brissac was roughly shaking Corncob out of his slumber.

The two white men gripped their Winchesters and Corncob the automatic that De Brissac had lent him. De Brissac thrust Yonita behind them into the deepest recess of the shallow cave, and stepped out into the darkness, his rifle poised ready.

'Stay, I beg you,' she pleaded, and a moment later he saw that there was no point in advancing farther. He could see nothing in the utter blackness that blanketed them in and it was sheer stupidity to risk being caught out in the open. The cave was hardly a cave in the true sense, since its greatest depth in the low wall of rock was no more than six feet, but at least the rock provided protection for their backs if some vile monster was coming up out of the weed at them.

Tap—tap—tap—the noise came again—and another slither of stones. Silence fell; for several moments they strained their ears, until they could hear the blood drumming in them from their quickened heart-beats.

'It's nothing,' muttered Basil, 'or whatever it was has gone.' He had hardly spoken when there came the sound of a loud splash, and further sharp, clear tapping so that it sounded now as though half a dozen small hammers were being beaten at the same time upon the ringing rock.

Corncob's knees began to knock together. The misty air about them was still damp and cold, but he was in a bath of perspiration; his teeth chattered, and his eyes bulged from his head. 'I'se scared, Bass, I'se scared,' he gibbered suddenly. 'Dem's unholy things—coming to get us—out o' de night.'

'Quiet!' said De Brissac sharply. Silence fell again; moments that seemed ages drifted by while they stood with muscles tensed, gripped by the stark fear of the unknown. The murk had lightened slightly; a faint, misty shimmer from the hidden moon low on the horizon gave just sufficient light for them to see each other's outlines indistinctly at close quarters.

The sounds came once more, nearer now, a loud, horrid tapping and clicking upon the rocks. Corncob was moaning softly in an extremity of terror. Suddenly, before the others could stop him, he threw down the revolver and dashed out of the cave, stumbling over the jagged rocks that he could not see, away from the creatures that were approaching.

'Come back!' yelled Basil. 'Come back, you fool!'

De Brissac plunged forward to pursue the negro; Yonita, sensing rather than seeing the Frenchman's intention, flung both arms round his waist and clung to him with all her might.

'Let go!' cried De Brissac furiously, 'let go! Anything may happen to that fool of a nigger unless I can get him back.'

'No, no, stay here, stay here. It's your only chance. You will be killed yourself,' she cried, fighting to maintain her hold on him like a small tiger-cat.

Even as they were struggling the tapping noise ceased and a great rushing slither took its place. The unseen horror passed some yards in front of them, no more than a long, irregular outline about twenty feet in length and nearly shoulder high. In a second it was gone again swiftly following on the heels of the flying negro.

De Brissac had given in to Yonita's pleadings, and for grim seconds they stood there huddled together, listening breathlessly as the slithering sound died away in the distance.

Suddenly a hoarse scream came muffled through the murk. Again and again it pierced the gloom, chilling their hearts by its sheer, unadulterated terror. The screams were followed by one long, whimpering wail—then there was again deadly silence.

The palms of Basil's hands were wet. De Brissac passed his handkerchief over his perspiring face. Yonita was sobbing softly as she clung to him. For a quarter of an hour they remained standing there, transfixed with an utter fear of the incredibly beastly thing which had come up out of the weed and slain the negro. There are few brave soldiers who have not known fear, and De Brissac's colonial experience had provided him with a fair share of tight corners, but never in his life had he been faced with any experience so frightful.

It was the awful fear of some nameless evil which held them

spellbound. If they could have seen the things that threatened them they would have at least been able to take some steps for their protection, but such creatures as might possibly live in this loathsome weed sea were utterly beyond all ordinary imagination. They could only wait, clinging to the scant shelter of their shallow cave, peering out into the darkness.

The moon had risen and its light filtered greyly through the mist which seemed to have lightened a little. At a distance of a couple of feet they could now make out each other's forms, and, vaguely, even each other's faces, but outside the radius of a couple of yards everything was hidden from them.

With unsteady fingers Basil fumbled for his cigarettes, got one out, and, forgetting the balloons, lit it.

'Put that out, you fool,' De Brissac snapped, as the match burst into flame. 'The thing is probably still on the island and you're giving our position away.'

'Sorry,' Basil murmured shakily, stubbing out the cigarette against the low cliff on his right. 'I don't think I've given anything away though. The thing that came out of the weed knows where we are. It came straight at us and would have attacked us by now if it hadn't been for that poor devil, Corncob, dashing out into the open.'

'That's true,' De Brissac muttered. 'I'm afraid I'm a bit jumpy.'

Basil gave a rueful laugh. 'Aren't we all. I'm in a bath of perspiration. What sort of brute d'you think it was?'

'God knows! It couldn't have been an octopus. Octopuses live among the rocks in caves under water but they never come up on land.'

Yonita ceased her sobbing. 'Methinks—methinks I know,' she stammered, but De Brissac checked her.

'Wait—there it is again.'

Once more the stealthy tap—tap—tap reached their straining ears; coming this time from the direction in which Corncob had fled. In an agony of apprehension they awaited the beast's approach. The tapping became a rapid, irregular tattoo. Pebbles and rocks tinkled and tumbled as the creature advanced and the awful scrambling noise came closer and closer.

Then it stopped—ten paces away. Suddenly it started again. Next moment a thing that seemed to have five great humps loomed up sideways-on out of the murk and came charging at them.

CHAPTER XIV

THE THINGS THAT TAPPED
IN THE NIGHT

THE rifles cracked. The roar of their explosion echoed and rever-berated against the rocky wall of the shallow cave. The flames from their barrels stabbed the black night and lit it for a second with the blinding glare of a photographer's flashlight.

An instant later the darkness, blacker than ever by contrast, blinded them utterly so that they could not see a single thing, but, in the moment of the flash, a clear and terrifying picture of their enemy had been indelibly imprinted upon the minds of them all. They were faced by five giant crabs.

The creatures were enormous beyond anything ever seen in any natural history museum. Reared up on their curved, hairy, back legs they stood shoulder high, their dead-black eyes protruding on thick, six-inch stalks over their flat backs, were as large as tennis balls. Their oval shells were from five to six feet wide across the back and above them in the air they waved huge pincers, of gigantic strength, as thick as a man's thigh.

Basil and De Brissac fired again, both aiming blind but firing low in the hope of hitting the creature's exposed bodies.

No sound came from the dumb brutes to show if any of them were hit, but a loud click suggested that a bullet had ricocheted off one of the creature's backs or claws. Both men knew that even armour-piercing bullets could not penetrate the solid shells of beasts of such a size. Their only hope of saving themselves from being torn to pieces by those terrific pincers, which could have clipped away a human limb as easily as one cuts the stem of a rose with a pair of garden scissors, lay in hitting them in their under parts, where softer shell covered their lungs and intestines.

At the blast of the rifles the creatures had drawn back a little, but now they came on again, scrambling sideways over the rocks with fierce determination, each waving one great claw high in the air. For a moment a rift in the mist enabled the gentle light of the rising moon to penetrate and outline these macabre monsters of the weed.

De Brissac fired at the upraised middle of the nearest brute. Its pincer flapped violently and it toppled forward. Immediately the others flung themselves upon it with cannibal lust. In its death agony it clipped off the pointed leg of one of the others but they threw it over on its back, nipped off its eyes and dug their claws deep into its body; tearing at it till it was completely disembowelled.

Basil was trembling violently, but, with a supreme effort, he steadied himself, took careful aim, and fired again. Both he and De Brissac had forgotten the danger of an explosion from the balloons which were only a few feet behind then. His bullet ripped away the soft shell under the throat of another of the huge crustaceans.

Two of the others, seeing it wounded, attacked it instantly. Pincer seized pincer, and a silent, gruesome fight began, but the third unwounded brute now came swiftly sideways at the human prey.

De Brissac and Basil fired at it simultaneously, but, in the bad light, their aim was uncertain and their bullets apparently had no effect. Next second the monster was right upon them, stretching out with one great claw for De Brissac's neck and with the other at Yonita.

De Brissac leapt aside, escaping the snap of the pincer by inches.

Yonita screamed and fell right under the beast's body. Basil clubbed his rifle, and leaping forward gave a mighty sideways sweep, bashing in both of the brute's eyes with one swift stroke.

Blinded now, it struck out right and left at them in terrible, silent fury. Basil stooped to drag Yonita from beneath it, but one of the claws caught him on the shoulder with such violence that it sent him spinning half a dozen feet away. De Brissac thrust the barrel of his Winchester right into the brute's slit-like, slavering mouth and pulled the trigger. It jerked back violently, clutched frantically at the air with its claws and collapsed, falling across Yonita's legs.

She screamed again as the two men flung themselves upon the beast and tried to lever it upwards, but the weight was so great that they could not shift it.

Next second they had to abandon their attempt as the two other brutes came slipping and sliding rapidly towards them. Yonita's piercing cries sank to a terrified whimper. Both the men

were grey-faced, ashen with fear; either would rather have faced a legion of savages than these silent, ferocious giants of the weed sea. An awful, reeking stench of dead fish came from the huge crabs and the flash of the rifles showed the sea-lice crawling in swarms upon them.

They fired again at the nearest of the creatures, Basil emptying the remaining contents of his magazine into the great brute's chest. It halted and sank down by the one which pinioned Yonita, tapping feebly with its great claws and long, sharp-pointed legs upon the rocks. The other came scrambling over it and made straight at Basil.

He pressed the trigger of his rifle but it was empty now and gave only a faint click. He tried to grab the barrel to use it again as a club, but the evil-smelling horror was right upon him, a huge pincer reaching out to nip off his head. In a frenzy of fear he ducked below it and came up inside the giant pincer. Almost before he realized what had happened he received a terrific blow across his back and felt himself forced up against the front of the brute, caught by the pressure of its claw as in a great spring-trap. Next moment, seized as in a vice against the dank, slimy chest of the foul monster, he was lifted from his feet and it began to scuttle away with him towards the weed.

Another bank of mist had drifted up, dimming the moonlight so that De Brissac was no longer able to see with any clearness. A breathless silence descended upon the frightful scene. It was broken only by Yonita's faint moaning and the slithering of the monster that was carrying Basil away until there came his sudden scream for help. The giant crab had covered fifteen yards before De Brissac realized what was happening. At Basil's scream he sprang forward towards the sound.

Plunging across the rocks he stumbled and fell, picked himself up again and raced on. The slithering sound was only just ahead of him and next minute he could make out the rough outline of the crab as it scuttled rapidly sideways towards the beach.

Basil was fast in its grip, his spine near breaking-point at the pressure the great claw exerted on him. His chin was just above the huge crab's shell and the fetid stench of decayed fish came up from the creature's mouth to him, nauseating him to such an extent that he vomited violently in the midst of his terrified cries for succour.

De Brissac ran on down the uneven slope, his fastest speed only just enabling him to outdistance the crab. It had covered

seventy yards and was within twenty of the waterline by the time
he caught up with it.

His Winchester was useless. To fire at the monster's back,
covered by the solid armour of its shell, would have had no more
effect than using a pea-shooter, and, even if he could have got in
front of it, all its vulnerable part was protected as it was hugging
Basil to its chest.

Without a second's hesitation De Brissac dropped his rifle,
flung himself headlong upon the brute's back and grabbing its
protruding eyeballs, one in each hand, gouged them out with his
fingers. The beast instantly dropped Basil, and waving its great
pincers high in the air, tried frantically to nip the man upon
its back.

Still clinging to its shell with one hand De Brissac wrenched his
big silver cigarette-case out of his pocket with the other and
thrust it with all the force he could into the creature's mouth
and right down its gullet.

The effort nearly cost him his arm as the huge claw descended
with a snap and he was only just able to get his hand away in
time. The crab reared up and De Brissac slid off its back, stumbling away, before it could turn, to try to find his rifle.

Basil had slipped from underneath it and was now a dozen feet
distant. The mist parted again and showed him wild-eyed and
panting as he lifted a great rock above his head. With the super-
strength of a madman he hurled it at the brute's chest.

The blinded crab began to gyrate wildly round and round
upon its needle-sharp, hairy, pointed legs, nipping the air again
and again with incredible swiftness.

De Brissac caught sight of his Winchester in the moonlight,
grabbed it up and knelt, taking careful aim. As the brute came
face to face with him he emptied the contents of the magazine
into its front and finished it.

Basil had collapsed upon the rocks. De Brissac stumbled over
and sank down beside him. For a few moments they lay there
panting; shaken by their terrible experience.

'You hurt?' De Brissac asked at last.

'No, thank God,' Basil gasped, 'only bruised. The brute had
the grip of a polar bear. I thought it 'ud crush my ribs in. How
about Yonita?'

'She's all right. Her legs are pinned under the second one we
killed. We'll free her directly we've got our breath back.'

Basil groaned. 'God, that was a near thing. If you hadn't

turned up when you did that devilish brute would be making a meal off me by now—somewhere down there in the weed. What a nightmare!'

De Brissac got slowly to his feet. 'Let's hope there are no more of them about. We must get back to Yonita and reload our rifles.'

'I hope to goodness she's all right,' Basil muttered.

'We'd have heard her screaming if she had been attacked by another of them,' De Brissac reassured him.

Back in the shallow cave they found her lying full length on the ground, sobbing quietly; her feet were still pinned under the soft body of the huge brute that had attacked her.

The dead crab was so heavy that at first they could not move it, but after half an hour's hard work with their clasp-knives they managed to cut through the rubbery tendons where the two great claws were jointed to hinge on to the body. Dragging these aside they got a shoulder each under the enormous shell and heaved it up the few inches necessary for Yonita to wriggle free.

Her legs were badly bruised from the feet to below the knees but she could stand without assistance and none of the bones in her feet seemed to have been broken. She told them then what she had been about to say when De Brissac checked her, just before the attack.

'I have never set eyes on any of the odious creatures, but our islanders speak of occasional encounters with them; it only occurred to me the moment they came at us that was what they must be. I vow I was near out of my wits with fright.'

De Brissac tried to comfort her by saying the night would soon be over, but looking at his wrist-watch he saw that it was only a quarter past two; they still had over two hours to wait for daylight. The mist had cleared entirely now, which was some comfort to them, as, by keeping a careful watch, they could overlook both beaches and have ample warning if any more of the great crustaceans came up out of the weed to attack them, and the moon, now high in the heavens and free of cloud, gave a bright, cold light which would enable them to shoot with some accuracy at a fair distance.

Nevertheless it was a grim and agonizing period of waiting. Had there been more of the brutes they would certainly have been overwhelmed and torn to pieces and they had every reason to suppose that the weed held hundreds of such monsters who might easily be attracted by the stench of their dead comrades or by whatever sense it is which guides crustaceans to the carrion of the beaches.

Time passed on with leaden feet. At half past three the uncanny, but friendly moonlight failed them. Shadows crept up about their refuge once again and only the faint radiance of the stars showed the rough outline of the bulkier rocks in the near distance.

The following hour was the tensest and most anxious of the whole terrible night. They constantly expected to hear again that loathsome scuffling sound down by the water's edge, but at last, after what seemed an interminable time, a faint greyness lit the eastern horizon, and ten minutes later it was light enough for them to see the shore.

Once daylight had fully come De Brissac found the automatic Corncob had thrown away, and they determined not to lose a moment but to leave the island where they had experienced such inexpressible terror with the utmost dispatch.

Yonita's legs and feet were so badly bruised that they feared she might not be able to manipulate her stilts, but she declared that she would rather risk falling into the weed than stay a moment longer. To give her additional support they lashed Corncob's gas balloon to hers and, adjusting their own, they began to hop gently down towards the beach.

The last crab that De Brissac had killed was still there, and a swarm of smaller ones, from tiny things the size of a thumbnail to ugly-looking brutes a foot across, were gorging themselves on its carcass. De Brissac drove them off with a couple of shots, aimed at the two largest, which scared the rest and sent them scuttling some twenty yards away where they remained, waving their claws and staring at the humans. Holding his nose with one hand because of the sickening stink, he ripped up the great crab's gullet and retrieved his cigarette-case.

In the meantime Basil had come upon a grim souvenir of the night's terror. It was ten inches of black-skinned human leg and a complete foot, sliced off as cleanly, halfway up the shin, as though it had been severed by the single stroke of a woodman's axe. One of the crabs must have nipped it from poor Corncob's body as he was flying in panic across the rocks.

Twenty yards farther on they came upon all that remained of his body; a hideous, bloody mess with little flesh remaining about the bones. The head had disappeared, having evidently been carried off by one of the monsters.

In that island of barren rock there was no place to give his remains burial, so they had to leave them where they were and set about the by no means easy task of launching themselves on to the weed.

De Brissac insisted that the other two should wait until he had made the first attempt. The difficulty lay in getting himself high enough into the air to operate his stilts as he could not jump because his legs were attached to them.

Retreating up the slope some fifty yards from the water's edge he lay down on a flat rock with the stilts dangling behind him. Holding his ski-sticks short he jumped awkwardly from his knees. His stilts dragged as he took off, but using his ski-sticks gripped short to force himself up into the air he managed to gain just enough height to come upright by the time he reached the weed. While he bobbed about there the others followed his example in turn and when they were all launched the two men took Yonita's arms so as to support her between them on account of the pain she was suffering in her feet.

For a little De Brissac chanted 'One, two—three!' as they hopped along in unison, but soon that was no longer necessary; by six o'clock they had landed safely on Yonita's island.

The shore had the same barren, deserted look as the island on which they had passed the night. Yonita said that her people rarely came down to the beaches. She had heard tell that each time a new batch of castaways reached the island they always attempted to vary their diet by catching fish, but soon abandoned the attempt. No boat could be poled more than fifty feet out into the weed without danger from the devil-fish, swarms of small but fierce sea-leaches infested the shallows, making bathing impossible, and occasionally giant crabs had been seen slithering from rock to rock at sundown.

They freed themselves of their stilts, and, partially supported by their balloons, clambered up a long, shelving cliff which rose to about sixty feet above sea-level. From its top Yonita was able to point out the nearest farmhouse almost concealed by a low coppice of trees some mile and a half away. Tethering the balloons securely in a sheltered pocket on the cliff top they set out for the farm.

Yonita protested that she could manage all right, but she was limping over the rough ground so painfully that De Brissac insisted on carrying her. In spite of her adorable little figure he found her no light weight, and after a time he had to pass her over to Basil. Carrying her in turns they covered the mile and a half, and, passing along the edge of a field of maize, came to an orchard of apple, pear and cherry trees amidst which the farm was set.

Its owner was just setting off to his fields for the day's work. Immediately he caught sight of them he dropped his farm implements and came towards them at a run; the look of amazement on his lean face giving place to one of excited pleasure as he recognized Yonita.

De Brissac set her down and she introduced her rescuers to the farmer, Silas Randel, who was the son of one of the American whaler crew that had reached the island in '79. He was a tall, gaunt man of fifty.

'Well, well, well!' he exclaimed again and again as he slapped the two strangers affectionately on their backs. 'If this isn't the best news ever. Come right along to the home now. We've scarce finished breakfast, but my little Elsa will cook you another and welcome. Well, well, well, just to think of you tricking them sons of Satan and getting back to your own folk like this.'

His *little* Elsa proved to be a buxom woman of forty-odd, the granddaughter of one of the Norwegian sailors and three of the earlier colonists. She fussed over Yonita like a distracted hen, endeavouring to bathe her guest's feet with some soothing lotion and cook a fresh meal at the same time. To help and hinder her she had her only son, a wildly excited, red-haired boy of twelve.

The meal was plain but abundant, cereals, ham and eggs, home-made bread and a cherry conserve; washed down by large mugs of steaming mint tea. Basil noted the absence of milk, butter and sugar from the table, and when he had explained what such things were, Yonita told him that they had no cows although she knew what a cow was from having seen a picture of one in a book that had been salvaged from a wreck. They also lacked both sugar-cane and beet, but had bees, and honey for sweetening things and making jam. Neither tea nor coffee could be grown in their island, even if they had had the plants, owing to the temperate climate and cold winters; the usual drinks were mint or verbena tea, and cider and perry made from the apples and pears in the orchards.

With breakfast over, much fortified and revived, they proposed to set out again at once; reluctant as their kind hosts were to let them go. Silas had already sent his small son off to the village in the centre of the island to let Sir Deveril Barthorne know of

Yonita's escape, and now he got out a hand-cart for her to travel in.

The road was no more than a narrow track as hand-carts were the only vehicles on the island, there being no horses or oxen to draw wagons. The Randels accompanied their guests, and half a mile from the farm they were met by young Sir Deveril and the whole population of the village, which had turned out to welcome them. The men were clad in old-fashioned, long-waisted coats and baggy breeches somewhat resembling plus-fours, the women in short pleated skirts like Yonita's.

Sir Deveril Barthorne was a fine, tall young man of twenty-six. He embraced Yonita again and again almost crying with delight at her safe return, while the others, men, women and children, crowded round Basil and De Brissac, wringing their hands, kissing them and hailing them with overwhelming gratitude as Yonita's rescuers.

The excitement took a good quarter of an hour to subside, but when it had died down a little they went on their way once more; the strangers now having some chance to observe the more highly cultivated portion of the island.

At this end it was mainly downland which lent itself to agriculture; broad fields of Indian corn and wheat were interspersed with well-planned orchards of apple, plum and cherry. Having no cattle the islanders devoted no land to grazing and there were no hedges, as all property was held in common. As they topped a rise dense woods showed in the distance, on higher ground across a park-like area in the shallow valley that lay below them.

Sir Deveril explained that the valley was roughly the centre of the island, and that his ancestors had deliberately left about ten acres surrounding their home uncultivated. There was no village in the ordinary sense of a narrow, crowded street, the houses being scattered through the park, each with its own garden.

Basil thought the arable land through which they had passed might well have been a portion of Kent or Sussex, and the park had something of the look of an English estate, largely owing to the magnificent cedars that graced it, but the houses had a queer, foreign air.

They were all built of thick logs, and with one exception were only one storey high, but there was nothing shack-like or impermanent about them. The majority were irregular in shape but of considerable size, obviously having been built on to from time to time and containing a dozen or more rooms. No farmyards or unsightly lean-tos marred their pleasant appearance as they lay there sleeping in the sun between the great cedars, and Sir Deveril explained that both the chicken and pig farms of the island commune were situated farther up the opposite slope of the valley towards the woods.

The whole party headed for the solitary two-storied building; it was windowless and presented the appearance of a huge barn. At first De Brissac supposed it was the church, but Yonita informed him that the church had been burnt down nearly a century before and they had never built another.

'Do you not follow any religion then?' he asked.

She shook her head. 'We have no religion as you understand it. For nearly two hundred years we lacked the benison of a priest in our land. Protestant and Catholic settlers each followed their religion according to their consciences and brought up their children in their faith, but neither sect had the temerity to build a church since none could officiate in it without being guilty of blasphemy and all held nonconformity in abhorrence. The Sir Deverils married and buried people as captains do on ships, but they could not give communion, and the people met on Sundays only to sing hymns and pray together. On the coming of Father Jerome they built a church owing to their particular regard for him, but no good came of it. The Protestants all became monstrous bigoted and refused to pray with the Catholics; and the Catholics began to detest the Protestants and call them heathens. For a few years there was bitter strife between the two factions until one night the church was burnt down and Father Jerome lost his life trying to save the sacred ornaments. After that the two sects made up their differences and decided not to hold any religious meetings at all so that there should be no further cause for trouble and dissension.'

'Yet you wear a crucifix,' remarked De Brissac.

'Ah, that is different,' she smiled. 'We all reverence God and pray in private when we have occasion to do so. Our mothers instruct us in the teachings of Jesus Christ and we follow them so far as we are able in our daily lives. For us, the Cross has a special significance. 'Tis scarce to be expected you will have observed it yet, but our island is shaped like a crucifix. We landed but now on the short, northern shore which forms its foot. Perchance you may say it is a folly in us but we believe that the Good God made it so; placing it in the very heart of this desolate sea which holds so much evil as a protection and a refuge for poor, shipwrecked people.'

As they entered the large building the newcomers saw that it consisted of a single, lofty room. From its rafters hung two rows of flags; the faded ensigns of the ships that had foundered in the bay to eastward. Sir Deveril pointed out his own ancestor's flag, the Leopards of England quartered with the Fleur-de-lis of France which he had flown as a Royalist Admiral in the Civil War against Cromwell, and, stranger still to behold, the Skull and Crossbones on a black ground that had waved over many a bloody fight from the masthead of the Red Barracuda, who had reached the island in 1744.

Other islanders were constantly arriving from the more distant houses as the news of Yonita's return spread. Her Uncle Cornelius, a tall, Spanish-looking man with a fine aquiline nose and sweeping black moustache, came hurrying into the hall and embraced his beautiful little niece with fervour. He assured Basil and De Brissac that never, if he lived to be a thousand, could he repay them for their services.

In the meantime long trestle tables were being erected and the olive-skinned women of the island were bustling about them setting out a meal. All of them wore costumes of home-woven stuffs, but the variety of colours and cut showed some individual taste; the men's coats and breeches were of the same materials. The visitors protested that they had eaten a hearty breakfast barely an hour before but they were forced to sit down and do their best to appear appreciative of the abundance of good things that were pressed upon them.

The meal provided one surprise after another for the principal guests, in the many articles in everyday use the islanders appeared to lack and the many others one would have supposed them unable to make, yet which they had managed to create by applying much ingenuity to their limited resources. Articles of their own manufacture supplied the needs of the table. Wooden spoons and forks took the place of cutlery, but no knives were used as there were no solid dishes of meat which needed cutting up. The drinking vessels consisted of gaily coloured, home-made pottery.

Yonita's uncle apologized that there was no wine as the island was too far south for them to grow vines, but a sparkling vintage cider was served with the meal and Basil declared that he had never tasted better. With the dessert a very palatable plum brandy made its appearance and numerous cordial toasts were drunk in it.

Having slept little over six hours in the last fifty Yonita was now absolutely dropping with fatigue, while Basil and De Brissac were also badly in need of rest. Sir Deveril seeing their plight, rescued them out of the hall, through a pretty garden, to his own residence which lay only a few hundred yards away.

The house was long, low and rambling with a wide veranda running all down the south side of it and a big lily pool beneath its principal windows; all but four of these being no more than salvaged cabin ports inserted in the tree-trunk walls.

The inside of the house intrigued the visitors even more than the outside had done. All the rooms had a strange atmosphere of the sea about them as so many things salvaged from the ships had gone to their furnishing. Each room had a huge, open fire-place on account of the cold winters and the walls were hung with canvas cut from ships' sails and awnings. Upon them for decorative purposes were a few cheap-looking coloured illustrations taken from old magazines, all neatly framed, a fine collection of ancient weapons and many lovely old maps.

When Basil asked if he could have a bath, his host looked a trifle worried, and it soon transpired that in such matters the islanders had not made any advance since Georgian days, but Sir Deveril assured him that it could be arranged.

He was shown to a spacious room and an ancient hip bath was carried in with numerous cans of hot water from the kitchen. De Brissac came in and shared the welcome tub. Ten minutes later both of them were tucked up on comfortable divans and no sooner had their heads touched their pillows than, with no further thought of their unusual surroundings, they fell asleep.

CHAPTER XV

THE GREEN DEVIL

WHEN De Brissac's party had left the ship most of the others went below, but Unity remained on deck watching the four figures bounding away across the weed into the distance until all trace of them was lost in the rising mist.

She tried to comfort herself with the thought that their journey to the shore would take only an hour, and that, as the balloons buoyed them up so easily, there was little chance of their falling into the weed; but now that the mist and twilight had come there was no means of witnessing their safe arrival. She knew she was in for a miserable night of worry over Basil's safety and would not be able to think of anything else until he returned to the ship on the following morning.

As she turned away from the rail she saw Harlem Joe grinning at her. The big stoker was leaning against a staunchion with his hands in his pockets. Since the mutiny he had given no trouble whatever, and, in fact, had even exerted himself to urge his black buddies to do their utmost in every fresh effort which was required for the safety of the whole company; yet Luvia always kept a wary eye upon the big negro fearing that he was only biding his time for a propitious opportunity to assert himself again.

'Mistah Sutherland hops very pretty over dat weed,' he remarked to Unity conversationally.

The man's tone was civil enough so she replied at once. 'Yes. Balloon-jumping's much simpler than it looks at first sight.'

'Ah'll say you's right,' Harlem nodded, 'but dere ain't much to it on dat island when a feller gets dere? Dat's what's bitin' me.'

'Oh, there are people and farms. Nothing very exciting, I'm afraid, but anyhow safety and no lack of food.'

'Shua, but one island's fer de white folks and one fer de coloured folks—so ai'se hearin'. What does you figger Mistah Luvia's goin' to do wid Corncob an' li'l Harlem?'

'I really don't know,' Unity said vaguely. 'It all depends which island we drift to. If we've got to stay here all our lives I expect you'd rather settle with your own people, wouldn't you?'

'Ah certainly would. Ah'se been talkin' with dem wounded fellers up in de poop-house. Dey's poor uneducated trash but one of dem can speak a li'l English and dat island life in his dorp certainly does sound de goods. De women does all de work an' de men get all de eats. Dat shua suits me.'

Unity smiled. 'You ought to be ashamed of yourself expecting the women to work for you. I thought you were supposed to be an educated man.'

'Oh, ah'se educated all right, but ah likes dese old-fashioned notions 'bout havin' plenty of wives an' lettin' dem work fer me, see. 'Sides seein' ah'se an educated feller dese fool island niggers might make me king or somethin'. Ain't dat so?'

'Perhaps they might,' said Unity uncertainly, 'but I shouldn't count too much on getting to the coloured men's island yet. From what Mr. Luvia said this afternoon it looks as though we're drifting in the direction of the other. If we once pile up on the shore there I'm afraid there won't be much chance for you to cross the channel.'

Harlem spat a long squirt of tobacco juice out of the corner of his mouth over the ship's rail with considerable dexterity. 'Do dey have cops in dis white folks's island?' he asked thoughtfully.

'I don't know. They probably have a police system of some sort just to keep law and order.'

'Den Mistah Luvia may go a handin' Corncob, Nudäa and me over to dem cops for de li'l argument we had way back in de boat when we was out in de open seas.'

'This island's not like a proper port where it would be his duty to do that so I don't think you need be afraid. All of you deserve a stretch for having tried to kill us but the circumstances were very exceptional. As you've all worked so well ever since I should think Mr. Luvia would be inclined to let you down lightly.'

The negro scratched his woolly head and regarded her with a cunning look from his bilious, close-set eyes. 'Dat's O.K. by me,' he said slowly. 'Ah'se willin' to let bygones be bygones but how 'bout de future—when we'se on dis white folks's island?'

'Well, you'll settle down and work on a farm, I suppose, just like the rest of us, if we can only get there safely.'

'Dat's not so hot. Ah bin at de grind bes' part o' der time ah kin remember. Ah'se orl fer de soft life now. Can't Mistah Luvia land us fellers some way on de coloured folks's island? We'd be sittin' pretty den.'

Unity shook her head. 'I don't see how he can unless we drift there. He seemed certain this afternoon that the current's carrying us to the south-west now. He means to use the ship's engines, too when we get further in, at a very slow speed to help us a little; or to keep the ship broadside-on to the wind if that looks like giving us any assistance.'

Harlem gave an evil grin. 'Shua, ah had a hunch it'd be dat way. Dey's not fond of whites in de coloured folks's island—so de poor trash nigger wid de scalp wound says. De white dames is plenty welcome but dey bumps off de men because dey's top dogs in dis part of de world and dere ain't no white cops to prevent dese niggers having' deir way.'

'Yes, they've reverted to a stage of complete barbarity, I hear,' said Unity acidly, and she turned abruptly on her heel, leaving the hulking great negro grinning after her.

When she joined the others she told Luvia of her conversation with Harlem and asked him what he intended to do about the ex-mutineers.

He shrugged his big shoulders. 'We don't want 'em. They'll only cause trouble among Yonita's people. Start raping white women and get lynched or something. It's not natural to expect healthy animals like that to go without a woman all the days of their lives. I'd give 'em a break if I could but how we'd put the three of them over to their heathen soul-mates I just don't see.'

'You do think it's quite certain that we'll beach on Yonita's island then?'

'I can't guarantee it but things are sure shaping that way. While you were having your party with Basil this afternoon I was on the job checking compass bearings. We're several hundred yards west of where we were this forenoon so Satan's Island's a little farther off than it was then. First thing tomorrow I mean to check up again. Even if I can't shove her through the weed, I'll be able to turn the ship a bit so as to get the advantage of what little breeze there is. That'll help carry us into the main current.'

'You don't think Harlem and his friends are likely to cut up rough again, do you?'

'They may try an' pull a quick one but I doubt it'll do them any good. Corncob's out of it with De Brissac so there's only Harlem and Nudäa left in the ship. Jansen, Hansie, Largertöf, Vicente, Li Foo and I could mighty soon put them in the can.'

'How about the wounded negroes from the island?' Unity asked.

'One cashed in his checks this afternoon and another is booked for the Golden Shore tonight. The thigh-bone of the third was smashed by a bullet near the groin so he's a cripple for keeps. That only leaves the guy who stopped one with his woolly pate, and I reckon his headache'll keep him thinking plenty for the next two days.'

Unity went off to the galley to help Synolda prepare supper and they all met again when it was served. Conversation that night was almost entirely about Yonita's island, how soon they were likely to reach the shore and what the future might hold for them as settlers there. Almost immediately after the meal Unity went to her cabin, leaving Synolda, Vicente and Luvia together.

Vicente had recovered from his mauling by the octopus the day before although he was still somewhat stiff and bruised. To prevent Luvia getting ahead of him with Synolda again he suggested at once that she might like to come out and sit up on the poop with him.

'No thanks,' she gave a little shudder. 'I'm not going on deck with anybody after dark again unless I have to. You seem to've forgotten pretty quickly what happened to poor Bremer in the early hours this morning.'

'But we would sit amidships,' he protested, 'and the octopus's tentacle is not so long that 'e should get us there.'

'I don't know so much,' she replied quickly. 'From what I've seen of them they look about forty feet of wriggling horror. You can risk it if you like. I'm not going to.'

'Come with me up to the bridge then, please.'

Luvia glanced across. 'Sorry to spoil your evening, Vedras, but I guess you've forgotten you're just about due for your watch below. We've got to keep the boilers going, else I won't be able to manœuvre the ship tomorrow.'

Vicente banged the table angrily. 'You take advantage, I am a passenger. Work in the stoke'ole is not for me.'

'Oh, shucks!' Luvia shrugged. 'We sorted all that long ago. Sutherland's been taking his turn at the furnaces and De Brissac would have too if he hadn't only just become fit again. As it is he's been employed on other jobs and he's risked his neck going out there on to the weed tonight. You're only on a two-hour shift, instead of four, now there's no other work to be done. You've got nothing to kick about.'

'I am a passenger,' Vicente snapped standing up. 'My passage monies is paid before I leave Cape Town. I refuse more of the shovelling coal. You are employed by the Company. Do it yourself.'

'What the hell's bitten you?' Luvia asked. 'All this talk of passengers and companies is just boloney now we've all got to stick around these parts for the rest of our lives. We're just a bunch of folks who've been darn lucky to escape so far from a whole lot of tight spots and we've only done that because we've hung together, taking an equal share in the jobs that had to be done.'

'I do not care,' cried Vicente flushing scarlet. 'If what you say is so and there are passengers no more, then there are officers no more also. We are equals. Why should I shovel coal for making boilers steam while you sit 'ere drinking at your pleasure? It is your turn to make the fire.'

'Sorry,' Luvia said coldly, 'but I'm afraid that's not quite how it pans out. If we get to Yonita's island we'll all have to work, I guess, and I'll be happy to do just the same share of hoeing and reaping as they hand you. But as long as we're on the *Gafelborg*, I'm running the outfit. It hasn't been all jam for me whatever you may think; and this past fortnight I've had a darn sight less sleep than you. I could do your job but you can't do mine. That's the way it is and that's the way it'll be till we're safe ashore, whether you like it or no.'

'So!—then I will make choose my own hour. I will work from two to four or four till six, but at the present I remain 'ere.'

'Oh, Vicente, don't be such a fool,' Synolda broke in. 'You're behaving like a perfect child.'

'You wish to get rid of me, eh?' he challenged suspiciously.

'Oh, no,' she protested quickly. 'Of course we don't. But it's so stupid to try and upset the running of everything like this when there's nothing to be gained by it.'

'I am the one to say that,' he snapped.

Luvia stood up, towering above the Venezuelan. 'Listen here, Vedras. I'm through. If you fix it to swop watches with one of the others any time I won't hold out on you for the necessary O.K., but it's a piker's trick on the rest of the bunch to fall down on your job without warning. Either you go below and get busy, or I'll have to take you by the seat of your pants and pitch you in the can. You won't find it any too pleasant trying to sleep off this pet of yours in irons.'

175

Vicente's face momentarily lost its rich colouring. 'Enough!' he cried. 'You threaten me! All right! I do the fires; but you shall 'ear more of this.' Angrily he swung away and stamped down the companionway.

Synolda smiled as she saw him go. She was no longer frightened of Vicente, only, in the darkness of her heart, a little sorry for him. She had never actively disliked him and understood so well the torture of jealousy he was suffering at the moment. Three nights before their situation had been very different; they had both expected then that a few more days might see the *Gafelborg* docking at a South American port. Now, there did not seem the faintest prospect that they would ever again reach the world that lay outside the weed continent.

'What about another drink?' Luvia suggested, breaking in on her thoughts.

'Grand,' she said. 'As we've been left all on our own don't you think we might run to a bottle of fizz?'

'Why, sure.' He gave a happy laugh. 'If you'd like it, honey. There's no more in Hansie's store but I'll go below and open up a case.'

Left to herself her mind reverted to the irate Venezuelan. The future was still a little uncertain, but the day's events pointed strongly to the *Gafelborg*'s company joining the colonists on Yonita's island and settling down there. Synolda had already decided in her mind exactly the sort of settling down that she would like to do. Men could be a bore when you didn't like them, but life without a man was quite unthinkable to her and, with a man one really liked to shoo off the others, a very delightful prospect indeed could be envisaged.

In Juhani Luvia she had met a man who really fulfilled her ideal of what a man should be—strong, kind, passionate, but not vicious; possessive, but not domineering—a Viking lover that any woman might envy her. Synolda's instinct told her that he was the faithful sort who would never look at another woman once he found one he truly cared about, and she meant to stick to him like glue. She had had much more experience than most women crammed into a lifetime, although she was only twenty-six, and she meant to make Juhani just the most faithful and adoring wife that any man could have, if, of course, he would have her.

She didn't think there was much doubt about that. It was hardly likely he would wish to remain single all his days, and beyond a pleasant friendliness he showed not the least interest in

176

Unity. There might be attractive girls on the island, but Synolda was quite prepared to nail her flag to the mast against all comers there. So many men had told her she understood the art of love to perfection that she had some reason to believe it, and, although she had been reluctant to stop painting her face at first, when she had made her bargain with Luvia, she had very soon come to see that with the healthy life on shipboard she was now looking years younger and infinitely more attractive.

She began to assess the possible harm that Vicente could do her if he turned really nasty. He might still tell Luvia and the rest what he knew about her past, but that did not unduly perturb her. If Juhani was in love with her he would understand all that, so, she thought, would the others. It was the police she was scared of, but no one could extradite her to South Africa from Yonita's island.

She made up her mind, there and then, that she would spike Vicente's guns by telling Juhani the whole truth about her flight from Cape Town at the first opportunity. For the next two hours there was little likelihood of their being disturbed so she would start working round to the subject directly he returned with the champagne.

A more tricky problem was the danger that if Vicente's jealousy led to another violent scene with Luvia the Venezuelan might announce that she had already given way to him. She wondered how Juhani would take that? He was a man of the world, so, if he was as fond of her as she supposed, she did not think that, apart from being naturally upset, he would hold it against her when he knew she had been forced to it. At the same time, Synolda was well aware that men were strange creatures and regarded the lapses of women they were in love with very differently from their own. The young Finn was such a straightforward fellow he might take it very badly indeed and refuse to have anything more to do with her.

That was a most unpleasant thought. She wondered if, perhaps, she had better tell Juhani about her reluctant surrender to Vicente as well as about being wanted by the police, but the shipboard episode was just the sort of thing that might linger and rankle in his mind. Much as she wanted to play fair with him she decided, out of the depths of her practical wisdom, that she had far better not risk it. Vicente could not show one atom of proof that he had ever spent a night in her cabin, and, if she denied it strongly enough, Juhani would certainly believe her rather than

177

him. The accusation could easily be attributed to jealous spite in view of the way Vicente so consistently dogged her footsteps.

Just as she had reached these decisions Juhani appeared with a bottle of champagne in each hand. Setting them down on the table he stooped and kissed her. She flung an arm round his neck, and, moving her mouth to his ear, whispered: 'Isn't it fun being on our own like this. We can make a night of it, can't we?'

He kissed her again and smiled down into her eyes. 'We certainly can, sweetheart, and I'll bet that's what Vicente's thinking. Poor sap, I passed him with the fizz in my hands just a moment back as he was going from his cabin down to the stokehold. He looked sicker than any dog.'

'Poor dear,' she laughed, 'he's not a bad sort. He's just terribly jealous, that's all.'

Luvia picked up one of the bottles and began to open it. 'Well, so'd I be if I thought you were interested in him.'

'How do you know I'm not?' Synolda smiled.

'Stop kidding now. How could you be, honey—a sweet thing like you—interested in that greasy wop, and—snakes alive—he's old enough to be your granddad!'

She shrugged impatiently and held her glass for him to fill. 'Nonsense, he's not much past the middle forties and I'm an old woman of twenty-six. Let's forget him and drink a toast.'

'Right; what'll we drink to?'

'Yonita's island,' she suggested.

'Sure—Yonita's island, and the happiness we'll be finding there.'

She leant towards him. 'How are you so certain we're going to find happiness?'

'It's just round the corner if you want it. I'll make you happy, Synolda, sweet, or I'll die in the attempt.'

For a moment she stared at him solemnly with her fine blue eyes. Her slant eyebrows tilted a little. 'D'you mean that, Juhani? You really want me for keeps?'

'I certainly do. You're the sweetest and loveliest thing I've ever set eyes on. To hell with the sea. It's all right for a single man but no sort of life when you're married. I'm mighty glad things have panned out just this way. I won't have to leave you, to go racketing round the world patching up engines any more, to make a living. My granddad was a farmer, home in Finland, and I spent a good bit of my boyhood on his farm. I know quite a piece about farming, and I'm not scared of having to till a hunk of land. These

178

islanders must be decent folk, too, from what that Spanish-looking kid said this forenoon; a simple, happy sort of crowd to live among. No taxes, no wars, no crook politicians, or any other darned thing to worry about. It'll be grand—simply grand!'

She smiled again. 'Juhani, I don't believe I've ever heard you make such a long speech before. But it sounds lovely and I'm going to adore it—adore every minute of it.'

He pulled her on to his lap. They kissed again, drank more champagne and he sighed contentedly. 'We'll get the local islander who does parson to hitch us up just as soon as we get ashore. No long engagements, or money to save, or furniture to buy, or anything. And you to make love to all day and all night too. Gee! What a break we're having after all.'

She stroked his fair hair gently. 'It is rather fun, isn't it? To think things have been made so simple for us compared with the trouble and waiting so many couples have to put up with before they can become man and wife. But I want you to be quite certain, Juhani darling, because I've had a bit of a past—two husbands already—you know.'

'Oh, shucks! What's that matter?'

'It doesn't really, I suppose, but I do think you ought to know all about me first.'

'Aw, what the hell! Haven't I got you in my arms right now? That's all that matters, honey. That and keeping you there.'

'You'll keep me there all right. You needn't be afraid about that. But you hardly know a thing about me and I've led a pretty hectic life. Juhani?'

'Yep.'

'Apart from my two husbands—there have been other men.'

'Plenty of girls have their fun before they're married, these days, so that doesn't cut any ice.'

'Yes, but with me it was afterwards.'

He wriggled uneasily. 'Well, let's not talk about that. Whoever they were we shan't be running up against them here. We're starting clean and fresh and straight so the past's a washout, and nothing in it can come between us.'

A rap on the door-jamb made them swing round quickly. Hansie was standing there; grimed with the dirt of the stokehold from which he had just come. 'Beg pardon, sir,' he said a little sheepishly, 'but Mr. Vedras 'as just relieved me and 'e asked me to give Mrs. Ortello this *billy doo*.'

Synolda slipped off Luvia's knee and took the white envelope

179

which had a greasy thumbmark smeared with coal dust on it. 'Thanks, Hansie,' she said laying it on the table.

'You're welcome, Mrs. Ortello,' Hansie grinned and disappeared again through the doorway.

She perched herself back on Juhani's knee, but he stretched out a hand, picked up the note from the table and gave it to her.

She hesitated, twisting it between her fingers, uncertain what sort of a message it might contain and feeling somehow vaguely reluctant to open it in front of him.

'Go on,' he said, 'don't mind me. What's poor old Vicente got to say?'

'It can't be anything of importance,' she smiled, letting it slip from her fingers to the floor as she turned her face to Juhani for another kiss.

He retrieved it quickly and handed it back to her. 'But, honey, if he didn't want you to have it at once, he wouldn't have bothered to send it up. Open it and have done.'

Synolda's heart began to beat heavily under her breast. She cursed her luck that the note should have arrived at the very moment when she had led the conversation so neatly to the point where she could tell Juhani the awful thing that had driven her to join the *Gafelborg* in such a hurry just as it was sailing. The letter might be nothing more than a simple request from Vicente for a chance to plead his cause with her alone, but she half-feared it would be one of abuse. She could hardly prevent Juhani seeing its contents if she opened it there sitting on his lap. With a little breathless movement she flung it back on to the table. 'It *can't* be anything that matters, and I want to talk to you. Vicente can tell me what it is himself in the morning.'

'Just as you say, sweetheart,' Luvia replied casually and Synolda suppressed a sigh of relief but, at that very moment, Hansie appeared in the doorway again wiping his hands upon a grimy towel.

'Beg pardon, Mrs. Ortello. I quite forgot, but Mr. Vedras said would I take him down an answer to that note.'

'Aw, hell!' exclaimed Luvia, snatching up the envelope again and thrusting it into Synolda's unwilling hands. 'Go on. Get it over with. What in heck does the fellow want!'

Synolda tried to stop her heart pounding as she slit the envelope with her thumb and drew out the single sheet of paper. Her scared glance took in the large clear writing.

'Synolda, my lovely one,

Your poor Vicente's heart is desolate because he sees that you mean to betray him. I love you so much that I forgive you in advance hoping that tomorrow night, or the next night, I shall be the lucky one again. If I am unjust to you, I beg so much that you will forgive me, and leave the light burning in your cabin so that I may see it through the chinks of the door when I come off the duties at midnight. To spare me agonies, if you can, send word by Hansie, just 'Yes' that I may come to you tonight. In the meantime I kiss again in my imagination that adorable mole placed so right below your heart.

Your despairing Vicente.'

At the sight of the first words Synolda endeavoured to crumple the note up but Juhani, without any deliberate attempt to read the letter, could not help catching sight of the last line. Instantly he gripped her hand that held the sheet of paper and kept it firm until every word of Vicente's pointed foreign writing had seared into his brain like drops of acid.

Slowly he let go her hand, thrust her gently from him, and stood up. Staring at Hansie he said in a thick voice, 'O.K. Hansie, tell Mr. Vedras the answer will be "Yes".'

'Sure, sir, sure.' Hansie gave a puzzled glance at the grey face of his officer and shuffled rapidly away.

The sound of Hansie's footsteps died out in the distance. For a few moments there was dead silence in the lounge; the utter quiet of the motionless ship at night caught fast in the dread, mysterious weed sea, completely cut off from all healthy, normal things. Synolda broke it. White-faced and shaking, she stared into the grim, golden-bearded mask that Juhani's handsome features had become.

'Juhani,' she stammered.

'You slut,' he roared, his blue eyes blazing. 'You slut. I wouldn't have believed it!'

'Juhani,' she pleaded, 'Juhani, let me explain.'

'There's nix to explain. You've had that blasted Venezuelan for your lover only a night or two ago. That's dead plain from the letter in your hand. Good God, how could you? That filthy wop! Just to think of it makes me so I could be sick right now.'

'Juhani,' she whispered. 'It isn't true. It isn't true.'

'Huh! sez you!' he sneered, and shooting out his big hand he seized the frail fabric of her dress at the neck, ripping it, in one savage tug, nearly down to her waist. Her right breast remained partially concealed by the torn dress but the left stood out round and perfect. Below it, clearly exposed to view, there showed the tell-tale red mole.

'There,' he pointed furiously. 'You can't wash that off any more than you can clean your lips of lies. God, just to think the very first time I fall good and proper it should be for a whore. And you made me think you loved me.'

'I do,' she whimpered, 'oh, I do, Juhani. *Please* let me explain. I don't care one snap of the fingers for Vicente—I——'

'That's another lie. You let him sleep with you.'

'I hate him—I swear I do.'

'Then you're more rotten than I thought. You hooked the poor devil just for fun and now you're driving him half-crazy with jealousy. I wouldn't have Vicente's leavings if you paid me and I'll not see him done dirt either. You led him up the garden. Since you've slept with him before you can darn well go on sleeping with him.'

'But, Juhani, I don't want to,' she gasped between her sobs. 'I'd die rather than have to do it again.'

'You can damn' well die then!' he raved. 'Vicente wants you—wants you like hell—but I don't. You're his woman by your own choice. Now he's got that message he'll be along to you at midnight. If he's not a spineless sap he'll beat you up for trying to double-cross him. Well, you can yell your head off, but you won't get any help from me.'

Synolda's tears ceased as suddenly as they had begun. 'I won't need your help,' she snapped. 'I'm not letting Vicente into my cabin tonight—or any other night. I don't belong to him.'

'Oh, yes you do!' In his demoniacal rage Juhani's blue eyes glinted hard as sapphires. 'No woman's got the right to do what you've done to Vicente and go cold on a man without giving him a break to work it off. I'm taking you down to your cabin now—get that. I'll have the bolt off the door and lock it—then I'll send him down the key.'

'You swine!' she flared, 'you rotten swine, how could you? I'll kill him before I let him touch me.'

He shrugged. 'Sorry you don't like the idea. P'raps it'll teach you not to try making a monkey out of a simple guy like me. Come on now!'

Synolda tried to evade his clutch but he grabbed her by the

back of the neck and ran her towards the companionway. As they slithered down it she called him every name she could lay her tongue to in both English and Spanish but, utterly insensible to her curses and tears, he hustled her into her cabin and flung her sobbing upon the bunk.

CHAPTER XVI

DEATH IN THE *GAFELBORG*

So BLIND and bitter was Juhani's rage he was hardly conscious of what he was doing when he carried out his threat of smashing the bolt of Synolda's door, locking it, and sending Vicente the key. The discovery that his girl was carrying on an intimate affair with a man like the Venezuelan would have proved a rude shock for any young man in love, however sophisticated. To Juhani, whose experience of women had been very limited, the thought was so unbelievably horrible that it temporarily sent him almost off his head.

The young Finn was not a very susceptible type and, owing to the difficulties of marriage which face a sailor, he had never allowed himself even to think of it until Synolda set her cap at him. The propinquity which had been forced upon them since the shipwreck had placed him in closer contact with her than he had known with any woman near his own age since he had been at sea and, having once fallen for her, he had fallen utterly and completely. Now, this beautiful idol he had placed upon so high a pedestal and clothed in the rose-tinted gauze of so many romantic fancies had turned to carrion at his touch.

He had not attempted to seek an explanation for her conduct. The fact of it was enough to fill him with a nausea that sapped the strength out of his body and left his mind a whirl of tortured emotions.

Returning to the lounge he sat there for some time, his big figure hunched forward, his head between his hands, almost stupefied by anguish. After a little he sat up and gazed round listlessly; his eyes fell upon the bottle of champagne he had been sharing with Synolda and its fellow which still remained unopened. Pouring the remaining contents of the ullaged bottle into a tumbler he tossed it off. Quite unconsciously he was soon following the normal reaction of any healthy young man in such a state of despair. He opened the other bottle, drank half of it, decided that it had not enough kick to alleviate his misery, got himself a bottle of whisky from the bar, and proceeded, since champagne and whisky do not mix, to get drunk.

How long he sat there he could not have told, but he finished the bottle of whisky and, staggering slightly, moved over to get himself another when he caught sight of the clock; it stood at ten past twelve.

As he opened up the second bottle and poured himself a handsome ration it came to him that, by now, Vicente would have done his shift at the furnaces and be with Synolda or, even if he delayed to wash himself, would be with her very soon. Vivid pictures of them together began to dance in macabre and horrible imagery through his brain.

At one moment he was laughing drunkenly. If she didn't want Vicente, serve her damn' well right. She'd made her bed with him before so she could lie and rot in it now. But he didn't believe her outburst about hating the Venezuelan. How could that be so if she'd already let him make love to her? Juhani felt he ought to have thought of that before; the beautiful slut was probably just beginning thoroughly to enjoy herself with the amorous dago. He gulped down another drink. Well, he didn't care. At least, he tried to pretend he didn't; although in fact the thought of the girl in Vicente's gorilla-like embrace was utterly maddening to him.

He began to wonder vaguely and painfully what had caused her to go all out with a man like Vicente in the first place. There could be only one reason; she must be one of those abnormal dames who were really medical cases; terribly over-sexed and eager to take on any man who came along. Perhaps she would have taken him that way too if he'd played his cards differently and not talked a lot of hot air about marrying her. She'd been full of warm passion every time he'd embraced her, and probably thought him a mug for having been so slow to take advantage of her obvious liking for him. He *had* been a mug. He saw that now through the fumes of the whisky that were mounting to his brain. If he hadn't been a romantic nit-wit, he would have been just about where Vicente was now, two hours ago. She liked him—he liked her. She was no schoolgirl, had been married twice, and had admitted herself to having had affairs apart from her two husbands. Plenty of women did, Juhani knew, although he had rarely come across them owing to the greater portion of his waking hours, these last eight years, having been spent in the engine-rooms of ships.

185

He began to rate himself for a prize sucker. Any smart guy would have taken the lovely gift God had seen fit to send him. Synolda with her beauty could offer a poor sailor man a better time than he could ever hope to have from some casual pick-up on a night ashore. He had been plumb crazy ever to think of her as a girl to marry.

The second bottle of whisky was now half empty. The lounge swayed tipsily before his gaze. For a little time his mind went blank until a new thought entered it. Was it too late? Why allow Vicente to have all the fun? Whether Synolda liked the wop or not she obviously preferred him—Luvia. He had been pretty tough with her, but she was not the type to bear malice. Surely she'd make allowances seeing it was her own doing he'd got so het up. Why shouldn't he go down, give Vicente the air and make his peace with her? Say she refused to play? Well, that shouldn't stop him. He'd go nuts if he sat there much longer. To take her body by hook or by crook now seemed the only way to get her image out of his brain.

Unsteadily he stood up, knocked over his tumbler, kicked it aside with a curse and lurched towards the companionway. He steadied himself on the rail, laughing inanely. God, he was pickled! Hadn't been as canned as this for a whale of a while, but what the hell! He'd suck down a pint of water when he got below and sober up a bit. Negotiating six stairs successfully he tripped and sprawled down the rest on his back. For a few moments he lay where he had fallen, propped against the lower stairs, not feeling his bruises, but quite bemused and temporarily unable to think why he had come below decks.

His brain cleared and staggering to his feet he swayed down the passageway until he came opposite Synolda's cabin. A light showed through the crack of the door and muffled, angry voices came vaguely to him from within. Lurching forward he banged his fist heavily upon the door, and shouted, 'Vedras, comeouto-there.'

Instantly there was silence in the cabin.

Juhani banged again, this time as though he meant to batter in the panel. A key clicked in the lock and Synolda flung the door open. She stared at him; her eyes inflamed and angry. 'What d'you want?'

'You,' said Juhani, with a tipsy grin.

'You're drunk,' she cried. 'Get out!'

He stood there in the doorway swaying gently backwards and

forwards. Focusing his glance with difficulty he stared over Synolda's shoulder at Vicente, who was sitting on the edge of her bunk. The Venezuelan had on an ornate silk dressing-gown over his trousers but his shirt showed open at the neck partly exposing his hairy chest. Synolda was fully dressed and, in addition, had a belted raincoat strapped tightly round her. Evidently she had meant it when she had said she did not want Vicente and he had been pleading or arguing with her.

Taking a clumsy step forward Juhani put one foot inside the cabin. Synolda tried to thrust him back.

'You drunken brute!' she stormed. 'How dare you try to force your way into my cabin! No one has any right here unless I ask them.'

Juhani took not the least notice of her protest. Putting out a hand the size of a ham he swept her aside and advanced on Vicente.

The Venezuelan rose to his feet. 'What game is this you play!' he asked angrily. 'You are drunk. Yes, beastly drunk. Get out and leave us in peace.'

'Ge' out yourself,' Juhani muttered thickly. 'Ge' out, you louse—before—I breakyourneck.'

Vicente faced up to him squarely. 'If Synolda says she wish that I go—I go. Otherwise it is *I* who throw you out.'

Juhani turned slowly. Synolda's face danced up and down indistinctly before his blurred gaze as he said:

'D'you want this bird—or do I—gi' him the works?'

'I want my cabin to myself,' she snapped. 'Get out—both of you!'

'There!' Juhani rounded on Vicente. 'The pretty lady says you're to go. I'm goin' to stay a while—want to-talk-to-her.'

With a clumsy movement Juhani stretched out to grab Vicente's shoulder. Vicente stepped swiftly back, jerked up the skirt of his silk dressing-gown, and pulled an automatic from his hip pocket.

His dark eyes glowed with hate and jealousy as he jerked up the gun, pointing it at the young Finn's chest. 'Now!' he cried. 'I lose patience. If I were in South America I kill you long before this. Young fools should be taught it is not good to make interference with grown men. Out—or I shoot.'

Juhani's jaw dropped open but he next second his teeth closed with a snap and he came stumbling forward like a charging bull.

With a gasp of fear Synolda flung herself at Vicente and seizing the gun with both hands tore it from his grip. It went off in that confined space with a deafening explosion which seemed to rock the ship. The bullet passed within an inch of Synolda's thigh and thudded into the skirting-board by the cabin door.

For a second they all remained rooted where they stood. The gun clattered on to the floor from Synolda's nerveless fingers and from its barrel a little wisp of blue smoke curled up.

Suddenly, with a loud shout, Juhani flung himself forward again on Vicente and, succeeding in getting both hands on his throat, forced him backwards.

Vicente crashed into the fitted washbasin, twisted violently, and wrenched himself free. Next second he had snatched up the water carafe from the shelf above the basin and, swinging it high in the air, brought it crashing down on Juhani's head.

The young engineer gave one grunt and collapsed, the water dripping from his golden beard and the pieces of glass tinkling on the cabin floor all round him.

Synolda screamed and flung herself upon the prostrate man. 'You brute!' she spat at Vicente. 'You may have killed him.'

'What if I 'ave!' Vicente shrugged. 'This great barbarian comes only to molest you, and who but I should defend you from 'im?'

'You swine!' she sobbed. 'This is your fault—all of it—all of it. If you hadn't behaved like a beast in the first place this would never have happened. Seeing that note of yours tonight sent the poor lamb half crazy—and—and he's been drowning his misery in drink.'

In the midst of her outburst she snatched a towel, raised Juhani's head and, propping it on her lap, began to dab away the water and blood from his fair curls.

Before Vicente had a chance to reply there came the sound of running feet from the passage outside. The shot and Synolda's scream had roused the crew. Li Foo was the first to appear. Harlem Joe arrived a second afterwards from the opposite direction, and a moment later the whole ship's company was crowded shouting angry questions in the doorway. With the exception of Harlem and Nudäa they were all devoted to their officer, and it was obvious that Vicente had struck him down.

Old Jansen shouldered his way through the crush, crying, 'Wait now, wait! I will see what it is they make here.' He turned quickly to Synolda. 'What hass happen, Missus? He is not dead, no? That is too ill.'

188

'Only stunned, I—I think,' she stammered, 'but Mr. Vedras attacked him—and broke a bottle over his head.'

'So!' The old carpenter favoured Vicente with a stony glare; the crew muttered threateningly in chorus.

'I was protecting Madame Ortello. 'E was drunk and made to molest 'er,' Vicente said defiantly.

'That's a lie,' Synolda cried. 'He was trying to get you out of my cabin.'

'It's a lie all right,' Hansie piped up. 'Mr. Luvia likes his drop of liquor, but 'e's got a head like a rock. I've been with him two years, and I sure ain't ever seen 'im over the odds yet.'

'Let us beat him oop,' shouted young Largertöf, and the remainder of the crew surged struggling in the doorway as they forced their way into the small cabin.

Vicente's face went deadly white. It looked as though the furious seamen meant to murder him. Dropping to his knees he grabbed the gun Synolda had snatched from him and let fall. Jansen, Largertöf and Hansie, all sprang at him together over Luvia's body. The gun went off with another earsplitting detonation. Old Jansen coughed, moaned, and toppled sideways on to Synolda's bunk; the other two landed right on top of Vicente and pinned him to the floor.

For one wild moment the cabin was chock-full of struggling cursing humanity while Synolda, still crouching on the floor, strove to protect Juhani's head from further damage by holding it tightly in her arms.

The writhing Laocoön unwound itself; Vicente was lugged kicking and bellowing out into the passage; only Li Foo remained behind. Jansen had slipped from the bunk face downward on to the floor. The Chinaman turned him over and one look at his fixed, staring eyeballs was quite enough to show that he was dead.

'Diss a hollible—hollible for Missie,' he lisped as, stooping down, he took the dead carpenter by the shoulders and hauled him out into the passageway.

A muffled cry came from near by. Unity had just arrived from her cabin on the far side of the ship.

'Heap tlubble, Missie, but oll over now,' Li Foo said gently, and he stood aside for her to pass through the narrow doorway.

'Oh, God!' she exclaimed as her glance fell on the second body. 'Poor Juhani's not dead too, is he?'

Synolda looked up. 'No, thank Heavens. That swine Vicente

bashed the poor darling over the head with my water bottle. Fortunately it was not one of the heavy kind and he's got a good, thick skull. This is only a skin cut and it's practically stopped bleeding already.'

'Betteh getum up on bunk,' suggested Li Foo and, with the help of the two girls, he succeeded in lifting Luvia's heavy body.

'What on earth happened?' Unity asked. 'I heard the most awful riot going on and two shots fired.'

Synolda gave her a brief, staccato explanation and, between them, they bathed and bandaged Luvia's head. He was breathing stertorously now and Synolda guessed that from unconsciousness he had passed straight into a drunken stupor.

'Poh Misteh Luvia,' lisped Li Foo. 'You two Missie go-away. Li Foo undlessum. Mekum oll topsides fine.'

'No, we'll stay and help you,' Unity volunteered promptly, and between them they undertook the awkward business of getting the young Finn out of his clothes.

When he was comfortably tucked up in the bunk Unity turned to Synolda. 'The cabin next to mine is empty. I think you'd better doss down there for the night.'

'No, thanks.' Synolda shook her head sadly. 'I'd rather remain here in case he wakes and wants something.'

'That's hardly necessary,' Unity said. 'When he does wake he won't have anything worse than a splitting head. You look absolutely all-in, my dear. But if you insist on sitting up I'll stay with you if you like.'

'No, please,' Synolda begged. 'All this frightful business is my fault. I can only be thankful that he wasn't killed. As it is Jansen's lost his life, and God knows what they've done with Vicente.'

'They've only locked him in his cabin, I think—after giving him a dusting-up. They were hustling him into it when I came along, but perhaps I'd better go and see.'

While Unity was gone Li Foo carried the old carpenter's body away and came back with a bucket and mop. Hansie and Largertöf appeared behind him to inquire how their officer was and were greatly relieved to hear that he was only stunned. Having asked if they could do anything and been assured that their help was not needed they both moved off. Unity returned a few moments later.

'Vicente's all right,' she announced. 'He was groaning like a stuck pig but I spoke to him through the door. They locked him in there when they realized Juhani was still alive. It's hardly likely they'll have another go at him now they've gone off to their own quarters.'

'Thank God for that,' Synolda murmured. 'You get back to bed, my dear. I'll be all right here now.'

Li Foo had been busy mopping up the spilt blood from the cabin floor. He gave Synolda his friendly grin. 'Yoh'l be ollight, li'l Missie. Li Foo go mek yoh veh good cuppa tea. Yoh dlink um tea while Li Foo sit veh close ou' side oll time—see yoh plenty safe.'

Unity hesitated. 'You're quite sure you wouldn't rather I stayed to keep you company.'

'Yes—honestly. He'll sleep easier without the light. I'll wrap up in a rug and lie down on the settee; then I can switch it out.'

'All right then. Li Foo'll look after you, I know. Do try and get some sleep if you can.'

'I'll try,' Synolda promised as Unity turned away. 'Good night.'

Li Foo brought the promised tea and Synolda drank it grate- fully. The warm, aromatic brew soothed her frayed and shat- tered nerves. She tried to persuade the solicitous Chinaman to go to his own cabin but he would not hear of it. He had brought along a mat and pillow upon which he proposed to doss down in the passage outside her door all night. When he left her she examined Juhani's bandages again, kissed him tenderly on the forehead, curled up on the settee, and put out the light.

Juhani woke early: the faint luminosity of morning lit the cabin greyly. He lifted a hand to his aching head and was amazed to find it a normal size; it felt heavy as a millstone on his shoulders, but pulpy, as though it had been beaten with a flail from every angle. It ached atrociously, and violent stabbing pains shot through it. Not daring to move it but swivelling his eyes slightly he caught sight of Synolda, sound asleep on the settee opposite. The events of the previous night came flooding back to him, and he wondered what had happened to Vicente. He remembered being knocked out but could recall little that had gone before except his scene with Synolda in the lounge and getting blind drunk afterwards.

He supposed that she had put him to bed after having got rid of Vicente. She looked younger than ever, asleep there with her golden hair tumbled about her pale face. There was something pathetic and wistful about the droop of her mouth which made him want to stretch out his arms and comfort her in them, but he hardened his heart. The girl was a wrong 'un; any man's plaything. He'd have no more to do with her.

Very gingerly he eased himself up in the bunk and slid one foot out on to the floor. He noted with satisfaction that he had no pains in his limbs. It was only his head that hurt him so abominably; his mouth tasted as if it had been filled with cinders, the result of his knocking back the liquor so heavily; the cut was nothing he decided.

Seeing his clothes, which were neatly folded in a little pile on the floor, he drew his other leg from beneath the bed-clothes, stooped and almost fell, as something that felt like ten pounds of loose duck-shot sloped forward in his head, hit the front of his skull and nearly overbalanced him. He grabbed at his clothes, thrust them under one arm and standing up, tip-toed towards the door.

Synolda slept on without moving a muscle as he carefully extracted the key, opened the door, and slipped outside.

Li Foo rose like a dark shadow to meet him but drew back as he saw Juhani's imperative gesture for silence. Closing the door gently behind him Juhani locked it, took the key out and walked down the passage beckoning the Chinaman to follow.

Once in his own cabin he soused his splitting head in cold water and, while he dried himself, shot a few questions at Li Foo. On learning of Jansen's death he was inexpressibly shocked; realizing at once that he was the main cause of it. The cold sluice had cleared his wits a little. Having learned all that he could from the impassive Chinaman he dismissed him abruptly, dressed, and went on deck to try to cool his fevered head further with a breath of early morning air.

He found Unity already up, pacing uneasily to and fro on the fore-deck. She was keeping well amidships, evidently not daring to go near either rail for fear a lurking octopus should snatch her up in the same way that one had taken poor Bremer. Juhani would have avoided her if he could but he came upon her too suddenly to withdraw without some sort of greeting.

'Mornin'. How's things?' he said awkwardly, wondering how much she knew of the previous night's events and feeling utterly shamed, under the gaze of her level grey eyes, by the part he had played in them.

'Not too good,' she replied quietly; 'they won't be for me until Basil's safely back again.'

'I doubt De Brissac quitting the island much before noon.

They'll be keen to see this hick dorp we've got to settle in and he knows there's no mighty hurry to get back.'

She nodded. 'I suppose that is so but I was hoping Basil might decide to do the return trip first thing this morning and tell us all about it. How's the head?'

'Not so hot.' Juhani looked away ashamedly. 'I guess you know all about the rough-house last night?'

'Quite a bit; although I only arrived on the scene when the worst of it was over. You must have fallen for Synolda pretty badly.'

'That . . . !' he checked himself and substituted: 'What, her? Oh, I was playing around a bit but she gave me a raspberry. I ought'a had more sense.'

'Poor Juhani.' Unity's smile was kind and sisterly and sympathetic. 'I'm so sorry there's been trouble between you two. If you'd only seen her cradling your injured head in her arms last night, after you were knocked out, you'd realize how fond she must be of you. The two of you were just made for each other.'

'Well, I had a yen that way,' Juhani admitted reluctantly, 'but it just didn't work out. She's dirty—that's what she is—dirty under the skin. I'm through with her.'

'That's not true. Synolda's had a past and she admits it; but she wouldn't play a dirty trick on anyone.'

'Now listen, Unity. I don't want to put her in wrong with you but I've got to blow off steam to someone. If I don't I'll go plumb crazy and you're the only person left in the old hooker I can talk to. I've a hell of a lot to answer for, getting canned like I did— I'm wise to that—but this is the way it was.'

They fell into step; pacing back and forth amidships while he poured out his tortured thoughts. He ended up with an angry burst: 'There! that's the kind she is—so what would any feller do?'

Unity was silent for a moment. 'It's not a pretty story,' she said at last. 'I don't blame you for getting tight but Synolda's different from most girls—it's the life she's led. If you love her you ought to make allowances.'

'I did love her—I was absolutely nuts about her up to last night—but now I don't know if I love her or hate her. Anyway, she's a danger to Vicente and to me. I'm going to keep her locked up in her cabin and send her meals down to her by Hansie or the Chink until we pile up on the island.'

'How about Vicente?'

'That goes for him, too. The swine shot poor old Jansen and if we were docking in any ordinary port I'd have to hand him over to stand his trial for murder.'

'He thought they were going to kill him and fired in self-defence. It would never have happened at all if you hadn't got drunk, so you're as much to blame as he is.'

'I know it,' Juhani's haggard features were lit up for a second with a rueful grin. 'I suppose I ought to lock myself up as well but someone's got to run the ship.'

'Perhaps it's as well that the three of you should not meet again for a time. It won't hurt the others to stay below for the day, anyhow,' Unity said thoughtfully; feeling that would at least stave off any further trouble until Basil and De Brissac were back in the ship. 'I think I'd better go and cook breakfast.'

Juhani left her at the entrance of the galley and went aft. Gietto Nudäa suddenly popped up in front of him from the engine-room hatch. The half-caste seemed surprised to see Juhani and said quickly: 'Didn't know you was about, Mistah Luvia.'

'Well,' said Juhani abruptly, 'what of it?'

The half-caste shuffled. 'I dort you was all in after dat rough-'ouse lars' night.'

'What the hell's that got to do with you?'

'I would have come rouse you out early on.'

'Why?'

' 'Cos a' Harlem. De big stiff dort you was a gonner. He's bin an' skipped ship wid dat nigger what stopped one in de knob. Dey beat it with de odder two balloons jus' arter sun up.'

'The devil they did!' Luvia exclaimed. 'Made off to Satan's Island, eh? Why didn't they take you with them?' he added suspiciously. 'There were three balloons.'

Nudäa flared up angrily. 'I'se a white man, least dats what dey say, an' dem island niggers croak all de whites dey gets hold of.'

'I see, and as they wouldn't have you along you would have spoilt their little game by getting hold of me, if you'd thought I was fit to tackle them.'

'Sure—I don't owe dem notin'. I don't owe no one notin'. May der ole white sot an' der coloured bitch what made me rot in hell!'

Luvia nodded slowly. Poor devil, he was thinking. Half-caste —outcast—no race, no nation, neither liked nor trusted by men of either colour. Aloud he said as he turned away:

'Well, they've gone now and good riddance. Harlem won't be able to make any more trouble here, at least.' Fortunately, perhaps, he was unable to foresee the future and visualize events that were to take place before another twenty-four hours had passed.

CHAPTER XVII

LOVE IN YONITA'S ISLAND

I**T** **W**A**S** late afternoon when Basil woke. After a second he recognized his strange surroundings and sat up. Owing to the dim light which was all that filtered through the two portholes in the wall he imagined that it was already evening.

Jumping from his bed he ran over to one of the ports and looked out. To his relief he saw that the sunshine still etched the shadows of the great cedars sharply across the park-land and threw up the bright colours of the flowers in the garden immediately below. He knew Unity would have expected him back that morning and felt she must now be desperately anxious about him. His one thought was to relieve her anxiety by returning to the ship as quickly as possible. Pulling on a few clothes he hurried into the next room and roused De Brissac.

The Frenchman blinked a little and raised himself among the comfortable pillows of the broad bed.

'Come along,' Basil urged him, 'up you get. We don't want darkness to catch us again on our way back.'

De Brissac yawned and glanced round the dim room. 'But it is night already, *mon ami*, or nearly so. We must wait now to return until tomorrow.'

'Not a bit of it. This light's deceptive,' Basil assured him. 'It's not much past half past four. We can do it easily if only you'll hurry.'

'But why should one hurry?' De Brissac smiled. 'It is very comfortable here. Sir Deveril and his friends are quite charming and will certainly wish us to stay at least one night. Tomorrow is surely time enough to leave them.'

'The others will be anxious about us. Surely you see that. They don't even know that we managed to get here safely.'

'You talk nonsense, *mon vieux*. They all took it for granted that we should—as we did ourselves—otherwise we should never

196

have set out. It was sheer bad luck that we had to spend the night on that ghastly island.'

'Well, I want to get back,' said Basil stubbornly. 'It's barely an hour's walk to the cliff where we left the balloons and another hour to cross the weed. We should be there by half past six.'

'We will see,' De Brissac agreed non-committally. He was already looking forward with much pleasurable anticipation to his next conversation with Yonita and had not the least desire to hurry off to the *Gafelborg*.

An old-fashioned bell-rope dangled above the bed. De Brissac pulled it sharply, and a few minutes later an elderly, dark-skinned manservant appeared bringing jugs of hot water for them to shave. Basil returned to his own room and got through the business speedily. Immediately he was fully dressed he hastened back to De Brissac and hung about him impatiently while the Frenchman made a leisurely toilet. They then walked together down a passage to the main hall of the house.

Sir Deveril rose smiling to greet them from a big armchair and asked how they had slept.

Having assured him that they had had every comfort and were now completely refreshed, Basil immediately began to speak of their setting out on their return journey.

'Gad, gentlemen,' Sir Deveril expostulated, 'I do protest. Your coming is a great happening in our uneventful lives, and we owe to you the return of my adorable betrothed. All of us are desperate eager to honour you as you deserve, and during the time you have been refreshing yourselves, preparations have been going forward for a banquet at which you will be our guests tonight.'

'That's terribly nice of you,' Basil said quickly, 'and we appreciate it tremendously, but really we must get back. Our friends in the ship will have expected us this morning and by now——'

'My dear fellow, you exaggerate,' De Brissac broke in. 'I never said anything to Luvia about our returning today, and as you know, he hoped to manœuvre the ship nearer in. I see no reason why we should go back to the ship at all; we might just as well wait here until the others are able to land.'

'What!' exclaimed Basil. 'But we can't possibly do that. It may be days until the *Gafelborg* beaches; and all that time the others won't know if we're alive or dead.'

'But they have not the least cause to believe any accident has befallen us and I would much prefer to stay here.'

'Well, you can please yourself,' said Basil stubbornly. 'I'm going back tonight.'

'If you insist . . .' the Frenchman shrugged, 'naturally I would not let you make the journey alone. We can only apologize to Sir Deveril, then, and ask him to make our excuses to his friends.'

Sir Deveril's young face showed deep disappointment but he did not seek to dissuade Basil further; only insisted that they should have some sort of meal before they set off.

Basil did not even wish to wait while food was prepared and De Brissac mocked him a trifle acidly. 'Yesterday it was you who must linger talking to Unity and delaying our departure while I was so anxious to be off. Today it seems I am not even to be permitted to take a meal before we start.'

'We could have sandwiches, perhaps,' Basil suggested, 'if Sir Deveril would be so kind; and eat them during our walk across the island.'

'I pray you command me,' Sir Deveril said. 'I will order them if you wish; but Yonita is not yet awake and she'd be monstrous angry if I let you depart without your taking leave of her.'

De Brissac frowned. 'She must need many hours sleep after all she has been through, so it seems a great pity to wake her. Really, Basil, I do think it would be better if we put off our return until tomorrow at least.'

'You stay by all means, I can manage quite well alone, but I mean to go back tonight.'

'No, no, either we stay or go together. Since you are adamant upon the point, Sir Deveril, I am sure, will make our farewells to Yonita.'

The young baronet laughed. 'Stap me, I wouldn't dare. She is the sweetest minx, but she has the very devil of a temper. I'll have them call her and prepare a cold collation for you.'

While he was gone they hung about examining the curios and old charts with which the comfortable room was decorated. His return was followed by the appearance of the manservant with two large packages of food.

'We may as well eat it while we're waiting for Yonita,' De Brissac suggested and they set-to on their picnic meal; Sir Deveril bringing them a selection of the island's fruit drinks to wash it down.

Time drifted by but Yonita failed to put in an appearance. De

198

Brissac chatted amicably with Sir Deveril but Basil showed constant irritation and impatience. At last he said:

'Look here, we simply must get off. We've nearly four miles to walk and nothing will induce me to spend the night fighting those foul crabs again.'

'Nor me,' De Brissac assured him, 'but since Sir Deveril has had Yonita called specially to say good-bye to us we cannot possibly depart without seeing her.'

'I will leave you to urge haste upon her,' Sir Deveril volunteered. 'But methinks she is contriving a very special toilet.'

He was away for over a quarter of an hour, yet when he came back Yonita was not with him. 'She prays your indulgence,' he smiled, 'but she refuses to be hurried.'

De Brissac laughed and settled himself more comfortably in his chair, apparently quite happily resigned to await her pleasure, but Basil paced up and down the room frowning angrily.

At last Yonita joined them. She looked an entirely different person to the little, shrinking, half-clad creature they had brought to the island that morning. Now she was dressed in a beautiful, old-fashioned, wide-skirted satin garment that was almost a crinoline; a design of sprigged flowers was embroidered on it and her golden arms and bosom looked like fragile china against the great puffed sleeves and shoulders. Her dark hair was carefully parted in the middle and curled into lovelocks which fell each side of her small, oval face in the manner of the late seventeenth century.

She swept them a mocking curtsy. 'Your servant, sirs! Am I not worth waiting to see in my gala costume?'

With a quick catch of the breath De Brissac stepped forward, and, taking one of her little hands, kissed it. 'You are enchanting, Mademoiselle, positively enchanting, but how did you ever manage to come by this lovely dress in your island prison?'

'It graced the fair form of one of my ancestresses and has passed down through the family. We keep such heirlooms with uncommon care and wear them only on memorable occasions. It scarce looks two hundred years of age, think you?'

'*Mais non*, and it fits you so perfectly.'

'I thank you for your good opinion since I altered it with my own needle.'

Fuming with impatience Basil stood by, while De Brissac bandied idle compliments with the girl and young Sir Deveril smiled indulgently. Quite obviously he adored his little fiancée but his attitude to her seemed much more that of a fond brother than a lover.

At length Basil could contain himself no longer but broke in abruptly saying that they simply must set off at once. Yonita's face lost its radiance and she began an astonished protest. It seemed that Sir Deveril had not informed her of the imminent departure of her two friends and, to Basil's intense annoyance, the argument as to whether they should go or remain started all over again.

By sheer stubbornness he forced the others to give way to him, but Yonita insisted that she must see them off, and as her legs were still paining her a little, more time was lost while a handcart was sent for to transport her with them to the distant shore.

Uncle Cornelius and a number of the islanders decided to go with them to the coast, so a small procession set out along the narrow track. Basil marched along in front with Sir Deveril, endeavouring to hurry their pace, but De Brissac insisted upon wheeling Yonita so that he could talk to her during the journey, and he refused to exhaust himself by pushing the cart at anything more than an easy walk. Uncle Cornelius and the other notables from the village brought up the rear of the party.

As they progressed Basil endeavoured to make polite conversation with Sir Deveril but his heart was sinking further with every quarter of a mile they advanced. Over two hours had elapsed since he and De Brissac had woken in their beds and the light was now beginning to fail. The previous day they had set off from the ship a little before six, and, glancing at his watch, he saw that it was already half past. By the time they reached the cleft in the cliff where they had cached their balloons it was after seven.

The foreshore of the island was as grim and deserted as ever in the evening light. From it the tideless waters, blotched all over with masses of the green weed, stretched east, north and west as far as the eye could see. In places it had a faintly bluish tinge as though drifting smoke was passing across its surface. The *Gafelborg* appeared to be considerably nearer in. De Brissac estimated that she must have drifted at least a couple of miles during the twenty-four hours since they had left her, but he shook his head when Basil began to pull out one of the balloons.

'I'm sorry, my friend. You were so set upon going I thought it best we should proceed to this cliff top so that you could see how things were for yourself. I did not intentionally delay you while we were at Sir Deveril's house but I knew before we started out that so much time had been lost it would not be safe for us to make the crossing tonight. Look at the mist which is already quite thick, low on the weed.'

'The mist comes up uncommon fast at sundown every evening during summer,' Deveril informed them, 'but it rarely rises more than thirty feet above the weed sea.'

Basil stared angrily at De Brissac and then at the ship. He wanted to insist on their attempting the crossing but, on the other hand, it would take them three-quarters of an hour at least to reach the *Gafelborg*, and the light would not last for more than half an hour at most. With acute reluctance he was forced to confess to himself that De Brissac was right; it would be sheer madness to venture now and risk missing the ship in the darkness and the rising mist.

With an angry gesture he pushed back the balloon. 'I give in, although I hate to confess myself beaten. We delayed too long and we daren't risk getting lost out there again. I wonder, though, if we could signal?'

They had no binoculars but peered out over the weed sea. In full daylight they might have been able to distinguish anyone moving on the *Gafelborg*'s deck, but now it was impossible to do so.

'I should have thought of that before,' De Brissac reproached himself. 'If we could have signalled them that would have assured them of our safety just as well as returning to the ship, but wait—even if we cannot see them they can see us against the skyline on this low headland. Anybody on the look-out should easily be able to as they have telescopes and glasses.'

'Plague on it! I might have brought flags to signal with, had I but thought,' frowned Sir Deveril.

'No matter. The ski-sticks will do and are even better because of the big balloons upon their tops. Quick, let us get them before the light grows worse.'

They snatched up the ski-sticks and De Brissac took three of them so that the balloons attached to their ends made a large black blob fifteen feet above his head. Running to the highest point of the headland he began to signal in the Mórse code, repeating a message slowly twice which ran: 'Corncob dead, rest safe; returning tomorrow.'

At the end of his second message a light began to wink on the *Gafelborg*, acknowledging his signals. As they watched he spelt out his reply from the ship: 'Trouble on board last night, Jansen and Harlem lost but all well now. Unity sends love to Basil, see you in morning.'

Basil heaved a sigh of relief at the knowledge that Unity was all right, but all of them were troubled by the thought of this new loss which had befallen the diminished ship's company, and speculated fruitlessly as to what fresh calamity had befallen the survivors in the *Gafelborg*.

By the time they had finished receiving the ship's signal the light was almost gone. The mist now totally obscured the tideless sea, hid the hull of the *Gafelborg* and was creeping up the rocky slope towards them in greyish billows; chill, dank and pregnant with the atmosphere of evil. Basil lingered a moment, thinking of Unity out there in the trapped ship, then reluctantly hurried after the others who had gladly turned their backs on the gloomy seascape and were already heading for the centre of the island.

Once they were over the rough and on the track, which started at the Randels' farm, they split up into the same formation they had used in making their outward journey. As Yonita climbed into her handcart she asked De Brissac if he was not too tired to push her all the way back to the village again.

He laughed, showing his even white teeth under the little black moustache. '*Mais non*, Mademoiselle. I am only too happy to be here to do it. I really feared that stupid friend of mine would drag me out across the weed.'

'Why was he so anxious to leave us?' she asked curiously.

'He had an admirable reason,' De Brissac smiled, leaning forward a little over her shoulder and lowering his voice so that the others should not hear. 'He is in love with Unity, the slim, brown-haired girl you met in the ship yesterday. Naturally he is anxious to get back to her.'

Yonita nodded her dark head wisely. 'Ah ha! that explains it; but I was equally determined that you should not go. My astonishment at your decision was only pretended as Deveril had told me of your purpose when he woke me. I do not really require anything approaching an hour for my toilet, even in these garments.'

De Brissac glanced swiftly at the young baronet who was walking some paces ahead with Basil; it seemed an unchivalrous thing to make love to his host's fiancée, yet Yonita was obviously asking for it, and the temptation proved irresistible.

'How much I wish that I might attribute the same reason to

your wish to detain us, Mademoiselle, as to my friend's for wanting to go,' he murmured.

'Mayhap you can,' she replied lightly. 'He is a handsome enough gentleman, although somewhat surly at the moment.'

De Brissac smiled in the semi-darkness. He knew that she was only mocking him, but he answered in a heartbroken voice: 'Mademoiselle, you desolate me beyond measure. Last night you allowed me to suppose that you found some interest in my unworthy self, and now you infer that my surly friend has already supplanted me. What can I possibly have done to deserve such cruel treatment?'

She turned and smiled back at him over her shoulder. 'I have a sufficiently good opinion of you both, and it is not in my disposition to be cruel. In truth, I am absurdly kind to handsome young men who flatter me by their devotion.'

'You were going to tell me last night things that it would much interest me to know about the way some of your customs differ from ours. Do you remember? Just as those horrible crabs interrupted us?'

'Now is not a good time for such conversation,' she said softly. 'Since you profess so great a curiosity I will enlighten you after the banquet tonight, perchance, should I feel so disposed.'

'The banquet is to take place after all then?'

'Assuredly, nothing was cancelled, once Deveril and I had formed the resolution that neither of you should leave the island yet. Credit us with some measure of finesse, I beg, sir. We contrived to delay the hour of your departure until such time as it would be too late for you to cross on account of the mist.'

It was eight o'clock when they reached Sir Deveril's house again and full night had set in. The gentle starlight faintly lit the fair park-land and showed the outline of the ancient cedars. The banquet had been postponed till nine o'clock, and, on reaching the house, the party split up to go and dress for it. Hook-nosed Uncle Cornelius left them for his own house, but Yonita had had her clothes sent over during the afternoon and meant to spend the night under her fiancé's roof. Sir Deveril went to his room while Yonita, who was already dressed, entertained the two visitors in the big lounge, which was now lit by shaded candles.

Twenty minutes later Sir Deveril rejoined them; a strikingly handsome figure in long, blue, cut-away coat and breeches of the Napoleonic period; other carefully preserved garments handed down by his forebears and kept by him for gala occasions. Fine

203

lace ruffles graced his throat and wrists, and the costume was completed by a pair of old-fashioned, square-toed shoes with silver buckles.

Basil had cheered up a little, endeavouring to put a bright face on his disappointment at being separated from Unity for another night, and De Brissac, completely happy in his semi-amorous sparring with Yonita, now appeared not to have a care in the world.

To occupy the time of waiting until they were due to walk over to the great hall where the feast was to be held, Sir Deveril showed his visitors some of his curiosities, including an old, iron-bound chest with many locks, which, as they saw with a little thrill when he opened it, contained a magnificent collection of old-fashioned jewels. ' 'Tis the loot,' he declared, 'which has come down to me through the many piracies of the first Sir Doveril Barthorne who became marooned here in 1680.'

'I didn't know he was a pirate,' Basil remarked.

The young man shrugged his shoulders. 'The glamour of his career somewhat excuses his depredations, the more particularly as they were all carried out against the shipping of nations then at war with England. He was a Cornish cavalier and he employed his early manhood fighting for the King during the Civil War. As you may know, some portion of the navy remained loyal to Charles I. When the Royalist cause was lost Barthorne fled to one of Prince Rupert's ships. Unable to obtain funds with which to pay his men, that romantic prince sailed down to the Spanish Main and turned his navy into a pirate fleet during Cromwell's usurpation.

'They all sailed home after the Restoration and my ancestor was then just over forty. For a few years, he played the rakehell in Whitehall with King Charles II, Buckingham, Rochester and the rest, but the idle life left him dissatisfied. In 1665 he fitted out a privateer with the King's Commission and set out upon his travels once more.

' 'Tis our belief he ne'er went home again but roamed the Spanish Main thereafter; sometimes in company with the famous Sir Henry Morgan, more often on his own; waylaying and robbing Spanish, French and Dutch vessels until he was caught in a violent hurricane. His ship was dismasted and trapped in the weed seas which surround these islands. He was a man of sixty then, yet lived on to the ripe old age of eighty-seven.'

'What happened then?' inquired Basil.

'He was succeeded as uncrowned king here by the son he begot, during the first year of his sojourn, upon the beautiful Spanish Contessa, Maria Silvestre a Costa. This son died at the age of forty-nine and was followed by the third Sir Deveril. He married the daughter of the French Governor of a West Indian Island, who arrived in a French warship which had become unmanageable through mutiny and the desertion of the greater portion of her crew, in 1726.

'The third Sir Deveril was, alas, a weakling and unable to resist a famous buccaneer known as the Red Barracuda, who was wrecked on our coast with a crew of thirty-three men and a number of women in 1744. His pirates sacked the island as though they were raiding some wretched township on the Spanish Main. They slew many of the male inhabitants, including the third Sir Deveril, but when they became sensible of the fact that they must spend the rest of their lives here, they began to settle down as peaceable colonists; much in the manner of the earlier arrivals upon whom they had brought so ill a fate.

' 'Twas an ungodly time for the islanders. The Red Barracuda lived up to the nickname given to him on account of his fiery red beard and temperamental likeness to the fish the Carib Indians call "the devil of the shallows". He proved a capricious and bloody tyrant. No petticoat was safe from him and he shot any man who refused to do his bidding, but the fourth Sir Deveril had fortunately been spared during the first massacre, as he was then but an infant. Fifteen years later, when he had grown to man's estate, he led a revolt which ended in the tyrant's kicking out his life suspended by three feet of rope from the rafter above the door of his own residence. From the time of that happy occurrence the Barthornes resumed their suzerainty of the island and we have ruled here ever since.'

Deveril having entertained them with some more episodes of the island's story the time came for them to attend the banquet, so they all walked across from the house to the great hall.

Here nearly the whole population had assembled, and the islanders gave the two guests a royal welcome. Sir Deveril led De Brissac and Basil to the top table and they looked round them in astonishment; the scene was almost like a pageant from English history, or a gathering for a fancy-dress ball. Both women and men had unearthed their most treasured clothes from old, cedar chests for the occasion, and the laughing crowd presented a most colourful spectacle. The costumes ranged from embroidered satins of a bygone century, through serviceable cloth uniform coats of numerous navies, to the black, formal best that the American whaling men had brought with them to the island in 1879, and the faded naval kit of the German sailors whose gunboat had reached there in 1904. Many of the women, Basil noted, wore little Chinese jackets with lovely, colourful designs of dragons and butterflies upon them. When he asked the reason for this, Sir Deveril told him that one of their most fortunate windfalls had been a shipment of these costumes which was on its way fr om China to Europe in the middle of the last century.

A band of six musicians tuned up in the gallery above the top ta ble, and the guests were delighted by the gentle airs of long-dead composers played with considerable skill. None of the islanders had ever heard a gramophone, and when De Brissac spoke with appreciation of the music, Sir Deveril told him that one of their principal recreations during the long winter evenings, when the island was snowbound, was part-singing and that there were very few people on the island who could not play some kind of instrument. He added modestly that he himself was reckoned quite an accomplished performer upon the harpsichord.

The hall was lit by torches in sconces round the walls, each guarded by a metal plate from setting fire to the timbers, and down each of the long tables were set rows of most strangely assorted candlesticks, many of them being of fine Georgian silver. Yonita laughed with her guests about the strange collection of plate that had been brought out in their honour. Instead of the earthenware utensils used at the morning meal a miscellaneous collection of glass and china decked the boards; ranging from old Bristol to cheap Victorian tumblers.

The feast was an admirable one, although its meat courses were confined to pork and chicken, and, to do their utmost honour to their guests, the island council, which arranged all affairs under Sir Deveril's chairmanship, had raided the common cellar, allocating a dozen assorted bottles to the feast from the small store of wine which had been saved from the wrecked ships.

The dozen bottles provided no more than a few thimblefuls for each person, and De Brissac knew that, except for the Madeira, the wine was long past its best, but they made up for its shortage by ample potations of the island's finest vintage champagne cider, and afterwards, having drunk the King's health in the wine, they broached flagons of excellent old plum, cherry and damson liqueur.

When the meal was done they were offered an entertainment, and the visitors were delighted by the admirable way in which the men and girls selected rendered the old-fashioned airs of a bygone generation. A party of glee-singers was particularly good. The centre of the hall was then cleared for dancing.

None of the islanders had ever heard of jazz, but they trod the barn dance with great gusto, enjoyed several sets of hilarious lancers, and waltzed most gracefully.

It was past one in the morning and the torches were guttering in their sconces when Yonita, having just finished a waltz with De Brissac, said to him: 'Pardon my frailty, I beg, but my poor feet will stand no more after having been half crushed by that vile crab last night. I do declare I must crave both your indulgence and your escort to Deveril's house.'

'*Certainement*,' he said, 'forgive me that I was not more thoughtful. I have enjoyed dancing with you so much that I had forgotten your injuries entirely. Let us go.'

' 'Tis unpardonable selfish that I should curtail your pleasure,' she smiled as they edged through the merry, laughing crowd. 'We can seldom afford such assemblies and methinks most of them will keep it up till morn.'

'I mean no insult to your friends, but it would be a dull and joyless affair for me once you were gone,' he assured her. He noted with considerable satisfaction that Deveril was flirting outrageously with a fair girl named Corisande. The young baronet had attached himself to her immediately after dinner, and, since, had hardly left her.

Yonita's hand was resting on De Brissac's arm and she pressed it slightly as they left the hall for the cool, soft darkness. ' 'Tis not that I am fatigued—only that my feet betray me by a scandalous lassitude. If you have no wish to retire permit me to entertain you as far as my abilities allow.'

Twenty yards from the hall he paused and looked down at her. 'I think for the sake of the little feet I should carry you.'

'Willingly, if you have strength to compass it,' she said wickedly. 'If not you can call on Master Sutherland for aid, as you did this morning.'

'I was played out then, and I only did so because he insisted. Now it is very different.' With a quick movement he picked her up and she nestled her head down on his shoulder. Her slight figure was no great burden to him in the rising excitement of the moment and he managed the few hundred yards to Sir Deveril's house without inconvenience.

As he set her down she put her hands on his shoulders and laughed up into his face. 'Have you nothing you would like to ask of me in return for your exertions?'

He hesitated a second. To kiss her seemed an appalling abuse of Sir Deveril's hospitality, but she hardly waited for an answer and the next moment, standing on tiptoe, she pressed her soft mouth firmly against his.

A little breathlessly they went into the house. She lit a single candle in the lounge and snuggled down in the corner of a big, old-fashioned chesterfield, pulling him down beside her. He put his arm about her and drew her to him. She sighed contentedly and began to stroke his cheek.

His heart was pounding as though it would burst.

He was filled with an overwhelming desire to crush her slender little body to him in a wild embrace, but suddenly he drew away from her and sat forward mopping the perspiration from his temples. He clasped his hands so tightly together that it hurt.

'Yonita,' he said in a half-strangled voice, 'this will not do. You will think me a prig and a fool. I adore you utterly but this is your fiancé's house. Every moment that I make love to you that thought makes me miserable beyond words.'

She gave a low, delightful ripple of laughter. 'I would have wagered that was what was troubling you, but is it not said that when you're in Rome you should do as the Romans do?'

'*Bon Dieu!*' he exclaimed, 'what is it you are driving at? You have hinted so much before. Explain, and put me out of my misery, I beg you.'

'You have shown patience enough, so I'll be kind.' She sat forward, took his clenched hands gently in hers and turned him towards her. 'Deveril was discoursing to you this evening of the brutal Red Barracuda, and how he raided our island many generations gone. The fifteen years that he held sway here altered our whole outlook. He was a horrid man, cruel and lecherous. At his death there was no single virgin in the island who was older than fifteen. For years he and his lieutenants had taken their pleasure of the womenfolk just as they listed. In cases where the men were old or ill-favoured that must have been prodigious horrid for the females, but in most instances it seems they confessed a naughty liking for it. We females are not so very different from you men,

208

but in the old days it was thought immodest to admit our natural pleasure in surrendering to a masterful lover.'

'How true!' exclaimed De Brissac. 'It was only through the old system by which men held women as property that there grew up the custom by which a man was free to have as much fun as he liked while a girl was supposed to remain chaste until her marriage and then continue content with one man, whether she liked him or not, for the rest of her life.'

Yonita nodded. 'While the Red Barracuda reigned here, a whole generation of young women became accustomed to "living in sin", as they used to term it, with a succession of men, and, although some of them were forced, most of them made their own choice and were protected from the others by the lovers with whom they were intimate for the time being.

'After the fourth Sir Deveril hanged the Red Barracuda, these forward females expressed the greatest repugnance to any return to the old system, so unrestricted gallantry became a custom in the island from the time the boys and girls were about sixteen or seventeen.'

'And did such unusual licence work out satisfactorily?' De Brissac asked curiously.

'Alas no, it tended to destroy family life, and no state, large or small, so the history books tell us, can prosper without that. Also, promiscuity, regardless of age, begot jealousy and quarrels. Few couples settled down together for more than a year or two, and the older men of the island saw that something must be done to stop such a parlous condition of affairs.

'You have been presented to all the members of the five leading families here tonight. As the natural leaders of the people are drawn from them it was thought important to preserve the aristocratic caste that had managed all affairs so successfully until the Red Barracuda turned the island into a state of anarchy. The men of our best families were leaving their wives, after a few years of marriage, to live with females of little breeding, the descendants of rough pirates or mulatto women, and begetting children by them, while their wives were consoling themselves by conducting amours with good-looking peasants, and getting children by them.'

'Yes—I see it—a bad business for all concerned.'

'Assuredly. Even prior to the coming of the Red Barracuda there had oft-times been trouble and scandal through husbands deceiving their wives with the wenches, and married women cuckolding their spouses, but afterwards the females insisted on retaining their freedom to love where they listed and go to bed with their gallants just as the men did with their mistresses.'

'And how did they get over such a difficult situation?'

Yonita smiled. 'A solemn council was held and a new resolution taken which has governed the relations of the sexes here ever since. To conserve the blood of the best families, parents arrange betrothals for each boy and girl when they reach the age of seventeen and are of an age to say whether they feel an inclination to the partners chosen for them or not. With our own consent these betrothals are made public, but the marriage is never celebrated until the girl is twenty-five. In the meantime the young couple are permitted to indulge any taste they may have for gallantry without reproaches on either side.'

De Brissac stared at her. 'But are there no—how about children?'

'If a young woman has the misfortune to find herself in an embarrassing condition, the doctor conveys her infant away at birth and it is reared in company with other offspring similarly begotten. Its mama is not even informed of its sex and later it becomes just one of the peasant population without any social status. By these means the infant does not at all affect her after-life when married.

'Knowing something of the customs of the outer world, I fear our apparent laxity must give you but a poor opinion of us,' she went on quickly, 'yet our system has proved adequate for close on two centuries and our women now would die rather than surrender their years of youthful freedom. The fashion of having a fiancé when quite young without serious obligation is a pleasant custom too, since he plays the role of an affectionate brother. Betrothed couples are not permitted any more familiar relationship because it would impair their freshness for each other when the time came for them to marry. 'Tis so that all craving for adventure and the ephemeral excitements offered by a variety of amorous experiences is got out of a young female's system before she marries, and the same applies to the men. Afterwards 'tis found the sexes are almost invariably content to settle down together, and, once they do, 'tis understood that a couple should be utterly and completely faithful to each other. No rule can offer perfection because human beings vary so in their temperaments, but methinks our marriages are of a more happy nature than yours in the great distant world, because they are based on a more enduring foundation than mere physical attraction. Here in our island, not once in a hundred times does a marriage break up or prove really unhappy.'

'I see,' said De Brissac slowly; 'so you are free as air until you are twenty-five.'

'La, sir. I am but twenty and have honoured only three gallants with my favours yet. I wearied of the last nigh on a month ago.' She smiled mischievously and raised her face to his. 'Now mayhap your tiresome conscience is set at rest and you will no longer scruple to provide me with a little diversion suitable to my age and our present situation.'

De Brissac could hardly believe he was not dreaming. He feared every moment that he would wake up, but he did not. He did not even fall asleep until the sun was stealing through the porthole windows the following morning; and when at last he did, Yonita's dark head was still resting on his shoulder while one of her soft little arms clung round his neck.

CHAPTER XVIII

THE SILENT SHIP

As YONITA had predicted, the party in the great hall was kept up until dawn was breaking in the east. Basil would have thoroughly enjoyed every moment of it had he not felt a vague anxiety about Unity which he could not altogether get out of the back of his mind. The message from the ship had clearly stated that all was well with them now and that Unity sent him her love, but the new calamity that had overtaken the small company in the loss of Jansen and Harlem remained unexplained. The sinister disappearance of Bremer three nights before and his own horrible experience with the giant crabs haunted his mind. What other evil thing might have come up out of the weed to cause the deaths of the old carpenter and the big negro? Perhaps at this very moment while he was waltzing with one of the bronze-skinned island girls a dire peril might be threatening those who still remained in the *Gafelborg*. They might be fighting for their lives against some hideous thing in the dark loneliness of that evil, tideless sea.

De Brissac having disappeared comparatively early, Basil felt that it was up to him to remain until the end of the party and do double duty as an appreciative guest, but, when at last the gathering broke up, he determined to get back to the ship as soon as it was practicable to do so.

Having had only a few hours' sleep the previous afternoon and been up all the preceding night, as well as the present one, he knew that it would be foolish to set off now, dropping with fatigue as he was, even if he could have roused out De Brissac to accompany him. The obvious course was to get at least a few hours' sleep and start about ten o'clock in the morning.

Deveril, like most of his friends and relatives, was mildly tipsy when the party broke up. Yonita's disappearance with De Brissac did not seem to bother him at all. The young man was in an exceedingly happy and affectionate frame of mind. During the party he had disappeared for a considerable time with the golden-haired Corisande and he kissed her with ardour in front of them all before she set off home, strange conduct in an engaged man to Basil's mind, but it was not his business to censor the conduct of his handsome young host, and he knew nothing of the somewhat unusual customs of the island.

Arm in arm the two men crossed the park-land in the pale light of early morning: the young islander babbling away with considerable cheerfulness upon the respective merits of blondes and brunettes. It was quite evident that, although he was extremely fond of Yonita, Corisande held first place in his thoughts, at all events for the moment.

When they reached the house Basil spoke of returning to the ship and asked if he could be called at nine o'clock.

'Plague take you for a restless fellow,' laughed Sir Deveril amiably. 'Here, you can stay up all night or in bed all day. Everyone does what they like in reason as you will soon find when you settle among us. Time, I believe, is a thing of moment in your strange great world, of which we know nothing, except what we have learned from the books and stories handed down to us; but here we set precious little store by it. Season drifts into season; providing the crops are sown and harvested, time is of small importance. Fresh settlers here, so my father used to tell me, invariably manifest a witless desire to add to their own toil by a multitude of pointless labours, but soon they become sensible of the futility of their exertions. We have abundant food, comfortable homes and work enough to prevent our becoming slothful. One of the German sailors who reached us in 1904 had some books by a man named Marx. He would talk for hours, I'm told about a thing called a "Proletarian State", but nobody here comprehended very fully what he had in mind although his description of the way in which the lower orders lived in European countries was curiously grim. His strange preoccupation with this subject became a harmless enough hobby, since, despite his attempts to upset everything here at first, he soon settled down like the rest of us to plough his few acres and drift quite happily from day to day. But I digress. If you wish to rise at nine o'clock, by all means do so. I will leave a message to that effect.'

When Basil woke, however, he found by his watch that it was nearly twelve, and when he reproached the old manservant who answered his ring with not having called him the man did not seem to appreciate the cause of his annoyance. He said he had found his master's message written on the slate, but thought it best that Basil should sleep on after being up so late. Moreover, he himself had only got up half an hour before.

Basil recalled Sir Deveril's remarks earlier that morning and was forced to realize that in this land where there were no telephones, posts, offices and business hours, time was honestly considered of not the least moment, but fresh fears for Unity urged him to spring out of bed and inquire if De Brissac were up.

'No, no,' replied the man with a cheerful smile, 'Mistress Yonita left word on my slate that she and the Captain were not to be called until they woke.'

Basil looked at him with blank astonishment, his mouth a little open at this extraordinary announcement, but he thought it hardly right to discuss the matter with the servant and directly the man had gone went to the door of De Brissac's room, on which he knocked gently.

As there was no reply he knocked again, then opened the door a crack, to find that the bedroom was unoccupied and the bed had not been slept in. Utterly bewildered by this strange conduct of his friend in Sir Deveril's house, he shaved, dressed himself and ran downstairs. The young baronet was not about so Basil made further inquiries of the old manservant, upon which he learnt that Sir Deveril had also left instructions that he was not to be called, and the man did not think it likely that his master would put in an appearance until the late afternoon.

'Is—er—Captain De Brissac—er—in Miss Yonita's room?' Basil inquired hesitatingly.

'Assuredly,' said the man. 'Did I not tell you so a moment back?'

'Perhaps you will show me where it is then,' Basil said, and the servant promptly led him down a corridor to it.

After repeated knockings Yonita's voice came sleepily and with a touch of temper from within. 'What wish you? Did I not say we were not to be roused? Begone!'

Basil then explained who it was and with some diffidence asked if she knew where De Brissac was.

'La, sir. Most certainly. He's here,' she said angrily. 'Be off with you. Are you not ashamed to disturb people's slumber in this unmasterly fashion?'

'I'm awfully sorry,' Basil shouted through the door, 'but it's getting on for one o'clock, and we simply must get back to the ship.'

There was a loud yawn and then De Brissac's voice. '*Mon ami!* have you no discretion? Leave us in peace, I beg. What does an hour or two matter? Be generous, my friend. We will go this afternoon, but do not bother me till then.'

'Oh, all right.' Basil grumbled as he turned away. There seemed nothing else that he could do, so he set himself to possess his soul in patience and wandered out into the grounds.

To occupy the time of waiting he walked down to the hall. It was deserted, with the big doors standing open and the remnants of the previous night's feast still not cleared away. Not a single house that he could see showed any sign of activity. They all lay drowsing in the sun, and it was quite clear that, like Sir Deveril and Yonita, their occupants had no thought of work on this morning after the big party.

Under the minstrels' gallery, in the big hall, he found another room which proved to be a library, and for some time he amused himself by going through the extraordinary collection of miscellaneous literature it contained. Evidently the islanders had made it a common depository for all the books which had been saved from the numerous ships that had reached their shores.

Upon one wall was a big chart of the two islands in the weed sea. Evidently the amateur cartographer had only a vague idea about the geography of Satan's Island; its nearest coastline was charted clearly, but the others were only roughly outlined. In its centre the word 'forest' was printed; about threequarters of the way along it the native village was marked, and beyond that came a thick line cutting off the whole of its southern end against which was written 'THE GREAT BARRIER'. The other island was etched in with the most detailed care. Its shape was that of a crucifix and they had landed at its foot. The village was in its centre and in a bay under its eastern arm, about two miles from Sir Deveril's house, Basil noticed that a number of wrecks were charted.

Having made a picnic meal off the abundance of cold foods that were still lying about on the tables and opened himself a fresh bottle of cider, he decided he would make a visit to the bay of wrecks, and set off at a leisurely walk.

When he came to the shore he saw that a long, low promontory forming the left arm of the cross stretched out for over a mile into the weed, and it was this evidently that caught the ships which were carried down the channel in the current. Opposite, about four miles away to the north-east, he could see the low

215

coastline of Satan's Island and, to its south, much clearer than he had seen it from the *Gafelborg*, the higher ground like a sheer cliff that rose at the far end of it; evidently 'the great barrier' marked on the map. It looked as though a sort of flat mountain occupied the whole of that portion of the island.

For a long time he stared at the numerous wrecks which had brought the colonists to Yonita's island. There were many more than she or Sir Deveril had mentioned, and he assumed that these were the ones which had arrived with only dead men on board.

As no serious storms ever agitated this tideless sea few of the wrecks had gone to pieces; many of the older ones were no more than hulks a few hundred feet out from the shore and had been entirely overgrown by the bright-green weed. Some of them had masts still standing, but of the majority the masts had been snapped off short by the hurricanes the ships had encountered before being driven into the weed sea.

One old hulk had an outline that, from its great, many-decked poop, suggested a Spanish galleon, and another quite near in to the shore, which for some obscure reason had no weed upon it so that its high, ornamented prow could still be seen, conjured up the almost impossible idea that it was the remains of a Phoenician or Norse galley. Basil did not think that even the stoutest timber could have withstood such aeons of time when partly submerged in water. Little of it remained, except the ribbed timbers of the hull and the great prow, and he was inclined to suppose that it might be the remnants of a ship from early Plantagenet times; a Moorish corsair, perhaps, that had got swept out from the African coast into mid-Atlantic and drifted down to the weed sea, months, or perhaps years, after its crew had died of thirst and starvation.

The more recent ships, including the small German gunboat, the American whaler and a dismasted barque, had not much wood upon them, but beastly patches of whitish mould showed here and there, giving their hulls a blotched, leprous appearance. A number of the ships had curious structures above their decks of rotting canvas or broken planking, partially covering them in. Basil guessed these must have been erected to protect their crews from the octopuses, as Yonita had said that sometimes ships drifted for weeks, embedded in the weed, before beaching on the island.

Leaving this strange graveyard of the seas that accounted for so many missing vessels long since written off in the musty ledgers of old shipping companies, many of which were, perhaps, no longer in existence, Basil walked slowly back to Sir Deveril's house, and was extremely glad to find that its inmates were at last up and dressed.

As he entered the lounge he came upon De Brissac teaching Yonita to foxtrot while Deveril struggled to play on the harpsichord the jazz tune the Frenchman hummed. They were all enjoying themselves to the utmost and, to Basil's relief, their host appeared not to bear the least resentment at the extraordinary conduct of his amorous guest.

'Well, what about it?' Basil asked.

'You impatient fellow,' laughed De Brissac, 'but I will hold you no longer, since you are so desperately anxious to get back to your Unity. After all, I shall only have to postpone Yonita's dancing lessons until tomorrow.'

'I hate to drag you away,' Basil said generously, 'but you insisted that I should not go on my own, and honestly, I am anxious about our friends.'

'Right then, we'll set off immediately we've had tea. Sir Deveril has decided to accompany us. He can do so by using Yonita's balloon and he wishes to welcome the others to his island.'

There was no further delay this time. After a quick meal they set off for the coast accompanied, as before, by quite a number of the islanders. As they topped the rise which hid the centre of the island from its northern shore, De Brissac halted to glance back at the view. The park-land in the valley had a blissful quiet, an ineffable peace, which made him recall Yonita's words about God having set his sign, even in the midst of these evil seas, as a refuge and protection for poor shipwrecked people; had De Brissac known that he was never to look upon that fair vista again he might have paused longer.

A quarter of an hour later they had recovered the balloons from the spot where they had cached them and were getting into their harness. De Brissac was a trifle worried as it seemed that they had lost a little gas in the two days since they had been captured from the negroes; but all three of the white men weighed considerably less than the blacks who had originally owned them and, after trying one out on the foreshore, De Brissac declared himself satisfied that the balloons would support them.

The day was bright and sunny, the time four o'clock, and

there was no trace of the nightly mist arising as yet, so it seemed that all was set fair for their journey. After affectionate farewells to Yonita and the rest the three men took off, this time quite easily as they were able to bound down the slope of the cliff and gain plenty of height before reaching the weed.

The going seemed much heavier than before and by the time they were a quarter of an hour out all three of them were acutely anxious. The balloons had lost more gas than they had supposed and were now barely sufficient to support them. With each bound they took their stilts and ski-sticks sank heavily into the dreaded weed and they had to exert all their strength to force themselves up again.

De Brissac was half-inclined to turn back. He would have had it not been for Basil and a little feeling at the back of his own mind that he really ought to have made more effort to hurry matters the day before so that they might have reached the ship the previous evening. If they abandoned their present attempt the balloons would lose still more gas and become completely useless. Then there would be no chance of getting to the ship until it beached upon the island, and none of them knew what might have been going on there. He set his teeth grimly and continued to advance.

They passed the island of the giant crabs, and all three men, now breathless and perspiring with their efforts, looked at it longingly, but they knew its terrible dangers far too well to think for a moment of taking refuge there for the night. Even if they had, once their balloons had further deflated they would have had no means of leaving it or their friends of rescuing them.

Grimly they pressed on, pushing and prodding at the weed, their ski-sticks sinking deeper with every stroke they made; the strain upon their muscles became appalling and the sweat trickled in rivulets down their faces.

Basil's mind was partially diverted from his danger by a fresh anxiety about the occupants of the *Gafelborg*. He had naturally supposed that somebody would be on the look-out, eagerly awaiting them. In any case it was strange that no one was to be seen about the ship's bridge or decks on such a pleasant, sunny afternoon.

De Brissac noticed the absence of a look-out too, and wondered about it. The *Gafelborg* was still nearer in; for which he thanked all his gods as he ploughed heavily along, rising no more than ten feet above the weed with every hop he took. The vessel lay there in the bright-green weed apparently lifeless and deserted· He began to fear that some new fatality must have overcome its survivors during the previous night, and reproached himself more than ever for having failed to join them the evening before.

Deveril was well in front of the other two. Although he was a tall, well-built young man, he was considerably slimmer than his companions and weighed less so he was making better progress but, even so, he was now acutely anxious. Each time he floated through the air his legs trailed out behind him so that he looked straight down into the weed. The hummocks and tangles of it which showed above the water-line glistened, sparkling wetly in the sun. The weed itself was by no means unpleasant to look on; but here and there he noticed a sudden, sinister disturbance in it and knew that some vile thing must be moving close under the spiky fonds of its countless tendrils. Plunging forward as he floated down the effort to draw his legs to the front and make another jump grew ever greater. His head was dizzy with the effort and he was half blinded by the perspiration that trickled into his eyes.

De Brissac, staggering along behind in a wild series of erratic hops, began to fear that they would never reach the ship, but he had a sudden inspiration now they were comparatively near to it. Luvia might be able to shoot them a lifeline from the rocket-gun if they fell and, if only their luck held, pull them aboard before one of the devil-fish got them. He gave a strangled cry for help.

The same thought came to Basil almost at the moment and he added his shout to De Brissac's but the *Gafelborg* remained dead and silent. Not a sign of life showed on board and now, as they leapt forward, they both saw the red of fresh-spilled blood upon her decks by the dark forms of huddled bodies.

With a gasp of relief Deveril reached the ship and flung himself over the rail. Basil was only a moment behind him. De Brissac nearly fell; he could not raise himself sufficiently to reach the deck in his last jump but, slipping, clutched frantically at the ship's anchor and managed to grab it.

For a moment he hung there suspended by one hand. The movements of the others were restricted by their stilts but Deveril thrust one of his ski-sticks over the side. De Brissac grasped it with his free hand and he was enabled to cling on until the other two could haul him aboard.

From the fo'c'sle head on which they had landed, the foredeck of the *Gafelborg* presented an appalling spectacle. They had all been almost blinded during the last few hundred yards to the ship by their terrific exertions for their own salvation so they had had little opportunity to take in details before. Now they saw that the negroes from Satan's Island must have attacked the *Gafelborg* again.

The corpses of half a dozen savages lay in grotesquely contorted attitudes below them on the for'ard well-deck. Great splodges of blood stained the planking near each of them. None of them made the faintest sound or movement, and all had that curious limp look which De Brissac, as an old campaigner, knew well to be an indication that no spark of life remained in their bodies. The pools of blood about them were already congealed, which made it obvious that they had been dead for some time.

With a terrible cry of anguish Basil jumped down into the well-deck and raced aft in search of Unity. Half-stunned by the shock and horror of the scene De Brissac and Deveril followed more slowly. The Frenchman glanced at one of the dead negroes. The man had a round puncture in his naked breast about which a little cluster of flies was buzzing. It was clear that he had been shot through the heart, yet his throat was cut from ear to ear so that his head was half-severed from his body.

They moved forward to the next and saw that he had been shot at close quarters through the face. An eye was missing and half his cheek was blown away. The carrion flies dispersed from the ghastly wound with an angry buzz then, greed overcoming fear, settled again. The second negro's throat was also cut.

Moving forward quickly now, in his anxiety to find out what was happening to Luvia and the rest, De Brissac did not pause to examine the twisted bodies on the port side of the fore-deck. Passing another dead negro on his way aft he saw that this one had had his throat cut too, but showed no other mortal wound, although his knee-cap had been shot away.

At the entrance to the lounge there were two more big savages; their dead eyes open and protruding horribly as they goggled at the sun. One had been shot through the thigh and the other through the stomach; both their throats gaped open at the neck where they had been slit below the Adam's apple.

The lounge looked as though a tornado had passed through it. Chairs and tables, previously secured to the deck by swivels, had been torn up and broken; smashed glass littered the floor in all directions, and a queer, strong perfume of mixed alcoholic spirits mingled with the smell of blood. Three more negroes were lying dead among the débris; one had been shot but the other two had jagged scalp wounds, which suggested that their heads had been smashed in with bottles. The sad explanation of this *débâcle* they found behind the bar—poor, fat, good-natured Hansie; dead from a dozen wounds, but still clasping an unbroken bottle half full of brandy in his right hand. Evidently he had made a last stand behind his bar using the bottles and glasses it contained with deadly effect upon at least two of his attackers.

Basil came dashing up the companionway. 'She isn't there— she isn't there,' he cried, his face contorted with anguish. 'Unity's cabin's been wrecked. Those fiends have dragged her off somewhere else and murdered her.'

He suddenly caught sight of Hansie and groaned. 'Poor old Hansie too. Such a good chap, and there's that girl he had a child by. He'll never be able to get back to her now.'

'I'm afraid he wouldn't have in any case,' De Brissac reminded him, 'but it's hard when, in another couple of days, he might have been safe ashore on the island. We'd better search the ship to see if we can find the others.'

Basil's face was white, his hands shaking. 'For God's sake give me a drink first. I'm about all-in.'

De Brissac pushed back the sliding shelves behind Hansie's bar but they disclosed only empty cupboards. 'Those black swine must have looted all the bottles Hansie didn't smash before they got him,' he muttered. 'But here, have a pull at this.'

He stooped and wriggled the bottle of cognac out of Hansie's dead hand.

Basil laughed hysterically as he took it. 'Poor old Hansie, his last service, eh, to provide a chap with a tot.' He gulped down a couple of mouthfuls of the neat brandy and shuddered. De Brissac and Deveril each had a pull at the bottle too; all three of them then proceeded upon their grim inspection.

The door of Unity's cabin had been broken in and it was empty as Basil had said. Further down the passage they came upon another slaughter. In the broken doorway of Vicente's cabin lay three more of the negroes, and all of them had had their throats cut. A fourth body lay across the bunk. It was that of Vicente Vedras, and his skull had been battered in. The door of Synolda's cabin hung crookedly from one hinge; that also was empty. Smashed furnishings and garments scattered about showed that a violent struggle had taken place there before she had been dragged out.

Next they went into the old dining-saloon below the lounge, which since their return to the *Gafelborg* after she had been abandoned in the hurricane had been used as a mess by the crew. In it they found the body of Gietto Nudäa, the half-caste seaman, spreadeagled on his back; a native spear thrust right through his body pinned him to the deck.

Appalled by the carnage, and the cloying, sickly scent of blood, they made their way up to the deck again and towards the stern of the ship. Five more negroes lay there lifeless; wounded in various parts of their bodies and, yet again, a mystery that intrigued the three searchers even in the midst of their horror, the throats of all five blacks were gashed from ear to ear.

Two of them had their gas bladders still strapped to their backs, but under the poop there was a number of balloons tethered, and evidently the negroes had used that place as a rallying-point at which to disembarrass themselves of their equipment before their final attack upon the centre of the ship. The big, dark, skin envelopes, piled high and hitched together, billowed up like a great stack of sausages.

A visit to the poop-house where the wounded natives had been quartered after the first attack, disclosed three empty bunks. The two who had died had, De Brissac supposed, been cast into the weed the previous day. There was no trace of the negro who had received a bullet under the scalp, but the fourth, who had been wounded in the thigh, still lay there. He had been slain by a great gash that gaped open, red and horrible, in his throat. Pints of his blood soaked the sheets and pillow which were dark and stiff; they judged that he had been dead for several hours at least.

Sadly, in grim silence, they made their way to the bridge. Behind the canvas windscreen they found young Largertöf. He had accounted for two more savages before some of the others had succeeded in braining him.

The chart-room was empty. De Brissac, led the way down the steep ladder from it to the captain's cabin which Luvia had been occupying since they had reboarded the ship.

As the Frenchman stepped on to the deck he gave an exclamation of surprise. Luvia was stretched out in the bunk, carefully tucked up with the sheets neatly folded below his chin.

His head was bandaged and they ran to him, fearing at first

that he, too, was dead but, to their relief, his heavy breathing soon showed that he was only asleep. With eager hands they tried to rouse him, but he slumbered on utterly unresponsive to their shouts and shakings.

'What the devil does it mean?' De Brissac growled. 'All these blacks, some dead from wounds, but others only winged by bullets, and every single one of them with his throat cut. Now, here is Luvia with, apparently, no more than a rap over the head, dressed in pyjamas, sound asleep in his bunk. It is a riddle in a nightmare.'

'God knows its answer,' Basil groaned. 'But the girls! Where are the girls? We've *got* to find them.'

De Brissac already had a shrewd idea what must have happened to them, from their smashed and empty cabins, but he did not like to voice his thoughts before the distracted Basil. They went below again to make a thorough search of the ship. No trace of the girls could be found or any other that would help to clear up the mystery of the cut throats and Luvia's coma, until they visited the galley. There, curled up on the floor asleep, they discovered Li Foo.

At the first touch he woke and, scrambling to his knees, began to jabber excitedly. He was pathetically glad to see them, but it was a good ten minutes before they could get a coherent account out of him of what had happened.

His version, pieced together, conveyed the main facts. There had been bad trouble two nights before between Luvia and Vicente. The Venezuelan had smashed the Finnish engineer over the head with a water carafe in Synolda's cabin. The crew, coming on the scene, had endeavoured to seize Vicente, but he had shot the old carpenter Jansen before they had been able to secure him. Luvia, it appeared, had been moody and silent when he came on deck the following morning. He had kept both Synolda and Vicente locked in their cabins, and apart from giving brief orders had spoken to no one except Unity.

In the meantime, after the scrap it seemed that Harlem, knowing Luvia to be out of action, had decided to desert the ship. He had gone off at daybreak with the negro who had been shot through the scalp, using two more of the balloons that had been left on the ship after the first attack, unobserved by the others until he was a mile away. The day had passed uneventfully although they had been anxious about De Brissac and Basil until they had picked up the signals from the island just before sundown the previous evening. They had turned in at the usual hour, but Li Foo had been up very early that morning and, in the dawn, had seen at least three hundred negroes crossing the weed towards the ship. He had roused Luvia and Largertöf in time for them to reach the bridge, but Hansie and Nudäa had been unable to get on deck before the blacks were swarming on board so they had endeavoured to hold the lounge.

Li Foo had no firearm and was cut off on his way to Synolda, but eluded his pursuers and took refuge in the for'ard galley. He witnessed part of the massacre but knew that he would be throwing away his life to no purpose if he went out into the crowd of blacks with nothing but his knife. Through the galley skyline he saw the negroes storm the bridge and Luvia scramble up to the top of the chart-house with his rifle. From there he managed to swing himself on to the ladder of the funnel and climbing to its top perched on it with the whole ship under his view. He shot down a number of the negroes but some of them had spears and one hurled with good aim caught him on the head and knocked him backwards so that he fell down inside the funnel.

Li Foo had succeeded in saving himself by wrenching out the plate of the galley ventilator, climbing up into it, and remaining there while the savages looted the ship. When all was quiet again he had crawled out and watched them hopping along half-way to their island with the two girls, balloons strapped to their backs, being carried away as prisoners amongst them. On the decks they had left a number of their dead and all those who were too seriously wounded to be helped across the weed. Li Foo had gone round conscientiously and carefully slitting the throats of every black on board, dead or alive, to make quite certain of them.

It had occurred to him that every ship's funnel had struts across its interior to strengthen it and hold its sections firmly in place. There was a chance that Luvia had been caught on one of these and could not get up or down. Climbing the funnel ladder Li Foo had found his officer lying doubled up across one of the struts. The spear had knocked him out but he was still very much alive by the time Li Foo had managed to get a bowline round his body and haul him up. The Chinaman had tried to persuade him to go to bed but he was in such a state of excited despair about the women that he flatly refused. Seeing him shivering and exhausted the cunning Li Foo had suggested a hot grog and doctored the drink with a strong dose of smuggled opium. It sent him off very soon after he had swallowed it. The Chinaman had then undressed his officer, washed him, rebandaged his head, and put him to bed.

'How soon will he wake?' De Brissac inquired.

'We go see 'um,' Li Foo replied. 'Dissa fella givum plentee heap dream dope in his dlink, but he sleepum long time, ten hour now.'

They went along to Luvia's cabin and found him still comatose but the Chinaman smiled blandly and produced a small phial from the inner pocket of his blue linen coat.

'You won' wake 'um,' he lisped. 'Me makeum plentee betteh soon,' and he dissolved a couple of pellets from the little bottle in half a glass of water.

They opened Luvia's mouth and forced the drug down his throat. 'Prap ten minute now,' said the Chinaman, 'prap half-hour—we see. Dissa veh good for fella wantum wakeup for duty watch. My flen givum me, I givum my flen, plentee time.'

'We'll have to wait a bit then,' remarked De Brissac, 'until he comes round.'

'But what the hell are we going to do?' moaned Basil. 'Unity—Synolda—just think of it, God knows what those swine'll do to them.'

Deveril placed a hand kindly on his shoulder. 'You have all my sympathy, sir. I well recall my sufferings the day before yesterday, and all through the night you spent on the island of the giant crabs, when I believed that those fiends had dearest Yonita at their mercy in their Marriage House.'

'Oh God, I shall go mad!' Basil exclaimed. 'What can we do? We must *do* something! We can't stand here!'

'I fear that there is little we can do,' Sir Deveril said sadly.

'On the contrary,' De Brissac took him up quickly, 'we have the balloons of all the blacks who have been killed. There's a great stack of them by the poop; we're going after those devils like smoke as soon as poor Luvia comes round.'

Basil's face suddenly lit up. 'Bless you for that. I'd forgotten the balloons. For heaven's sake let's get going.'

'Try to be patient for a little,' De Brissac said softly. 'Luvia will be as anxious about the girls as you are, and it would not be right or sensible to go without him. We shall need every gun we can get.'

Sir Deveril slowly shook his head. 'I fear you will only be

throwing your lives away. It is true that the blacks have no firearms, but how can three of you, however brave, hope to overcome such scores of them?'

'Frankly, I was counting on your help.' The Frènchman gave him a sharp glance.

'Gad, yes! I will accompany you willingly if you can devise a plan which shows some prospect of our succouring your ladies, but there's little sense in throwing our lives away to no purpose. If the four of us land on Satan's Island, what chance have we against such odds?'

'This is my plan,' De Brissac announced. 'It came to me immediately we found the girls' cabins were empty. I felt certain they had been carried off. There must be anything from fifteen to twenty freshly filled gas bladders in that great stack on the after-deck of the ship. I see no reason why each of them should not be weighed down so that it floats about ten feet above the weed. You could then tow a whole string of them back to your island carrying the ski-sticks and stilts strapped across your shoulders. If you could take a dozen balloons they would transport eleven of your friends or relatives and yourself across the channel to Satan's Island. One of you could tow the string back again and so bring over another eleven men. The process could be repeated until we had assembled all your people, who are capable of bearing arms, on the enemy's shore. Even then we should be nothing like equal in numbers to the blacks, but we have firearms and they have not. If we march on their village in a body and make a surprise attack I think we may succeed in rescuing the women.'

'Why, stap me!' exclaimed Sir Deveril, 'but 'tis a marvellous notion. Our ancestors have suffered for nearly eighty years from the negro raids. There's not a man among us who would not welcome the chance of having a cut at these heathens. We would have wiped them out long since had it not been that never before have we captured more than a couple of their balloons at one time.'

'The plan's sound enough,' Basil agreed, 'but I was looking at a rough sketch map of Satan's Island this afternoon. The village is miles away—nearly at its other end—and if our attack succeeds we've got to get the girls away.'

'You mean the blacks will surround us and cut us off before we can get back to the shore?' De Brissac asked.

'Yes. I'm game, anyhow, but it's going to be a pretty desperate business even if Sir Deveril can muster three of four dozen men with guns or rifles.'

'Is there no way in which we can spread terror among them so that we can get a clear start after our rescue,' Sir Deveril suggested.

'*Ciel!* I have it!' cried De Brissac. 'My machine-gun! My invention which is packed up down in the hold. With it there are a thousand rounds of ammunition supplied to me to make my quick-firing tests for heat, which I had no time to do before leaving Madagascar. The gun is light, and it will take me no great time to assemble it. If we could transport that to the island we should have a weapon as good as a hundred bayonets with which to spread the terror you speak of.'

Basil started for the doorway. 'Come on, let's get it!'

'Wait!' called Sir Deveril. 'None of my people will be able to do aught until I return. Surely the first thing is for me to set forth with these balloons.'

'You're right,' De Brissac agreed quickly. 'Quick—to the after-deck!'

Working with frantic speed they sorted out the great tangle of gas-filled bladders and found that, including the two which were still strapped to the backs of the dead natives, they had altogether twenty-one, but two of them had been shot through and were useless. De Brissac tethered six of them. The largest was strapped on to Sir Deveril's back and the remaining twelve were hitched one to another, on to long lengths of line and each weighted down with sacks of potatoes from the store. They were a little uncertain whether Sir Deveril's weight and that of the potatoes would be sufficient to keep the whole string down, but tried out the arrangement along the length of the ship and after adjusting the contents of some of the sacks found that it worked well enough.

The evening mist was now rising from the weed and they hurried forward their preparations with the utmost speed, but no cloud obscured the sun this evening and the ship had come so much nearer to Yonita's island in the past two days that there did not seem any risk of Sir Deveril becoming lost on his way ashore as the others had been two nights before.

It was agreed that the machine-gun party should take lanterns with them and place these at a point well up from the weed and above the mist on the shore of Satan's Island to show Sir Deveril where they were, so that he could land his men without having to hunt a mile of coast to find the advance-guard.

An hour and a half had slipped by since they had reached the *Gafelborg* but by half past six all was ready and Deveril launched himself out on to the weed with the long string of balloons trailing behind him. At first they feared that he would lose his balance owing to the extra buoyancy which the additional balloons gave him, but there was no wind upon the silent sea to carry him off his course, and he soon adjusted his strokes with stilts and ski-sticks to suit the slower motion necessitated by the long chain of bladders.

Directly they had assured themselves that he was progressing safely, Basil and De Brissac hurried back with Li Foo to Luvia's cabin. He had woken in their absence and was sitting on the edge of his bunk with his head buried in his hands. As they came in he started up and grabbed at a revolver that lay on a shelf at his bunk side, but immediately he realized who it was a look of immeasurable relief spread over his tired face.

They told him, as briefly as possible, what had occurred since he had been knocked out and fallen down the funnel, while he berated himself miserably; cursing at his own folly as having been the cause of all the terrible events which had taken place since they left the ship.

Basil tried to hearten him by saying that Harlem had probably intended to make off to Satan's Island in any case, but Luvia was difficult to cheer. He felt that Jansen's death lay at his door and that he would have been in a better case to defend the ship if he had not been suffering from such an appalling hang-over.

While Luvia was dressing, De Brissac and Li Foo went down to the hold to get the machine-gun and ammunition, but Basil remained to learn further particulars of the raid.

Juhani had little to add to Li Foo's version of the massacre, but in jerky sentences gave an account of events the night of the scrap. He blamed himself entirely for the row with Vicente although it seemed to Basil that Synolda was really the cause of the trouble through having led both men on to such a pitch of jealousy. Luvia could give no explanation of her conduct as he had not seen or spoken to her the following day.

'I don't wonder you were sick,' Basil remarked; 'she seems to have behaved abominably.'

Luvia looked up suddenly from pulling on a sock. 'What the dame's done doesn't matter two hoots now. She's right to amuse herself her own way I reckon, and anyhow I was the mug. The thing that's been biting me ever since I came up for air is what those devils of niggers'll do to her tonight. I'd risk my neck to get any dame out of their clutches however much dirt she'd done me.'

'I know, I know,' moaned Basil. 'For God's sake don't talk of it. Unity's there too.'

They fell into a miserable silence until De Brissac and Li Foo joined them. The Frenchman rapidly set about assembling the parts of his gun while Li Foo went down again with Basil into the hold to bring up the ammunition. They all worked with feverish haste but it was a quarter to eight before the gun was assembled, and darkness had fallen by the time they got out on deck again.

There was one balloon left for each of the four men and two over, to which they tethered the heavy cases containing the belts of machine-gun bullets. De Brissac decided to carry the precious gun himself and the others lashed it across his shoulders under the balloon. The two bladders supporting the ammunition were attached by lines to Luvia and Basil, who, with Li Foo, each took two of the six rifles and a knife or cutlass from one of the dead negroes on the deck. It was pitch dark now except for the bright patch of light made by the two lanterns which Li Foo had strapped to his waist.

De Brissac told the Chinaman to put them out so that any of the savages watching from the island should not be warned of their approach. They had no fear of being lost in the mist and darkness this time as Satan's Island presented a much longer stretch of coastline than the promontory at the foot of the cross that formed Yonita's island, and the *Gafelborg* had now drifted to within half a mile of the entrance of the channel that separated the two.

About the ship was all the silence of the night with only an occasional plop to show that some vile creature was stirring in the weed beneath them. After a last look round to see that nothing had been forgotten they left the deck of the *Gafelborg* with its cargo of dead men.

It was half past eight when they landed on Satan's Island and they had a mile of dark foreshore to cover in rounding the curve of the island until they could reach the beach nearest to the promontory from which Deveril's people would set off. Keeping as far as possible from the water-line, from fear of giant crabs that might come up out of it, they struggled forward over the rough ground in single file; by nine they had reached the beach where they hoped that Deveril's force would be able to land.

Scrambling up the slope away from the weed De Brissac chose a promontory well above the mist. They weighed down their balloons and showed a light.

Almost at once an answering flash came from the opposite shore. It went out but then came on again flickering rhythmically.

'They're Morsing us,' exclaimed Luvia. 'Fancy their knowing Morse.'

'Nothing strange in that,' said Basil; 'all of them are the children or descendants of sailors.'

'Hi! Give me that lamp.' Luvia snatched the lantern from Li Foo and pulling off his coat flung it over the steady light so as to obscure it entirely for the moment. By lifting the coat up and down, so as to show the light in long and short intervals, he was able to reply.

Sir Deveril signalled that he had six men with him and that another forty-one men and youths were being fetched from various parts of the island. All would carry firearms although some of these would be of an oldfashioned kind. As soon as enough men arrived to form a first detachment of thirteen he would send them across but as it would probably be the best part of half an hour before the first lot had collected and set off, he did not think they could reach Satan's Island under the hour.

'An hour,' gasped Basil, 'but just think what may be happening to those girls!'

'The natives will almost certainly hold a feast of victory and the girls will be all right till then.' De Brissac tried to comfort him.

'But it's nine o'clock already and we've got to cross the island.'

'An' the balloons'll have to make seven trips before all four lots of Deveril's folk get over,' Luvia added. 'Holy Mike! I hadn't thought of that. It'll be close on two before they've all landed.'

'We can't possibly wait all that time,' Basil broke out. 'I'll go mad if I stay here.'

De Brissac made a wry grimace. 'I know what you must feel, *mon vieux*, but what else can we do?'

'Go ahead without waiting for the rest; spy out the land and try to create some sort of demonstration to keep those devils busy until Deveril's people come up.'

'That would be a forlorn hope indeed,' De Brissac shrugged. 'We are almost certain to be caught and killed and, in any case, having the best part of five hours' start of the main body how could we possibly occupy the natives for so long?'

'If we can find a good hiding-place near their village we could shoot down into it. That would give them something to think about. If we wait for the rest we won't get there before daybreak and God knows what will have happened to the girls by then. We must go on—*we must*.'

'I'm with you,' Luvia muttered thickly, 'but how'll we know the way to go?'

'I've an idea of it,' Basil said. 'There's a great barrier cliff at the far end of the island and the native village lies just below it —a little nearer to the eastern coast than to the west.'

'Right,' agreed De Brissac with sudden decision; 'in that case we'll go ahead. It is sheer madness but, as you say, the only chance of helping the girls before morning.'

Luvia began to flash a message to the opposite shore letting Deveril know what they meant to do, while the others loaded up their burdens. Leaving one of the lanterns to guide Sir Deveril in they set off on their march. De Brissac led the way with his machine-gun strapped to his shoulders. The others followed humping the heavy cases of ammunition and two rifles apiece.

A few hundred yards inland they passed some scattered trees. As they penetrated farther the land became more thickly wooded. None of them spoke but each was busy with thoughts which centred round the captive women. Within five minutes of leaving the shore the little forlorn hope was deep in the dark, silent forest.

CHAPTER XIX

THE FORLORN HOPE

THE forest was mainly pine and larch with occasional tall cedars. They found the going to be comparatively easy as there was little undergrowth. Apart from large patches of bramble, which delayed them for a little here and there, they were able to move forward in a straight line, at a good speed, over the springy carpet formed by the fallen pine-needles of countless years.

The machine-gun, rifles, and cases of bullets which they carried weighed heavily upon them, and De Brissac decreed that, to avoid wearing themselves out, they must halt regularly every ten minutes for a short rest. Occasionally they struck thicker patches of the forest where the night sky was shut out entirely, but, for the most part, they were able to catch glimpses of star clusters in one direction or another and several times they caught sight of the Southern Cross gleaming high in the heavens to the southward.

De Brissac was not relying upon the stars for guidance as he had brought his prismatic compass with its luminous needle. Knowing the metal of the machine-gun he carried would seriously affect its orientation he laid the gun down each time they halted and walked some distance from it with his compass before checking their direction.

Basil alone had a rough idea of the geography of the island and, from the scale to which the map in the great hall had been drawn, he estimated that they had about seven miles to go.

The three white men were all muscular and in excellent condition, while Li Foo, was of the thin, sinewy type that can stand up to tremendous exertions without showing any trace of fatigue, so De Brissac was able to push forward at a steady speed that ate up the miles without fear that any of his companions would find the pace too hot; yet, loaded down as they were, and having to rest every ten minutes, the journey seemed interminable.

They spoke little. Each was busy with his thoughts. Basil and

Luvia were wrought up to such a pitch of sickening anxiety about what might be happening to the girls that they felt no weariness and were constantly pressing De Brissac to curtail the short periods of rest on which he insisted.

The Frenchman was too good a soldier to give way to them. The pace he set was too swift to keep up over a long distance without regular halts; he knew that the only chance of their arriving at their destination still in a condition to undertake the desperate exertions of a fight lay in their forced march being carried out with military precision.

Half an hour after they had started the moon came up and its light glimmered ghostlike in the wider clearings. Their footsteps were muffled by the thick carpet of pine-needles and an eerie silence caused them to speak, when they spoke at all, in lowered voices. Only the occasional snapping of a twig under foot and their laboured breathing broke the hushed quiet, except once or twice when a small animal scurried away at their approach, until, during their fifth halt, Basil whispered 'Listen!'

They remained stock-still, and, faintly through the windless night, there came to them the muffled throb of native drums: 'Hell!' exclaimed Luvia, 'the party's started.'

De Brissac nodded. 'They've been waiting for the moon to get up. Savages nearly always depend on moonlight to illuminate their midnight gatherings.'

'We must hurry—hurry!' cried Basil, grabbing up his cases of ammunition.

'Put those down,' ordered De Brissac sharply. 'We've another minute to go yet. You'll need all the strength you've got when we arrive.'

'But we must get on—*we must!*' Basil reiterated. 'Just think what the girls are going through.'

'I know, *mon ami*, I know. But we have only covered about half the distance. It is imperative that we should arrive as strong and fit as we are now. By exhausting yourself you will only defeat your own purpose.'

'You no wolly, Misteh,' Li Foo said soothingly. 'Black devil eat and dlink first. Takum Missie after.'

'That sounds sense, Chinkee,' agreed Luvia brightening a little. 'The girls'll be all O.K. for a bit yet, I reckon.'

'I only hope to God you're right,' Basil muttered, and they set off again.

As they advanced the war drums grew louder, a steady,

233

rhythmic tattoo that beat with maddening insistence upon their ears as they hurried forward.

Some five miles from the shore the forest ended abruptly and they came out upon an open stretch of downland which sloped gently upward. The drums had now taken on a more rapid beat and the night air seemed to quiver with their throbbing. De Brissac's party were beginning to feel the strain of their exertions; the guns and ammunition cases seemed to have doubled in weight since they set out. The night was mild and fine but all four men were sweating profusely as they laboured up the slope.

Another mile and they reached its crest, which De Brissac estimated must be a good hundred feet above sea level. Immediately they breasted the rise they could see the light of a great fire in the distance, far below them down in the valley. De Brissac called a halt and scanned the moonlit panorama through his night-glasses. Against the glow of the fire he could just make out a number of low buildings and some darker patches a little to the east which, thrown up in the moonlight, suggested a big cluster of hutments rather than a patch of trees. Beyond the native village there rose a solid black patch clearly outlined against the starlit sky to southward, which they knew must be the great cliff with the high table-land that occupied the whole of the southern end of the island.

Grabbing up their weighty burdens they hurried on again down the slope and a hundred yards farther came upon a patch of mealies. To its left they struck a track which led in the direction of the village and, from this point, they found that the land on either side of them was in a state of rough cultivation. Every few hundred yards, at some distance from the track, there showed the outline of a native kraal, but all of these were deserted and it was obvious that their inmates had left them to attend the gathering about the fire.

Half a mile farther on they came to another slight rise which hid the fire from them for a few moments and, when they reached its top, they halted once again. The village was now only a quarter of a mile distant and could be seen in some detail. The huts to the east numbered a good two hundred. No light showed among them and all the natives were congregated in a big, open space which was ringed about by half a dozen larger shacks. In its centre the fire was burning brightly, and against the lurid flames the outline of a long, snake-like chain of natives could be seen as they wound in and out following their leader in a slow, rhythmic dance. Each man took two steps forward, one step back, then stamped with all his force upon the earth in time to the beat of the tom-toms. Their stamping echoed dully across the valley, but no other sound came from them; they danced with vigorous gestures, shaking their spears and knobkerries above their heads but maintaining complete silence.

A hundred yards to the west of the open space there was a single building forming three sides of a square and far greater in extent than any of the others. Round it the moonlight showed a high palisade fencing in a great compound. Without any of the watchers remarking on it each knew, as he gazed at the big, dark building, that it must be the dreaded Marriage House, and that in it the negroes kept the concubines, common to the whole community, which they either captured or reared there in slavery, apart from their own women.

De Brissac was studying the terrain through his glasses to select the most suitable spot for the forlorn hope that he led to make its attack. He knew that the natives did not lack courage. After having been beaten off with serious loss from the *Gafelborg* by rifle and revolver fire two mornings before, they had attacked the ship again, knowing that they must face heavy casualties if they were to succeed in looting the vessel of its drink and women. Once he set up his machine-gun and opened fire upon them, it was quite certain that they would charge it, and there were several hundreds of them. It was vital that the rescue party should choose their position with the utmost care in order to have a clear field of fire and such protection as the ground on the best chosen site could offer.

He made up his mind at once that, even at the expense of further time, they must make a wide circle round the village so that they could get the towering cliff as a protection for their backs.

When he told the others of his decision they could not possibly argue with its wisdom and, humping the ammunition cases again, they set off in a diagonal direction, across a field, towards the westernmost corner of the palisade that fenced in the compound of the Marriage House.

When they were within a hundred yards of it De Brissac turned further westward again to give it a wide berth and so avoid being seen by any sentries who might be posted about it; but Basil checked him.

'The girls are in that place somewhere. There doesn't seem to be anyone about. We could scale that palisade if one of us stood on the other's shoulders. Now's our chance to get them out while those devils are still busy dancing.'

De Brissac shook off his hand impatiently. '*Mon Dieu!* You must be crazy. There are probably two or three hundred other women inside that place as well as the girls. Even if there are no sentries and you got inside, the women would start screaming and we should all be massacred within ten minutes.'

Reluctantly Basil followed him in the new direction he had taken. They filed across lower ground where the fire was hidden from them for some distance by the western side of the compound.

As the ground rose again and they came opposite the northwest corner of the palisade, Luvia suddenly whispered 'Wait!' and sank down on to his knees. The others followed his example; from where they crouched he pointed out the tall, dark silhouette of a solitary negro who was standing near the corner of the palisade leaning upon a spear.

They crawled a hundred yards farther away, so as to get out of his range of vision, before rising to their feet again and plodding up on the higher ground towards the cliff.

At last they reached it and stood panting there. It rose almost sheer above their heads, apparently unscalable, with broken patches on its face only in the higher parts, which were thrown up by the moonlight. Farther to the east and almost opposite the bonfire De Brissac could see some big rocks just at the foot of the cliff, and he decided that somewhere there he should be able to find the well-protected position for which he was seeking.

Gasping and sweating they covered the last four hundred yards till they came to the great pile of rock and stone which formed part of a landslide. This broken ground was higher than the rest, shelving steeply away at each side and gently down in front towards the village, which lay about six hundred yards distant. They scrambled up to the highest rocks and found a large flat piece in front of which rose two higher peaks forming a small natural fort; it seemed to have been placed there for them by Providence.

De Brissac set up his gun while the others prepared the belts of ammunition for it and laid out in a row the six Winchesters they had brought with them.

From their new elevation they could see the village much more clearly than before. Hundreds of men and women formed a great

circle round the fire. All crouched cross-legged upon the ground
except in one place where a canopy had been erected and an
enormously fat negro in gaudy trappings was sitting on a sort of
throne. He was evidently the chief. Round him were gathered his
principal councillors and a number of witch-doctors in fantastic
costumes with grotesque animal masks upon their heads. Among
them Harlem could be clearly distinguished as he was still
clothed in his dungarees and an old tweed jacket.

The dance had changed, having become much more violent,
while the dancers no longer maintained their silence; instead,
each man was emitting wild blood-curdling howls at irregular
intervals. The rapid tattoo of the war-drums was inciting them
to a positive frenzy.

De Brissac had been quickly thinking out a plan of campaign.
He knew, from the many negro war-dances he had witnessed, that
the natives could not maintain this wild pace for long. Another
ten minutes or so and the dance would be over. Anything might
happen after that, and he could not hope that Sir Deveril would
be able to bring his force of forty-seven armed whites into action
for another three hours at least; even allowing for the fact that,
not having to carry the gun and ammunition, or make the circuit
of the village before attacking, which had taken his own party
the best part of threequarters of an hour, they would march more
quickly. If his party were to hold the fort for three hours and keep
the natives occupied for so long it was essential that Sir Deveril
should know the best way to relieve them if they were still alive
when he came up. Turning to Li Foo, De Brissac placed his hand
upon the Chinaman's shoulder.

'You are a brave fellow and a clever one. I'm going to give
you a special mission, which may save our lives if you do it
properly.'

'Ho, yess! Jus' yo tellum dissa fella,' said Li Foo promptly.

'Good. I want you to go back the way we came for about two
miles, until you reach the rising ground that overlooks the village
on the opposite side of the valley from here. The high part from
which we first caught sight of the village is threequarters of a mile
or a mile from the woods. You are to remain there until you
see Sir Deveril and his people coming out of the woods up the
slope. You can hardly miss them as there will be the best part of
fifty men, and they must cross the bare ground of the crest on
their way to the village. The chances are that by the time Sir
Deveril arrives we shall either be fighting here—in which case

you'll be able to see the flash of our arms—or dead; but you'll know if we have been in action because you'll hear the sound of our firing quite clearly across the valley. If we have not attacked or been attacked, you are to lead Sir Deveril and his men to us here by the way we came; then we can all act together and surprise the village. If we have already been in action and our firing has ceased you'll know that we have been killed or captured and Sir Deveril must use his own discretion as to what plan he adopts, but, if we are still fighting when Sir Deveril comes up, this is what I want him to do.

'He is to send a small party of his men south-east, down into that main maze of hutments you can see there, which is now deserted. The few men that he sends are to set those huts on fire, which should draw off the natives who are attacking us. In the meantime he is to march his main body to the south-west until he reaches the point where we saw the sentry guarding the Marriage House. It is practically undefended so he should be able to take it by a surprise attack and save the women from being butchered out of spite; then he can use it as a rallying-point if the blacks prove too numerous for his men. Once he gets inside it should not be difficult to hold owing to the strong stockade all round it. If he succeeds in capturing the Marriage House without difficulty he is to press on east, straight through the circle where the natives are dancing now towards the place where his small party have set the main group of huts on fire. In that way he should be able to take the natives in the rear while they are trying to save their goods from being burnt. Is that all clear?'

'Ho yess, Misteh. I tellum. His flen's mek plentee fire in black devil town but you wantum him come flom west-way. Li Foo heap savvy velly good.'

De Brissac nodded. '*Bien!* Off you go. Be as quick as you can but don't take the least chance of getting caught.'

With a smile the Chinaman picked up his rifle, slipped out from the cover of the rocks and disappeared into the shadows thrown by the cliff.

'Those niggers are getting pretty het up now,' said Juhani thoughtfully. 'God, how I am hating this! Can't we do something?'

'I don't want to fire on them before we've got to,' De Brissac replied. 'Once we open up, we'll have to face the whole lot and be prepared to die, literally, with our backs to the wall. There are easily five or six hundred of them and every moment they

238

remain dancing there means that Deveril is a few yards nearer to us.'

'But he won't be here for hours,' Basil expostulated, 'and think what the girls must be suffering in anticipation. Once the dance is over you can bet your life those devils will make straight for the compound and the women. We'll be able to give them something to think about with this machine-gun but, even if we scatter them, we daren't leave our position here to come out in the open. Some of them'll murder the girls for certain before Deveril can reach us.'

'That's so,' Luvia declared. 'Once they stop their dancing we won't have a hope in hell of getting the women out alive. We've got to do something—and that mighty quick.'

'The only thing for it is to raid the Marriage House while the men are still occupied.' Basil went on hurriedly. 'We only saw one sentry on it and they can't possibly have any idea that a rescue-party has set out. The sentry's probably there only to see to it that Unity and Synolda don't escape with the connivance of the other women. Even if there're a couple of men on guard we ought to be able to tackle them and get inside.'

'Sure,' Luvia backed him up. 'That's the way it is and that's what we're going to do; but you'd best stay here, De Brissac, with the gun, and blow merry hell out of them if there's trouble.'

'All right,' De Brissac agreed. 'I would come with you willingly were it not that I shall be more use to you here. From this position I can sweep the whole village with my fire; whereas if we all went and took the gun with us it would lose threequarters of its value. I shall not shoot until I see that your attempt has been discovered or hear it from their cries. You're almost certain to be killed, but you're right about it being the one hope now of saving the girls. You must hurry too—if you mean to do it—as the dance will soon be over.'

Leaving their rifles so that they should not be encumbered and taking only their cutlasses and pistols, Basil and Juhani gave De Brissac's hand a quick clasp and slithered down among the tumbled rocks to follow the path that Li Foo had taken a few moments before. Now that they were freed from their heavy burdens and moving downhill they were able to make rapid going. The beating of the drums and stamping of the earth by the black warriors drowned the noise of their footsteps so they had no need to exercise caution during the first part of their journey and were able to trot along side by side.

In five minutes they were back again in the hollow to the south-west of the compound. The solitary sentry had moved to the north-west corner of the stockade, but he was again standing motionless, leaning on his spear.

The two white men sank to their knees directly they saw him and began to crawl cautiously forward. Basil stretched out a hand and halted Juhani. 'We'd better separate,' he whispered, 'and advance on him from opposite sides in the shadow of the palisade. He's almost certain to hear one of us creeping up on him. Directly he turns to face that one, the other can rush him from behind.'

'O.K.' muttered Juhani, and he set off to crawl in a semi-circle round the solitary negro, while Basil flattened himself out on his stomach and wriggled straight forward up to the stockade.

It was made of thick tree trunks, so closely set that it was impossible to see between them, and he judged its height to be about ten feet. Each trunk had been sharpened to an ugly point as he could see from the serrated edge against the skyline, and it looked as though it would be a stiff job of work getting over it.

But Napoleon's phrase, 'It is time to think of the Vistula when we are over the Rhine', flashed into his mind. The negro sentry must be got out of the way first.

Fortunately the moon was in the east so the high paling threw a heavy belt of shadow about two yards wide, and Basil was able to worm his way along with little fear of being seen by anyone who was not keeping a very active watch.

The negro stood there motionless and silent, about twenty yards from the angle of the compound, staring out dreamily on to the moonlit vale; doubtless cursing his luck that he had been picked upon for this duty, while the others were feasting on the far side of the Marriage House. The wild, excited cries of the native dancers, the rhythmic stamping of their feet, and the rapid tattoo of the drums came clearly, drowning all other sounds, and enabling Basil to get to within ten yards of the sentry unobserved.

Basil saw a deeper patch of blackness that he knew must be Juhani take form at the corner beyond the man. Another yard and his knee caught a stone which clicked sharply against another. The negro swung round and caught sight of him. He rose swiftly to his feet and drew his cutlass.

The black's mouth opened and his white teeth gleamed; he was about to yell a warning. His spear lifted and came level with

Basil's face. Next second there was a sudden scuffling of feet and Juhani leapt upon the man's back, locking one arm tight round his neck. They went down in a heap together.

There was a short, wild flurry of whirling arms and legs, while Basil stood there, his cutlass raised, but fearing to strike in case his blow caught Juhani.

The two figures on the ground straightened out with a jerk. The negro gave a queer gurgle. Juhani shook himself free and stood up. 'I've broken his blasted neck,' he said in a hoarse whisper.

'Good,' Basil muttered. 'Now for the fence.'

Juhani spread out his legs and put his hands against the palisade. 'Up on my back,' he panted. 'Quick!'

Thrusting the cutlass into its sheath, Basil sprang on to Juhani's broad shoulders, gripped two of the points in the stout palisade and hoisted himself up to them. Luckily the tree trunks were so large that he was able to find a perch between them with one leg on each side of the stockade.

Juhani did not wait to be pulled up. As a sailor he was an expert climber and his height helped him. In one spring he had gripped two of the points of the great stakes and next moment he was perched beside Basil. Without a word they lowered themselves to the ground on the far side.

The Marriage House was a long, low building, forming three sides of a square, and large enough to accommodate at least a couple of hundred people. Lights were burning inside it and the murmur of voices drifted out to them quite distinctly. Evidently the women were waiting there for the visit they knew that the warriors would pay them on this gala night after the dance had been completed. The compound was deserted; its emptiness broken only by a few coarse wood tables and things that appeared to be washing troughs. Very cautiously, crouching a little, Basil and Juhani crept towards the nearest building.

CHAPTER XX

IN THE MARRIAGE HOUSE

DE BRISSAC watched the open space about the bonfires anxiously. It was nearly a quarter of an hour since his friends had left him. The dance had changed again; the warriors were now formed up thirty deep, in irregular lines, facing the fat old negro under the canopy. In unison they were chanting some wild song of victory, stamping the earth so furiously that the dust rose in a little cloud half obscuring their lower limbs; the upper portion of their naked bodies glistened with sweat in the light of the flames.

Every few minutes the dancers surged forward, raising their weapons on high and emitting hideous howls as they charged across the open to within a few feet of their chief. They receded again some twenty paces each time, recommenced their chant, and stamped more furiously than ever. De Brissac knew that in a few moments now, at most, the climax would come; a last mock charge when they would halt with their weapons poised, apparently to kill, only a few inches from the watchers' faces. Instinctively he found himself praying each time a charge was made that it would not be the last, and that the dance would continue yet a little longer, giving time, precious time, to his friends.

Inside the stockade Basil and Juhani crept forward on tiptoe. As they came nearer to the long, low building that formed one side of the open square, they saw that it was raised a few feet from the ground on piles. Every ten yards or so a rickety flight of steps led up to a doorway. Of the four that they could see clearly two were open and two shut, but both of the open ones had curtains of some coarse material hanging across them.

The two men reached the hut and crept along it to the nearest doorway. An irregular, two-inch gap showed between the bottom of the curtain of the floorboards, which were just on a level with Juhani's chest. Reaching the steps he leant forward and, stooping, peered under the curtain. A horrible stench of greasy, unwashed human bodies was wafted out into his nostrils, but he scarcely noticed it in his eagerness to find Synolda.

From the loud murmur of sound he judged that the long building consisted of one large room although he could see only a portion of it. Its interior showed a squalor which beggared all description. There were no beds or furniture. The women lay or squatted on filthy, ragged mattresses, from which ends of straw protruded at the seams. Their colour varied from darkish brown to near-white, and they were of every age from children suckling at the breast, to women who looked forty, but might be younger.

He seemed to remember Sir Deveril saying that the negroes strangled their concubines when they were too old for further service in order to save food. Father Jerome had reported a continual shortage after his brief visit to Satan's Island and, from the ragged patches of ill-cultivated land Juhani had seen that night, he had already gathered that the negroes were a lazy, thriftless tribe. Owing to the climate, which was far harsher than that of their native Africa, crops needed more attention and labour to grow, so in the bad seasons such a people would certainly suffer famine.

Some of the women were talking listlessly in low voices; others were sleeping with tattered coverlets drawn round them. As he watched, heavy footfalls sounded on the floor and an enormous, full-blooded negress with powerful, gorilla-like arms plodded slowly down the centre of the room. In her right hand she grasped a cat-o'-nine-tails; the coffee-coloured women fell silent and shrank away as she walked by; evidently she was some sort of wardress or mistress of the house who kept the concubines in order. Juhani drew back and shook his head conveying dumbly to Basil that the girls were not there.

Easing their way along the side of the building they passed the next door, which was shut, and paused at a farther one which only had a ragged curtain across it. This time the curtain fell to the floor, but it had a large rent in it, about three feet up, and by standing on tiptoe Juhani was easily able to get another glimpse of the big room's occupants.

Here a little group of the women showed more animation. They formed a small kneeling circle and were chattering shrilly as they played some primitive game of dice. One girl among them was of unusual beauty; a 'high-yaller' with blue eyes, light bronze skin, and near-gold hair. She was about nineteen and her lithe figure had just reached perfection. The greater part of it was exposed to view as, like the rest, she had little on except a soiled and ill-patched shift. The other women looked blowsy and unwholesome beside her. The hair of them all was tousled and their bodies ill-cared-for. In the ten seconds Juhani was staring at the fair girl he saw her pull down the shift from her shoulder and kill a louse.

His survey had occupied no more than a minute. They moved on more swiftly now, round the corner of the building to that which joined it with the one on the far side of the courtyard. Here again some doors were shut and others only veiled by curtains.

As they approached the nearest a scream rang out from inside the building. Basil leapt forward impulsively and, stopping, raised the curtain an inch with his finger so that he could peer beneath it. The sight he saw filled him with a fierce desire to draw his pistol and rush inside. Two more huge, full-blooded negresses stood one on either side of a fair-skinned young girl of about seventeen. They were holding her down while a third, whose face was contorted with sadistic hate, wielded a cat-o'-nine-tails above her head.

The girl was kicking out with her bare legs but her body was held by the two great black women, as though in a vice, and a second later the nine lashes descended through the air on to her back with a sickening whistle. She let out another scream; Basil swayed forward, but Luvia, who was peering through a gap at the side of the curtain, wrenched him back. Their own women needed all the help they had to give and must come first; pushing Basil slightly he urged him on to the next doorway.

A third wail of agony came quavering through the night. Silence fell again, broken only by the wild cries of the dancing savages in the near distance, the beat of the tom-toms and the constant mutter that came from inside the evil Marriage House.

They passed two more closed doorways but the third was again covered only by a piece of tattered stuff. Basil caught the first glimpse of the interior and instantly gripped Luvia's arm. Juhani bent and peered in, rapidly glimpsing what Basil had seen before him. Almost opposite to them Unity and Synolda were lying on one of the filthy mattresses with their backs propped against the further wall. Their faces were grimed and tear-stained. Great red semi-circles showed under the eyes of both girls from constant weeping, but they were dry-eyed now, having perhaps no more tears to shed. They were huddled together tightly clasped in each other's arms. An awful look of despair and terror was on both their faces.

Juhani wondered why they did not endeavour to escape through the open doorway, but it occurred to him that they had probably attempted to do so and been hauled back. The reason they were not making any attempt at the moment was plain to him a second after as, shifting his position a little, he saw another of the huge negresses squatting on her haunches only a couple of yards away with a cat-o'-nine-tails laid across her lap. Behind the negress stood a long-limbed, coffee-coloured child who was busily engaged in picking vermin out of the hideous old woman's tight, black curls.

Stepping softly back Juhani gave Basil another chance to look and pointed with his finger in the direction of the huge black woman. Basil gave her one glance before rivetting his eyes on Unity. She moved a little at that second and he saw that the right sleeve of her dress had been completely ripped away; on her bare arm there showed three angry, red weals. The sight inflamed him to the point of madness; drawing his cutlass he wrenched aside the curtain and leapt into the room.

Red rage distorting his features, Basil swung his blade high and in one stroke almost severed the hideous head of the negress from her obese body. Juhani, bounding after him, dashed straight over to the girls.

Next second pandemonium was loose in the long, low barrack. The half-caste women sprang up from their palliasses gibbering excitedly. A big negress, who had been sitting about fifty feet down the room, gave an angry bellow and came lumbering heavily towards them, but the concubines saw their chance to revenge themselves upon their tormentors in this unprecedented invasion of their quarters. One of them tripped the negress and the others fell upon her like a pack of wolves, tearing the flesh from her face and body in gory shreds.

In the opposite direction further sounds of strife broke out. The two wardresses who had been thrashing the young girl advanced side by side, laying about them lustily with their nine-tailed whips at the crowd of slatternly women who tried to bar their progress. A strapping young girl threw an earthen pot which caught one of the negresses in the face and she went down with a howl of pain. Basil saw no more of the affray. He had snatched Unity up in his arms and half-lugged, half-carried her out of the vile building. Juhani was behind him with Synolda flung over his shoulder.

'You all right?' Basil gasped as he drew the clean wholesome air of the dark night thankfully into his lungs.

'Yes,' breathed Unity. 'Oh, Basil! bless you!'

'Can you run?' he cried, hustling her along by the arm.

'Yes, yes,' she shouted, breaking from him and tearing towards the distant palisade as though all the devils in hell were after her.

'Put me down, put me down,' Synolda's voice came from just behind them; but Juhani took no notice and raced on, his great strength being more than equal to the burden.

Suddenly it came to him that the night was changed. What was it? What had happened? A second later the truth flashed on him. For nearly three hours now the monotonous tattoo of the war-drums had been beating in their ears. They had ceased; so, too, had the war-cries of the natives.

The same thought penetrated Basil's mind just as they reached the palisade. There was a chance that the savages would rest for a while after their exertions, or pause to eat and drink, but it was equally likely that in a few moments they would come streaming through the gates of the compound into the courtyard.

Luvia came bounding up and, dropping Synolda on her feet, bent down, his hands planted on his knees.

'Up you go,' he panted. 'Quick, for God's sake!'

Basil scrambled on to his back. A second swift movement brought him astride the palisade between two of the great spikes. Synolda had followed him on to Juhani's wide shoulders. Basil seized her hands and drew her up beside him. Lifting her right clear of the spike in front of him he dropped her down on the other side.

With feverish haste he stooped for Unity. She gave a spring and landed in his arms; her face on a level with his own. He pressed one fierce, swift kiss on her mouth and, tilting her over, let her drop beside Synolda.

The girls had hardly picked themselves up when their men thudded down almost on to them. Basil realized only then that in the excitement they had lost their sense of direction and, instead of heading for the western side of the compound, they had come out to its south. The error had brought them a good two hundred yards nearer to De Brissac but, on the other hand, they were no more than a hundred yards from the nearest native

246

hutments and in plain sight of any of the savages round the fire who chanced to glance in their direction.

Up on his hill of rock, at the foot of the landslide, De Brissac was still peering anxiously through his night-glasses. In dismay he had witnessed the war-dance come to an end with a final mock charge right up to the very faces of the onlookers, and heard the last wild cry that heralded an almost complete silence. To his relief the sweating dancers sank down on the ground and young negresses moved out from among the crowd bringing them earthenware pitchers from which they drank. There seemed a chance that the warriors' visit to the Marriage House still might be postponed a little longer.

In the new silence that had fallen over the great gathering fresh sounds now became perceptible to him. A single scream echoed from the Marriage House and then the shrill falsetto of many women's upraised voices. At any moment he feared the big negro under the canopy might send somebody to investigate the trouble but none of the crowd in the clearing appeared to take any notice. Probably they were used to quarrelling among their concubines.

He focused his glasses on the compound, wondering if Basil and Juhani had managed to get inside or if the excitement there was caused by some ordinary upset. It was too dark for him to see anything but the faint glimmer from some of the curtained doorways, and in the valley beyond, to the west, all was darkness and silence.

For two minutes he peered through his night-glasses; then he fancied that he could make out a vague movement down there by the south side of the stockade, which was nearest to him. A moment later he was certain of it and his heart bounded joyfully. Four figures bunched together were moving cautiously up towards the cliff. It could only be Basil and Juhani, with the two girls; but why in the name of thunder, he wondered, had they taken the risk of passing so horribly near the great gathering of negroes? As he watched he could see the pale blur of the girls' light-coloured dresses even at that distance.

Suddenly a shout went up from one of the blacks on the edge of the crowd. The whole body of natives seemed to turn as one. The white women and their rescuers had been spotted. Instantly the warriors were upon their feet shrieking madly. The tightly packed mass broke out of its circle; those farthest away, streaming across the open space, silhouetted plainly against the blazing

247

fire while those nearest the compound rushed forward to head off the little party that was coming up the hill.

De Brissac's machine-gun was aimed and sighted. At the same instant that Juhani and Basil fired their pistols into the oncoming crowd De Brissac pressed down the lever and a stream of lead streaked from his gun. The night became hideous with its clatter and the screams of the wounded as the first burst' took its victims among the witch-doctors and elders who surrounded the big negro chief.

Shrieks, yells and curses came up from the valley and echoed back from the cliff-face. Utter confusion reigned in the lighted circle. A score of dead and dying lay writhing upon the ground. The chief himself had been hit in the groin and was howling frantically with the pain of his wound.

The unexpected attack momentarily halted the natives nearest to the little party of whites. Taking advantage of it, the four of them began to run, but after a moment, the nearest savages charged towards them again.

De Brissac swivelled his machine-gun and fired another burst, doing deadly execution among the negroes who were nearest to his friends, but hordes of them seemed to be sweeping up the hillside from every direction. He kept the lever of the gun down and traversed it swiftly from side to side. The blacks were so numerous and crowded together that practically every bullet found a mark; the night became a horrid din of wailing, flesh-torn humans.

Juhani was half-way up the hill, dragging Synolda by the arm; Basil and Unity were running level, only a few yards behind them. A group of burly warriors was less than a dozen yards away, racing to cut them off. One flung a spear that sailed within two inches of Synolda's shoulder; a flight of spears followed and Basil was pierced by one in the fleshy part of his thigh. He wrenched it out and, whipping round, pistolled the man who had thrown it.

Luvia shot down two more of the nearest negroes, but the others would have overwhelmed them had not De Brissac concentrated his fire on their aggressors. Mown down by the blast of lead the blacks pitched and tumbled as they were hit, toppling backwards down the hillside.

The four whites raced on. Another moment brought them to the foot of the rocks, Juhani took a flying leap and landed half on the ledge beside De Brissac. Wriggling round he stretched out his long arms and, grabbing each of the girls by a hand, hauled them up beside him. Gasping and cursing, Basil stumbled up the broken, jagged slope and flinging himself down beside De Brissac snatched up a rifle. Luvia seized another and, as fresh hordes of savages charged yelling up the hill, the three white men commenced the grim fight for their lives and those of the girls they had rescued.

CHAPTER XXI

UNDER THE CLIFF

BRIGHT moonlight lit the prospect of the whole low valley. From the natural fort, formed by the great jagged rocks at the base of the landslide, its defenders could see the dense mass of native hutments away in the dip to their right front; before them, six hundred yards away, the great bonfire still burned in the clearing, its light a little subdued by the cold silver of the moonbeams. To its left the Marriage House compound was now full of screaming, running figures.

In a great semi-circle, from cliff-face to cliff-face on either side of them, countless dark forms were racing up the gentle rise. It seemed utterly impossible that the whites could withstand such numbers and there was no possibility of retreat. Behind them, at an angle of forty-five degrees, there rose a fifty-foot gradient of loose earth and shale which had come down from the mountain mass with the great rocks amongst which they crouched. Above it loomed a black cavity. The moonlit landscape and the towering cliff behind them had no cloud, only degrees of shade and darkness, with here and there a silvery edge of jutting rock.

De Brissac had fitted a new belt of ammunition to his machine-gun. As the howling crowd of natives surged up the slope he pressed down its lever. The gun spat flame like an acetylene blow-lamp and the staccato rat-tat-tat of its automatic explosions drowned the dull trampling of the advancing savages on the matted earth.

Standing out from the cliff the natural fort formed a semi-circle and could be attacked on its sides as well as its front. Luvia was crouched between two large boulders with Synolda beside him to De Brissac's right while Basil lay prone upon the flat slab of rock, with Unity to the Frenchman's left. The two girls had hardly recovered from their desperate effort to escape being cut off but they did their best to help their men by loading the three spare Winchesters and placing ammunition ready to hand for the machine-gun.

Traversing the gun slowly from side to side De Brissac took a terrible toll of the black attackers, mowing them down by the score before they were near enough to throw their spears, but along each cliff-face the negroes were able to advance without exposing themselves to the decimating fire. Basil and Luvia found themselves faced by a mob of warriors who came pounding up towards them. Both the white men used their rifles until the magazines were exhausted then snatched the ready-loaded spares from the girls.

On each side of the redoubt their bullets dealt death and destruction among the foremost of their aggressors but the others came hurtling on, and the spears they flung came clattering down among the rocks. Unity screamed as one pierced the soft flesh of her arm. Basil turned quickly, but she made a desperate gesture which he knew at once meant that she was not seriously wounded and that he must not relax, for a second, in his efforts to drive off the howling band who were now scrambling up the lower rocks.

The front was clear. Not a single black had succeeded in getting to within two hundred yards. The ground beyond was littered with dead and dying. The unwounded were beating a precipitate retreat; rushing in panic to save themselves from a further rain of death-dealing lead. In the nick of time De Brissac abandoned his gun and came to Basil's assistance with his automatic; shooting the foremost savage through the head. His intervention enabled Basil to grab up the fifth rifle. He plugged another two negroes at close range; the rest scuttled back in terror and made off into the darkness.

On his side Luvia had been more fortunate as he had better cover and the rocks in front of him were more difficult to scale. He had succeeded in shooting down five of the natives and the others had abandoned any further attempt to rush him for the moment.

In the lull that followed they sorted themselves out and attended to the casualties. Basil's thigh-wound was not serious as the spear had caught him in the fleshy part on the outer side of the leg and only ripped away a piece of skin. By tearing out one of his shirtsleeves he was able to make a bandage for it which De Brissac adjusted with practised skill. The spear-wound in

Unity's arm was more serious as the point had pierced the muscle above the elbow and it was bleeding freely. They applied a tourniquet and bound up the wound to stop the bleeding while Synolda made a sling out of a scarf she was wearing, to keep the arm in place.

'I'll say we came out of that mighty well,' Juhani remarked gruffly. 'Take a look at all those stiffs in the valley there. That ought to teach 'em.'

'I hope to God it does,' Basil murmured. 'It was touch and go. We may not be so lucky next time.'

'I doubt if there'll be a next,' Juhani said more cheerfully. 'They've had a bellyful, and they know what's coming to them if they try the same stuff again.'

De Brissac said nothing; having no wish to depress the others. Now that the natives had learnt what they were up against, after their first mad, unplanned onslaught, he did not think they would make any further attack while the moonlight lasted; but a dark patch in the sky to the north-eastward told him clouds there were blotting out the stars and he feared that in another ten minutes or so they might obscure the moon.

For a little time they sat, almost in silence. The terrible experience which the girls had been through was too recent for them to speak of with any uneasiness yet; the men were all tired after their long forced march and knew that they must conserve their remaining strength in case they had to face fresh fighting.

Basil sat with his back against a rock and Unity lay in the crook of his arm. Juhani and Synolda were perched side by side upon a ledge but a strange shyness seemed to have come between them now that they were suddenly reunited. They had not spoken more than a dozen words to each other since their bitter quarrel and the shooting of old Jansen. Both of them sat awkwardly silent with their eyes cast down; not daring to catch each other's glance in the soft moonlight.

After a period of quietness, broken only by the groaning of the wounded negroes, Basil spoke: 'Deveril and his people ought to be well on their way by now and we'll be able to chip in with good effect when they start setting light to the kraals.'

De Brissac shook his head. 'We've got a long time to go before we can hope for that. A lot has happened since we reached here but it's surprising how much action can be crammed into a single minute. It's barely half an hour yet since we reached the shelter of these rocks and then, if you remember, we reckoned that the islanders would be a good three hours before they could come up with us.'

As he spoke he was studying the low ground of the valley through his night-glasses. The bonfire still burned brightly in the open space but the savages had vanished to a man. Not a tremor of movement showed among the dark hutments and the Marriage House compound was now empty. During the fight he had glimpsed the half-caste concubines streaming out of the great gates in the palisade and round its north-eastern corner into the patchy blackness of the maize-fields. Evidently they had succeeded in overcoming their gaolers and, by this time, had probably taken to the forest. He wondered how Li Foo was faring, and judged that if he had followed their old track he should, by now, be reaching the higher ground on the far side of the valley where he could take up some advantageous position from which to watch the whole line of the woods for the approach of Sir Deveril and his company.

A film passed across the moon. The silver vanished from the crags and bulging overhang above them. Their range of vision was curtailed, so that the native village was now only a blur in the shadows, and none of the houses could be seen distinctly except those near the big fire. An unbroken hush hung over the darkened sweep of country before them. Not a shadow moved giving the least indication of the place to which the savages had retreated. The minutes crawled by. Gradually the film across the moon thickened until a big bank of cloud blotted it out entirely. They were now dependent on the faint starlight by which they could just make out each other's faces vaguely, but they could not see more than fifty feet from their redoubt into the surrounding murk.

De Brissac took up his position behind his gun again. Without a word Basil and Juhani picked up their rifles and, posting themselves on his flanks, stood straining their eyes into the darkness. Their muscles tensed, they listened anxiously for the least sound which might indicate a renewal of hostilities. At last it came; the sharp tinkle of a stone as it glanced on a piece of rock and rattled down the slope away to the left in front of Basil.

'Hold your fire!' whispered De Brissac. 'Keep calm and take them one by one. Shoot for their bodies once you can see them.'

'O.K.,' muttered Luvia, and suddenly his rifle cracked.

A second later the other two came into action as their eyes

focused on black humps of deeper shadow stealthily moving up towards them.

Instantly the rifles and machine-gun flashed the blacks leaped to their feet and launched themselves at the redoubt. The blast of fire from De Brissac's gun checked the advance in front even more quickly than before but, once again, the two sides of the rocky fort became points of peril. A score of blacks reached the lower boulders in spite of Basil's and Luvia's good marksmanship, but De Brissac was equal to the occasion. He stood up, with his machine-gun in his arms, and poured a stream of bullets across Luvia's front, annihilating the yelling savages there. Swinging round, he brought it to bear on the other group with equal fatal effect.

One huge negro escaped his fire and was already up on the land-slide behind them, but Synolda snatched up a loose slab of rock and hurled it at him, catching him in the midriff. With a grunt he doubled up and, slipping, somersaulted down the rocks on top of his dead and wounded comrades.

The attack was over and they sat back again; mopping their perspiring faces before hastily setting about the reloading of their weapons. De Brissac frowned anxiously as he fitted a new belt of ammunition to his machine-gun. With it he had done enormous execution but he was down to his last belt and once that had been fired any further attack would render their situation desperate. To his relief the shadows lightened just then and the moon came out from behind the bank of clouds, but another bank shut out the stars further to the north and was drifting slowly towards it.

For a few minutes they sat there, resting their tired limbs and praying fervently that the moonlight might endure a little longer. All too soon the moon was veiled again and the shadows crept forward, like living things, out of the valley, hiding its landmarks in a cloak of inky blackness.

The third attack developed very shortly after the disappearance of the moon; the enemy had evidently been waiting for it and preparing to make a new assault directly they could count on darkness to cover their activities.

Again for breathless seconds the flashes stabbed the murk; the machine-gun chattered and the acrid fumes of cordite were strong in their nostrils; but the tattoo of the gun ceased abruptly. De Brissac's last belt of ammunition was finished and all that remained from the heavy cases they had humped so laboriously were the chains of miniature brass shell-cases which tinkled as they knocked against each other. Yet for the third time the gun had done its work. The horde of blacks was flying down the hill leaving their dead and dying piled high upon the earth at the edge of the nearest boulders.

'I'll say you've got guts,' Luvia panted. 'They must be stark crazy to charge that gun of yours the way they do.'

'It won't help us next time,' De Brissac said grimly. 'The ammunition's run out.'

Their new peril caused them acute anxiety as they tried to pierce the surrounding gloom for signs of a further assault. There was silence no longer. In the last two attacks many of the natives had got right up to the rocks on either side before being shot down and their groans of agony now wrung the heart-strings.

'Here they come!' cried Juhani raising his rifle and aiming for a dark figure no more than twenty feet away.

Basil stood ready on his side but their front was now totally unprotected. De Brissac could only clutch a spare rifle that Unity thrust towards him and empty its magazine into the advancing mass. They all felt that their last hour had come. In a few moments they must be borne down by sheer weight of numbers and massacred, but before the attack had a chance to develop fully relief came from an unexpected quarter.

A flame spurted up away down in the blackness of the valley to their right where they knew the thickest cluster of the native huts to be and, as though it were a signal, the rattle of musketry came clearly from beyond the Marriage House.

'*Dieu merci!*' De Brissac gasped. 'Deveril and his men!'

The blacks had also seen the flames; they hesitated, broke off their attack on the stony fort, and turning, ran down the hill, leaving the defenders of the redoubt to witness the scene in the valley unmolested.

From the native village great spurts of flame were now going up as the frail dwellings of dried mud, grass and wattle burned like tinder while the north-east corner of the stockade round the Marriage House compound was lit, intermittently, by the flash of firearms.

'Well done, Deveril!' Basil gasped. 'By Jove, he's got here quickly!'

'Nearly two hours before his time,' De Brissac supplemented.

'Oh, thank God! Thank God!' Unity sighed; letting her head fall on Basil's shoulder.

A few moments later, while the fight in the valley was still raging, the moon came out again and they could see the rescue party. Deveril and his men had fought their way out of the compound and were advancing up the slope firing to either hand, upon shadowy groups of blacks, as they came.

De Brissac stared down at them anxiously. 'That can't be all his force. It's no more than ten to a dozen men. Where the devil have the others got to?'

'Making a bonfire of the niggers' homesteads,' Juhani said quickly. 'There're lots of folks moving down there. Look, man! you can see them against the flames.'

Dense clouds of smoke and sparks were rising from the native village and wild confusion reigned as indistinct figures dashed back and forth, glimpsed only for seconds in the lurid glare.

Deveril's men were half-way up the slope. Standing up, now, in their front, De Brissac's party gave them a rousing cheer. An answering shout came from the rescuers and their firing ceased as the blacks gave back on either side, enabling them to cover the last two hundred yards at the double. Willing hands hauled them up into the redoubt as soon as they reached the boulders at its foot.

Panting, laughing, exclaiming, they exchanged breathless greetings and, to De Brissac's amazement, he found Yonita was among the rescue party.

'What in the world are you doing here?' he cried, seizing both her hands and kissing them violently.

'She was so plaguey insistent,' Deveril shrugged. 'With our thirteen balloons we can land twelve men each journey. Four trips will see the forty-seven men I have raised over and leave two balloons spare on the last crossing. Knowing that, Yonita blackguarded me into letting her accompany our vanguard.'

'But why are you so few?' asked Basil hurriedly. 'Are all the rest of your people down in the village?'

Deveril shook his head. 'Gad! No. Only Li Foo whom you sent to meet us and one other. The eleven of us here, including Yonita, and the fellow who is with the Chinaman, were the first company to make the crossing. 'Twas Yonita's notion that we should not wait for the rest but set out to your assistance instantly.'

'Thank God you did.' Unity flung her sound arm round Yonita's shoulders. 'We should all be dead now if you'd waited; we should have been dead long ago if it hadn't been for the machine-gun and our ammunition, for that has just run out.'

Deveril's young face suddenly lost its cheerful look.

256

'We heard the gun, miles distant in the forest, and saw it in action from the far side of the valley, but we wondered why you did not fire it again to succour us when we were hard-pressed down by the compound. Heaven forfend that the negroes should attack again until the rest of my people come up.'

'Oh, shucks.' Juhani laughed for the first time for hours. 'Now there are more than a dozen of us we'll hold this place easily with our rifles.'

'Think you it will be so easy?' Yonita broke in. 'We have a great variety of arms in our island but many of them are of considerable antiquity and for some types we lack ammunition. All that was saved by their first owners was used up long since on occasions when these heathens first raided us.'

'Dang me! 'Tis the truth,' Deveril agreed. 'We are in a sad pass for modern weapons and have only the dozen carbines that came off the German gunboat; and the munition for those is no more than twenty rounds apiece. My people are armed with the most ill-assorted pieces and few of them have more than a score of bullets.'

The relief of the survivors from the *Gafelborg* at the appearance of the rescue party was sadly damped. It seemed that their situation was little better than before, even though their numbers were greater, and De Brissac had the added anxiety of Yonita's presence.

The tumbled black bodies that littered the slope in all directions and the unceasing groans which came up from the rocks just below them showed that they had done enormous execution among the enemy, but De Brissac recalled the great number of natives he had seen performing the war dance and he had estimated then that not less than five hundred fighting men were present. The remaining ammunition was checked over and Sir Deveril's men told that they should count every remaining bullet as worth its weight in gold and not fire a single shot until they could see the whites of the negroes' eyeballs.

The sky was clear now and gave them a welcome half-hour's respite. Deveril and his men had brought flasks of applejack and packets of emergency rations in their pockets. These, being shared out, heartened and revived the little company.

While the moon was shining no further attempt was made on the stronghold of the whites but it was now low upon the horizon and soon would pass behind the cliff-face to east of them before sinking into the sea. As they waited there, watching it decline in the heavens, the roaring of the flames in the native village came clearly to them. A heavy pall of smoke hung above it in the windless night but the incendiaries had proved so efficient that it looked as if every building in it would be consumed.

De Brissac had just glanced at the luminous dial of his watch and noted that it was five minutes past two when a hail came from under the cliff to their right. Li Foo and his companion, having fired the village, had fled to the east, almost down to the coast a mile away, to escape capture, but had afterwards succeeded in creeping along the wall of cliff to rejoin them. Their delight at the Chinaman's safe return was increased by the fact that he was still carrying his rifle and the best part of a hundred rounds. They shared out his store among those who had Winchesters and settled down again to watch.

Twenty minutes later the moon had passed behind the cliff and lit only the farther slope of the valley. A blanket of darkness enshrouded them and they knew that there was no hope of it lifting until the coming of dawn. Silence fell again except for the pitiful whimpering of the wounded and a period of tense, expectant waiting set in. The hush continued for so long that they began to believe that the blacks had had enough, and, knowing nothing of their shortage of ammunition, decided not to renew the attack now that the original party had received reinforcements. The thought had almost lulled them into a false sense of security when they clearly heard the hoot of an owl away out in the darkness. It was a signal, and, without further warning, the warriors came hurtling, ten deep, towards them.

For five awful minutes chaos reigned. The whites blazed off their last rounds of ammunition, and, clubbing their guns, smashed at the woolly heads that seemed to rise in waves above the rocky parapet. For moments that seemed endless they fought hand to hand with the brawny, semi-naked savages, but at last they succeeded in throwing them back and they retreated, vanishing like ghosts for the fifth time, into the lower levels.

Having got to such close quarters in this last attack the negroes had succeeded in inflicting casualties. The head of one of Sir Deveril's men had been laid open with a club and the fingers of another had been broken. The first man was dead, the other had his hurt bandaged and stood up to the pain of his wounds with excellent fortitude.

'I'm right out of shot,' Luvia declared. 'How about you other folks?'

A chorus of murmurs greeted his inquiry. There were only five bullets left which fitted the Winchesters and Deveril's party were reduced to seven rounds between them.

Basil turned and looked up the dark slope of the landslide. 'There's only one thing for it,' he declared. 'If they rush us again it'll be the end of us. God knows if we can do it but we've got to have a shot at scaling this cliff.'

'*Mais non!*' De Brissac exclaimed. '*Ce n'est pas possible.* From one third of the way up it hangs almost sheer above us.'

'We've got to try,' Basil insisted doggedly. 'There may be a chimney or gully up there which can't be seen from here. I'll bet I'd find my way up somehow, if I only had proper climbing gear.'

'That's all very well for you, darling,' Unity said softly. 'At one time you were a crack mountaineer, but I don't suppose many of the rest of us have had any experience and the darkness would make it doubly difficult.'

'My middle name's Tarzan,' Juhani broke in. 'I used to climb house-walls for recreation when I was a kid and a masthead in a gale isn't so funny. If we stay here we'll be bumped off for certain.'

'If only we had some rope we might attempt it,' De Brissac said doubtfully.

'There's some on the ammunition carriers,' Basil pointed out. 'Enough to string the girls between Juhani and me, anyhow.'

With swift fingers they knotted the cords and found that there was sufficient to hitch up four people. It was agreed that Basil should lead the party. Unity, who had done a little climbing in Switzerland one year, volunteered to go next. The wound in her arm was still numb and had not yet begun to pain her seriously so she removed it from the sling, knowing that she would need both hands to help herself. De Brissac was the next to be roped and Yonita was the fourth on the string. Juhani, being both a climber and a powerful man, took responsibility for Synolda. He said that by hook or by crook he would get her up behind him anywhere the four ahead could climb, and would bear her weight, if she slipped, on the sling of one of the Winchesters buckled through his belt and hers.

The rest sorted themselves out into couples utilizing every oddment they had with them in the way of scarves, slings, belts and braces, so that each pair would be able to help each other take a strain at a dangerous point.

Regarded soberly the exploit was a mad one, but in their peril they underestimated its difficulty and feverishly completed their preparations, spurred on by the knowledge that, at any moment, the negroes might attack again.

Basil led the way upward and the going for the first fifty feet was comparatively easy. Loose earth and stones slithered from under their feet, but, bent forward and with their hands outstretched before them, they made the ascent until they reached the naked rock above.

Here, while the others paused, Basil moved swiftly along the overhang. To the right a rock wall shelved outwards smooth and bald so that it was quite impossible to pass it to the broken cliff which showed faintly in the starlight beyond, but the left rock-face at the top of the landslide showed a better prospect. In the middle of the apparently solid cliff a dozen feet above his head he caught a glimpse of the glow in the sky reflected from the flaming village and saw that, from a spur, a tall tower of rock rose close against the face of the main precipice. If he could only reach the fork from which the tower started it looked as though he might be able to make his way up the chimney between it and the cliff-face. While the others rested, half-lying on the steep slope, he called Luvia up to him and, when the Finn had planted himself firmly, clambered on to his shoulders. From there he was able to wriggle forward into the hollow of the fork.

He had no sooner reached it than a fresh commotion broke out below. The negroes had crept forward right up to the edge of the redoubt and suddenly rushed it with victorious war cries, only to find that its defenders had disappeared.

After the blood-curdling yells had died down there was an angry chattering for a moment; until one of the blacks spotted the girls' light dresses gleaming faintly against the dark background above. With a fresh outburst of screaming hate they began to scale the landslide. The whites were in a difficult position for aiming their rifles as their foothold was so insecure but they had the big advantage of being at the top of the cascade of scree.

'Aim carefully!' cried De Brissac, and those who had ammunition left let fly at their assailants. Half a dozen of the savages were hit, and, pitching backwards, rolled down among their comrades carrying many of the others with them. The affray was short and sharp. By the time it was over the whites had used their last bullets, but, yet again, the negroes had been driven off with heavy losses.

With Juhani's help from below Basil hauled Unity up to him

by the rope and Yonita after her. In the fork where he sat with his feet firmly wedged against two jutting tongues of stone, to take the strain on the rope, there was room for about eight people standing wedged together. They got Juhani and Synolda up and two of Deveril's men; after that Basil was forced to seek a way to climb higher so that the leaders of the party could make room for the rest to follow.

Calling on the others to wait he untied himself and went ahead alone, straddling up the chimney with his hands and feet pressed against opposite sides of the narrow, rocky walls. The tower rose for nearly fifty feet, and no way up showed on either side of it until he was within ten feet of its top. Here, to the left again, there was a narrow platform in the main cliff sloping gently upwards and apparently unbroken. It led to a black patch of shadow about twenty yards farther on which looked as though it might be a cavern where they could take refuge.

The platform was a mere ledge no more than eighteen inches wide, and as he made his way along it he wondered anxiously whether the others would be able to negotiate it, or be seized by vertigo.

In one place the rock ledge narrowed to a mere six inches and the darkness added to the danger of the passage as the edge where it ended could only just be seen. When he reached the patch of shadow it proved to be, not a cave, as he had hoped, but jagged broken rock, easy to climb, but impossible to rest on for any length of time without acute discomfort. He decided that before prospecting a further way of ascent they must make the best of it and risk the passage of the narrow ledge, since it was impossible to leave Deveril and his remaining men at the top of the landslide exposed to any renewal of hostilities by the savages.

Making his way swiftly but carefully back to the chimney he clambered down it, untied Unity from the others and re-roped her to himself; then, taking up the slack of the rope each time she moved, he led her stage by stage up the funnel. When they reached the little platform he stood her up on it with her face to the wall and said:

'It's pretty narrow farther on. Think you can make it?'

'Yes,' she said, evenly. 'I'm not afraid.'

'Bless you.' He pressed her hand. 'It's too much to hope all the others will be as little trouble.'

'They'll be all right, darling. In this darkness one can't see how far there is to fall.'

'That's true. We'd never be able to get them up here in day-light.' He stretched his arm across her shoulders and they edged along feeling their way from one handhold crack to another until they reached the jagged patch where he could leave her to rest in safety. Returning, he repeated the process with Yonita; but when Synolda's turn came she proved more difficult. By the time he had her up to the shelf she was trembling in every limb. She declared she had always been terrified of heights and that her legs felt like giving way under her.

Basil called down to Juhani, who came scrambling up to help him, and nerve-racking moments for both of them followed. One on each side of Synolda and both roped to her they gradually shuffled their way along. She was so near fainting with terror that she could hardly move her feet, and, between them, they had to half drag and half carry her. At the narrowest part of the path, where the precipice fell sheer away, the sweat poured down Basil's forehead in rivulets. He knew that one unexpected clutch from the trembling girl would send all three of them hurtling down into the abyss.

At last the frightful business was accomplished and the two other girls, clinging to their precarious perches in the steep ravine that rent the cliff-face, were able to receive Synolda, sobbing, in their arms.

One by one Deveril's men, Li Foo and De Brissac followed; not without many moments of acute anxiety for the two practised climbers who had to make a dozen journeys, back and forth, to encourage and help them. Deveril brought up the rear, making the passage without assistance, and at length the whole party was assembled on the broken surface in the wide cleft.

Basil was half dead with fatigue and nerve strain. Juhani was little better, but, after a brief rest, the two of them made their way upwards again, as the present position of the party only gave it a temporary security. They were all spreadeagled clinging to lumps of outcrop or splinters of straight stone and would not be able to retain their hold there indefinitely.

At the top of the gully the two leaders were faced by slanting slabs of smooth rock but these were cracked with jagged fissures, and both men felt that, if the party used the ropes in turn, they should be able to cross them on a diagonal slant, heading up again to what appeared to be a small plateau.

While Basil returned to the others to prepare them for this fresh ascent Juhani went on, his chest pressed close to the rock, his fingers feeling for every niche and cranny, worming his way upward until he reached the broad shelf they had made out from below. It proved to be a fair-sized, level plateau forming the top of a shoulder which jutted out into the void.

Basil meanwhile led the main body up the craggy tangle of rocks in the steep gully until he met Juhani, just returned from his reconnaissance, at its top.

A grim time ensued for the two mountaineers. Sweating and straining they laboured on the dangerously short lengths of rope, driving and encouraging the weaker members of the party by turns. Two of Deveril's men slipped on the glassy boiler-plates and were only saved from destruction by the prompt action and great strength of Juhani.

The hearts of all of them played a devil's tattoo in their chests. Their nails were broken, the toes of their boots torn and their muscles aching excruciatingly, but by four o'clock, after an hour spent crossing the smooth, sharply tilted slabs, they had all reached the little plateau, three sides of which beetled over the abyss. There was room enough for the whole party to stretch at full length there, and, for some time, they lay almost comatose. Luvia had made an examination of their situation on his first journey to the plateau and he knew that there was no way of progressing further upward from it. A steep wall of rock, rising to the cliff-top forty feet above, which showed no break for hand or foothold, cut them off entirely, but for the moment they were content to rest.

For nearly two hours their every thought had been concentrated on the emergency of the moment and none of them had had any opportunity to wonder what had become of the rest of the rescue-party from Yonita's island, but the sound of a shot, down in the valley, recalled its existence to them.

Eagerly they all scrambled to their knees, their fatigue forgotten, and peered down into the depths below. The fire in the native village had burnt itself out and showed only as heaps of smouldering embers scattered over a wide area. The bonfire about which the native warriors had danced had died down so that it gave little light, but beyond it intermittent flashes pierced the blackness and the rattle of musketry echoed clearly up the cliff.

'Uncle Cornelius!' Yonita cried. 'Uncle Cornelius! At last, he has arrived with the others.'

Anxiously they watched the new battle raging in the valley. Deveril and his advance party had had the advantage of surprise and the additional diversion caused by Li Foo firing the village at the moment of their arrival, but evidently the negroes had sighted the main body of the whites almost as soon as they crossed the crest on the far side of the valley. They were fighting in the open, and, by the semi-circle of flashes from their arms, it looked as though they were partially surrounded.

As the moments sped the hearts of the watchers on the cliff-face sank. It was obvious that instead of gaining ground their friends were losing it. Uncle Cornelius's men were gradually being driven towards the west. As they came opposite the Marriage House they seemed to rally, and, with a sudden movement, surged forward. The din of battle grew nearer. Flashes lit up the high palisade and soon it was clear that the whites had fought their way into the compound.

Another ten minutes and it became obvious that their intention was to hold it as occasional shots kept coming from various points along all four sides of the enclosure. Gradually these grew more infrequent; the blacks, weakened by their many losses sustained that night, had given up trying to storm the compound. The firing died away altogether and silence fell over the valley.

De Brissac and some of the others with him realized to the full the gravity of their situation. They could not ascend the cliff any farther and only darkness had nerved most of the party to the ascent. In daylight hysteria would almost certainly overcome many of them if they attempted to climb down and the only method of getting them back to the valley would be to lower them from stage to stage, until they could be received into friendly hands. All of them had counted upon Uncle Cornelius defeating their savage enemy and being able, at least, to help them in the last stages of their descent. Now, it seemed, his attack had failed and he was cut off there below them, surrounded and besieged, in the Marriage House compound. Even if they could have got down the cliff their weapons were of little use now they had run out of ammunition; they could give no assistance to Uncle Cornelius, or he to them and, worst of all, Deveril's men had made their desperate gamble and lost, since there was no possibility of further help arriving from their island.

CHAPTER XXII

BEYOND THE BARRIER

EVERY one of the little party on the plateau in the cliff-face was absolutely dropping with fatigue. The exertions of all of them for the last sixty hours had been prodigious, and eveh Sir Deveril's people had been up merrymaking all the previous night in addition to having made their forced march from the shore, fought heroically and scaled threequarters of the mountainous rampart that shut off the southern extremity of Satan's Island from the low-lying land forming the bulk of it.

De Brissac knew that nothing further could be done for their own preservation, or to assist Uncle Cornelius's besieged force in the valley, until daylight came. He urged the rest to sleep if they could, and, curling himself up in a little hollow, dropped off immediately. Yonita had already fallen into a heavy sleep with her head across Deveril's knees, and very soon nearly all the others had followed their example, too utterly wearied for the hard rock on which they lay to prevent nature taking its toll of their tired bodies.

Only Juhani and Synolda, seated side by side with their backs against the cliff, remained awake; their minds still active with their own problem. Neither had had a chance to speak to the other during the stress of the girls' escape and the events that followed, and if they had they would not have cared to do so in the presence of the others, but now the quiet, regular breathing which came from all sides of them, punctuated by an occasional snore, assured them that for all practical purposes they were utterly alone up there in their eyrie.

'Not asleep yet?' Juhani asked in a low voice as he heard Synolda ease her position.

'No. A quarter of an hour ago I was dead beat, but now I'm too overtired to sleep, I think. Anyway, leaning against this rock is so damned uncomfortable.'

He stretched out a long arm and drew her towards him 'Lean on me. You'll be better so.'

Without a word she snuggled up against him, resting her head on his shoulder.

'Juhani,' she whispered, after a moment, 'what happened to Vicente?'

'He's dead. I had him locked in his cabin, same as I locked you, and the niggers did him in there, poor devil, when they sacked the ship. I'm afraid that's bad news for you—isn't it?'

'I *am* sorry he's dead, in one way,' she murmured. 'He wasn't such a bad sort really but I never cared for him the way you thought I did.'

'Well, you've certainly an extraordinary way of showing ordinary friendship—do you behave with all your men friends as you did with him?'

'Of course I don't!' she whispered angrily. 'But Vicente was a sort of legacy left over from my second husband.'

'I'm afraid I don't get you.'

'It's not easy to explain and it's a long story.'

'I don't mind that if you don't. I'm darn tired but I'm not sleepy.'

'All right. I'll tell you. I can hardly expect you to believe me, but I lived in Caracas for seven years, you know, and life's pretty queer for lots of people who live in these little South American republics, like Venezuela. Particularly for a girl who's good looking and happens to be married to a Venezuelan.

'Piet Brendon, my first husband, took me to Caracas when I was quite young and he died when I was only twenty. Ortello was a rich man and quite attractive. I've never cared much for work, and, like a fool, I decided to marry him instead of going back to South Africa where I would have had to earn my own living.

'In those days the tyrant Gomez was the dictator of Venezuela. He only died in 1935 and right up to that time he ruled just like any robber baron, only carrying on the business in a very big way. His army was simply a collection of legalized gangsters. They ran the whole country as though it was their private property. There was no law and no justice outside the old man's will. People were shot, imprisoned or fined by the thousand without any sort of trial, and the old Catfish's lieutenants were every bit as bloodthirsty and cruel as he was himself. Not a woman in the country, except the few Europeans in the Consulates and oilfields, was safe from them, and I should think you can guess what the bad kind of Portuguese-South Americans can be like with women.

'As Ortello's wife I was a Venezuelan subject and to keep his business going he had to hobnob with a lot of these blackguards who ran the country. He managed to conceal me from them for the best part of eighteen months, but a Colonel Diaz came to the house on business unexpectedly one day and saw me. After that he resorted to all sorts of ruses to see me again, and, when he found that I wouldn't have anything to do with him behind my husband's back, he trumped up a charge of conspiracy against Ortello, who was immediately arrested and thrown into prison.

'You can imagine what happened then. Diaz came to see me and gave me the choice of being pleasant to him or having my husband shot. There was no question of its being an empty threat because people were shot every day in Caracas at that time, Ortello had been kind to me so what else could I do.

'If I'd know what was to happen afterwards I'd never've done it because that wasn't the end of the wretched business—only a beginning. Diaz told his friends about me and I was forced to give way to them too during an awful six months while they kept Ortello in prison. But worst of all Ortello wasn't worth it. Soon after they released him I found out that he'd been having a succession of mistresses ever since our marriage. In the blow-up that followed, I learned that he knew all about what had been happening to me but was tired of me anyway, so, instead of being grateful, he was brutally cynical about it.

'I suppose I could have got to South Africa then, if I'd really made an effort. But that six-months' experience with half a dozen different lovers, some of whom I liked and others whom I hated, but all of whom I'd been compelled to take by force of circumstances, hardened me in a way it may be difficult for you to understand.

'I lived in every comfort. In fact I had all the luxuries any woman could have outside Europe or the States. In a way, it seemed to be cutting off my nose to spite my face, to throw it all up; particularly as by then I'd realized that physical relations don't really mean much. It may sound awfully cynical but they're soon forgotten unless there is love too.

'I wouldn't have anything more to do with Ortello himself but he wanted me to stay, and, while I was trying to make up my mind, I met a young Spanish official with whom I fell in love. Ortello was quite happy with his mistresses and encouraged me to go ahead with my affair because my young lover could help him in his business by giving him big Government contracts.

'The Spaniard was killed a year later in a mining accident and I was utterly heartbroken—until I discovered I was going to have a child. I told Ortello and offered to leave him. He said nobody would know the child wasn't his so there was no reason why we should separate, and I thought, at the time, that he was behaving very generously.

'Really he wasn't being generous to me at all because he lost his Government contracts after my lover died, and he had suddenly realized my value to him as a financial asset. He wanted me to have the child, and become fond of it, so that he could use it as a lever for blackmail against me later on.

'That's just what happened. I adored my baby boy, and for a few months I was completely happy. Then Ortello introduced another Government official to me, and, very soon, I saw the wretched position in which I'd placed myself. Legally the child was Ortello's, and in Venezuela a father still has absolute rights over his children. He told me, quite bluntly, that unless I was prepared to be complacent to his friends, which would enable him to get back his contracts, he'd take the boy away from me and send it to an orphanage where I should never see it again.'

Synolda paused, shrugging her shoulders with a weary little gesture. 'Well—there you are. I'm not asking for pity. I've had some good times as well as bad and it wasn't all quite so terrible as it sounds, just put baldly like that, but there were some pretty grim moments, and, towards the end, I got to hate Ortello more than I'd ever thought it possible to hate anybody. My affair with Vicente was forced upon me, like the others, a last link in my life with Ortello.'

'You poor kid,' said Juhani softly. 'You've had one hell of a time. But he's out of it now and you'll never see Venezuela again.'

'Oh, God!' she groaned. 'I'm tired—desperately tired.'

Juhani was nodding too and far too weary to seek for a more detailed explanation of her recent conduct. All that seemed to matter was that they were together again. In the hours of his desperate march across the island to rescue her he had realized that he loved her for herself, no matter what she might have done, and he had felt an actual physical ache to have his arms round her again. That desire, at least, was realized whatever morning might bring. Sleepily he turned her face up to his and gave her a long, gentle kiss. Almost as their lips parted both of them fell asleep.

The whole party would probably have slept far into the morning if the sound of a loud explosion had not roused them. Staring about them sleepily they sat up, and, craning over the edge of the precipice, peered down into the valley.

Daylight had come and a glance at his watch showed De Brissac that it was nearly eight o'clock. The valley below them lay clear as a map in the sunlight. Little wisps of smoke still curled up from the native village to their front. To their left they could see a number of the white islanders, evidently perched on makeshift stands, manning the palisade of the Marriage House compound, but another group of whites had appeared from a big maize field on the opposite side of the open space which lay between the compound and the village. Round it were the larger hutments, the only ones which had not been destroyed in the previous night's fire.

As those on the plateau high up on the cliff watched, one of the party by the maize field hurled something dark into the air. A second explosion followed and half of one of the hutments disappeared in a burst of flame and smoke.

The natives who had taken refuge in the buildings round the open space after the burning of their village were tumbling pell-mell out of them to resist this new attack. Meanwhile the whites manning the stockade opened a brisk fire, shooting down into the mass of running savages.

More bombs were hurled, and, falling among the blacks, did appalling execution. As the islanders advanced from the maize fields their comrades manning the stockade slipped down from their posts, flung open the gates of the compound, and came charging out. The two parties converged on the yelling mob of blacks and drove them back with frightful slaughter. Bomb after bomb was flung into their midst and suddenly they broke.

Basil let out a loud 'hurrah!' and all those with him, standing up in their excitement, crowded to the edge of the cliff; cheering the advance of the little body of victorious whites, which was now driving the mass of negroes helter-skelter before them.

The cheer echoed back from the rock-face, and, as the echo ceased, there came another from higher up on the cliff.

Juhani looked round, 'What in thunder was that?'

The others scarcely heeded him. All their thoughts were concentrated on the rout of their enemies below, but another cheer, coming from somewhere to the right, above them, caused them all to turn and stare up the bleak rock.

'Hullo there!' Basil hailed excitedly. 'Hullo! above!'

Next moment an English voice with a strong Cockney accent floated down to them.

'Hullo! down there! . . . where are yer?'

'Here!' bellowed the whole party on the big ledge. 'Here!'

With intense excitement De Brissac and his friends stared up the cliff. They continued shouting and shouts came in reply until a bright ginger head appeared over the cliff top almost directly above them.

'Who are you?' shouted Basil.

'Bo'sun of the *Sally Ann*, stuck here these two years,' replied the red-head. ' 'Oo are you?'

'Survivors of the Swedish ship *Gafelborg*,' Basil called back.

' 'Ow the 'ell d'yer get up there?' inquired the stranger.

'Climbed,' replied Basil promptly, 'but how we'll get down again God knows!'

' 'Ang on a moment,' shouted the bo'sun. 'I'll fetch the mate and we'll 'aul you up.'

The red-head disappeared and Deveril's men began to speculate about this new party of survivors from another wreck. They knew nothing of any ships that might have reached Satan's Island since Father Jerome's time but had always supposed that the current carried all vessels in the weed sea to one or other of the two big bays on opposite sides of the channel. It now appeared that a third bay existed which was protected from the murderous negroes by the great barrier which shut off the southern end of their island.

While Deveril's party waited they divided their attention between the cliff-top and the valley below. There, Uncle Cornelius was now inflicting a final defeat upon the savages. Fifty or sixty of them had taken to their heels and were making off in various directions through the maize fields. The main body, of some two hundred, were driven up against the mighty barrier of rock and were flinging down their arms in token of surrender.

A tall figure which they could clearly recognize as Yonita's uncle left the white force, and, walking some way away from it, began to signal in semaphore with his arms.

Several of them spelt out the message. They learned that it had been Uncle Cornelius's idea to bring over a store of explosives salvaged from the German gunboat. The old man had feared that they would never be able to overcome such a superior force with so little ammunition, so sent the second party, which had got boxed up in the compound, ahead to help Deveril, while waiting for the explosives to be landed before coming on with the main body himself. Their casualties totalled four killed and nine wounded, but the remaining negroes had now surrendered except for the few who had fled, so there was no further fear of their being surprised and overwhelmed.

Deveril signalled back, giving particulars of what had happened to his party and De Brissac's. He said that, with the aid of ropes from above they would be able to make their way down later, but, for the time being, most of them were too done-up to hazard the descent, so they proposed to take advantage of the succour offered by the castaway who had so unexpectedly appeared on the cliff-top.

Before he had completed his signals the red-headed bo'sun hailed them again. With him, this time, there were several other bearded men who called greetings to the marooned party. A good stout rope was lowered and Deveril insisted on being hauled up first to test its strength. One by one the others were drawn up after him, and, when they arrived, they found him in close conversation with a stocky little man whom he introduced as Mr. Thomas, the only surviving officer of the *Sally Ann*.

Thomas related that his ship, a 2,400-ton tramp steamer with a cargo of canned goods, agricultural implements and silk stockings, when outward bound from New York to Buenos Aires two years before had sustained a breakdown in her engines. She had been caught in a hurricane while disabled and driven down into the weed sea. Ever since, she had been lying derelict in a small bay to the south of Satan's Island. Her crew had suffered many casualties during the hurricane and afterwards, while for three weeks they drifted fast in the weed. On reaching the island their captain had landed with the bulk of the survivors to explore and they had camped on the beach. The party had been attacked that night by giant crabs, and only the bo'sun, with one other, had escaped. They had succeeded in getting back to the ship the following morning, where Thomas and five more men had been left. From that time onward they had never been ashore except in the day time and only then to gather seaweeds and other things to help out their store of supplies.

'Didn't you ever attempt to get down the cliff to the negro village?' Basil inquired.

271

'Yes, indeed,' replied Mr. Thomas indignantly. 'In the first week we explored all the high tableland hereabout, and, seeing the natives in the valley there, we brought good stout hawsers from the ship and lowered one of our chaps. The murderous devils just pulled him off the rope as he touched ground and butchered him before our eyes. Think of it, man!'

De Brissac nodded. 'They are worse than genuine savages. Having had just a touch of civilization makes them vicious. But have they never attempted to get up the cliff at you?'

'Indeed no. It's no easy climb whatever and none of them has tried it since we've been here. But the ladies look all-in and every one of you could do with a good square meal. Let us get back to the *Sally Ann*.'

His invitation was a welcome one and they set off across the mile-wide plateau which sloped down a little at its south-eastern edge. The tableland ended in sheer cliff, falling straight to the sea, except at one spot where two or three hundred yards of beach showed below and a break in the cliffs formed a miniature bay. In the middle of it the *Sally Ann* rode at anchor.

As the newcomers gazed down they exclaimed in surprise; for the bay and the sea beyond it presented a most curious spectacle. On either hand the weed stretched as far as they could see but the bay itself, and a channel several hundred yards wide running out to southward, was completely free of it. Instead the still water shone, iridescent in the sunlight, reflecting every shade of brilliant colour as though a portion of rainbow had been pinned down to make a roadway through it.

Thomas laughed at their exclamations. 'That's oil,' he said. 'There's a gusher here and three times since we've been stuck in the bay it has overflowed. Look at the black streaks of it down that cliff yonder. The oil kills everything that lives in the sea, or else they get away from it. Indeed even the weed shrinks back to give it passage. Ever since we got here the bay's been clear and each time the oil gushes like this there's a channel of open water as far as we can see, but the weed closes up again in a day or two after the oil stops flowing.'

'Good Heavens!' exclaimed Basil. 'Why the devil do you stay here then? Surely you can make your way out to sea if you want to and sail away home?'

Thomas shook his head. 'Didn't I tell you, man, it was a breakdown of our engines led to us getting carried into this devilish place, and from one mishap after another we lost every engineer in the ship. None of my chaps understands anything about engines and they're double-dutch to me.'

'You could have made sails out of your awnings,' Basil suggested.

'We tried it,' Thomas told him. 'But there's little wind in these parts and to sail a ship you've got to have room to manœuvre. There's never a free channel of more than two hundred yards in width; we got stuck in the weed half a mile out and had to kedge the ship back again.'

Juhani laughed. 'I'm an engineer. Just get me aboard and let me look at that engine. I'll put it right if it's mendable.'

A chorus of excited joy went up from the red-headed bo'sun and the rest of the *Sally Ann*'s small company. Basil's eyes met Unity's and they clasped hands with a sudden thrill. If Juhani *could* repair the *Sally Ann*'s engines it meant—escape—home— England. De Brissac shot a swift glance at Yonita. Could he persuade her to sail with him to France? But Synolda went deathly white. If they sailed she must lose Juhani or face extra- dition from the first port they touched and trial in South Africa.

The whole party made its way down a rough track in the cliff- side, piled into a lifeboat which was beached on the shore, pulled out through the oily water and was soon on board the tramp.

Their first thought was food, and Thomas provided them with a fine stew of corned beef and vegetables from the stock of tinned goods in the cargo on which, eked out by sun-dried fish and boiled seaweed, he had kept himself and his men alive for the past two years.

After this belated breakfast Juhani went to the *Sally Ann*'s engine-room. He returned from his inspection positively trembling with excitement, declaring enthusiastically that with the help of a dozen strong men and a block and tackle he felt confident he could make the necessary repairs.

'How long d'you reckon it'll take you?' Thomas asked.

'Six hours, maybe eight. Not more, since you've had the sense to keep your engines well greased. I'll be through by sundown.'

The survivors of the *Sally Ann* numbered seven but all the new- comers volunteered to help, so Juhani did not lack assistance. Thomas's men were overjoyed at the thought that they might see their homes again after having long given up any such hope.

Deveril pressed them not to hurry and to accept his hospitality for a few weeks, at least, but Thomas shook his head gravely.

273

'We'd all like to see your island, sir, but indeed it can't be done. It is a week since the oil started gushing and it gave out two days ago. The channel will be closed within twenty-four hours now and the oil may not gush again for another nine months or a year. If we're going to make a bid for our homelands we must not delay sailing later than tonight.'

'Holy smoke! I'd best get busy on those engines then,' Juhani cut in. 'Come on, boys!' and with a party of eager volunteers crowding after him, he hurried below.

As Juhani had more help than he needed Deveril, De Brissac, Thomas, Basil and the three girls decided to land again, cross the high plateau and see how Uncle Cornelius was faring. De Brissac had the good sense not to rush his fences. Instead of asking Yonita right away to accompany him on the voyage, he exerted every atom of his wonderful power to charm and fascinate her. Never had he cut a more gallant figure or displayed a more brilliant wit than on their climb and walk. Synolda alone among the party remained unsmiling at his sallies; she scarcely heard them, her brain half-numbed by the misery in her heart.

A few minutes after they arrived at the further cliff edge, Uncle Cornelius caught sight of them against the skyline and signalled up to report that all was well.

He had discovered the fissures in the cliff farther west from which, by a rude apparatus, the negroes filled their balloons with natural gas, and he proposed that half a dozen of Deveril's men should form a permanent guard there, being relieved at regular intervals. They could act as a local police force to the remaining natives who should be left in possession of their own lands but never again allowed arms or balloons, and so rendered harmless. Their chief and principal witch doctors were dead.

Deveril signalled back telling him of the presence of the *Sally Ann*. He added that an attempt would be made that night by her crew to sail for the outer world and asked if any of his own people wished to accompany them.

There was a short consultation among the whites down in the valley and the reply came up, 'Good fortune to those who adventure forth, but we are all resolved to remain.'

The men with Deveril held the same view, which he duly reported to Uncle Cornelius; informing him that they would remain to see the *Sally Ann* on her way and descend the cliff by ropes the following morning.

The party on the cliff-top made its way back to the ship in time for a high tea at which the islanders much enjoyed the strange foods that came out of Thomas's cargo of canned goods. He added to their joy by presenting Deveril with several cases of agricultural implements for their use, and Yonita with twenty gross of silk stockings for herself and the women.

After the meal De Brissac skilfully drew Yonita aside from the rest and took her up to the after-deck.

'Listen!' he said urgently, his voice strained with anxiety now that the time had come to make his bid for her. 'I hate to rush things so—but we are sailing tonight. Yonita, you must come with me.'

Slowly she shook her head. 'Methinks you are joking. How could I possibly abandon Deveril?'

'*Peste!*' he exclaimed. 'You do not love him?'

'You wrong me there,' she said gravely.

'You cannot,' he urged. 'How can you say such a thing seeing what we were to each other two nights ago?'

She raised her eyebrows. 'That was not love—only youth. Love is something very different.'

He made an angry gesture with his shoulders. 'You are so young, Yonita. You do not understand. Come with me to France. All the world lies before us. I am not rich but my family do not lack money. We shall have everything that anyone could wish for. My machine-gun is lost, down there on the rocks, but I have the plans of it with me and when my Government see it they will honour me and give me rapid promotion. There are a million things I want to show you. *La Belle France* is so beautiful. Paris! It is the loveliest city in the world. The buildings, the cafés, the shops——'

'Shops?' she broke in curiously. 'What are shops? Ah, yes! I recall reading of one in a book. They are places where people toil all day selling things, are they not? No, I do not think I should like that.'

'But you would not work in them,' he urged. 'You would only go to them to buy pretty things. Lovely dresses, hats, lingerie. You should see the races at Auteuil, the Opera, the theatres, the beautiful *plages* with all the smart people—Biarritz and Deauville.'

'It must all be prodigious diverting; yet life in the outer world sounds monstrous complicated if report be true, whereas here simple pleasures readily content us.' She smiled a wicked little smile and began to fiddle with a button on his grimy blue tunic.

'Tis but a poor compliment to me that you do not wish to remain. Did you not enjoy your one night as my guest?'

'How can you ask?' he stammered. 'But there is my gun . . you would not understand . . . but it means so much to my country since every week these days we never know when there will be another war in Europe.'

'Ah! War,' she sighed, 'how horrible! 'Tis passing strange that two white races should be so desperate eager to massacre each other. What can excuse such atrocious barbarity? Soulless heathen as those negroes are, I could scarce help feeling for them when I beheld so great a number all broken and dying in the valley. Thanks largely to your coming the only war we can be called upon to wage is over. Why do you not stay and make your life with us?'

In miserable indecision he clenched his hands until the fingernails cut into his palms. The temptation was almost irresistible. Yonita, small, supple, golden-skinned, with her wicked merry eyes—adorable beyond words. 'Would you . . . would you . . ?' he stammered.

'La! Yes,' she smiled. 'Why not? I think you are still the most pleasing gallant I have ever had. We should be very happy together for mayhap even so much as a year.'

'Only a year?' he frowned. 'I cannot—*ce n'est pas possible*, yet if I did stay surely you would marry me?'

'Nay.' She shook her head again, slowly but firmly. 'I am promised to Deveril and 'tis Deveril that I love. My adult life will not begin until I am old enough to be married to him. 'Tis wondrous gratifying to pleasure oneself with a new beau, yet such youthful follies are no more than part of our education here and all of us are passing glad to reach maturity in due season so that we may share the joys of children and a home with our own man.'

Sadly he took her in his arms and kissed her. Instinct told him now that it was quite useless to plead with her further. Her upbringing and outlook were so utterly different from those of a modern girl in the great world outside the weed continent, he would never be able to persuade her to go with him, and his own duty lay in returning to France. Once the *Sally Ann* had sailed it was extremely unlikely that any other chance to leave the island would occur during his lifetime.

They lingered there a little, while the shadows of twilight fell, but the flavour had gone from their kisses and with mingled feelings of regret and a strange, unexpected relief they strolled back to join the others, who had congregated in the ship's dining-saloon.

A meal was served at eight o'clock, and as they were sitting down to table Juhani came up with his companions from the engine room to announce that their work was completed.

Thomas had saved the coal in his bunkers in the vague hope that some unforeseen chance might arise for them to put to sea again, and all cooking and heating since the ship had arrived had been done on oil fuel collected from the island. While Juhani had been at work some of the men with him had been getting the fires going and filling up the boilers. He said that by the time the moon rose they should have enough steam to get under way.

One Scotsman among the crew had proved a particularly able helper, and he had shown such a grasp of the engine that Juhani decided he would make an excellent second engineer. The other five men with Thomas and the party from the *Gafelborg* would be quite sufficient as an emergency crew to run the little tramp up to a South American port where a full complement could be secured.

The party in the saloon was a merry one. Only Yonita and De Brissac were a little silent at the thought of their parting, and Synolda, who appeared deplorably unenthusiastic about the prospect of getting home again.

Juhani was discussing some arrangements with Thomas, but as soon as they had done he came over and sat down beside her, beaming happily. 'Well, it looks as though we'll have to get hitched up in Finland and find the money for some furnishings, after all, honey. I'll have to land another job and get to sea again to keep the home fires burning, but there'll be the period between ships and it's worth a lot to get back to one's own folk.'

'Juhani!' she whispered in a strangled voice. 'Come outside, I've got to speak to you.'

'Have a heart,' he smiled. 'I'm needing a sit-down what with last night and eight hours solid below only just——'

'Please,' she interrupted. 'I've been wanting to talk to you every moment of that time.'

He stood up and made way for her with an indulgent shrug. Outside on the deserted deck it was now quite dark; the sky was bright with stars but the moon had not yet risen.

'Juhani,' she said breathlessly the moment they were alone. 'I'm not coming with you—I'm staying here.'

'Not coming!' he swung upon her. 'Snakes alive! what's bitten you?'

'I'm going to stay here,' she repeated.

'But—honey!' He threw his arm round her shoulders. 'You can't expect me to go giving you up like this—and—and although the island's all right in its way—well——'

'The island *is* all right,' she broke in swiftly. 'I haven't seen it but I've heard enough to realize everyone's happy on it. You can't say that about Europe or anywhere else in the world we know.'

'Well, maybe you can't,' he said slowly, 'but it's unnatural somehow not to want to get back home.'

'I've got no home,' Synolda declared bitterly, 'and I *can't* go back. I wouldn't be able to marry you even if I did.'

He frowned suddenly. 'God, is that blackguard husband of yours—still alive?'

'Juhani,' she said very quietly, 'I had no chance to tell you everything last night. It was over seven years since I'd seen my own people when I induced Ortello to take me on a holiday trip to South Africa—a few months ago. We took my little boy with us, and seeing Ortello among my own people made me hate him more than ever. My old desire to cut and run surged up again. My sister had married a rich farmer but they haven't got any children and she simply doted on my boy. I talked it over with her and she and her husband were quite willing to give us both a home.'

'You deserted him, but he's still alive, eh?' Juhani interrupted.

'Wait,' she pleaded, 'wait. We were all staying at Muizenburg together. One day, I came into our bedroom at the hotel. Ortello was there, walking up and down in a most violent rage because some business arrangement he had made had gone wrong. My boy ran in front of his feet to rescue a toy aeroplane. Ortello kicked him away as a brute might kick a dog. All I had suffered through him boiled up in me then and I simply saw red. There was a Spanish dagger that I used for fancy dress on the side-table I snatched it up and—and——'

'Yes? . . .' said Juhani hoarsely, staring down into her eyes.

'I—I killed him. I didn't mean to but the one stab was enough. When I realized what I'd done I was horrified—horrified. I tried to pull my wits together to save myself. I snatched up the child and fled to my sister's room and I told her what I'd done. She's only two years older than I am and looks very like me. She agreed to take the child and go back to Johannesburg in the hope that when the police circulated my description they'd believe her to be me—and I think that's what they did. I flung a few things into my dressing-case, locked the door of the bedroom, and fled to Cape Town. No ship was leaving the harbour before the following morning. I spent a ghastly night and joined the *Gafelborg* just a few moments before she sailed. In the meantime the murder had been discovered. It was in the morning paper and that's where Vicente came in. He'd seen me with my husband at Muizenburg the previous afternoon and he saw the paper before sailing, next day. That night, when we were already at sea, he recognized me and threatened to have me arrested at the first port we touched unless . . . Oh, good-bye, Juhani! good-bye! I'm desperately sorry I've brought so much trouble on you.'

Juhani heaved a deep sigh, and through the tears that filled her eyes she suddenly saw that he was smiling.

'Ortello had that coming to him,' he said firmly. 'If you hadn't done it I'd have given that devil the works myself for all he did to you. You're right about the island—we'll make a new start there.' Her tears came freely then, until he kissed them from her eyes.

An hour and a half later the moon was up. It was a sad blow to Thomas that he was losing Luvia as an engineer, but De Brissac had a considerable knowledge of machinery so between him and the Scot, who had helped Juhani with the repairs, they felt confident they would be able to manage. With many expressions of goodwill Deveril and his men, Yonita, Synolda, and Juhani piled into the boat and were rowed ashore.

It was only when they reached the cliff-top where they were to camp for the night they realized that the devoted Li Foo was still with them. Nothing, he declared, would induce him to leave the beautiful Missie Synolda.

The little *Sally Ann* blew a long blast on her siren as the anchor was weighed. Her bow turned slowly towards the oily channel where the moonlight silvered the still surface. In the stern of the ship Unity leaned over the rail with Basil's arm round her. The debonair De Brissac stood on her other side, already half-consoled for his loss of the adorable Yonita by the thought of returning to his beloved France and the possibility of fresh adventures.

The sound of turning turbines sounded strangely over that grim, silent sea while the party on the cliff-top watched the people on the *Sally Ann*'s decks gradually merge into the shadows. At last the little ship was lost to sight and only the dimming light at her masthead showed that she was well on her way towards the open ocean.

This book, designed by
William B. Taylor
is a production of
Edito-Service S.A., Geneva

Printed in France
Bound in Switzerland